A TIMELESS KISS

Jolie sighed, looking Cole over again. Maybe if she was really lucky, she mused, this wish-come-true business was her big chance to prove herself. To herself. And to him. And maybe her reward in the end would be the kind of love she'd wished for while playing an incredible song on an impossibly powerful piano.

Or maybe she'd just gone around the bend. *After all,* Jolie told herself, *you know perfectly well you never learned to play the piano.*

Or even to read music.

"Hmm?" Cole prompted. His gaze lowered to her lips . . . and lingered in a way that sent her pulse through the roof.

Wowsers. He still meant to kiss her! The gentle upward tilt of her face in his hand left no doubt of that. So did the slow, seductive way he drew her closer.

Their bodies pressed together beneath the quilt, defying the wintry weather—and common sense, too. Jolie had never fallen for a man this quickly. Had never even considered kissing someone she'd met only hours before.

Until now.

—from "Winter Song" by Lisa Plumley

BOOK YOUR PLACE ON OUR WEBSITE AND MAKE THE READING CONNECTION!

We've created a customized website just for our very special readers, where you can get the inside scoop on everything that's going on with Zebra, Pinnacle and Kensington books.

When you come online, you'll have the exciting opportunity to:

- View covers of upcoming books
- Read sample chapters
- Learn about our future publishing schedule (listed by publication month *and author*)
- Find out when your favorite authors will be visiting a city near you
- Search for and order backlist books from our online catalog
- Check out author bios and background information
- Send e-mail to your favorite authors
- Meet the Kensington staff online
- Join us in weekly chats with authors, readers and other guests
- Get writing guidelines
- AND MUCH MORE!

Visit our website at
http://www.zebrabooks.com

TIMELESS WINTER

SANDRA DAVIDSON
KATHRYN HOCKETT
LISA PLUMLEY

Zebra Books
Kensington Publishing Corp.

http://www.zebrabooks.com

ZEBRA BOOKS are published by

Kensington Publishing Corp.
850 Third Avenue
New York, NY 10022

First Printing: December, 1999
10 9 8 7 6 5 4 3 2 1

Printed in the United States of America

CONTENTS

WINTER'S BRIDE

SANDRA DAVIDSON

PROLOGUE

Massachusetts
January 21, 1980

It was all Miss Fortunata's fault, Sheena Stewart thought as she trudged across the barren peak of Lost Mountain with the rest of her Girl Scout troop. They could have been snug and warm now in their cozy homes, but no, their leader had wanted them to prove their mettle by hiking up this lonely mountain in the dead of winter.

They could have made the hike in the fall when the mountains were ablaze with orange and gold, or in the summer when the wind was friendly instead of an icy slap in the face. But thanks to Miss Fortunata, they had to walk it when it was cold and damp and the air was thick with ghostly threads of mist that made the mountain seem spooky and forbidding.

To make matters worse, there were no guardrails. Nothing to keep them from tumbling over the sheer cliff to the valley 3,000 feet below if they ventured too close to the edge. And as if all that wasn't bad enough, she had to pee.

Lagging behind the others, she looked for a sheltered spot where she could relieve herself. Scanning the desolate landscape, she decided that the huge outcropping of boulders several feet away was her best bet. The thought of undressing in the frigid air was not very inviting, but she gritted her teeth, walked to the wall of standing rocks, and started to unzip her pants.

"My, my, my, what do we have here?"

Sheena spun around to see an old woman sitting on a boulder that looked for all the world like some ancient faery throne. She blinked her eyes, not sure she was seeing right, but the woman was still there, looking strangely out of place in a long skirt made of some coarse gray fabric and a hooded woolen cloak of the same color. No wonder she hadn't seen her; the old woman's clothing and hair were the same color as the surrounding rocks.

"Ma'am, what are you doing up here? Are you all right?"

"Just fine, thank you. I been waiting, is all."

"Waiting? For who?"

"For the Silver Storm. Mark my words, it'll be here any time now." Wetting the tip of her finger, she held it up to the wind. Then frowning, she said, "Still blowing the wrong way, dang it. Guess I'll be here a mite longer than I expected. But there's nothing to be done about it. Nobody tells the wind when to blow."

"No, ma'am." Sheena stared at the wrinkled face with lines etched so deep they looked carved into her skin. She'd never met anyone so ancient before.

"You expect to be here long? Do you have any idea where you are?" Sheena was afraid this might be one of those old people from a nursing home who sometimes wondered off and got lost.

"Oh, I know where I be. Just don't know when I can go home. Could be I'll be stuck here another day or two."

Scolding her in a voice much like her mother's, Sheena said, "Ma'am, you need to go home right now. You'll freeze to death out here."

"It is a mite cold—I'll give you that. But I didn't

expect to tarry so long. The Silver Storm has become mighty unrealiable of late. Don't know what to make of it.''

Sheena had no idea what the woman was talking about. But she did know that she couldn't let an old lady stay out in the cold like that. Though she was only twelve, she was smart enough to know you could freeze to death real fast in this awful weather.

Taking the backpack from her shoulders, she untied a blue woolen blanket and handed it to the woman. ''If you're going to be up here awhile, you better have this.''

The old one's eyes lit up. ''Why, that's mighty kindly of you, child. What did you say your name was?''

''Sheena Stewart. What's yours?''

''You just call me Old Lucy, or *Nekomes*. That's Abenaki for grandmother.''

''What's an aba-nakie?''

''Don't they teach you 'bout them in school? For shame. The Abenaki were—are—a great Indian tribe. Pardon me, I mean Native American tribe. Ain't that what they're called nowadays?''

Sheena's eyes opened wide in wonder. ''Are you a real-life Indian?''

Lucinda laughed and slapped her knee. ''Not a bit, but I've picked up some of their language, living close to 'em as I do.''

''Wow. I didn't know there were any Indians left around these parts.''

The old woman smiled slyly, then murmured, ''The Abenaki have fooled their enemies into thinking that for centuries. Thought they killed 'em off with their poxes and their wars, but Injuns have the power to melt away, scatter into small bands, and then regroup when danger passes.''

Sheena almost peed her pants then. Peering around the landscape, she expected to see the remnants of some ancient Indian tribe staring back at her. Her excitement made the urgency to go even stronger, and she danced around, trying to keep from having an accident.

Old Lucy shook her head. "For heaven's sake, child, the way you fidget so, I think I'll call you *Nanatasis.* That's Abenaki for hummingbird. Never did see a humming-bird that could stay still for a moment."

Sheena repeated the name. *Nanatasis.* Then a broad smile played across her face. "Wait till I tell the others I have an Indian name. They'll be so jealous."

"Will they now?" Lucinda's eyes sparkled with glee. "Like I was saying, the Injuns call me Nekomes, but amongst the whites, there are some who call me witch woman because I have the old magic. They come to me when they *ail.* I know what herbs will take away their bellyaches, their warts, their pain in childbirth." Sniffing at the air, she crooked her head at Sheena. "You got food in that sack?"

"Yes, ma'am." Sheena foraged through her backpack and drew out a plastic bag filled with foil-wrapped pack-ages of chicken salad sandwiches. "I guess this will get you through a day or two. Maybe by then your Silver Storm will come take you home." Sheena decided Silver Storm must be the name of a beautiful Abenaki Indian maiden. She could see her clearly in her head, a lovely young maiden with hair down to her waist and a silver band around her forehead.

The old lady sniffed at the offered food, then cackled with delight. "What a treat. What a treat. I tasted me one of them sandy witches last time I got stranded here. Some lonely soul out wandering over the mountains shared his with me. Very tasty, very tasty. Had me some chocolate Devil Dogs too. Now there's a real treat. What I wouldn't do for a mouthful of them right now."

"You've done this before?" Sheena cried, her voice elevating to a high pitch. "Doesn't your family try to stop you? Someone your age shouldn't be up here all alone."

"Pshaw! Nothing to it when you ride the Silver Storm."

Ride the Silver Storm? Her image of the lovely Indian maiden faded away and in her place stood a prancing white horse decked out in a sparkling silver saddle. Yes, Silver Storm must be the name of her horse. Had he run away from her? "Ma'am, maybe I should run ahead and tell Miss Fortunata about you. We could help you down the mountain. Our Girl Scout camp is in the valley, just a short hike down the northern slope. You could stay there until your family comes to get you."

"Now there, no need to worry your sweet little head 'bout me. I'm right at home here. And now that I have food for my belly and a blanket to keep me warm—well, I'll be just fine. You just run along and catch up to your friends."

Sheena started to walk away, but the old lady wasn't through with her yet. "Afore you go, I want to give you something as a token of my gratitude." Tugging on her pinky finger, the woman removed a silver ring and handed it to Sheena.

The wind suddenly kicked up, blowing Sheena's hair into her face. She brushed it away, then reached for the ring. Holding it in the palm of her gloved hand, she stared down at an intricate design of tiny silver snowflakes that circled the ring. "Holy shoot! I've never seen anything so pretty and delicate. But, ma'am, I can't take it. It must be very valuable."

"Oh, tush. I can make another. It's time well spent on a cold winter's eve."

Slipping the ring inside her glove, Sheena felt the tiny circle of metal against her skin and was oddly comforted. "Thank you, ma'am. I'll cherish it. It's the nicest ring I ever had."

"You remember that, then, and take care of it and someday . . . well, someday it might just lead you to your destiny. Now you run along before you lose your friends in the fog."

Sheena stared at the woman in awe. She wanted to ask Nekomes just what her destiny would be, but something kept her from it. Anyhow, she already knew what it was. She was destined to be a famous writer. "You sure you don't want to come with me?"

Nekomes shook her head, then holding up her finger to the wind again said, "The wind is shifting. Won't be long now. *Wlipamkaani.* That means travel well."

Sheena started off in search of her troop, but the need to pee was too great to deny any longer, so she ducked behind a large boulder and relieved herself. A sudden gust of wind blew snow onto her bare skin, making her wish all the more she was home snug and warm in her own bed. She thought about the old woman then, and became ashamed of walking away from her. How could she think of leaving her in this wild place? Someone her age needed more than a blanket and a few sandwiches to survive.

With that thought in mind, she headed back toward the standing rocks. The wind was stronger now, bringing with it a flurry of snow, and she paused to survey the landscape, feeling suddenly uneasy. From where she stood, she had a clear view of the rocks, but there was no sign of Old Lucy. The blanket and packet of food were gone too.

Where had she gone? No one could disappear so quickly. Especially someone that old. Unless . . . Had her Silver Storm come back for her? The horse could have come while she was behind the rocks, peeing. That was the only thing that made any sense. And it sure made her feel less guilty to believe that, for it would mean Old Lucy didn't need her help after all.

She turned back to the trail in time to see Miss Fortunata appear out of the mist.

"There you are, Sheena. You gave me such a fright. What in the world possessed you to take off like that?"

Sheena started to tell her about the quaint old woman, but changed her mind. One look at the Girl Scout leader's face and she knew she wouldn't believe her story. Sheena did have the reputation for telling tall tales. Well, darn it all, it wasn't her fault she was born with a vivid imagination, was it? She needed a creative mind if she was ever going to be a writer.

Feeling the silver snowflake ring inside her glove, she made up her mind to keep her encounter a secret. But she could hardly wait to get home and write about it in her journal. She might even put the scene with Old Lucy in a book someday. Then the whole world would know about Lost Mountain and the old lady who rode on a Silver Storm.

CHAPTER ONE

December, 2000

From the cockpit of the helicopter, Sheena Stewart stared down at the cliff that jutted out from the top of Lost Mountain and understood how it got its name. Surrounded by much taller mountain peaks, it was hidden from view at ground level, except from the western side.

Seeing it from the air for the first time, she was struck by the desolation of the ragged cliff. Compared to the rest of the mountain and all the other dense, tree-covered peaks nearby, Lost Mountain could only be described as bleak. Had something cataclysmic happened here long ago?

That was very likely, since only the cliff side was devoid of vegetation. A shiver crawled up her spine as her imaginative mind invented different scenarios to explain the barren cliff.

But she was still thinking like a twelve-year-old. There was nothing mysterious about Lost Mountain except for its name. She had hiked up and down the gentle north side of Lost Mountain many times without fear. In fact, the well-worn path ended in the peaceful, secluded valley where her old Girl Scout camp still stood.

From this altitude she could just make out the many buildings of the camp, looking like tiny dollhouses in the pretty winter setting. *Pretty winter setting, my foot.* Remembering the winter hike when she was twelve, she knew just how cold it actually was down there.

What had ever possessed her to choose this place for her photo shoot? Deep in thought, Sheena unconsciously twirled the snowflake ring around and around her finger. Hmm, she had to admit that something about Lost Mountain called to her spirit, and much as she might want to, she couldn't deny it.

Jared Jones must have been having second thoughts too, for he suddenly declared, "Hey, babe. You sure you want to go through with this? It looks wicked cold down there, not to mention slippery."

Sheena tried to take a deep breath before answering, but the beaded, silver-embroidered bodice of the wedding gown she wore was too tight. She settled for a reassuring smile. "Piece of cake, right, Tony? Helicopters land on mountaintops all the time. Carolyn told me you had to rescue some hikers from Mount Greylock just last week."

"That doesn't mean it's safe," the pilot, Tony Absolem, answered stoically. "Hey, the only reason I agreed to this harebrained stunt is because you and my wife are such good friends. I would have been relegated to the sofa for the next two weeks if I had refused. Like Jared said, it's pretty slippery down there and the wind's picking up. That fancy gown you're wearing could billow out like a sail and take you right over the cliff."

"Stop trying to scare me, Tony. It's a little late for that." Lifting her voluminous skirt, she wiggled her foot. "And besides, I came prepared. These are my lucky hiking boots. They saved my hide more than once. Don't worry. I know what I'm doing."

"The jury's still out on that," Jared answered. "I still think you should have chosen the Bahamas for the setting

of your next book. What were you thinking? We could
be relaxing on the beach as we speak, instead of freezing
our tushes off up here in the frozen North.''

"Hey, I have to go where my muse takes me. *Winter's
Bride* could hardly be set on some balmy tropical shore,
now could it? Admit it. You're looking forward to this.
What other photographer would be given such an opportunity to express himself so outrageously?''

"What other photographer would be crazy enough to
freeze his balls off, dangling out the door of a helicopter
to take those shots? Only one—that's who. Yours truly.''

"You don't fool me, Jared. You love this kind of stuff,
and you know it.''

"You're right about that, kiddo. If this shoot works
out the way I want, they'll be talking about this picture
for a long time. It's a great publicity stunt.''

Sheena thought about that for a moment. "It's not just
for publicity, Jared. I really like posing in costumes for
my covers. My readers have come to expect to see me
dressed like my heroines on the back cover of my books.
I'll never forget the first one I did for *Rosefire*. I thought
I was being very outlandish dressed in a Scottish tartan
and holding a sword, and I was afraid it would backfire
on me, but the readers loved it and—''

"We're about to descend," the pilot interjected.
"Remember everything I told you. And make sure you
keep your headset hooked up, so we can communicate.
Under no circumstances are you to remove the battery pack.
And, Sheena, let's make this quick. I just got a report of a
snowstorm heading this way.''

"Roger," Sheena quipped, trying to sound lighthearted
and confident, while butterflies were doing barrel rolls in
her stomach. She braced herself as the copter descended,
glad that the noise drowned out the frantic beat of her
heart. She didn't want Jared or Tony to know just how
scared she was.

But then, she was just being foolish. What could possibly go wrong? Jared didn't even have to leave the helicop-

ter. He was going to take the pictures from the air. They had agreed that a photo of her in a wedding gown, complete with attached fur cape instead of the usual veil, and a matching fake rabbit fur muff instead of a bouquet of flowers, would be spectacular against the raw beauty of the snowy mountain.

The helicopter bumped to a stop, settling near the edge of the cliff, and when Tony gave the word, she opened the door scooped up her skirt, and stepped outside. The cold blast of air that hit her almost made her change her mind, but the thought of disappointing her readers kept her from turning back. Giving a thumbs-up sign to Jared and Tony, she ducked her head and stepped gingerly through the snow, aware with every step she took that there was no guardrail at the edge of the cliff.

When she was far enough back to feel secure, she waved off the helicopter and it began to rise slowly, its whirling blades kicking up snow furiously in her face. Digging her feet in until she felt solid rock beneath her shoes, she told herself, *I can do this.* Smoothing out the skirt of her gown, she made sure it was positioned attractively, then stuck one hand inside the fur muff and smiled up at the helicopter.

The copter was far enough away now not to blow snow in her face, and yet it was still dancing about her. It took a moment for her to realize it had begun to snow. Perfect. If Jared could capture the snow in the picture, all the better.

She almost laughed seeing Jared poised precariously out the open door of the copter, and she moved from pose to pose as he snapped away, while relaying instructions to her through the small receiver in her ear. She did as he asked until the frigid air penetrated the very marrow of her bones and her eyes wept from the cold. "Hey, Jared. You got enough? The cold is really starting to get to me."

"I hear you, babe. Just one more. I want a shot from

higher up so we can get more of the scenery in. You game?''

Her teeth chattered, distorting her answer. "One more and make it a good one. I can't take this cold any longer."

She watched as the copter rose higher in the air, in awe that such a heavy chunk of metal could actually defy gravity. Suddenly battered by a blast of icy wind, Sheena lost her balance and fell backwards. With her heart in her throat, she started sliding toward the cliff's edge. Frantically, she dug her hiking boots into the snow and came to a halt just inches from the edge. If the snow had been any deeper she would have gone over the edge, but lucky for her it was only a couple of inches deep. Just enough to color the mountain white. *Just enough to get her killed.*

When she stopped shaking, she spoke into the microphone attached to her shoulder. "Well, Jared, I sure hope you got that shot."

The expected expletive-filled retort from Jared never came. The noise of the engine sounded different now, and curious, she looked up at the copter. The sun blinded her for a moment, and when her eyes adjusted to the brightness, her heart stopped. Why was the helicopter tilted at such an odd angle? "Tony. Jared. What's wrong with the copter? It's . . ."

Before she had time to finish the sentence, she saw it careen out of control and she watched in disbelief as it started to spiral downward. She kept waiting for it to right itself, thinking, *This can't be happening. It can't.*

But it was.

She watched in horror as the copter circled lower and lower until the cockpit was below the cliff and the knife-like blades were slicing into the rock, breaking off and catapulting through the air helter-skelter.

Sheena plastered her body against the snow-covered ground, afraid of being hit by the flying metal, and heard the terrible sound of the copter hitting the cliff walls repeatedly in its deadly descent. The muffled thud that followed told her it had crashed.

"Oh, God! No! *No!*"

Still lying flat against the snow-covered ground, she used her elbows to help pull herself to the edge of the cliff. The long skirt of her gown made it difficult to move. But she had to know. She had to see for herself what had happened to her friends.

Peering over the edge she saw the copter crumpled and split, and feared the worst. How could anyone survive such a terrible accident? But they had to. They just had to.

"Jared! Tony! Please answer me. Please. Tell me you're all right. Oh, God, let me hear your voice."

But the world was deadly silent.

This can't be happening. It can't be happening.

Her body started to tremble violently. In shock she struggled to her feet and gazed down at the devastation. A sense of helplessness drew over her like a black shroud. What was she to do? She had to go down to them. Help them. Pull them from the wreckage. But how? There was no quick way to get down. She'd have to hike down the northern slope, then around the bottom of the mountain to reach them. That would take hours. By then, surely a rescue team would have been there and gone. There was nothing she could do but wait. Hope that they were found before it was too late.

She tried to tell herself that everything would be all right. That very soon now someone would find them. *Alive.* A road wound around the base of the mountain, clearly visible from the cliff. Surely someone would drive by soon and see the fallen copter. They had to. *Oh, please, someone come right now. Right now. Right now.*

But though she willed it mightily, no one came. Nothing moved on the horizon. It was as if she were the only one left in the world. And she had never felt so lonely in her life.

Gazing down at the wreckage with a heart breaking in

two, she waited for the tears to come. Waited for the
sense of guilt to overtake her, knowing it was her fault
they had crashed. And she waited for someone to come
and take her away so she wouldn't have to look at the
devastation she had caused with her vanity.

Her violent trembling continued, tiring her quickly, and
she pulled her cape tight around her to warm herself. But
it was little protection from the cold. It was strictly a
costume prop, a pretty ornament. If the rescue team didn't
come soon, she'd freeze to death.

She thought about hiking down to the shelter of the
Girl Scout camp, but quickly dismissed that idea. She'd
never make it through the snow weighed down by her
heavy, ice-stiffened gown. As it was, it was nearly impossible to move in it. How ironic that a beautiful wedding
gown, the symbol of love, life and happiness, could con-
tribute to her death instead.

But no need to dwell on that. There was another compelling reason why she should stay where she was. It would
be easier for the rescue team to find her up here on the
cliff. Dressed in white, she blended in too much with the
snowy landscape. They might never find her and she'd
perish for sure.

Thank heaven she had been smart enough to wear her
old battered hiking boots. Her feet were the only part of
her that was warm. She half-laughed, half-cried, thinking
about the old adage of dying with your boots on. Well,
she wasn't ready to give up yet. She was going to die of
old age, sleeping in the warm comfort of her bed.

Time passed slowly, agonizingly, and still there was
no sign of rescue. Surely someone had noticed the helicopter was overdue back at the airport. Tony must have
filed a flight plan. She remembered Carolyn mentioning
something like that. Oh, why hadn't she paid more attention?

But what if he hadn't? What if no one knew where
they were? What then? Hysterical laughter bubbled up
and then escaped, turning quickly into wild sobs. "Jared.

Tony. I'm so sorry for getting you into this mess. Oh, God, I'm so sorry."

Trying to bolster her spirits, she looked around and saw the familiar outcropping of boulders and the faery seat where Old Lucy—Nekomes—had sat so many years ago, and she realized she had a better chance of survival waiting in the shelter of the boulders.

Making her way over to the stone seat, she sat down, feeling the coldness of the rock seep into her bottom. She tried to think straight, to figure out what she should be doing to save herself, but her mind was numb. How could this have happened? Why had she been so foolish, so frivolous to attempt this venture?

And . . . oh, dear God, how could she face Carolyn? She'd rather die out here in the cold than have to tell her that her husband and brother were dead.

Oh, great. Now she was feeling sorry for herself. A long time ago she vowed never to feel sorry for herself no matter how tough things got. And she had kept that vow when her parents died two years ago, and through the long, drawn-out divorce from Peter last year. she wasn't going to give in to self-pity now. She was a survivor. She just had to use her head. That was all.

And the first thing she had to do was get warm. Rising to her feet, she danced around to keep the blood circulating, and remembered the Indian name the old woman had given her. *Nanatasis. Hummingbird. Where are you now, old woman? Did you get back home safely, or did you die up here too?*

Touching the snowflake ring on her finger, she whispered, "Help me, Nekomes. Send your Silver Storm to rescue me."

The thought of a beautiful white stallion appearing like magic and carrying her effortlessly down the mountain was strangely comforting. Sitting back down on the stone seat, she closed her eyes and escaped into a fantasy world where such things were possible.

It had always been her gift to conjure up scenes in her

head as if she were watching a movie, and that talent had helped in her career as a writer. And now, it helped her forget how cold she was. Playing the scene of her fairy tale–like rescue over and over in her mind, she drifted off to a world caught halfway between sleep and consciousness.

But eventually, even that didn't help ward off the numbing cold, so she opened her eyes and was surprised to see that it was dark. How had she lost track of so much time? She knew how dangerous that could be. She had heard that people who died of exposure just drifted off to sleep and never awoke again. She couldn't let that happen.

Shivering, she walked over to the edge of the cliff and looked out to the horizon. In the distance she could see a light flickering on and off, but before she could even begin to hope it was a rescue team, she realized it was only the beacon light flashing from a mountain peak. A beam of light to keep airplanes from crashing into the mountain.

Another, brighter light compelled her to look up, and overhead she saw the pastel lemon-slice moon. How lovely and lonely, at the same time. How uncaring of what was happening to her and to her friends tangled in the wreck below her.

And then, a sound traveled to her on the night air, and she strained her ears, hoping to hear it again. Praying it wasn't her imagination. Daring to believe she was about to be rescued. Ahh, there it was again. The nickering of a horse. Was she imagining it? Or ... had she truly conjured up Nekomes's Silver Storm?

Hanging on to a thread of hope, she turned very slowly, her heart in her throat.

Blinking back her surprise, she saw a gentle cyclone of snow. It was as if the wind were blowing only in that one spot. And emerging from the very center of the swirling snow was a white horse. A *silvery* white horse. Sparkling silver specks of snow twinkled and shimmered and circled around the magnificent animal as if caught in some ancient rhythm of nature, while bright moonlit snowflakes glistened on the stallion's sleek back.

The Silver Storm.

Her wish had come true. He had come for her just as he had for Old Lucy so many years ago.

For just a moment, reason overtook her, and she realized it couldn't be the same horse the old woman had waited for. That horse would be ancient now, and this one was in the prime of life, his muscled body rippling with the strength and energy of vigorous youth. But her imagination countered with the Son of the Silver Storm. That was who it was. *Son of the Silver Storm.* What a great title that would be for a book.

If only Jared could see this. Wouldn't he love to capture this beautiful scene on film?

The sudden remembrance of him and the terrible accident brought reality back to her cruelly, swiftly, and she felt herself close to collapsing. She struggled to keep standing, struggled to move away from the treacherous cliff behind her. Struggled to move toward the life force disguised as a magical horse.

With her gaze still locked onto the animal and the swirling silver snow, she took a step and then another and another, moving toward the shimmering creature. In truth, she could do nothing else. Drawn by the stallion's beauty and the glow of the moon reflected on the silvery snow, she likened it to gazing at the white light people claimed to see in near-death experiences. Perhaps the swirling snow was the tunnel you had to travel through to get to the white light.

She came to a halt. *No. Don't even think it. I'm not ready to die yet. I'm not ready to go to the white light*

Ah, but the white light was coming to her. It bobbed along toward her as if floating in air. As it got closer she could see it was no specter, but a lantern held in the hand of a dark figure dressed in furs.

Was she imagining that too? She couldn't bear it if she

was imagining this. Not quite trusting what she saw, she
started moving toward the light.

Strong arms closed around her as the man clad in fur
caught her in his arms, then lifted and carried her. Clutching at the man's jacket, she held on to him for dear life.

Dear life. Oh, yes, it was. And thanks to this wonderful
man, she would go on living it.

Staring up at the man's face, she realized he was more
than just a rescuer, he was her lifeline to reality, her
lifeline to the world of warmth and safety, for she would
surely have lost her mind or died from the cold, not to
mention the terrible aloneness that had pressed down on
her.

Setting her on his horse, the man removed his fur jacket
and wrapped it around her, and the sudden warmth sent
violent shivers coursing through her. The man looked up
at her then, with eyes that burned through to her soul,
and in the warmth of that gaze, the shivering stopped.

And then he was leading the horse toward the center
of the cyclone of snow, and though she thought it odd,
she wasn't frightened. Not anymore. Not as long as she
could gaze into eyes that drew her more compellingly
than any white light ever could.

CHAPTER TWO

Unsure whether she was dreaming or hallucinating or really experiencing the incredible fairy tale rescue, complete with knight and white horse, Sheena prayed she wouldn't suddenly find herself alone, still sitting on the cold stone seat, her only companion the pale face of the moon.

But it must be real. How else could she feel the warmth from the horse's body against her shivering legs? How else could she smell the man's masculine scent radiating from the fur jacket?

But where was he taking her? She knew this mountain. There was no refuge anywhere on it. The nearest shelter was the Girl Scout camp in the valley. Needing reassurance, she compelled him with her thoughts to look at her, and he did, staring back at her steadfastly.

Wondrously, without saying a word, he conveyed to her the reassurance she needed. Even in the pale lantern light she could see his incredibly mesmerizing eyes, and she trusted what she saw in them. He would take care of her. He would take her someplace warm. He would stay with her forever.

Forever? Where had that thought come from? She was really losing it now. Poor man would be surprised to find she had claimed him for her own. But then, she was a dreamer and dreamers could dream anything they liked, couldn't they? And right now she needed to dream of a happily ever after so she wouldn't have to face bitter reality.

She knew she wasn't being rational, but then it wasn't every day a crazy woman posed for a picture on a frozen cliff in a satin wedding gown. It wasn't every day someone experienced the horror of seeing friends plummet to the ground from a great height, and it wasn't every day someone nearly froze to death. Hadn't she earned the right to a little fantasy?

They were in front of the silvery cyclone of snow now, and she became suddenly uneasy, despite his reassuring presence. Why was he leading her into the snow? Hadn't she experienced enough stormy weather to last a lifetime? She started to protest, but before she could speak they were inside the cone, and the fierce wind was taking her breath away.

She felt as if she were on a wild elevator ride to the bottom of a tall building. But there was no skyscraper. There was nothing but a cold mountain, a deep sorrow, and the hypnotizing eyes of a stranger.

She must have blacked out, for when she came to her senses they were no longer on the mountain, but riding toward a pale orange light that flickered and glowed in the distance.

And the man no longer walked beside her but was seated behind her on the silvery horse, his hands on either side of her holding the reins. Grateful for his presence, she leaned into him, finding comfort in the solid wall of his body.

The horse suddenly broke into a gallop, and in a moment they were close enough to the light for her to make out it was coming from a picturesque cottage made of stone.

A feathery stream of smoke rose gently from the chimney, and she shivered in anticipation of the warmth it promised.

The cottage looked inviting, and cozy, nestled in the valley between the mountains, and she supposed the man lived there. What a potent combination. Cozy home and strong, protective male. Thinking of that inviting image, she started to drift again, but the sudden jerking stop of the horse pulled her back to reality. *Or what she prayed was reality.*

"We're home," the man said, talking to her for the first time, and the deep masculine resonance of his voice thrilled her. In those mere two words, he seemed to be letting her know she belonged to him, that this beautiful stone cottage was to be her home from this moment forward.

She told herself her imagination was really working overtime. Either that, or the deep loneliness she had experienced on the mountain had addled her brain. How could anyone convey all that with just two little words? But it nagged at her that he really meant it that way. Who was this mysterious, charismatic man?

Then he was lifting her from the horse and carrying her inside, and her misgivings flew from her mind as the delicious warmth of an open fire surrounded her like the comfort blanket she had as a child. She was safe. Soon she would be warm. That was all that mattered for the moment.

No! Not true! She had to get help for Jared and Tony. What was she thinking? How could she have forgotten about their plight for even a moment? What was happening to her?

"My friends . . . We have to get help for my friends. Will you call 911 and see if they know about the crash yet?"

For a moment, she feared he didn't understand what she was saying, but she must have misread the expression on his face for he answered, "It's been taken care of."

Relief flooded over her and she cried, "Thank God. Are they all right?"

"I couldn't say."

Her uneasiness crept back. Why was he being so vague? "May I use your phone? I need to know how they are. Do you know what hospital they were taken to?"

"Phone? I don't know what you mean."

It was her turn to look at him with a strange expression. "Surely you have a phone?"

He stared at her for a long uncomfortable moment as if trying to decide the right thing to say. "Forgive me. You're tired after your ordeal. It's no wonder you're not making any sense. I'll have my servant prepare a bed for you." With that, he took a candle from the mantel and walked from the room. Sheena stared after him in shock. Not making any sense? How could she have been any clearer? What was going on? Was she losing her mind?

Looking around the room helplessly, as if searching for an answer to her dilemma, she became aware of her surroundings for the first time. The inside of the cottage was every bit as inviting as the outside, but there was something very odd about it. The furniture was ruggedly built, as if hewn from trees on that very spot, and something else ... Gazing at the flickering light from the myriad of candles that glowed from tables and shelves, she realized what it was. There was no electricity. No switches on the wall, no overhead lights, no lamps or radios or television sets.

But there was nothing very odd about that. After all, they were out in the wilderness, weren't they? Miles from a town. True, but she knew firsthand that the Girl Scout camp had electricity and at least one telephone that worked even in the winter. And the camp had to be close by. Perhaps he didn't want anything to do with modern technology. Perhaps he was some kind of history nut who wanted to live as his ancestors had. She had heard about people like that, had even met some of them while doing research for her books.

It came to her then that, if there was no electricity, there wouldn't be any telephones either. But if that were true . . . how had he called 911?

Maybe he hadn't. Maybe he had seen the rescue from atop the mountain. Of course he had. If she hadn't drifted off to sleep she would have seen it too. That explained why he didn't know whether they had survived or not. He was too far away to see their condition.

Content that she had solved the mystery, she waited for him to return. She was still shaking from the cold, and from the trauma of everything that had happened, and the need of sinking into a warm bed was becoming more and more urgent. She wanted to sleep dreamless, mind-numbing sleep and forget all about today, if just for a little while.

He appeared in the doorway saying, "My mother and the servant have both retired for the night, and I don't want to disturb them. I'll just see to your bed myself."

Sheena followed him up the staircase to the second floor. He opened the door and she stepped inside, shivering again when she saw their shadows climb up the wall as if trying to escape.

Carrying the candle over to a chest of drawers, he set it down. "I'll find you something to wear so you can get out of that wet gown. I'm afraid one of my shirts will have to do until morning."

"That will be fine."

"I'll just be a moment then."

When he returned, he was carrying a long, voluminous white shirt, and she was struck by the archaic style of it. He had strange taste in clothing. That thought prompted her to look closely at him. Not his face, which she knew by heart now, but the way he was dressed. She hadn't had time to notice before, but he was wearing a shirt very similar to the one he handed to her, and breeches instead of pants, tall boots instead of shoes.

She had seen men dressed like that at various historical reenactments, and she had certainly done enough research on period clothing to know he was dressed like an early-seventeenth-century man.

Curious, she started to ask him why he wore such outdated clothing, but changed her mind, afraid of the answer. A violent shiver chattered through her, and she decided she would deal with her curiosity when she wasn't feeling quite so vulnerable.

He handed her the shirt. "Good night then. Try not to worry about your friends. Their fate is in God's hands now."

He turned to leave, and an unsettling foreboding fell over her. The incredible aloneness she had felt on the cliff came back to haunt her. Holding her hand out to him, she said, "Please . . . would you stay with me awhile? I can't bear being alone again."

Taking her offered hand, he silently walked her over to the bed. "Turn around; I'll unbutton your dress so you can get out of it. You'll feel better once you're dry."

She did as she was told, standing as still as her shivering body allowed, while he struggled with the tiny pearl buttons. His closeness was reassuring, yet at the same time disconcerting, and she wondered if he too was affected by the intimacy of his actions. Now, what compelled her to think of that? He was just being kind and she did need help getting undressed. That was all there was to it.

When he was done, he took a quilt from atop a chest and wrapped it around her. "Step out of your dress now."

Another deep shiver coursed through her as her body reacted to the lovely warmth of the blanket. At least, that was what she told herself, but in truth it could have been his close proximity that caused her reaction. There was something about him that made her feel more alive, more female, more unsettled, than she had ever felt before. But then, having just escaped death, she was bound to feel that way, wasn't she?

The gown fell in a puddle around her ankles, and she was amazed to see that parts of it were still stiff and frozen. She realized again how lucky she was to be alive.

He slipped his shirt over her head while she held the quilt tight around her, and when she put her arms into the sleeves, she let the quilt fall to the floor and quickly climbed into bed.

A deep sigh escaped her throat. She should be jubilant that she had survived the cold. That she hadn't been on the copter when it went down. That she was warm and safe in a dream cottage, with a man as beautiful to look at as any she had ever seen. Yet she felt as if she were tottering on the edge of an abyss. Clearly she was still traumatized.

"Will you stay with me until I fall asleep?"

He whispered his answer, as if he didn't want her to hear, but she could swear he said, "I'll stay with you forever."

Forever. She sighed, and snuggled into the covers, and her eyelids, too heavy to stay open, slowly closed. Just before sleep came, she thought, *I don't even know his name.* Then, letting go of the last thread of consciousness, she fell into a deep sleep.

Michael Winters stared into the blazing fire, his mind as frenzied as the dancing flames. No use going to bed now. He'd never sleep. Thinking of the girl upstairs, he knew he had a chance to have the life that such a short time ago seemed closed to him forever. He'd be a fool not to take advantage of the situation.

Even now, it was hard to believe he had found *her.* It was enough to make him believe in miracles. Thinking of the way she was dressed in that incredible wedding gown, he knew there could be no more potent omen that she was meant to be his bride. A bride to warm his bed, to share his life, to bear his children. How long had he dreamt of that? Too long. Too long.

To think he might not have found her if his stallion

hadn't sailed over the corral fence and raced up the mountain path! Tired as he was, he almost didn't go after him right away, since in an hour's time he'd have to make the trek anyway, when it was his turn for sentry duty. And after all, where could Pale Warrior go on that lonely peak? *Nowhere but the dangerous cliff.*

Horses were such stupid, unpredictable animals, it was possible he might gallop right over the edge in the dark, and he couldn't afford to lose such a valuable animal.

He could have saddled a horse for the trek up the mountain, but he had declined to trust an animal with the delicate task of making it up the icy, narrow path. And he was glad of that decision when he saw how slippery it was.

What had compelled Pale Warrior to gallop up the mountain? It was almost as if he had set out to lead him to the girl. But that was just romantic nonsense. The horse had no more knowledge of her being up there than he did.

Absentmindedly, he placed another log on the fire, then leaned back on the settle to think about what he should do next. No, not what he *should do,* what he *wanted* to do, which was an entirely different thing. He had already lied to her about her friends. But it was for her own sake. Telling her they were taken care of had eased her mind enough to let her get the sleep she needed to recover from her ordeal.

Still, it was a lie, and one he could benefit from greatly. Damn it all, he abhorred lies and the people who spoke them. But if lying was the only way he could keep her in his life, then so be it. He should be used to lying by now, having done it before to others who wandered into Lost Valley. But thankfully, it was a rare day indeed when someone wandered here.

Thank God she had.

The moment he had seen her in the pale moonlight,

dressed in the shimmering white gown, he knew he wanted her for his bride.

He'd remember that lovely sight the rest of his life, for surely it was the most beautiful scene he had ever witnessed, not to mention the most bizarre. What kind of woman strolled across the top of a lonely mountain in the dead of winter dressed like that? *His kind of woman, for certain.*

He had wanted to take a wife for over three years now, and his desperation had driven him to travel to Plymouth, and the risk of being murdered by the superstitious folk there, all for the sake of finding a wife. But he had returned with only an indentured servant for his mother.

He should have realized he'd find no wife in Plymouth. Conditions were deplorable there, and with so few women, none could be spared to marry a stranger from the mountains.

They acted as if the mountains of Massachusetts were far removed from them, but in truth they were only a three-day ride away. They had been wary of him, until he explained that he was from Jamestown. It wasn't true, but he knew they had been visited many times by men from the Virginia colony and were more apt to accept him that way.

Still, it had been a mistake to go there. Even if there had been women aplenty to choose from, he doubted that any Puritan woman would be suitable for his unusual life. He needed a woman with the same sense of obligation to the future of mankind that had driven him to live in a place so isolated from the very people he hoped to save.

But he didn't want to clutter his mind with such serious thoughts right now. Instead, he'd think of the magical creature who would become his bride.

Winters's bride, in more ways than one.

For hadn't she dropped out of the skies to be with him in the very heart of a winter storm? Even an ungodly man such as he could think of her as a gift from heaven.

Ah, yes, a gift from heaven, that was the way to think

of it. Then he wouldn't have to contemplate where she came from, or for whom she had worn a wedding dress. Not that it mattered anymore. She was in his world now, and by all that was right and holy in *this* world, she'd stay. He'd do anything, risk anything, to make her his.

CHAPTER THREE

The night was full of stars, winking at her from above as she skated on the frozen river that meandered through Lost Valley. Her skating partner held her waist snugly, and they skated in perfect harmony to the music of "River of No Return," the haunting song from the old Marilyn Monroe movie by the same name. Had it been only a few days since she and Carolyn had watched it on the small TV in her bedroom, while Jared and Tony watched a football game on the giant screen in their den?

She had never been able to master the art of ice-skating before. Her ankles had always been too weak to hold her up on the thin blades. How weird that she could skate so well now. But here she was, arm in arm with the handsome man who had rescued her from the cliff, ice dancing every bit as masterfully as an Olympic pairs team.

She laughed out loud at the thought, and he looked down at her with eyes that twinkled as brightly as the stars overhead.

"I'll stay with you forever," he said, and she nodded her head, wanting to please him.

He started guiding her out to the middle of the river,

but she was suddenly hesitant, remembering a sign at the river's edge that said, THIN ICE. "No. I don't want to go out there."

"Too late," he answered, and she heard the ice begin to crack. "Toooo laaate."

Sheena awoke with a start, still hearing the words echoing in her head, but now they were being spoken in a woman's voice.

Searching for the source of the voice, she saw a toothpick of a woman standing in the doorway. Her heart sank when she saw the seventeenth-century clothing she wore. Was this a dream within a dream? Or was it a nightmare?

"Too late, mistress. Ye have stayed abed too late. 'Tis a sin before God to waste the day in such an indulgent way."

Sheena felt the urge to protest. What business was it of this stranger how late she stayed in bed?

" 'Tis seven o'clock in the morning. Long past time to get up. But Master Michael thought ye'd benefit from a little extra sleep, considering the ordeal ye have been through. Hmph. He's a good one to talk. 'Twas past dawn before he left to do his chores."

Sheena swung her legs out of bed and sat up. "Is there any news of my friends? I need to know what happened to them."

Seeing her distress, the woman's voice softened. "Be not fearful, mistress. The master has the reputation for finding lost souls."

How odd to hear the woman call someone master. Things just kept getting stranger and stranger. *"The master?"*

"Master Michael Winters. This be his home. His and his mother's, though ye'd never know it. She spends more time at the neighbors' dwellings than her own. I'm Sarah. Been here no more than a year, m'self. Traveled through this wild, heathen territory from Plymouth Colony, I did, to my deep regret. If someone had but told me when I signed on as an indentured servant that I would have to leave the goodly Puritans of Plymouth and serve my time in the bowels of the wilderness, I would have thought them daft. But here I be, and here I'm forced to stay for near on three more years.''

Sheena stared at the woman in disbelief. *Puritans? Plymouth Colony? Indentured servant? If she mentions the* Mayflower, *I'll know I'm dreaming for sure.*

''I tell thee, the day I stepped on that cursed ship *Mayflower* was the worst day of my life. I had a premonition it would be a disastrous journey, and it surely was. 'Twas my fate to board the ship at the last moment. I discovered later my name was never added to the register. Can ye believe that? As far as me family back in England knows, I've disappeared from the face of the earth.''

Sheena stared at the woman in shock. This had to be a dream.

''But enough of my sad story. We'll have plenty of time to talk and get to know each other, now won't we? What else will there be to do all winter long?''

Sheena felt her sanity slipping. She struggled to understand what was happening and grasped at the idea that the people here were reenactors who took their hobby very seriously, living the roles of their ancestors in their everyday lives. How else to explain the way they dressed and spoke? As strange as that was, it was easier to accept than the idea she had somehow traveled back in time to the days of the Pilgrims.

There was only one way to find out the truth.

Clearing her throat, she spoke timidly. ''I know this is going to sound silly, but could you tell me what year this is?''

''Mistress, there be nothing silly about that. Living in the wilderness, 'tis easy to forget what day it is, there being no meeting house or preacher here to keep us straight. 'Tis the twenty-first day of January in the year of our Lord sixteen hundred and thirty.''

Sheena blinked back her surprise. 1630? Seven years after the Pilgrims landed? Somehow that seemed more frighteningly real to her than if the woman had said it was the year the *Mayflower* actually landed at Plymouth Rock.

"When Master Michael told me ye arrived from Jamestown late last night, well, 'twas beyond belief, but here ye be. Imagine losing your traveling companions and surviving the wilderness on your own. God must surely have been watching over ye, to have come through such an ordeal."

Sheena felt as if she were in never-never land. Nothing made any sense. Why would Michael Winters tell this woman she came from Jamestown? Seeing the expectant look on her face, she realized Sarah was waiting for an answer. In shock, she couldn't think of a thing to say.

To her relief, the sudden barking of dogs drew the woman to the window, making a reply unnecessary. "Master's home. And me with no breakfast ready."

The woman flew out the door, prompting Sheena to go to the window and peer out. The glare of snow from the wintry world outside caused her to close her eyes, but they popped open when it registered on her brain that the view of the mountains was very familiar.

It was the same view she had enjoyed when she had attended the Girl Scout camp. But then ... where were the buildings? The pool and the tennis court? Where was the flagpole where they recited the Pledge of Allegiance every morning?

All she could see now was a barn and a corral, and in the distance a few more quaint houses at the edge of the river, but nothing that remotely resembled the Girl Scout camp. What was happening to her? The camp couldn't have disappeared. *No. It couldn't have. But ... if it is really 1630, the buildings wouldn't have been built for another three hundreds years yet.* But that was crazy. Cra-zee.

There had to be an explanation. In desperate need to know the truth, she pulled on her hiking boots, now toasty warm from sitting by the fire, and without another thought, she flung open the door and ran out to the snow-covered world.

As she gazed first at the familiar mountain, and then at the unfamiliar surroundings nestled below it, a terrible sinking feeling came over her. Nothing was as it should be.

Hearing the crunch of footsteps in the snow, she spun around to face the man who had rescued her. Ohhh! He was even more handsome than she remembered. But more than that, there was something about him that pulled at her heart. Something that called to her on the wind, warning her that if she gazed into his eyes too long, she would be forever lost. No wonder she had dreamed about him last night. Just being in his presence was like being on thin ice.

Taking in her makeshift nightgown, he said, "Mistress, you have the strangest way of dressing for cold weather I ever did see."

Sheena looked down at the long shirt she wore and felt a blush rise on her face. Still confused and dazed, she stared up at his face, and felt suddenly reassured. The smile he gave her was so open and sweet, she immediately felt much better.

Her gaze would have lingered, taking in all that male beauty, but over his shoulder she saw what at first she took as a large dog, then realized was a wolf.

"Don't let my friend scare you. He'll not harm you. We have an understanding. He would never harm anything belonging to me."

Sheena looked at Michael, puzzled and a little frightened by his words, but he smiled again and her fears vanished. Surely he didn't know how possessive his words sounded. He was just generalizing, not speaking specifically of her. Of course he wasn't. She didn't belong to him. She wasn't an indentured servant bought and paid for to do his bidding.

He was still smiling at her, as if expecting her to respond with a smile of her own, so she obliged him. His smile widened, and his eyes lit up like amber crystals. She'd have to watch herself around him, for certain. Not only was he the most handsome man she had ever met, but he had the most beguiling smile she had ever seen. It was a thrill just to look at him. Struggling to hide his effect on her, she said, "Does he belong to you? The wolf, I mean."

"Not any more than I could own the wind. Silver Fang stops by from time to time to be fed. He's not able to hunt as well anymore since losing most of his teeth to the butt of a fur trader's rifle."

She started to shiver, and Michael took off his jacket and wrapped it around her. "One of us is going to end up dead from the cold if you insist on going outside dressed so poorly, and I fear it will be me."

She heard laughter and was surprised to find it was from her own mouth. After everything that had happened, she was glad to know she could still laugh.

Taking her arm, he escorted her inside. Uneasily, she looked over her shoulder and was relieved to see the wolf lope off toward the river.

Once inside, she slipped out of his jacket and handed it back to him. "I promise not to deprive you of your jacket again. It should please you to know I don't usually act like this. It's just . . . just . . ."

Suddenly and unexpectedly, everything that had happened bore down on her as if she had been saving up for this moment, and she became so choked up she couldn't speak. He was really going to think she was crazy now.

Michael spoke to his servant woman in a gruff voice. "Sarah, bring hot tea for my guest, please."

Turning back to Michael, Sheena said, "I'm sorry. I didn't mean to get emotional. I'll be fine now."

Michael took her hand and escorted her to the settle by the fireplace. "You're entitled to a good cry . . . Mistress . . . I'm sorry. I don't believe you told me your name."

Sheena sat down, then gazing into Michael's eyes, said,

"I'm Sheena Stewart, bona fide crazy woman. What else could I be, standing on a snowy mountain in a wedding dress?"

Michael grinned mischievously. "The thought had crossed my mind."

"I'll just bet it did. I do have an explanation, believe it or not, if you'd care to hear it."

"I have to admit I'm curious about how you got up there. For the life of me I couldn't figure out how your tracks started and ended up there on the cliff. It was as if you descended from the heavens."

"I did. In a way. I was doing a photo shoot for the back cover of my new book, *Winter's Bride*. I'm an author, you see," she added, as if that explained everything.

Sheena saw something flash in Michael's eyes, but it was gone before she could make out what it was. She might have thought she was imagining it, but seeing Michael grow suddenly quiet, she knew she had said something that disturbed him.

"I have pictures taken in costume for all my books. It's my signature. My readers expect it of me."

Michael stared at her so intently, Sheena knew he must still be disturbed. Maybe what she was saying was incomprehensible to a seventeenth-century mind. "You don't know what I'm talking about, do you? How could you? If this is 1630 you couldn't possibly understand about helicopters and cameras and photographs. It is 1630, isn't it? I mean if it isn't, I'll be vastly relieved, but I'll feel like an utter fool for believing for even one moment that I had traveled back in time."

Michael sat down beside her and took both her hands in his. Gazing into her eyes, he said, "Sheena, I could never take you for a fool. It *is* the year of our Lord sixteen hundred and thirty. Be sure of that. And be sure of this. If you say you come from another time, I believe you. For I cannot think of any other way for you to suddenly appear on a mountain top dressed the way you were."

Sheena shook her head. "Michael Winters, you are an

extraordinary man to take me at face value. I don't imagine many people would believe such a crazy story, even if it is the truth."

"Don't start thanking me yet. I still want to know how you descended from the heavens."

"How can I explain? It was a *hel-i-cop-ter*. A ship that floats through the air. Well, not actually floats, too rough a ride for that, but it is an airship with the power of flying up to the top of the mountain where it left me off. It crashed shortly after that, and I don't know whether my friends on board survived."

"This time you come from must be truly a wondrous era to have such ships as that."

Sheena felt a cold shiver climb up her spine, and a sense of utter loneliness came over her as the enormity of it all washed over her. It was true. It was really true. She had traveled back in time.

Sheena was desolate. She had lost everything that ever meant anything to her. Her family had been lost to her already and now she had no friends, no home, and certainly no career. There were no romance writers in the seventeenth century. Nowhere to publish her novels and no one to read them. The puritanical people of these times were hardly the right audience for her sexy stories.

But she had never been fatalistic. If she could travel to 1630 from her century, then she could travel back. The door through time surely must swing both ways. All she had to do was figure out where it was and how it worked, and then what a story she'd have to tell.

The pressure of his hand on hers suddenly made her hand tingle, and she looked into his eyes. "I'm afraid I'll have to take advantage of your hospitality until I can find a way back home."

"This is your home ..." he said emphatically, then his voice softened, "... for as long as you want. When Mother returns, she'll welcome you as openly as I do."

"You don't understand. I have to get back soon. I have a book coming out next month, and a book tour to promote it. People are depending on me. I must find my way back. Oh, do you understand anything I'm saying?''

Lifting her hand to his lips, he kissed it. "I understand perfectly. You must find your way home, but if it turns out you cannot do that, well then, you are most welcome to stay with me."

The warm touch of his lips brought a rush of heat to her core and a blush to her face. What was happening to her? She had never felt this way before. But as delicious as the feeling was, it was also unsettling. Michael Winters was a very intense man, despite his open face. And he was an enigma. She had no idea what to make of him. But it seemed she'd have plenty of time to figure him out.

Time. Before today she had taken it for granted. She never would again.

Pulling herself together, she smiled at the seventeenth-century male who had rescued her. If she had to travel through time, she was glad it was to this place, to this man. She'd never met anyone like him. So handsome, so trustworthy, so completely kind and generous. With his help and support, surely she'd find a way to return home.

CHAPTER FOUR

February, 1630

Sheena watched as Michael slung an ax over his shoulder and went out into the cold to split logs for the fire, a potent reminder that life went on no matter the time period you found yourself in.

She had been here two short weeks and had already learned how much harder it was to live in the past. It awed her to see how much work was involved in the day-to-day living. The only thing that made life here tolerable was Michael Winters. With each passing day she found herself growing more attached to him.

Everything about him was endearing, from his wildly handsome looks, to his charming attentiveness to her every need, to his strong, protective nature. Perhaps in her time he would have been considered too possessive, but here in this scary world of wild Indians and boundless wilderness, his passionate attention offered her the protection she so desperately needed to feel secure.

And after seeing how small the community was, she had good reason to feel insecure. Michael had introduced her to the folk who lived here, and she was appalled to find that only five families lived in Lost Valley. *Five families!* How in the world did they defend themselves against hostile Indians, or whatever else threatened them?

She had met most of the residents except for Michael's sister Elizabeth and her Native American husband Snow Eagle, and oh, yes, she still hadn't met the sick old woman, Mistress Nims, whom Michael's mother was caring for.

Although she had yet to meet Mistress Nims, her two sons were becoming very familiar. She found them to be interesting rustic individuals with flaming red hair and untamed beards and alert, piercing blue eyes that seemed never to blink. They came knocking on the door to Michael's cottage one day carrying twin baby deer in their arms. It seemed they had accidentally shot the mother deer and wanted to know if Sheena would take on the chore of caring for the fawns until they were old enough to survive on their own.

Sheena saw it as a gesture of acceptance in this tight-knit community, and it moved her so deeply she agreed to the responsibility. Michael and the two brothers made a small covered pen for the deer against the outside wall that housed the fireplace. The warmth radiating from the stones was enough to keep the small animals warm.

The other families in the valley were the Petries and the Proctors, the only families with small children. It seemed an incredible act of faith to raise children in the wilderness. Stranger yet, both these families were peopled by folk who seemed more like college professors than the rugged individuals you would expect to find so far from civilization. But that just showed that you couldn't judge a book by its cover.

She finally met Michael's mother, Kathleen, when she came home after several days of caring for the Mistress Nims. But she only stayed long enough to introduce herself and gather more clothing. Her patient was still very sick. In that short visit, though, Sheena had taken an instant liking to Michael's mother, and looked forward to getting to know her better.

Despite her desire to return to her own time, Sheena had to admit there were some things she enjoyed about this era, and one of them was her new clothing. Sarah had taken it upon herself to give her one of Kathleen Winters's dresses to wear, and Sheena had been surprised to find it a deep, flattering shade of violet. So much for the theory that Pilgrims only wore dull blacks and browns. She wondered what other myths she'd shatter as time went on.

Remembering it was time to feed the fawns, she warmed milk for the makeshift bottles she had fashioned, then went outside to feed them.

She was surprised to see the sun was already in the western sky. How fast the hours flew by. Between Michael's exciting presence and chatterbox Sarah's endless stories about her trek across the frozen wilderness from Plymouth colony, she was certainly kept entertained.

It amused her to see that whenever Michael left the room, Sarah's tales would switch to those of the Winters family.

The first revelation Sarah made came as no surprise. Michael was not a Puritan or even a Pilgrim from the *Mayflower*. But then, she had figured that out already. His speech pattern was very different from Sarah's.

Michael, Sarah said, was originally from Jamestown, Virginia, and lived in the mountains with his mother and sister instead of one of the civilized coastal villages because he wanted to start an independent colony.

Though Sarah said it in a disparaging voice, Sheena couldn't help admiring Michael for going after his dream. He certainly had the determination and strength for it. In fact, as the long winter days passed she was pleased to discover he had many qualities she admired in men but rarely found. No doubt about it, Michael Winters was an exceptional man.

When she was done feeding the fawns, she led them

outside for a romp. The male fawn was particularly playful
and when she bent over, he butted her in the behind,
knocking her into the snow. Hearing a laugh behind her,
she turned her head to see Michael with a load of wood
in his arms.

Wiping the snow off her face, she rose to her feet and
put her hands on her hips in mock anger. But how could
she ever get mad at him? Just looking at his handsome
face, all red-cheeked and sparkling-eyed from the cold,
her heart quickened, as it did every time he was near.
"Do you enjoy seeing me get beat up by baby deer?"

"I enjoy everything about you. Do you have any idea
how much grace and beauty you've brought to my life?"

Sheena didn't know what to make of that extraordinary
statement. Michael Winters was a man of many surprises.
Not knowing how to answer him, she grabbed hold of
the female deer and led it back to the pen, feeling the
heat of his gaze as she walked away from him.

When Sheena emerged from the pen, Michael had gone
inside with his armful of wood, so she set about capturing
the elusive male deer. Not an easy chore today. The male
fawn was extra frisky and was giving her a bad time.

Hearing laughter behind her, she turned to see an
amused Michael leaning against a tree. "Well, don't just
stand there. Give me a hand," she groaned.

"Looks like you need more than one hand to control
the little devil." He joined in, and in no time at all they
had the small animal safely in his pen. They both reached
out to close the door to the pen at the same time and their
hands touched, sending a jolt of electricity between them.

"Your hands are cold. Let me warm you," he said,
folding her into his arms.

As if he left her a choice. But she wasn't complaining.
Far from it. Closing her eyes, she snuggled against his
warmth and breathed in the musky, male scent that worked
on her like a potent aphrodisiac. No man had the right
to be so sexy. What chance did she have against all his
confident maleness?

His mouth found her ear, and in a husky voice he whispered, "Can't you feel it, Sheena? This powerful thing between us?"

Sheena felt his breath upon her face and drew it into her lungs, into the very marrow of her bones, fighting the urge to melt into him. Feeling as she did, she knew it wouldn't be long before she found herself in his bed.

Michael tilted her head up with a gentle hand under her chin. "Sheena, darling Sheena, haven't you figured out yet just how much your being here means to me? When I first saw you in your wedding gown, I thought I was dreaming, that God was playing a cruel trick on me, but you are really here, and as each day passes I realize all the more what a miracle you are."

Sheena gazed into eyes dancing with light, and her heart turned to butter. "Michael . . ."

His lips came down on hers, cold and moist at first, then warming as the heat between them rose in the icy air, and the day suddenly became more alive. Her arms circled his neck, holding tight to him, wanting nothing more than to be in his arms forever.

But he broke the kiss and looked at her seriously. "I want you to be my wife."

It wasn't a question, but a statement of fact. Almost a demand, she thought. So typically Michael. And yet, the idea of being with him was so compelling she didn't know if she had the strength to turn him down.

She had never met a man like him in her own world, and doubted there was anyone else like him in this one. He was warm, caring, intelligent, and as if that were not enough, he had the rugged good looks of a movie star. It occurred to her that she had made a living writing about men just like him. In fact, he could have been the model for all the heroes in her books.

But if she said yes to him, she would have to give up all hope of going back to her own life, and she wasn't ready to accept that. "Michael, it would be no hardship marrying you. You're all any woman could ever dream of in a husband—''

"Then why the hesitation? Surely you have to know how it would be between us? You want me too. I know you do."

"Michael. As easy as it would be to love you, and God knows it would be, it's just as hard for me to love this place and time. After the life I've led, it's very difficult for me to accept life in such a primitive wilderness."

"That's ridiculous. You need never lift a finger. If Sarah isn't enough, I'll hire other servants. You can live like a princess in my domain."

"Your domain? Is that how you think of it? You really do believe yourself some kind of emperor or king, don't you? Look around you, Michael. This is no kingdom. It's a tiny flyspeck of a place on the earth. There's nothing here but disease and hardship and an early death."

"Is that truly all you see?"

"Oh, Michael, I don't mean to hurt you. It's got nothing to do with you. Don't you see? I still hold out a small, dim hope that I can go back to my own world. *It's where I belong.* I know you can't possibly imagine how it was there. It's beyond anything your seventeenth-century mind can conceive of. But no matter, before I can say yes to you, I have to be certain there's no way back to my own time."

"And just how do you expect to accomplish that?"

"The mountain, Michael. The barren cliff. That's where I crossed through the time portal. I have to go back up there and see for myself whether I can go home or not. I should have gone as soon as I had the strength, and I would have if I had not been so irresistibly drawn to you. But I must know the truth. I have to know if the other world is lost to me before I can put all my energy into a new life, here with you. Don't you see that's the only way we can ever find happiness together?"

Sarah came around the corner of the house then. "Uh, beg your pardon, sir, but your mother sent word that she left her keys behind and wants me to fetch them for her. Can you imagine that? Why would she need the keys to the storage room when she's not even here? Only one reason, I'm thinking: She's afraid I'll go peeking in there and see for meself what dark secret you and she be keeping.''

Michael frowned. ''Sarah, for the last time, there is no dark secret hidden behind those walls. It's just the place I store arms. Mother just wants the keys so they don't get lost, and she trusts you to bring them to her.''

Sarah didn't look convinced. ''Hmmm. There's stew simmering in the pot for your supper. And I'm to tell you that Mistress Elizabeth is back, and will be stopping in later. Your sister is most eager to meet Mistress Sheena before she reports for sentry duty.''

With that, Sarah was off.

Sheena watched her go, suddenly feeling uneasy. Michael had given her the same runaround when she had asked him about the locked room. What was going on? One thing was certain. There was no use asking him again. She'd have to learn the truth some other way. Then remembering something else Sarah had said, Sheena asked, ''Sentry duty? What's that all about?''

Michael looked at her blankly for a moment; then taking her arm, he escorted her inside. ''We can talk over supper. I'm hungry. How about you?''

Sheena didn't know if he was trying to change the subject or not, but she acquiesced, and sat down at the kitchen table, feeling a little uneasy with this talk of locked doors and dark secrets. Who was Michael Winters, and what was she getting herself into?

CHAPTER FIVE

Michael seemed to gather his thoughts, then said to her, "Everyone in our little community takes turns guarding the village from atop Lost Mountain. As you know, the view of the surrounding territory is quite expansive up there."

Oh, yes, she knew very well what the view was like. She also knew that was where she needed to go.

"What is it, Sheena? You look so far away."

"I am. Almost four centuries away. Michael, I want to go back up on the mountain and see if I can find my way home again. Will you come with me?"

Michael stiffened, then walked over to the fireplace and began stirring the stew.

Realizing she had offended him, she said, softly, "Michael, for my own peace of mind I have to know. Can you understand that? I can't just throw away my career as a writer. My next book is coming out very soon now, and *Winter's Bride* shortly after that. You can't expect me to just give up without even trying. If I find out there's no way, well then, I'll marry you without any reservations. But it would be unfair to marry you with that question in my mind. How can I get on with my life until I know which century I'll be living in?"

Michael's hand tightened on the wooden spoon, and he stirred the stew so hard some of it sloshed over into the fire where it sizzled and smoked. Then suddenly he set the spoon on an iron trivet and turned to her. "You're right. I've been selfish, just thinking of my own happiness. You have every right to know what awaits you on the mountain."

A burst of laughter broke from Sheena's throat, relieving the great tension she had been feeling. "Thank you for understanding. You had me worried for a moment. You do have the tendency to act as if the only right way to do anything is *your* way."

"You're not the first one who's told me that. Sorry. Sometimes I get carried away. It's just that I take my responsibility very seriously."

"Responsibility?"

"For the safety of the folk here in Lost Valley."

"You make it sound dangerous living here."

"It is no more dangerous here than in Plymouth, or Jamestown. In truth, I fear nothing but the unknown, for I have no control over that."

"In my time they'd call you a control freak."

"That doesn't sound very flattering. I pray you do not see me in that light."

A soft rapping sounded on the door then, giving Sheena no time to answer. Michael opened the door and a young woman came in, followed by an Indian warrior. Oh, my, why hadn't Sarah mentioned that Elizabeth was pregnant? Was it too delicate a subject for a Puritan woman to talk about? Probably so.

"So 'tis true. I could scarce believe it when Sarah told me about the angel who dropped out of the skies."

"Elizabeth, this is Sheena Stewart. Sheena, my sister, Elizabeth, and her husband, Snow Eagle."

"Sheena. Such a pretty name. What does it mean?"

"I've been told it means God's grace."

Elizabeth took Sheena's hand and squeezed it. "Then we are truly blessed to have you."

Sheena stared at the young couple in fascination. Elizabeth had an open, friendly face just like her brother's, and indeed, the same twinkle in her eyes. Underneath the fur jacket she wore, Sheena could see a dress much like the one she herself was wearing, but on her tiny feet she wore tall deerskin boots, each painted with an eagle in flight.

Her husband, Snow Eagle, was tall and well formed, and had an aristocratic air about him. *A chief's son,* Sheena thought. And very handsome. They made a charming couple.

"I'm very happy to meet you. Actually, your coming at this moment is providential. I was just telling Michael how much I wanted to go up to the cliff and look around, see if I can't find the way back to my own time."

Elizabeth gave her brother a wary look. "Why not give Lost Valley a chance? You might find life in this century more interesting than your own. Why meddle in things you don't understand? Didn't you almost die up there?"

"Yes, I did, but thanks to your brother and the beautiful Silver Storm, I came through adm—"

Sheena stopped, seeing the astonished looks on all three faces. "What is it? What did I say?"

"What do you know of the Silver Storm?" Michael said, his voice steely.

Sheena had no idea why he looked so upset. "Isn't that the name of your horse?"

"I never told you that. My stallion's name is Pale Warrior."

"Oh! Really? I don't know why I thought he was Silver Storm. Well, actually, I do. A long time ago I met an old lady who rode a horse named Silver Storm. I guess I was thinking of him. Isn't that strange? You have to admit, though, it's the perfect name for a horse so white it shimmers."

The relief in the air was palpable. Sheena had no idea

why everyone had been so tense at mention of the Silver Storm, but she was sure of one thing: They weren't about to tell her the reason. It was as if they had reached some mutual agreement to keep it secret from her. But how could they have accomplished that? As far as she knew, Snow Eagle and Elizabeth hadn't talked with Michael since she got here. They had been visiting the Abenaki Indian village since before her arrival.

But one thing was certain: Whatever it was they were keeping from her must be very important. Dear God, had she stumbled into a nest of horse thieves or, even worse, murderers? What other reason could they have for being so secretive?

Elizabeth broke the awkward silence with, "Well then, shall we go? I've brought along supper for Onotoquos and I'm sure he'd appreciate it still warm from the fire."

It was Sheena's turn to look puzzled.

Elizabeth smiled. "Onotoquos is Snow Eagle's father. A great shaman. He goes to the mountain often. I can't imagine why. Secret shaman business, I expect."

Michael took a woolen cape from a peg on the wall and wrapped it around Sheena. "This should keep you warm."

Captured in the circle of his arms, Sheena's heart beat raggedly. Gazing into his eyes, so warm and yet so commanding, a jolt of desire coursed through her. "Thank you."

She felt the loss of his arms when he moved away from her, and wanted them back around her. *Snap out of it,* she thought. *You're acting like a silly teenager with her first crush.*

In a few moments they were mounted on horses and riding up the moonlit mountain trail. Most of the snow had melted by now, but as cold as it was, the earth was firm instead of muddy, making it easier for the animals to make the ascent.

As mountains went, Lost Mountain wasn't very high, more like a hill really, like most of the Massachusetts landscape, and it didn't take long to reach the cliff. Sheena was grateful for the hooded woolen cape she wore, which kept her considerably warmer than her own fake fur cape. But it was too painful remembering that awful day, so she tried to push it from her mind. An impossible task with the cliff looming before her.

Michael helped her off her horse and walked her over to the boulders where she had first met the old woman Nekomes so many years ago. In the light of the moon she saw a man sitting on the stone seat. He was as ancient as Nekomes had been, and by his dress she knew he must be the shaman Onotoquos.

He beckoned her to come closer, and when she did, she looked into his eyes and saw wisdom and understanding, and some other unfathomable trait that made her feel uneasy. It was as if . . . as if he could see right through to her very soul.

Perhaps he could.

"Ah. See. Michael Winters, you will believe my prophecy now. The woman of air has substance now. She has come to you just as I foretold."

Sheena looked at Michael questioningly.

"Onotoquos foresaw your coming. He saw a women dressed in white descend from the heavens. I'll never doubt you again, wise one." Nodding his head in homage to the shaman, Michael took Sheena's hand and led her to the edge of the cliff.

It might have been the edge of the world for all she knew, for suddenly she felt as if she were floating, drifting away from reality.

With a hard lump in her throat, she forced herself to gaze out at the familiar wintry landscape. The moon was overhead now, and cast enough light for her to pick out the landmarks she was so familiar with. Familiar, and yet alien as well, for when she looked down where the road that wound around the mountain should be, she saw nothing but wilderness, and when she looked over to the other mountain peak, where the beacon light had winked at her, it too was gone.

And then she looked down at the spot where the helicopter lay broken and she saw it . . . but only in her mind's eye. It too had disappeared, and with it all hope that she might go back to her own time, her own life.

Jared. Tony. Where are you now?

The answer came to her inside her head, in a voice gruff and blunted by age. *My child, they are alive and safe.*

Sheena looked back to the standing rocks. Had the shaman spoken to her?

For a fleeting moment she thought she saw a glint of merriment on his face, but it disappeared so quickly she couldn't be sure. Had he read her mind and relayed an answer to her psychically? He was a shaman, after all. Who knew what powers existed in this time before civilization infringed on wild, open minds.

Wherever the voice came from, she believed what it had said, and for the first time since the terrible accident, peace washed over her.

Michael squeezed her hand tight, and she knew she must share the good news with him. "They survived the crash. I know now that they did. You wouldn't believe me if I told you how I know. I think this mountain must have great magic."

"Of course it does. It brought you to me. Can you not be glad of that?

Sheena returned his squeeze, staring at his beautiful face. "If not for you I don't think I'd want to live anymore. It would be too lonely a place here in your world without you."

Michael's face took on a solemn look. "You give me hope then. For the first time, you give me hope that we might be together always."

Sheena was shocked to see his vulnerability. She had thought him so strong, so sure of himself, yet here he was, showing that he was human after all. Unbidden, tears formed in her eyes. "Oh, Michael, I don't know what to say. God knows, I don't know what to do. Nothing in my life ever prepared me for this moment. I feel so helpless, so—"

Michael pulled her into his arms. "Let me take care of you. Protect you. *Love you.*"

Sheena buried her face against his chest, and his words were a balm to her spirit. In his embrace she feared nothing. With him at her side she felt as if she could start to live again.

And then he was kissing her, and lightning leapt between them. She wrapped her arms around his neck and kissed him back, immersing herself in the strength, the power that radiated from him. They kissed until they were breathless, and when their lips parted she saw tears in his eyes too. The sight of this strong male crying touched her heart, and she was compelled to caress his cheek.

He took her hand from his face and kissed the center of her palm, and the warmth of it shot through her, leaving her hungering for even more intimate touches.

"Marry me. Be my winter's bride. Right here. Right now."

Sheena laughed at Michael's enthusiasm. "Not even the mighty emperor Michael can make that happen. Or have you forgotten, you need a minister or priest to perform the ceremony?"

"Will a shaman do? He married my sister to Snow Eagle—he can do the same for us."

Sheena's eyes opened wide. "Are you serious?"

Hugging her tight, he said, "I've never been more serious in my life. This is the perfect spot for a wedding. For wasn't it here I saw you for the first time, dressed as Winters's bride should be?"

"But I'm not wearing that wedding gown now. I'm—"

"But you are! In my mind I can still see you in it, the moon behind you, turning you into a shimmering vision. Say yes! Life's too precious to waste the smallest particle of it."

His words wrapped around her heart, almost stopping her from breathing. Overcome with emotion, she blurted out, "No!"

Michael's body jerked as if he had received a blow.

Fearing he was off balance and would fall from the cliff, she clutched his arm. "I meant, *no,* let's not waste another precious moment. I'll marry you now."

Then he was lifting her off her feet and carrying her over to the others who watched in silent awe.

Setting her down in front of the shaman, he said, "Great Onotoquos, bind me to this woman who descended from the heavens."

A sudden gust of icy air hit them, and the small group of people huddled closer together, Michael and Sheena at the center, as Onotoquos spoke the words that joined them together. And when it was over, Michael crushed her to his chest, and she felt his body shake as if he were sobbing. Once more she marveled that a man such as he could express his emotion so openly.

All the tension, the utter loneliness and desperation she had felt drained out of her, and she clung to her new husband as a fresh emotion washed over her.

Joy.

Joy that she had found this wonderful man at the moment she most needed him in her life.

CHAPTER SIX

Returning to the cottage, Michael left Sheena sitting beside the fire while he impatiently took care of the horses, so eager was he to get back to his bride. He rushed back to the cottage, only to pause outside the rugged wooden door.

Suddenly he was overwhelmed with remorse. Sheena was so open, so completely without guile, and he had taken advantage of those wonderful traits, deliberately deceiving her. If she ever found out the truth, would she hate him forever?

Grasping the door handle firmly, he banished those thoughts from his head. Time was too precious to waste on negative thoughts. And it was never so precious as now, this very moment, since he knew she was waiting for him. It was almost midnight, a fitting hour to take his bride to bed, for it marked more than the beginning of a new day—it marked the beginning of a new life.

When he entered the room, she looked up at him with such bright eyes, so expectantly, so sweetly, it gave him hope that everything would turn out all right.

But something was different about her now—ah, yes,

she was wrapped in the quilt from his bed. He watched as she rose to her feet, and a thrill surged through him, seeing that she was naked beneath the blanket. This was no coy maiden standing before him but a genuine woman, confident and ready to meet him halfway. As great as his desire for her was at this moment, the pride he felt at having her for his wife was even greater.

She took a step toward him, the expression on her face one of such serenity, such beauty, he was in awe. To think that this lovely vision, this incredible woman, belonged to him now.

She smiled and loosened her grip on the quilt. Slowly it slid down her body, caressing her skin on its journey until it lay at her feet. By then, he had ceased to breathe.

But, oh, he was thankful that his eyes still functioned well, for the sight of her in all her female glory was the most exquisite thing his eyes had ever witnessed.

And then she was in his arms and he was carrying her to his bed. He didn't remember undressing, but somehow he had, for the next thing he knew he was under the covers as naked as she, and the touch of her skin on his was sending him straight to heaven. Was there anything beneath the moon and stars that could compare to the sweet touch of a naked man and woman united?

His hands, greedy to possess more of her, ranged over her soft body, claiming everything they touched as his treasure.

Treasure that would never be seen by another man.

Treasure that was his alone.

Treasure that he would keep forever.

Her breathing quickened and he rejoiced, eager for her to experience their lovemaking as fully as he. He wanted to make her his in every possible way. To make her a slave to his desire, to possess her body and soul.

His hand strayed down to the heat between her legs, to the seat of pleasure, his and hers, and it was almost more than he could bear to touch her there. He wanted to last as long as he could, to wait until she was ready for him, and he stroked her to hasten that goal.

She nuzzled her head against his neck, and emboldened, his finger moved inside her. Oh, God. The warmth, the silky wetness. Nothing felt as good as this. He caressed her, inside and out, and her breathing quickened until it was no more than little gasps.

In great need, he mounted her, moaning as the sweet agony drove him crazy with desire. She stared up at him with love and trust shining in her eyes, and he entered her, pushing deep, closing his eyes to the sweet acceptance she so openly displayed. And then all was forgotten but the moment and the woman, the incredible act of loving.

She was his, now and forever, and he would cherish her and keep her safe. But right now, all he wanted was to make endless love to her.

He moved inside her, reveling in each silky plunge, each soul-splitting retreat, until he was no longer master but slave to his need. He rode her faster, as the world shrank to the size of his bed, encompassing only the two of them. And then she was writhing beneath him, and he was calling her name, and the world turned white with ecstasy as the boundaries between them disappeared and they became one.

It was as if one heart beat between them, one soul bound them together, one ecstasy was shared—expressed—enjoyed, and after every ounce of passion was strained from their mortal coil, they lay exhausted in each other's arms.

But not for long.

Gazing into Sheena's eyes, shining with love, he came to life again and the lovemaking began once more.

There would be no sleep this night.

CHAPTER SEVEN

Just before dawn they fell into a deep slumber, their bodies entwined, and Sheena slept until the crowing of a rooster woke her with a start.

Still caught in Michael's arm, she could feel the gentle rhythm of his breathing. Tired and sore from her incredible wedding night, she wished she could escape into sleep once more, but there were too many disturbing thoughts swirling around in her mind. Things that she had buried last night, in hope of escaping from reality.

But what good would it do to think of her past life now? It wasn't as if there were anything she could do to bring it back. She had a chance now at a happy new life with a man as wonderful as any in her books, and she would be a fool to dwell on a world that was lost to her. It wasn't fair to Michael.

Michael. Such a beautiful name, such a beautiful man. To think she might never have met him if time hadn't been ripped asunder.

She had never believed in destiny though she had written about it many times, but she was a believer now. For hadn't she traveled through time to meet the one man she was meant to love?

Michael stirred then, pulling her closer and murmuring in her ear, "You're really here. For a moment I feared I had only dreamed you."

"Maybe you did. Maybe life is nothing more than a dream," she answered. Then, thinking of the accident and her loneliness on the mountain, she added, "But I fear it can be a nightmare too."

Michael's muscled arm became taut against her back. "And where do you reside at this moment—in a dream or a nightmare?"

Feeling the need to reassure him, she ran her fingers through his dark hair. "It's been a fantastic dream from the moment I came to your bed."

Another part of him stiffened now, and Sheena knew exactly what that meant. Feeling his hand between her legs, she smiled to herself.

In a husky voice, Michael murmured, "Then let's dream on. We'll stay in bed all day."

Sheena pushed against his chest. "Oh no you don't. All that exertion has made me hungry, but first, I really need a nice hot bath." Then remembering where she was, she said, "Will you fetch the tub for me?"

"If I say no, will you stay in bed with me?"

"If I tell you I must freshen up before I can possibly make love again, and that I will need to have food in my stomach to help keep up my strength, will you bathe me and feed me?"

Fondling her round bottom, he answered, "Aye, you've said the magic words for certain. I'll just set the tub before the fireplace so you can stay warm whilst you bathe."

"I knew you'd see it my way. Lead me to it."

"Not so fast. First I have to add wood to the fire and fill a cauldron with water to heat upon the flame. Can you see now why I wanted to stay in bed?"

Sheena was constantly amazed at the length Michael had to go to get her a bath, but sticky and sweaty from a night of lovemaking, she wasn't about to give in to him. Sighing, she said, "While you're doing all that, I'll just lie here and think up ways I can repay you for your effort."

Michael groaned and pulled her into his arms again. "I'm thinking I should demand payment in advance."

"I'm thinking I'll roll over and go back to sleep."

Groaning again, Michael climbed out of bed. "Say no more. I know when I'm beaten. One hot bath coming up."

Sheena rolled over on her stomach, and content, dozed off again. She awakened to the touch of a warm hand massaging her back. "Your bath awaits, madam."

Rolling over, she stared up at her husband and was surprised to see he was still naked. Gazing at his wonderful body, she took in his wide shoulders and flat stomach, his narrow hips and long, muscular legs. He had the body of an Olympic swimmer. She would have told him so, but before she could say anything, he was lifting her into his arms and carrying her over to the fireplace.

In front of the roaring fire, she saw a deep wooden tub, filled with steaming water. "Mmm, that looks inviting."

Expecting to be set down in the water, she was taken by surprise when Michael stepped into the tub with her still in his arms. He lowered himself into the water and set her on his lap.

"No fair. This was supposed to be *my* bath."

"Fair, wench? Life is never fair, but . . . it can be very rewarding. This is my reward for hauling all that water."

Taking a bar of soap from the stool beside the tub, he proceeded to lather her, and his hands quickly slid up her body to encase her breasts. The exquisite agony brought a groan to her lips. Reaching for the masculine hands that held her engorged nipples captive, she cried, "Oh no, you don't. Give me that soap. You're not getting your way with me until I'm done bathing."

She grabbed for the soap, but slippery as it was it catapulted out of her hand and flew threw the air, then skidded along the floor before coming to rest against the door.

"Now you've done it," Michael proclaimed.

"Me? You're the one who stole my bath from me. You go get the soap."

"And just how am I supposed to do that? I hate to be the one to tell you, but you're not exactly as light as a feather. You'll have to climb off me before I can get out, so you might as well get the soap while you're up."

"No fair. It's too cold and drafty by the door."

Reaching between her legs, he whispered huskily, "Remember what I said. Life is never fair."

A sudden knocking on the door brought their conversation to an end as both Michael and Sheena froze. And then a high-pitched feminine voice carried to them through the door. "Yoo-hoo. Michael. Sheena. It's just me. I come bearing gifts."

Sheena stared at the door in horror. Then in a panic she quickly climbed out of the tub, with Michael following suit. Sheena grabbed for the strip of fabric they used to dry themselves and ran for the bedroom, leaving behind a tub full of agitated water that splashed all over the floor.

Unknowingly, she slammed the door in Michael's face, and he cried out in pain. Hearing this, Sheena yanked the door open and pulled him inside, then slammed the door shut again.

Michael was rubbing his nose. "If my nose was any longer, it would be broken now."

"Shush! She'll hear us."

"Darling, it's only my mother. She's not going to eat you, you know."

"I know. I just didn't want her to catch us in the tub. Oh, no, I heard the door open, Mike. I know she's waiting for us out there. You go entertain her while I get dressed." Sheena pushed Michael toward the door.

"Not so fast. She'll be more than a little entertained if I go out there like this."

Sheena gazed down at Michael's nakedness and giggled. "That's for sure."

Michael dressed quickly, then went out to greet his mother. Sheena breathed a sigh of relief, then dressed as swiftly as she could. Steeling herself, she put a smile on her face before going out to join the others. Her smile froze when she saw Kathleen down on her hands and knees, cleaning up the puddle of water on the floor.

Completely mortified, Sheena cried, "Here, let me do that." Grabbing a rag, she joined Kathleen on the floor.

"My dear," Kathleen replied, "no need to treat me like a guest. This is still my home too, you'll remember."

Fearing she had hurt her mother-in-law's feelings, Sheena quickly said, "Of course. It's just that I made the mess, so I should clean it up. I don't want my being here to be an added burden to you."

Kathleen rose to her feet and, holding out her hand to Sheena, helped her up. When Sheena was standing, Kathleen embraced her. "My dear, you could never be a burden."

Over Kathleen's shoulder, Sheena saw Michael wink at her, then leave the room. Obviously he was going to leave them alone to work things out by themselves. The coward.

Kathleen brushed a strand of hair from Sheena's hair. "You're being here is a blessing. You've made my son very happy, and for that I'll always be grateful. I just wish I had more time to spend getting to know you, but what with Old Lucy being so ill, and—"

Sheena stared at Kathleen in shock. "Old Lucy? I know that name."

Kathleen looked startled. "You must be mistaken, dear. Lucinda Nims came to this valley when she was but a child and was adopted by the Abenaki Indians who lived here. How could you possibly know her?"

How indeed? If Old Lucy was the one she had met on the cliff when she was twelve, then it meant the old lady who rode a Silver Storm had traveled through time in *both* directions. And that meant there might be a way for Sheena to do so too.

"That sounds like her. She mentioned Indians when she was with me, and called me Nanatasis. Hummingbird. It's her. I know it is. She calls herself by the Indian name Nekomes."

Kathleen averted her eyes. "I . . . I don't know what to say."

"Will you take me to her? I must talk with her. She can tell me how I can go back to my own time."

"But, my dear, you're married to my son now. How can you think of deserting him?"

"But there's no need to. Don't you see? He can come with me. You too. You and your daughter and her husband. Oh, you'll love my time. My world is full of wonders—"

"You don't understand. Michael can't—"

The door opened then and Michael came in, looking handsomer than ever in a crisp white shirt and leather vest. "I can't what?"

Michael's gaze traveled from one female to the other.

"Michael! It's so exciting! Old Lucy can tell me how to go back to my time. You'll come with me, of course, and we'll be so hap—"

The look on Michael's face stopped Sheena cold. "What is it? Why are you looking at me like that? Of course I want to go home. Surely you can understand that."

"It's out of the question."

"What do you mean, out of the question? I'm not your indentured servant. You can't tell me what to do."

"Indentured servant? Do you think so little of being my wife that you could liken it to servitude?"

"Michael, why won't you consider living in my time? If you only understood how wondrous a place it was—"

"And you don't seem to understand that *this is my home*. Your home now too. And this is where we'll stay."

"Oh, you're acting like a typical male now. I thought you were above that."

"Enough! I don't want to discuss this any longer. You're my wife now, and you'll live here with me." Michael strode out of the house, slamming the door.

Running to the window, Sheena watched as he mounted his horse and rode toward the small cluster of homes in the distance.

Kathleen joined her at the window. Patting Sheena on the shoulder, she said, "Let the matter lie for now. Give him a chance to calm down and I'm sure he'll come to the right decision."

"Right decision? You don't understand. It's not his decision to make. It's mine!"

Through the window Sheena watched as Michael dismounted in front of the Nims cottage. Why would he go to Old Lucy's house after their fight? Why indeed? To keep Lucinda from telling her the truth. Whatever that might be.

She had to go there, now. Before he convinced Old Lucy to keep the secret of time travel from her. She was about to reach for her warm cloak when the door flew open and Sarah appeared in the doorway, ashen.

Addressing Kathleen, Sarah said, "Mistress, you must come at once. Old Lucy says it's urgent."

Kathleen wrapped her cloak around her shoulders and raced for the door. Fearing the worst, Sheena followed after her. With her heart in her throat she started running toward the distant cottage by the river, and was halfway there before she realized she had forgotten to put on her warm cloak.

But there was no time to go back for it, no time for anything but reaching the old woman before she died. Would she be too late? Would the secret of traveling through time die with the old woman?

CHAPTER EIGHT

Still reeling from Sheena's stubborn insistence on going back to her own time, Michael tied Pale Warrior to the hitching post outside Lucinda's cottage. How could she even consider going back after marrying him? After their night of lovemaking? Had it all been just an act to put him off guard?

He didn't want to believe that.

No, he *couldn't* believe that. Their lovemaking had been the real thing—he was sure of it. And ... if that were true, then what he did couldn't be so very wrong. In time, she would love being here as much as he.

Entering the Nims home, he felt a moment of fear. Why had Sarah raced past him on the road? What was she doing leaving Lucy alone? Had something happened to the old woman?

Bracing himself, he rapped softly on the door to Lucinda's bedchamber, then entered. Lucinda was sitting up in bed, slurping on a cup of soup.

Though she was small and frail-looking, he was relieved to see she seemed as full of life as ever. He smiled, a great weight lifting from his shoulders. Lucinda would outlive them all.

The dear old woman raised her eyes to meet his gaze. "So you come at last. I knew you'd not let me leave this world without a last good-bye."

Michael forced a laugh. "And what's so different about this time? You say the same thing every time I visit you, and yet you're here still, looking more robust than ever."

Lucinda's head wobbled as she raised herself up in bed. "Robust, you say? How can you speak so falsely to an old woman? Why, there's not enough of me to feed that wolf of yours. I have no doubt he'd pass me over for a plump rabbit."

"So, I take it you're on your deathbed once again? How many times does this make? Eleven? Twelve?"

"It's not nice to make sport of an old woman. I'm perfectly serious. At my age, each breath I take could be my last. But I'm happy you're here all the same. There's something I've been meaning to tell you. Something I've already told the rest of the folks."

"What is it this time, old woman? Have you changed your will again? Who is to be disinherited this time? Onotoquos, I suppose. Have you two been feuding again?"

"Ha. Wrong again. When will you learn not to try and outguess me? But you do well to speak of Onotoquos now, for what I say comes from him too." In a whispered voice, she said, " 'Tis very serious."

Michael knew better than to go on with his joking. "What is it, Nekomes? Have you had another vision?"

"Aye, that I have, and Onotoquos too. It is rare indeed to share a vision with that wise old owl. It is certain to be true. Son, the time portal will soon close forever."

"How could you know that? Why is it you've never mentioned it before?"

"Because I didn't know it before. But now I do, and everyone in Lost Valley will soon have to decide on which side of time they wish to live."

"I see."

"Is that all you have to say? Methinks you would be jubilant that you no longer have to guard the portal."

"Give me a chance to digest the news, old woman. I never expected to hear those words. Never believed it would ever happen. After all these years of worrying. All the lonely years of standing guard to see that no unsavory characters breached time and wreaked havoc on the future. Sweet Jesus, can it really be true?"

"This is no time to doubt my visions, son. Remember, Onotoquos saw it too. I know which side of the portal you will choose to live in, but what about your new bride? Does she feel the same as you?"

"I'm afraid not. In fact, she'll be here soon, to learn the truth from you. Damn it all. Why did this have to come now? I want Sheena to love this time, this place, as much as I. If she learns about the portal closing, she'll leave here for sure. When will it happen?"

Michael prayed she'd say it would happen this very day, so that he could keep his wife. He thought about what that would mean. Sheena here with him forever, never having to worry about her stumbling onto the Silver Storm again.

" 'Tis impossible to say the exact hour. But the day is upon us. It will happen the first day of spring. The signs are there for all to see. Have you not noticed that the portal has been staying open for shorter and shorter periods of times the last few years? It started the year I got caught on the other side. That's when I met the winsome young woman who has become your wife."

Michael laughed bitterly. "My wife? For one brief shining moment, she was. Just long enough for me to fall in love with her. Onotoquos told me she would descend from the heavens, but 'twas more like from hell, for all the heartache she's caused."

"Women troubles already, son? Might as well get used to 'em. Nanatasis is much like her namesake, the hummingbird. You could crush her with one squeeze of your hand, but you cannot make her obey you. She will fly where and when she pleases. But take heart. When I gave her my snowflake ring, I sensed she would know the right time to fly to you. And hasn't she shown up at the moment when she is most needed? Just before the portal closes forever? I do believe 'twas written in the stars. Mayhap even butterflies and hummingbirds must follow the call of destiny.''

"Ah, I wish it were so easy. But Sheena is determined to go back to her century. What am I to do? Go with her?''

"How troubling for you, a man who loathes the very idea of living in the twenty-first century. I taught you too well, I think, to love this valley, this time of all times.''

"Yes, old woman, you did your job well. I can't imagine living anywhere but here and now.''

Lucinda was silent a long moment before she spoke. When she reached out to him, he moved closer to the bed, and she grasped his hand, squeezing it hard. "You love her very much. I see that now. and though I might go straight to Hades for it, I'll tell your beloved that I am too old to remember how to ride the Silver Storm.''

Michael lifted the old woman's wrinkled, brown-speckled hand to his mouth and pressed his lips to it. He had come to Lucy's house to ask her to do just that, but looking at the frail old woman, he knew he couldn't let her compromise her principles. She had always been a woman of great honesty, and he couldn't let her leave the earth with a lie on her lips. "You are very dear to me, Lucinda, and much as I want my wife on this side of the portal when it closes, I can't let you lie for me. I'll find some other way to keep her here. She has no family on the other side. They've all passed on. There's no reason why she can't be happy here. It's written in the stars, remember? I'll find a way to keep her.''

* * *

Sheena opened Lucinda's door in time to hear the bubble of laughter. Michael and Old Lucy laughing heartily. Leaning up against the wall, she struggled to catch her breath.

By the sound of it, Lucy was far from dying, and that eased her mind considerably. She might yet have the chance to go back to her time, or at the very least, decide for herself where she wanted to live. If she chose to stay here, then at least it would be her decision and not her egotistical husband's.

Kathleen, too, seemed eased by the laughter, for she breathed a deep sigh, then taking Sheena's hand led her into Lucinda's bedchamber. "Well, now, Nekomes, look at this. It seems Michael's presence is all you needed to get better."

"I am feeling much better, 'tis true. Perhaps I'll live another day. And what a great day it is, too. For at last I shall meet Michael's new bride."

"So you shall." Kathleen's eyes sparkled as she turned to Sheena. "My dear, this is Lucinda. Prophet, seeress, healer, and great friend to everyone in the valley. Lucinda, this is Sheena Stewart."

Sheena took a tentative step toward the bed, avoiding Michael's intense gaze. Did he have to look at her that way? Just being in the same room with him made her heart ache. It wasn't fair. Why couldn't they have met in her own time? She would be the happiest woman in the world then.

"Come closer, my dear, so that I may see you better. My eyes aren't what they used to be."

With her heart in her throat, Sheena whispered, "Do you remember me, *Nekomes*?"

Lucinda gazed at Michael before answering. "Nekomes, is it? What a strange word. Do you know what it means?"

Sheena's heart sank. "It's the name the Abenaki Indians

called you. Grandmother. That's what it means." Sheena stared at the old woman closely. "Don't you remember? I gave you a blanket and some sandwiches, and ..." Sheena's throat was so tight she could barely talk. Had she reached a dead end? No. She couldn't give up yet. There must be a way to trigger the old woman's memory.

Then remembering her snowflake ring, she pulled it off her finger and held it out to Lucinda. "Look at this, Nekomes. You gave it to me. You made it yourself."

Lucinda stared at the ring, and suddenly tears flooded her ancient eyes. Taking her right hand from beneath the covers, she held it up for Sheena to see. "I do remember you. How could I forget your kindness to a strange old woman?"

Sheena stared at Lucinda's ring, a twin to her own, and relief washed over her like a gentle summer rain. "Thank God! Please tell me how you traveled back and forth through time. I have to know. Please. I know how easy it is for Michael to influence people, but I pray you don't give in to him. Don't let him keep you from telling me the truth."

"Child. Child. You're so young, and beautiful, but you know nothing of the human heart. Michael never asked me to keep my knowledge from you. He couldn't do it, though it was his greatest desire."

Sheena looked into Michael's fervent eyes, and though she tried to repress it, a surge of love coursed through her. "He . . . he didn't? But I thought . . . Oh, Michael, I'm so glad you didn't do it. I could forgive you almost anything but that."

Michael stared silently at her, and that was much worse than if he had spoken hateful words. Why was he so quiet? Why didn't he gloat and brag about his innocence?

"Child, though he will not defend himself, I tell you that you blame the wrong one, for it was I who brought you here."

Still gazing into Michael's eyes, Sheena saw he was

as startled at that news as she was. "Lucinda, even you don't have that kind of power!"

"Don't I, then? That ring you're wearing. Have you not worn it all these years? Do you not feel restless whenever it's not on your finger, even for a little time? I used old magic on that ring the day I gave it to you. I made it bring you back to the mountain that wintry day. For when I saw you at the cliff when you were a child, I knew that you and Michael would be perfect for each other. I imbued into that silver ring the desire that you should be Winters's bride. That you should come to the mountain on a day when the portal was open and meet your future husband."

Michael and Sheena both stared at the old woman in astonishment.

"Look at the two of you. So perfect for each other. Was I wrong to bring you here, my dear? Do you not love the man I chose for you?"

Sheena took a deep breath to clear her head. "Lucinda, even if I believed you, which I don't, I can't allow you or anyone else to dictate to me whom to love, where to live. Tell me where the time portal is, and let me make up my own mind whether to stay or go."

Lucinda sighed, then shook her head. "My dear, you were a kind and generous little girl. I only wish I could repay your kindness with the answer you are seeking. But I will not. And I pray you can accept that, for there be very little for me to hold on to anymore but a farthing's worth of dignity. Don't leave me bereft even of that."

"Why can't you repay me for my kindness? What's holding you back? Help me understand."

"My dear child, when I held your hand a moment ago, a vision came to me. A daughter will be born to you on winter's solstice. A little girl with her mother's creative mind and her father's strong will. Now do you understand?"

Sheena shook her head in disbelief. "I don't believe your vision. I don't believe anything you say. You're just a foolish, superstitious old woman! I don't need you! I don't need anyone to help me find my way back!''

Sheena ran out of the house, and seeing Pale Warrior, climbed onto his back, desperate to escape Michael and Lucy. Desperate to gain control of her life once more.

Michael came running out as she galloped off and tried to stop her by catching hold of the bridle, but she veered off and he missed it by inches.

Seeing the stricken look on Michael's face when he couldn't reach her, Sheena almost turned back. It would be so easy just to give in to his strong will. But no, she couldn't let anyone decide her fate. It was and always would be in her own hands.

She rode up the mountain pass, knowing there was little chance of finding her way home, but she had to try. And if she failed again to find the portal, well then, she thought bitterly, what was her hurry? She had all the time in the world to find it.

No. That wasn't true. If she didn't leave now, she'd never find the strength to leave Michael. His hold on her grew more powerful every day. *Damn you, Lucinda! Damn you and your old magic!*

Reaching the top of the mountain, she steered the horse over to the side that looked down upon Lost Valley and the ribbon of water that wound its way through it. She wanted to avoid the barren area near the cliff because it was too painful a reminder of the awful accident and the terrible loneliness she had felt there such a short time ago. Was it only two months since she came here? It seemed like a lifetime ago.

Spying a fallen log lying nearby, she sat on it and gazed down at the river. *River of No Return.* She choked back a sob.

River of No Return. That was certainly true. There would be no return for her. Not to her life, her career, or her old friends.

Shifting her gaze, she sought out Michael's cottage, looking serene and inviting in the valley. What was wrong with her? Surely she could be happy in that cozy place? Why did she need to escape? Was she so self-indulgent she had to have all the trappings of the twenty-first century around her to be happy?

She had never thought of herself as so shallow. Then what? What was eating at her? Tears suddenly clogged her eyes. Oh, great. *Now* she could cry. Not when the helicopter crashed, or when she thought she'd die of exposure, but now.

Turning her back on the scenery, she faced the path that led down to Lost Valley, and saw a dark figure riding toward her on a black horse, and she understood everything. Because of *him*. That's why she cried.

He had complicated her life so thoroughly she didn't know what she wanted anymore. But as he dismounted and made his way over to her, as his long legs ate up the distance between them, she knew that wasn't true. She did know what she wanted.

She had known it from the beginning, but couldn't accept it because it meant staying in this primitive time.

She wanted *him*.

Michael fell to his knees and buried his face in her lap, and her heart danced a wild tattoo. Oh, God, she loved him. There was no longer any doubt of that.

Her hand hovered over his head, wanting, needing to caress his hair. Knowing that if she gave in, if she made that small gesture, she would be forever condemned to stay in this century. There would be no turning back after that, for her heart couldn't bear to go through this agony again.

Unbidden, her hand slowly descended, to rest on the head of the man she would love throughout eternity.

CHAPTER NINE

March, 1630

A sense of peace settled over Sheena as the cold winter days mellowed into more temperate ones, a hint of the coming spring. The snow had melted by now, but the ground was still frozen, the earth still barren of greenery.

She looked forward to the summer when fresh fruits and vegetables would be in season. The variety of foods available in winter left something to be desired. If not for Michael and the Proctor brothers' hunting ability, their diet would have been even more constricted. They existed on bread and meat, a few shriveled vegetables, and mead.

It seemed strange to her, but no one drank water in this time. They lived on mead, a drink she despised. But she drank it too, because she believed Michael when he told her the water caused too many sicknesses.

Michael and the others seemed to enjoy drinking the fermented liquid, but she longed for a nice wine or a frothy, bubbly Coke. But no use dwelling on the impossible. She had learned that as long as Michael was by her side, she could be content.

Since she didn't believe Lucinda when she claimed responsibility for Sheena's traveling through time, she didn't stay angry at her very long. In fact, she was grateful to the old one for helping her realize just where she belonged.

She wondered now why she had fought so hard to leave Michael. Perhaps because she loved him too quickly, or too powerfully. Nothing in life had prepared her for the strong love she felt for him. Every time she looked at him, she wanted to devour him with her eyes. Every time his hand brushed hers, she burned with desire, and every morning when she awoke, she thanked God for the gift of Michael's love.

And yet as wonderful as he was, there was some part of Michael that was closed off from her every bit as much as the room he kept locked from her. At times he would become distant and restless, as if he were holding something back from her, and she wished she knew what was troubling him so.

But as curious as she was to know what he was keeping from her, both in his mind and behind the locked door, the subject was never mentioned between them. *Let sleeping dogs lie,* she thought.

Surely nothing could ever come between them. What did it matter what was behind the locked door? All that mattered was the happiness she shared with Michael. The joy of living with such an incredible, loving man.

Loving and *protective.* It was almost as if he were afraid to let her out of his sight. Especially on days when it snowed. Did he think her too fragile to go out in a storm? He should know better than that. Hadn't she survived the bitter cold in nothing more than a flimsy wedding gown? He would have to learn to trust her ability more.

Maybe he was afraid she might leave him if she discovered how to go back to her own time. But that wasn't about to happen, since the only one who could show her the way was a stubborn old woman who held her secret close. And even if she did know the secret, how could she ever leave her stubborn husband? Loving him as she did, she could never bring herself to force him to leave this time and place he loved so much.

That revelation surprised her. She never knew she could be so noble. Especially now when there was a baby on the way.

Just yesterday she had realized that she was pregnant, and the reality of it hadn't sunk in yet. Caressing her stomach, she thought of the new life growing inside her and prayed that it would be healthy. Then remembering Lucinda's prediction, she immediately counted the months and days until her child would be born, and was astounded to find the wise old woman had been right: Her baby could very well he born on winter's solstice. What a fitting birthday for Winters's child.

How wondrous to be able to see into the future like that. Why was it the two oldest residents of Lost Valley should have such powers? Perhaps in earlier days it was more common. Had the advance of civilization bred the gift out of mankind?

Scary though it might be, she wished she too had the gift of prophecy, for she longed to see into the future, to know how her life would turn out. To see if they would have more children. If she and Michael would be as much in love ten years from now, or twenty, or thirty. But then, she already knew the answer to that. They would love each other for eternity.

She wanted to tell Michael about the baby right away, but something held her back. She told herself it was too soon. That she needed to keep it a secret until she got used to the idea herself. Too many overwhelming things had already happened and she needed time to digest it all. But if the truth be known, she wanted to hold this precious secret close to her heart awhile longer for yet another reason.

Michael was such a dynamic personality, she feared he'd take over even her pregnancy. As protective as he was, he was sure to treat her like a porcelain doll, and she didn't want that.

Ah, but if she didn't tell him now, she'd be just as secretive as Michael and his mother were about the locked room. What contents did it hold that needed to be kept under lock and key? Every time she passed by the room, she was tempted to try the door handle, to see if it would open.

Of course, she didn't try it very often. Certainly not when anyone was around. But it always frustrated her when she did, to find herself barred from entering the room. She didn't like feeling left out. It was too, too lonely.

She had mentioned it to Michael a couple of times, to no avail. He always repeated that the room held a store of firearms. But that answer didn't satisfy her. Why would they lock away the very weapons they might need someday to defend their home from invasion?

Oh, what was the use of thinking about it? It was getting dark out and she had to feed the deer.

Warming some goat milk over the fire, she poured it into her makeshift bottles, then went outside to the pen.

The fawns wagged their tails at her, as if they were puppies instead of baby deer, and she felt a rush of love for them. They thought of her as their mother, and in a very real sense she was. She was the one who nurtured and cared for them.

When they had drained their bottles, she led them outside and on impulse decided to bring them down to the river. Michael had told her that deer went to the water at dusk every night to drink, and she wanted her deer to behave as they would in the wild, for she knew that when they were old enough she would have to set them free.

She called out Michael's name, then remembered he

had gone to Lucinda's house on an errand. Well, she would just go without him. She had grown to rely on him too much and feared she was in danger of losing a part of herself.

Here was the perfect chance to show him she was quite capable of doing things on her own. Feeling lighthearted and almost giddy at asserting her independence, she ran down the path leading to the river's edge, the deer frolicking around her.

When she arrived at the river, she decided to continue on, but which way to go? Gazing to the right, she looked downriver to the cluster of homes that made up the settlement; then she headed instead in the opposite direction.

She had never ventured so far from the cottage, not without Michael anyway, and seeing how fast it was getting dark, she suddenly doubted the wisdom of asserting herself at this particular moment.

Clicking her tongue at the fawns, her signal for them to come to her, she watched as they gamboled toward her, kicking their heels in the air. They were so full of life, it was a joy to watch them at play. If she hadn't traveled back in time, she would never have known such pleasure. Which gave her two great reasons to live in the here and now: Michael and her sweet little fawns.

She watched as the female sprinted ahead of the male, cheering her on, but the laugh that bubbled to the surface was suddenly cut off when she saw a streak of tawny fury cut in front of the male fawn and pin it to the ground.

It happened so fast, Sheena barely had time to understand what was happening before the sleek mountain lion bit into the fawn's throat with its powerful jaws, and started carrying the young deer away.

Coming to her senses, Sheena grabbed a stout tree branch and started after the lion, screaming at the animal. But the mountain lion barely deigned to notice her as it ambled off with the bleeding deer.

Though it seemed impossible to catch it, she continued

to run after it, until the lion suddenly lost his grip on the squirming deer and it fell to the ground.

Seeing her chance, Sheena swung the tree branch, hitting the mountain lion on its rump, but instead of scaring it off, the infuriated animal rose on its hind legs and swiped at her with its paw.

She swung again, but the lion dodged out of the way easily, then, having had enough of her, slunk away and was swallowed up by the night.

Sheena ran to the fallen fawn and sank to her knees. She knew at once it was too late. The fawn was dead. No animal could have survived such a grievous wound.

Staring down at the small, lifeless body, she felt the need to stroke the animal's soft fur, but it was matted with sticky blood now, so she quickly removed her hand and dissolved into a sea of scalding tears and heartache.

Her stomach churned at the sight of the poor baby fawn, and she suddenly felt nauseated as she thought about the baby she carried. What if it had been her child beside her, instead of the deer? My God, how could she even think of raising a child in this wilderness?

The next thing she knew, Michael was there and she was crying in his arms. He kissed her face and hair, murmuring, "I never saw anything so brave in my life. My sweet angel, I'm so proud of—"

Sheena pushed him away. "Don't say it. For God's sake, Michael, don't say it. Because of me the fawn is dead. Don't act so condescending. I don't deserve that any more than I deserve your praise."

Michael held her at arm's length. "Condescending? Surely you know better than that. I *am* proud of you for standing up to the puma. He could have ripped your heart out, and you well knew it, yet you still tried to save the deer."

"But I didn't succeed, did I? My God, Michael, what if it had been our child with me? I couldn't have saved it any more than I was able to save the fawn."

Sheena started to blurt out her secret, but a fierce scream cut off any chance of that. It was the mountain lion, crying out its frustration at having lost its prey. The animal's fierce cry reminded her that her child was not safe in this savage place. Reminded her there was yet another fawn that could fall prey to it. "Michael, what if he comes back for the other fawn?"

"I'll handle him. You take the female to the pen."

"No. I can't just leave the poor little thing to be ravaged."

"I'll not leave him here. You go. I'll bury him."

Sheena gazed into Michael's eyes and saw sorrow there. The fawn's death had affected him, too. "I'm sorry, Michael. I didn't mean to take it out on you."

Michael kissed her forehead, then nudged her toward the waiting fawn. Unwilling to take a chance on it wandering off, she picked it up and carried it. By the time she reached the pen, she was exhausted. As soon as the fawn was safely enclosed, she sank to the ground and folded her arms across her stomach, as if protecting her unborn child.

Indeed, she felt a great responsibility to protect her baby from harm. What was she going to do?

Michael returned, and without a word lifted her in his arms and carried her inside the house. Sitting down on the rugged rocking chair by the fire, he rocked her and crooned to her. She should have been content in his arms. She should have been happy he loved her so much, but all she could think of was the fawn with his neck torn open, and how swiftly life could change from idyllic to disastrous in this savage time.

Next morning, Michael and Snow Eagle left at dawn to hunt for the mountain lion, and Sheena turned her attention to the remaining fawn. But she didn't get much time to spend with it before Kathleen and Elizabeth came for a visit. They were obviously concerned about her well-being after the ordeal with the mountain lion. Touched by their sympathy, she assured them she was fine, and began preparing lunch.

Kathleen watched her closely all through the meal, and Sheena felt the need to reassure her once again. "I'm fine, really. You can stop worrying about me."

"Oh, dear. I didn't mean to stare. It's just there's something very different about you today."

Caressing her swollen stomach, Elizabeth smiled mischievously. "That's what you said to me just before I told you about my pregnancy."

Sheena feared they'd guess her secret now, and rose from the table to fetch more stew so they couldn't see her face until she composed herself.

"Come to think of it, you're right, dear. That's exactly what I said to you." Kathleen went to Sheena and took her hand. "You're with child. I can see it in your eyes."

"You might as well confess, Sheena. Mother won't let loose of you until you do. I swear she gets more like Old Lucy every day. Can you imagine how hard it's been for me to have a life of my own with Mother and Nekomes scratching through my brain all the time?"

Sheena forced a laugh. "Really, it's too soon to even think about having a baby. Let me enjoy being a bride for a while longer. After all, having a child is a huge responsibility."

Elizabeth's face suddenly turned ashen, and she let out a little groan.

Kathleen immediately rose from her chair and went to her. "Elizabeth, what is it? Is it the baby? Oh, dear, don't tell me it's coming so soon?"

Elizabeth rocked back and forth in her chair, then suddenly let out a loud breath. "I'm fine, Mother. Your grandchild was just making his presence known with a sharp kick straight down. I thought for sure his little foot would do a little dance on the chair."

Kathleen laughed nervously. "I swear, I don't know how I'm going to last until the baby's born. I worry constantly that something will go wrong." Kathleen reached into her pocket and drew out a handkerchief, dabbing at her eyes with it.

Elizabeth stroked her mother's arm. "You're just being a loving mother. That's all. To tell the truth, I don't know what I'd do if you weren't here. I depend on you so."

Sheena swallowed hard, seeing the love flow between mother and daughter. She envied them their wonderful bond. Perhaps, if she were very lucky, she'd have it someday with a daughter of her own.

A while later, after Kathleen and her daughter left, happily babbling about the future and eager to make more baby clothes for Elizabeth's child, the silence of the house pressed in on her. She decided to spend time with the fawn. She must be very lonely now without her brother.

She was about to walk out the door when she felt something beneath her shoe. Lifting her skirt, she looked down and saw a large metal key. Kathleen's. It must have fallen from her pocket when she removed the hanky. No one heard it fall because it landed silently on the soft braided rug on the floor.

Kneeling down, she picked it up. As she stared at the key in the palm of her hand, a shiver of excitement thrilled through her.

Could this key unlock the secret Michael so doggedly kept from her?

There was only one way to find out.

But something held her back. Michael had made it clear he didn't want her to see what was in the locked room, and knowing how protective he was, she feared what she might find there. Maybe it was something she was better off not knowing.

Darn it all, she wasn't a child. She was perfectly capable of making her own decisions. And it was past time for Michael to realize that.

Fortified with that thought, she clasped the key tightly and with great determination went upstairs to the door that had always been barred to her.

With trembling hands, she put the key in the lock and slowly turned it.

CHAPTER TEN

Sheena opened the door and peered into the room, but could see very little in the dim light. *There were no windows in there.* That didn't exactly inspire her to go any farther. She hesitated, torn between fear and her eagerness to know Michael's secret.

But a myriad of friendly smells wafted her way, instead of the menacing acid smell of gunpowder that she had been expecting. She felt easier about going inside. In fact, her sensitive nose was sorting out several different odors, and among them she swore she was picking up the delicate scent of chocolate.

But then, it must have been just wishful thinking, for she had been craving chocolate ever since she became pregnant. She wished it were true, wished the forbidden room was filled with all her favorites. Godiva, rich and yummy, creamy Cadbury bars, and tasty Swiss chocolate with raspberry filling.

Pushing her desire for chocolate out of her mind, she ventured farther into the room, coming to a halt when her eyes became adjusted to the dark and she could make out objects all around her.

But, but, this was too incredible. She couldn't be seeing what she thought she was seeing. It was impossible.

In the light from the doorway splashing across the opposite wall were shelves and shelves of staples. Packages of elbow macaroni, spaghetti, and cereal, containers of tea and coffee, cans of vegetables and fruits, all bearing familiar labels. And there staring her in the face were boxes of Godiva chocolates, and . . . and . . .

How could it be? How could there be twenty-first-century packaged foods in a seventeenth-century home? Reeling, her gaze traveled around the room, trying to take it all in, trying to make sense of what she saw.

On a small table she spied a portable CD player and alongside it stacks of CD's and packages of batteries needed to operate it. And there, a wine rack stocked with bottles of wine from deep burgundy to pale champagne.

If that weren't enough to boggle her mind, another wall was covered with sturdy shelves filled with books she recognized. Her gaze swept across the titles, picking out novels by best-selling authors and . . . and . . .

Oh, no, this was impossible. *A row of her own novels.* She had never dared hope to see copies of her books again.

Taking one from the shelf, she stared down at the cover, and a chill coursed through her. No. This was too much. Too much. *The Gilded Cage* had been published just this month. *Since she disappeared.* How could it be here? But then, how could any of her books be here?

Trying to make sense of it all, she picked up a large leather-bound book and saw it was a photo album. Dreading what she'd find in it, but compelled to look, she opened it up.

Michael smiled back at her, dressed in twenty-first-century clothing.

She could deny the truth no longer. Michael Winters was a first-class liar and cheat. He had cheated her out of her life as a writer. Had cheated her out of the era she was born into. He had known all along how she could go back to her own time, and he had deliberately withheld it from her.

Oh, he knew all right, because he had obviously traveled through the portal many times to bring back all these goodies. He knew it because he was not the seventeenth-century man he pretended to be, protective and loving, considerate and kind. No. He was the heartless twenty-first-century time-bandit who had held her captive in a time and place she never wanted to be in. He was the thief who had literally stolen time from her.

No wonder he was so attentive. No wonder he was at her side wherever she went. He knew that if he didn't keep an eye on her, sooner or later she'd find the way to go home. And he couldn't let that happen. Oh, no. He had decided she belonged to him.

To think she had found his possessiveness endearing! To think she thought such a cold-blooded male was warm and wonderful! How could she have let him deceive her like that? How could she have been so blind?

No, more than blind. In her case, love was blind, deaf, and incredibly warped.

Infuriated, she started out of the room, then went back to grab a bottle of wine and a copy of *The Gilded Cage*. If ever there was a moment in her life when she wanted to get drunk, this was it.

Slamming the door behind her, she locked it, then, furious, kicked at the heavy wooden door. Limping down the stairs, she sat before the fire, furiously rocking, trying to dissipate her pent-up anger. Just wait until she got her hands on that conceited, selfish bastard.

But much as she'd have liked to do violence to him, she knew that wasn't the answer. Revenge was. And . . . she knew that to accomplish that she'd have to calm down and use her head.

He said he was going to Lucinda's, but how could she believe anything he said anymore? For all she knew, he could be back in twenty-first-century Boston, enjoying a gourmet meal at a fancy restaurant. How often did he travel back and forth anyway? Judging by the contents of the room, it had to be pretty often.

What a hypocrite! He professed to love this time period too much to leave it, and when she had begged him to go with her, he had so self-righteously turned her down. To think she had thought him noble for wanting to stay in so harsh an era, when all the while he had the best of both worlds. Had he ever planned to tell her the truth?

Then remembering that the key belonged to Kathleen, she felt even more betrayed. Obviously, Michael wasn't the only one who had lied to her. Kathleen had too. Sheena was sure the chocolate and all the other feminine things she had seen in the room were there for Michael's mother and sister. So they had to be apart of the deception too.

And what about Lucinda? Sheena knew for certain the old woman had traveled back and forth across the time portal. Who else? Were the Petries and Proctors also from her time? She remembered thinking they didn't look as if they belonged. Well, she was right—they didn't.

Dear God, were they all a bunch of time-traveling bandits using the past as a hideout? Of course that idea was ridiculous. But still, there had to be some reason why they were all so willing to live in an era so distant from their own.

Whatever they were up to, it was obvious Michael was their ring leader. And he was the one she was most angry with. She had trusted him, had given her love freely, had really believed he had devoted his life to her. Now she realized he was probably the most selfish human being she had ever met.

Forcing her anger down, she decided that the best way to handle it was to take him completely by surprise, and to that end, she began cooking supper. Setting two tankards on the table, she filled them with the wine she had taken from the locked room. She could hardly wait to see his face when he tasted the delicate wine in his cup, instead of the miserable-tasting mead they usually drank. But then, he didn't have to drink mead all the time,

did he? He had his choice of fine wines whenever the
mood struck him. Whenever he got a hankering for a
special twenty-first-century food, all he had to do was
visit his storeroom. Damn him to hell!

While supper was cooking, she went to the window
and stared out at the bleak winter world. It was snowing
again. The hint of spring had been only a tease. But that
made what she was about to do all the more perfect. She
had come to this world in the midst of a snowstorm, so
it was only fitting she should leave the same way. This
time, though, she'd be dressed for the weather.

But, of course, she was forgetting one thing. She still
didn't know how to go through the time portal.

Would Michael still withhold that information from her
once he knew she was on to him? If he did, her only
other option was to talk to his mother. Surely that gentle
woman wouldn't go on protecting her son once she realized their secret was out.

But she'd just have to cross that bridge when she got
to it. One thing was certain, someone would tell her what
she needed to know, if she had to beat it out of them.

Still seething, Sheena finished making supper, and as
if on cue the outer door opened and with a forced smile
on her face, she turned to face her husband.

Seeing his wife standing before the hearth, Michael
was struck by the beauty of the tranquil domestic scene.
A scene he never believed he would be witness to. Thank
God, Sheena had come into his life.

Drawing closer to his lovely wife, he realized something
was wrong. Sheena's smile was taut and strained, her
hands clenched tightly at her sides. Suddenly uneasy, he
decided to test the waters. Pretending not to notice anything was wrong, he walked over to her, drew her into
his arms, and kissed her. She stiffened, confirming his
suspicions that she was angry.

Pushing him away, Sheena said, "Supper's ready. Sit down and eat before it gets cold."

It was worse than he thought. She was as frosty as the winter air. Sitting down at the head of the table, he forced his voice to sound lighthearted. "What is that delicious smell?"

Sheena didn't answer, but instead lifted a large chunk of venison from a pot and unceremoniously plopped it on his plate.

Still hopeful that he could coax her out of her nasty mood, he sliced into the meat and ate a piece of it, murmuring his approval. She seemed to like that, for she suddenly smiled brightly and said, "Why don't you wash it down with a drink from your tankard? I'll join you in a toast."

Michael's spirits lifted. "Fine idea. Let's make a toast to our future."

Lifting her tankard, Sheena said, "To the future, *yours* and mine."

For some reason he couldn't fathom, her toast troubled him. Why had she worded it that way? It was almost as if she meant they would have separate futures. Still puzzling over that, he swallowed a large gulp of mead.

As the liquid washed over his tongue, he realized it didn't taste a thing like mead. It tasted more like . . . wine! It was wine, but where would she get . . . And then he knew. He understood her anger now. She had gone into the locked room.

Michael set his tankard down and slowly raised his head to look at his wife, words of rebuttal forming in his head. But he didn't get a chance to say them, for without warning, Sheena splashed the wine from her cup into his face and stormed out of the room.

Wiping his face, Michael followed after Sheena, climbing the stairs two at a time to catch up to her. Grabbing her by the arm, he said, "Hold on! We need to talk."

Sheena wrestled herself out of his grip. "Go to hell!"

Determined to make her understand, he took her by the

arm again. "Angel, I can understand the shock you must be feeling, but—"

"Shock? That's putting it mildly. You can't begin to understand what I'm feeling right now. How could you, you cold-blooded bastard!" Sheena ran into the bedroom and slammed the door, and taking a deep breath, Michael yanked the door open, then ducked when a boot came sailing toward him. He started in once again, and the second boot hit him on the shoulder.

Still determined to reach her, he started toward her again, and she retreated backwards until she bumped into the wall. "Stay away from me. I'm too angry to talk with you right now. Just go away."

"I'm not going away until I know what has you so upset. So I kept you in the dark about the contents of my storeroom. That's nothing to get so upset about. Lucinda collected all that stuff on her journeys from the other side of the portal and—"

"Do you really think I'm naive enough to believe that? Lucinda has been in bed for weeks now—she couldn't possibly have gotten *this*." Sheena thrust a book in his face, and his heart sank. She knew. Of course she knew. She was an intelligent woman; it wasn't hard for her to figure out.

Throwing the book at him, she cried, "Explain this!"

Michael caught the book in his hand and gently set it on the table by the bed. He knew he couldn't explain the book away. He had no choice but to tell her the truth now. He knew, had always known, that what he had done was reprehensible. But still, he had to make her see that what he had done was out of love and for no other reason.

Taking her cold hands in his, he drew them up to his lips, kissing them in turn. "Sheena, I'm so sorry. I wish I could have told you sooner. But I was afraid of losing you. Can you forgive me for loving you so much?"

Sheena pulled her hands free. "Is that what you call it—love? That's funny. I don't see it that way. I see it as a very selfish act. You didn't consider for a moment that I didn't want to be here, that I wanted my own life, and, by God, was entitled to it. No, you lied and lied and lied. I understand now why you accepted my story about traveling through time so easily. Of course you did! You knew it was true because you had traveled through time yourself. And not just once, either, but over and over again.''

"I won't deny it. You know the truth now. But not all of it. If you'll put your anger aside for a moment and let me explain, I'm sure you'll understand why I had to lie to you.''

Sheena pressed her hands over her ears. "No! I don't want to hear it. I don't care what noble reason you had for lying. You deliberately deprived me of my life, and I can never forgive you for that.''

Taking her by the shoulders, he pulled her up against his chest. "Sheena, you can't mean that. We were so happy together. How could what I did be so wrong if it brought us such happiness?''

"Can't you see? It wasn't real! It was all based on lies. I can never trust you again.''

Michael's heart constricted. How could he turn her around? What would he do if he lost her? There had to be a way to make her see. "I can't blame you for that. But if you'll just listen to what I have to say with an open mind, then, I swear, after you've heard my story, if you still want to leave, I won't try to stop you.''

Struggling out of his arms, Sheena said sarcastically, "Very well, Michael. Tell me your story, if you insist. Actually I'm curious to hear what you have to say. I want to know how perverted your brain really is.''

Michael walked over to the window, his head framed against the falling snow. "Did you know my father died on my nineteenth birthday?''

"What does that have to do with your deceit? If you think you can play on my sympathy, you're—''

"Listen and you'll understand. After his death, I felt the need to get away, and wandered up to the top of Lost

Mountain to be alone. I certainly didn't expect to find anyone up there in the middle of winter. But there she was, Lucinda Nims, sitting on a large boulder almost as if she had been waiting for me.''

Despite her anger, Michael had her full attention now. "That's how I met her, too."

"Then you'll understand how easy it was for her to engage me in conversation. Before I knew it, she was telling me a strange story about a swirling vortex of snow she called the Silver Storm."

Sheena gasped. "You mean it was a real storm all along?"

"I'll explain. Lucinda asked me if I'd like to go on an exciting adventure with her, and the idea was irresistible to my young mind. She told me she could bring me to the far-distant past, and though I didn't believe her at first, I went along out of curiosity. What could it hurt to humor an old woman?

"I suppose if I had known what lay ahead of me, I might not have gone, but young and reckless, I walked through the Silver Storm with her and emerged in the valley below. A very different valley than I was familiar with. Very different from the way it is now, too. Then, there was only a small wooden hut standing close to the water's edge, and around the bend in the river, a small Abenaki village.

"Lucinda told me she had come through the time portal for the first time when she was only seven. The year was 1902. She had been crossing the mountains with her family, on their way from West Virginia to Boston to start a new life. Her mother had the promise of a job in a shirt factory, and her father a job as a milkman. She said they had spent the night on the mountain after a long trek and were planning on continuing on to Boston the next day.

"But Lucinda never traveled any farther. In the middle of the night, she awoke and saw the shimmer of the Silver Storm and was drawn to it, like a moth to a flame.

Mesmerized, she stepped inside it without hesitation and when she emerged found herself in the valley, surrounded by the Abenaki.

"It was several years before she learned how it had all come to be. By then she had been assimilated into the tribe. And by then she had become close to her adopted brother Onotoquos, for their spirits were remarkably alike.

"As she grew into adulthood, she traveled back and forth through the time portal, and it was on one of those trips that I met her."

Michael walked over to Sheena and sat beside her. "The rest is history. At first I stayed because of the thrill of adventure, but as time passed, I became more and more concerned about what could happen if the wrong people traveled through the portal.

"I was horrified at the thought of someone with AIDS traveling to this time and spreading the disease amongst America's earliest residents. Can you imagine the devastating effect it would have in a time when even measles and chicken pox could wipe out a whole village? Not to mention what might happen if a terrorist group happened upon the portal. Who knows how the future might be changed because of their actions?

"And I wasn't the only one concerned. Snow Eagle and Onotoquos were aware of the dangers too and had already taken precautions to protect the portal from being breached."

"But if they were so protective, why did Lucinda let you through?"

"Lucinda got it in her head that I would make a good addition to the small community, and I was excited by the prospect. Remember, I was only nineteen. The whole idea of living in the past was very appealing to me. But I couldn't leave my mother and sister behind. I was the man of the family now. They needed me.

"Lucinda trusted me to go back through the portal to get my family, warning me that the Silver Storm only appeared when the wind was from the northwest and was bringing snow along with it. If either element was missing, the portal would remain closed.''

So that was the information she had been waiting so long to hear. She had the key now, so she could travel back to her own time. But what about Michael?

Needing the impetus of anger to walk away from him, she cried, ''And did you deceive them too, the way you deceived me? Did they know what they were getting into when they walked through the portal?''

''I'm not a complete monster, Sheena. Of course I told them. And of course they didn't believe me, and it wasn't until the following winter that I was able to convince them to at least come to the mountain and see for themselves. They finally agreed, and luckily the Silver Storm appeared while we were there.''

''I can't believe they agreed to stay, once they discovered they really had gone back in time.''

''Why is that so hard to believe? You have to remember, my father had just died, and all three of us had been struggling with the idea of a life without his powerful presence. They were just as eager as I to start a new life, and what better way than here where the future was all laid out before us? It's rather a unique way to start over, don't you think?''

''Unique? I think it's cowardly. It was a way of escaping your father's death. Why couldn't you just do what everyone else does when faced with the death of a loved one? Just go on and learn to live again. That's what I had to do after my parents died.''

''But don't you see? That's what we were doing. Learning to live again, in the most meaningful way possible. My mother and Elizabeth felt just as strongly as I did, that for the sake of the future of mankind, we had to protect the portal. Over the years, we added to our little colony, choosing people from our life in the twenty-first century that would be of help to our cause.''

''I don't understand that at all. Why couldn't you protect

mankind just as well from the other side of the portal? Why did you have to go back in time to do it?''

''Think about it and you'll understand. What were we to do? We couldn't build a home or even so much as a guard shed on the mountain. First of all, we didn't own the land; second of all, any building there would just call attention to the area. The last thing we needed were curious people milling around and discovering the Silver Storm. We were just lucky the portal appeared in such a barren, isolated place.

''No, it was better to guard it from the seventeenth-century side. We were among friendly Indians here. People just as dedicated as we to protecting the portal. And remember, we were only here during the winter months, when there was a possibility of the portal opening. We lived a double life for many years, going back and forth between the two times, but it became a burden after a while, and frankly, we all agreed we preferred the past, where life was more peaceful. No threat of nuclear war, no threat of a deadly disease spread by some madman's chemical weapons. And, of course, we had the peace of knowing exactly what would be happening in future years, so there was no anxiety.

''In truth, we thought it was an idyllic time to live in. Here, civilization is still just a dream. There are only a few small colonies spread beyond the coast, and after the crowded living in Boston, we found life here tranquil. Surely you do as well? Haven't you been happy?''

Michael searched her face, seeking, praying, that he would find the answer he sought, but her face was unreadable and he went on with his story. ''When I saw you standing in the moonlight, dressed in a wedding gown, I thought Lucinda and Onotoquos had used their magic to bring you to me. I didn't stop to think you might have been wrenched from a life you were happy with.

''I wasn't thinking very clearly at all. I realize that now. I fell in love with you the moment I first saw you, and I still haven't regained my equilibrium. I thought of you as a gift, a wondrous gift that I was entitled to. I know that sounds egotistical, and it is, but after years of dedicating my life to guarding the portal, I really believed you were my reward.

"But in truth you are so much more than that. You are my life, my whole world. Sheena. Forgive me. Please. Don't throw away what we have."

Sheena walked over to the window to gaze out at the falling snow, and Michael wondered if she was thinking of the Silver Storm. He had given her the key to leaving; would she take it and go, destroying him in the process? His fate was in her hands.

CHAPTER ELEVEN

Sheena's mind was churning. How could she hope to make the right decision when so many conflicting emotions were tearing her apart? The one thing she knew for certain was that she loved Michael, despite his egotistical and selfish ways. But then, nothing was completely black or white, was it? He had sacrificed his life for a noble cause, which meant he wasn't totally selfish. Knowing that should make it easier to forgive him.

But it didn't. Not now. Not with the baby to think of. She had to put her child's welfare above everything else. And the bottom line was, she feared raising it in the wilderness. Michael might feel comfortable living in the wilds of early America, but she certainly didn't. She wanted to raise her child in a civilized world. A world where it had a chance of growing up to be anything it wanted to be. And that wasn't possible here.

But, and this was a big but, if she did leave, her child would never know its father. Oh, why did life have to be so darned complicated?

"Sheena, listen to me. For God's sake, don't make up your mind now, in the heat of anger. Promise me you'll take a week to think it through—that's all I ask. One week, and then if you still want to leave, I won't try to stop you."

Michael's fervent plea was interrupted by a loud knocking on the door. It was his mother and sister. Michael drew them inside, and Sheena was glad for the diversion. He had thrown her off guard by offering her a week to think it over. That was so unlike the Michael she knew. She was actually surprised at how reasonable he was acting. Surely she could spare one week to make up her mind. One week, then no one could say she acted in haste.

"Oh, dear, are we interrupting something?"

Michael embraced his mother. "Of course not, Mother. This is your house too, though you'd never know it lately. Has Lucinda convinced you to move in with her?"

"No, son. And don't tell me you've missed me. Not with a beautiful new wife to keep you company. I'm just a little concerned about Lucy and want to be with her as much as I'm able. After all, she won't be with us forever."

The door was suddenly flung open again and a grim-faced Snow Eagle stepped inside. "Silver Fang has been injured. He's caught in the metal trap set for the puma."

Michael grabbed his jacket, but before rushing out he turned to Sheena. "Will you be here when I get back?"

Sheena nodded, and, reassured, Michael left with Snow Eagle. Kathleen stayed only a few moments longer and then headed back to Old Lucy's, leaving Elizabeth and Sheena alone.

Elizabeth sank into a chair. "Poor Michael. I've seen the damage those traps can do. It won't be easy for him. He's very fond of Silver Fang."

Seeing how pale Elizabeth was, Sheena poured a little wine into a goblet and handed it to her. "Here, drink this. It'll bring the color back to your cheeks."

Elizabeth took a sip and then gave Sheena a puzzled look. "Wine? Where in the world did it come from?"

Sheena sat across the table from Elizabeth. "You know

where it came from. There's no need for secrets anymore. Michael has told me the whole story.''

Elizabeth reached across the table to take Sheena's hand. ''You have no idea how relieved I am to hear that. It's been such a burden keeping the truth from you. I'm so glad Michael finally told you. I don't know why he was so insistent on keeping it from you in the first place. Afraid of losing you, I suppose. But then, I can understand that. I know how I'd feel if I were to lose my husband.''

''Is that why you went along with Michael? Why you didn't let me know you too were from the twenty-first century?''

''Sheena, you have to realize, I love my brother. Seeing he had a chance for happiness with you, I kept my silence. The same with everyone else in the valley. We wanted to give your love a chance to grow. And in the end, you'll have to agree that fate had a hand in it. You arrived here just in the nick of time, didn't you?''

''Just in time? What do you mean?''

''Well, it's pretty ironic that the portal will be closing forever so soon after you've come. You would never have had a chance to meet Michael if your photo shoot had been the day after tomorrow.''

Sheena felt as if she had been punched in the stomach. Struggling to keep from showing her shock, she forced a smile and said, ''Yes. It certainly is amazing. The portal closes tomorrow, you said? Michael must have forgotten the date. He thought it was more than a week away.''

''How could he forget something so awesome? It was thoroughly discussed at the council meeting just yesterday. My goodness, it boggles my mind to think everyone in Lost Valley voted to stay here, knowing they could never leave once the portal closed. But then, they've had over a month to think about it.''

Michael has known for over a month the portal would close tomorrow? That diabolical . . . Ohhhh! But she mustn't think about that now. She didn't want Elizabeth to know how upset she was. ''Even you, Elizabeth? With a baby about to be born? How can you choose this time to raise your child in?''

"Where else would I want to raise him but among his father's people? Onotoquos says my son will grow up to be a great chief of the Abenaki. If I left, that future would never come to pass. I could never do that to Snow Eagle's people.''

"I never realized till this moment how much alike you and your brother are. You're both so devoted to some lofty ideal that you're practically playing God.''

With the taint of bitterness in Sheena's voice, understanding slowly dawned on Elizabeth. "Oh, no. What have I done? You didn't know the portal was closing, did you?''

"Your brother lied to me about that too. No more than a minute ago he stood right in this room and ever so sweetly, ever so understandingly, asked me to promise I'd stay just one more week. *One more week.* Can you believe the nerve of him? And to think I actually considered it. He was just buying time because he knew that in *one day,* just one little day, I wouldn't be able to go back to my own time. Ohhh, I can't believe he would lie to me yet again. That he would manipulate me like that. Well, this time he won't get away with it.''

"What will you do?''

"What do you think I'm going to do? It's snowing now. I'm going through the portal before its too late.'' Slipping into her warm jacket, Sheena said, "Don't look at me like that. Not everyone is as noble as you and your brother. Damn it all. What's so wrong about wanting to go back where I belong?''

Elizabeth suddenly embraced Sheena, holding her tight. "Oh, Sheena, there's nothing wrong with it. But I'll miss you. Terribly. I understand your feelings. The time we live in is harsh. Not everyone is cut out for it. But what will I say to Michael? It will break his heart if you leave.''

"Heart? What heart? He certainly didn't have one when he forced his will on me. He could have told me the truth and let me make up my own mind. That would have been the right thing to do, the honest thing to do, but then, he doesn't know the meaning of the word, does he?''

''You must love him very much to be so hurt. I'm sorry for that. Are you so sure you're doing the right thing by leaving? Can't you find it in your heart to stay for Michael's sake? I know you could be as happy here as mother and I are. We would never think of leaving anymore.''

Sheena thought of Michael's poor mother. She'd never get the chance to know one of her grandchildren. But she couldn't think about that. It was hard enough to think of her baby without its father.

Still in Elizabeth's embrace, Sheena squeezed her tight, then stepped away. ''Please don't make it any harder on me than it already is. I've got to go now. Michael could return at any moment.''

Tears sprang to Elizabeth's eyes. ''Then I wish you Godspeed and pray you find happiness in your world.''

Pulling her jacket close, Sheena opened the door and quickly disappeared from sight. She didn't breathe an easy breath until she was halfway up the mountain pass. By the time she reached the top, the winds were beginning to shift, and the snow was little more than flurries.

Oh, please. Don't let it be too late. Let the Silver Storm still be there.

And there it was, sparkling in the light of the moon, looking for all the world like a miniature silver tornado. Afraid it would disappear before her eyes, she ran toward it, her heart in her throat.

In a moment she was inside the vortex and the world was slipping away.

Away . . .

Away . . .

Sheena closed her eyes for just a moment, and when she opened them she was standing in the moonlight. The Silver Storm was gone and the world was eerily quiet. Looking around her, she saw that she was back in the valley again, and for one heart-stopping moment she thought she was still in the past. But as her senses returned, she realized she was in the midst of the Girl Scout camp. She had made it. She was back in her own time.

She thought it strange to find herself down in the valley instead of on the mountain, but remembered this was where she had emerged the last time too. Would she ever understand it all?

Heading toward the camp office, she tried the door, but it was locked. There had to be a way inside. She knew there was a phone in there, and she prayed it was still in service. It seemed likely, considering that the scouts sometimes used the facilities in the winter.

The wind whistled around the corner of the building, and she followed the sound to the south side of the log structure and the long row of windows. She tried each one in turn, finding them all locked. Then, in desperation, she grasped a fallen tree branch in her hand and smashed the glass from one of the windows.

The noise was so loud that if anyone had been nearby, they would have heard. But no one came running, and she knew she was alone. She climbed through the window into the camp office, where her gaze swept over the dark room. The phone was on an ancient mahogany desk, and she picked it up and listened. Thank goodness, there was a dial tone.

Suddenly overwhelmed, she started shaking all over, and sank into a deep upholstered chair to compose herself.

Michael . . . Would she really never see him again? Gazing out the window, she saw the mountain looming overhead, and the loneliness that swept over her that first day at the edge of the cliff came back to her. Was it just two months ago? It seemed like a lifetime. So much had happened in such a short time.

Now here she was all alone, and once again she could blame no one but herself. Was she wrong to leave Michael? She didn't know anymore. All she knew was that once again her fate was in her own hands, and that couldn't be wrong.

Feeling a sudden chill, she rubbed her hands together to warm them, and thought about who she should call. Who was there to call but Carolyn? She didn't have many friends. Writers lived such solitary lives. But Carolyn had made sure they stayed in touch with each other, no matter how deeply Sheena emersed herself in her writing. Yes, Carolyn was the right one to call, and for more than one reason.

Sheena dialed the number with shaking hands, almost dreading to hear her friend's voice, for then she'd know whether Onotoquos was right. Whether Tony and Jared really had survived the helicopter crash.

Carolyn's lilting *hello* lit up the dark office, and with a hard lump in her throat, Sheena cried, "Carolyn, it's Sheena."

CHAPTER TWELVE

One look at Silver Fang, and Michael's stomach churned. It was bad. The animal's leg was so mangled there was no hope of saving it. Kneeling beside the wolf, he spoke to it in a gentle tone, drawing his hand back when the wolf started growling.

"He's crazy with pain," Snow Eagle said. "He wouldn't let me near him."

"Easy, boy. I know it hurts, but I just want to help you." Michael reached out to stroke the animal's back, and the wolf's muscles rippled beneath his thick coat. Placing one booted foot against one jaw of the trap, he pulled with all his strength on the other, forcing it open enough to free the mangled leg. Silver Fang responded with an unearthly howl, and Michael knew the animal's pain must be unbearable.

Looking up at Snow Eagle, Michael said, "I'm going to need your help."

Snow Eagle answered. "Of course. I'll get my rifle and—"

"Rifle? No. You don't understand. I don't want to kill him. I'm going to amputate his hurt leg."

"Michael! No! You cannot do this. Silver Fang has a wild nature. It would be terrible for him to live without his leg. How could he hunt? How could he run? Better to set his spirit free."

"But I care too much about him to lose him. And there's no need. No need. He'll be fine without his leg. I'll take care of him. In no time he'll be content to sleep by my hearth. That's not such a terrible fate, now is it?"

"Michael. For once in your life think of the needs of others instead of your own. Put yourself in his place and think what it would be like for him."

"My God, man, you sound just like Sheena. Am I really that selfish? I *am* thinking of Silver Fang. Every living thing deserves a chance to live. You taught me that."

"It is so. But everything must also die when it is time. And it is Silver Fang's time now. He has led a full life. Let him go. He would be miserable sitting by your fire, hearing the howls of the wild wolves in the distance. Wanting to join them, to ride free with the wind. He was not meant to be tamed. Did I not also tell you that?"

Michael gazed down at the suffering wolf. What Snow Eagle said was true. It had been a selfish act to hold on to a creature born to be free. Look at the consequences. This terrible accident would never have happened if he hadn't tried to make the wolf his pet. Stretching out his arm to Snow Eagle, he said, "Give me your rifle."

Snow Eagle hesitated. "Let me do this for you."

"No. I brought him to this. I'll be the one to take him out of it. I pray you and your father are right, that spirits live on after the flesh decays. I want Silver Fang's spirit to run free."

Taking the rifle from Snow Eagle, he called Silver Fang's name in a calm, measured voice. The wolf looked up at Michael with golden eyes. Wise eyes. Forgiving eyes. Michael squeezed the trigger.

In the distance, a sound carried through the air, a sound that started so low, that at first Michael thought it was the wind, but as it grew and grew. There was no mistaking the howling of a wolf, and then another and another, until the glen rang with the eerie music.

Michael and Snow Eagle stood silently, listening. Letting the sacredness of the moment into their very souls. It was as if the wolves were singing their comrade into eternity.

And when the howling stopped and the world was silent again, the two men knew they had shared a profound experience. There was no need for words, only the need to be with their loved ones.

Michael's thoughts turned to Sheena, and he knew he had been as unfair to her as he had been to the wolf. Her spirit needed to be free too. It had been wrong to deceive her, to hold on to her against her will. He had known from the beginning how much she deplored living in the seventeenth century, and yet, because of his own selfish needs, he had persisted in forcing his will on her.

How different he had been when he first came to the valley. He had high ideals then. What happened to them? How had he lost his way? He had convinced himself that since his mother and sister had adjusted well, Sheena would too. But it was a wrong assumption. She cherished her life in the twenty-first century.

After tomorrow the portal would close forever and there'd be no more need for deception, no more need for anyone to guard the portal. He would be free of his responsibility then, and could go with Sheena to the century she longed to live in. That was little enough to sacrifice for the woman he loved. Hadn't he already put the foundation of that life in place right from the start?

Thanks to his father's insurance money, he and his mother had bought the last remaining land in Lost Valley and donated it to the Girl Scouts to enlarge their camp. The only stipulation was that he could maintain a garage there for his vehicle, which they needed to pick up supplies whenever they visited modern times. But of course, the Girl Scout council knew nothing about the portal or his real reason for needing the garage. They rarely even saw him, and since the camp was hardly ever used in the winter, the arrangement worked out very nicely.

But there would be no more traveling back and forth between times after tomorrow. What a relief to know that no one could ever breach time again. Pray God, the portal would never return. At least not until men grew beyond violence, and were able to live in peace with their neighbors.

Snow Eagle clasped Michael's shoulder and walked him toward their horses. "My father taught me that when you listen to your heart, you will always do the right thing. And you, my friend, have done the right thing."

Michael nodded solemnly. "Your father is right. But damn it all, does it have to hurt so much?" Mounting his horse, he murmured, "There's one more painful thing I must do. Tell Sheena the truth."

They rode to the cottage in silence, and when they arrived, Michael turned to his friend and said, "Pray for me, Snow Eagle. I may lose more than Silver Fang today—I may lose my wife."

Gritting his teeth together, he opened the door and went inside. Elizabeth turned to look at him, her face ashen, and he knew something was very wrong.

His eyes scanned the room looking for his wife, knowing in his heart he would not find her. She was gone. Not to a neighbor's, not for a walk, but to the other side. Oh, God, he was too late. Why couldn't she have waited one more day? He would have told her the truth and things would have been healed between them.

With a heavy heart he asked, "When did she leave?"

"Right after you left with Snow Eagle. I couldn't stop her."

"It's all right, Liz. It's not your fault. I should have faced Sheena and resolved the problem when she first came here. Don't blame yourself. I'm going after her, but . . . I won't be coming back this time. I've decided

I'd rather be with her in a time that I despise than be alone in a time I love. It's as simple as that."

Elizabeth flew into his arms. "I know, Michael. For I feel the same way about Snow Eagle. I could never leave here. Go. Fly to her before the portal closes. I'll say good-bye to Mother for you. She'll understand."

Michael squeezed his sister tight, knowing it would be the last time he would ever be with her. Over her shoulder, he spoke to Snow Eagle in a voice choked with emotion. "Snow Eagle, it gives me peace to know that my mother and sister will be under your care. You've been like a brother to me, and I'll always be grateful for your friendship."

Snow Eagle nodded his head. "I will guard them with my life."

Holding his sister at arm's length, Michael said, "Saying good-bye is never easy, but this time it's almost too much to bear. I'll miss you and Mom so . . . Damn it all, I wish there was a way we could—" And then a glimmer of an idea came to him. It was a long shot, but it might work. "Elizabeth, Snow Eagle. I know a way we might still communicate. It's not a perfect way, and you won't be able to receive anything from me, but I can receive letters from you."

"But . . . how can we communicate once the portal closes?"

"Do you remember confiding in me once about the secret hiding place where you and Snow Eagle used to leave messages for each other when you were courting?"

"Of course I do. But I still don't understand."

Snow Eagle's eyebrows raised. "Ah. I think I do. It might work."

Elizabeth gazed quizzically at the two men. "What might work?"

"You and mother can write to me, then hide the letters in the crevice where you once hid your letters to Snow Eagle. Don't you see? No one will find them there, and they'll be well protected from the elements. In the twenty-first century, there is nothing to prevent me from going to the crevice and finding your messages to me. That way I can at least know what's going on with you and Mother, and it will make our separation more bearable.''

Elizabeth started sobbing, as much from joy as from sadness. ''Oh, Michael. I think it will work. That way, you'll always be a part of our lives.''

Taking hope from this, he kissed Elizabeth's forehead three times. ''One kiss for you, one for Mother, and one for your son soon to be born. Tell me all about him in your letters. Take a picture of him for me. There's plenty of film and cameras in the storeroom.''

With those last, promising words, Michael left with Snow Eagle. Mounting Pale Warrior, he said, ''Snow Eagle, I'm leaving Pale Warrior on this side of the portal. Will you give him to Onotoquos after I'm gone? He's always admired him.''

''My father will be well pleased. I thank you for him.''

Michael rode up the mountain without looking back. It was easier that way. And he had other things to think about. The Silver Storm. What if it was gone? What if it was too late to go to Sheena? But he couldn't believe that. Surely they were destined to be together.

To his relief, the storm was still churning and swirling as he dismounted. Slapping the flank of his horse, he sent it galloping back toward the valley, toward Snow Eagle and Onotoquos and all the people he loved and would never see again. But there was someone who drew him more than all the others, and with her name on his lips, he stepped into the time portal.

When he emerged, he headed for the garage where his Ford Explorer was stored, then changed his mind and went to the camp office instead. Sheena didn't know about the garage and had no idea there was any mode of transportation at the isolated camp. She would have gone to the office in search of a phone.

Taking a key from a hook on a nearby tree, he unlocked

the door and entered the darkened room. But the question was, who would she have called? How would he find her now? But then, he wasn't too worried about that. How hard could it be to find an author of many published books?

How hard indeed. All he had to do was push the redial button and he'd know who she called. Picking up the phone, he tapped the proper key and waited while it rang several times. His heart quickened when he heard a lilting voice. "You have reached the residence of Tony and Carolyn Absolem. Sorry we're not home right now, but if you'd like you can leave a message after the beep."

Damn. It was only an answering machine, but at least he knew where Sheena had gone. To Boston. Disappointed, but determined to find Sheena that very night, he called Information and gave the operator Carolyn's name, hoping there would be an address where he could find her. The operator obliged him, and he quickly wrote it down, and with spirits soaring, went back to the garage.

The Explorer started up right away, a good omen, he hoped, that everything was going to turn out all right. Lighthearted, he started the long ride to Boston. He estimated it would take an hour to get out of the mountains and another hour on the Mass Pike before he reached Boston, but time meant nothing to him anymore. He'd have the rest of his life to be with Sheena.

Since he was lost in thought, it took him a while to realize the car was coasting. The engine had stopped. Pulling over to the side of the road, he put on the brakes, then looked at the gas gauge. Empty. Damn it all. Now what? It was the middle of the night, on an isolated country road, and he knew for a fact there wasn't a gas station around for miles and miles.

But nothing was going to dampen his spirits. He'd just take a little nap and hail someone down in the morning. Hell, if he had to, he'd just start hitchhiking toward Boston at first light.

* * *

Carolyn and Sheena talked into the wee hours of the morning after Carolyn picked her up at the Girl Scout camp. At first Sheena had felt awkward, afraid to ask Carolyn about her husband and brother, but, unable to bear the suspense any longer, she finally blurted out, "I'm to blame for everything that happened. Can you ever forgive me, Carolyn?"

Carolyn responded with a hug, and then a long story about the rescue after the helicopter crash. "Miraculously, Tony was able to walk away from the crash with no more than crushed ribs and a broken nose, but it was touch and go with Jared for a while. He suffered a broken back, broken pelvis, and other injuries, but he's recuperating just fine now. Funny thing, he held on to his camera so tight the medics couldn't pry it from his fingers. Photographers! They're all a crazy breed. But then, he did get some great shots of you on the cliff. One of them actually made the cover of *People* magazine."

"How wonderful for Jared! He must be in seventh heaven."

"His feet haven't touched the ground yet. And he'll be so glad to know you're alive. He was so worried. We all were. Your disappearance made the headlines. No one could figure out what happened to you. There were no tracks leading down from the cliff. It was as if you disappeared into thin air."

Relieved to know she hadn't caused her friends' deaths, she told Carolyn her story, and although her friend had a hard time accepting it, she knew Sheena well enough to know she was telling the truth. Exhausted, they had gone to bed with a promise from Carolyn that she would dig up a copy of the photographs from the photo shoot in the morning.

Next morning, Sheena arose to find Tony returned from a chartered trip with his new helicopter, and tears sprang to her eyes when she embraced him. It was so good to hold him, to know that she hadn't caused his death.

Teary-eyed herself, Carolyn embraced them both. "Sheena, let's go to the Chowder House tonight to celebrate your return."

Unexpectedly, Sheena's tears turned into an anguished torrent.

"What is it, Sheena? Did I say something wrong?"

"It's not you, Carolyn—it's me. I've just lost my husband, and my unborn child will never know its father. I'm in no mood to celebrate."

"Sweetheart, don't beat yourself up over this. Michael's the one who did wrong, not you."

"Then why do I feel so bad? I've been here less than twenty-four hours and I'm miserable without him already. I didn't sleep a wink last night, thinking about everything that's happened, and I realized that all I want in this world is to be with Michael. Oh, why didn't he love me enough to come after me? I waited and waited for the knock on the door, so sure that he would come."

"Maybe he will. Give him time."

"Carolyn, don't you see? There is no time! The portal is going to close forever today. If he was going to come, he'd be here by now."

Sheena's heart raced at the thought that it might already be too late. The portal might already have closed. What a fool she had been! How did she think she could be happy without Michael in her life?

Grasping at Carolyn's clothing, Sheena cried, "What am I going to do? I've made a terrible mistake, and I'm afraid it's too late to change it."

"Honey, I was afraid you'd change your mind. After everything you told me yesterday, I figured you'd eventually come to realize that what you really needed was not the comfort of modern-day Boston, but the comfort of Michael Winters's arms."

Sheena gazed at her friend in amazement. "How did

you get so much smarter than me? Why didn't I realize that before it was too late?''

Tony rose from the table. ''What makes you think it's too late?''

''Well, if it's not, it soon will be. The portal could close before I get there.''

''True, but you'll have a fighting chance in my helicopter. Shall we give it a try?''

''Oh, Tony, do you mean it? Of course I want to. Damn Michael and his stubborn soul! Why didn't he come after me? I stayed awake all night just listening for his knock on the door, so sure he would follow me here.''

Michael's feet were starting to hurt now, and he gave up hope that anyone would stop for him. What was wrong with these modern people anyway? In his time—or at least the time he had claimed as his own—it would have been unheard of not to help someone in need. But then there was no need to hurry anymore. Sheena was in Boston, and very soon he'd be with her.

The only thing he worried about was whether she would forgive him. She had to. She *would*. After all, he had sacrificed his chosen life for hers. She would realize that when she saw him, and everything would be all right.

A shiver snaked up his spine, and he wondered who was walking over his grave, but he quickly forgot about it when, miraculously, a woman stopped to pick him up. An elderly woman with a sparkling helmet of blue-white hair.

''If you're heading for Boston, son, hop in. I'm heading for the reenactment myself.''

Michael wondered what she was talking about until he realized how out of place his clothing was. No wonder no one had picked him up; they must have thought him some kind of nut. ''Thanks, ma'am. I appreciate it. My car broke down a few miles back, and I was afraid I'd be late for the, uh, celebration.''

"Well, I'd hardly call rehearsing for the Patriots Day event a celebration, but then, I suppose every time we get into Colonial costume we celebrate our ancestors."

"Yes, ma'am."

"This your first time?"

Michael almost laughed at that. He'd been living in the seventeenth-century life for over ten years. The stories he could tell this kindly old woman. The instruction he could give to the reenactors on the way people really lived. Maybe someday he would do just that. Maybe someday his own children would take part in a reenactment. It pleased him to know that in some small way, he might still capture his past life.

It was close to noon when the woman dropped him off, and as she pulled away, the bumper sticker caught his eye. Emblazoned in gold over black were the words "Time traveler." *Time Traveler*. In truth, she was, for dressing in costume and reenacting the past was surely the closest way to travel through time without benefit of the Silver Storm.

Then, eager to find Sheena, he got his bearings and headed in the direction of Carolyn's street, rehearsing in his head what he would say to Sheena. But as soon as he found the right house, everything went out of his head and he became anxious. What if she refused to forgive him?

He pushed that thought out of his head and stabbed the doorbell with his finger, waiting as the faint sounds of someone moving inside drifted through the door. And then it was opening, and a pleasant-faced young woman appeared. Suddenly her face went white. "You're Michael. Oh, my God!"

Michael hadn't been expecting such a dramatic greeting, but at least he knew he had come to the right place. How else would she know his name?

"And you're Carolyn. Sheena has told me so much about you."

"Oh, God, Sheena! What are we going to do?"

"What . . . what do you mean? Isn't she here?"

Michael's heart stopped beating as he waited to hear the awful news. He knew it had to be bad by the look of distress on Carolyn's face.

"Michael, she's gone. She went back through the portal to find you."

CHAPTER THIRTEEN

In Michael's worst nightmare, he could never have thought up a worse scenario. Had he come all this way only to lose what he wanted most in the world? His wife, by his side, in his arms, where she belonged? Was he destined to spend the rest of his life deprived of the one person who could make living in the twenty-first century worthwhile?

"It can't be true. She couldn't have gone back. She hated it there. My God, she hated it there! Why would she do that?"

"Isn't the answer obvious, Michael? She loves you."

Michael tore his fingers through his hair. "This can't be happening. Didn't she realize I would come after her? Why didn't she wait for me?"

"Michael, if you don't mind my saying so, it took you bloody long enough to get here."

"My car ran out of gas. That's why it took so long. I crossed over last night, and had to wait it out in the car. If I had thought for one minute she'd pull a stunt like that, I would have walked here last night, even if it took me all night. Damn it all, why couldn't she have been more patient? She's condemned us both now.''

Carolyn's husband suddenly appeared in the doorway. ''It's too early to give up, man. The Silver Storm was there when I dropped her off; it might still be there now, if you hurry.''

Michael laughed bitterly. ''Hurry? It's a two-hour drive to the mountains. I can't possibly make it in time.''

''You can if you fly.''

''Fly? You mean by helicopter? My God, do you still have it? I thought it was destroyed in the crash.''

''Oh, it was. Completely, but I was well insured. I replaced the old one with a state-of-the-art Huey. Flies like an angel. I can hit 150 miles an hour in an emergency.''

One hundred fifty miles? Just about the distance to Lost Mountain. Maybe they could make it in an hour. Would that be enough time? It had to be. Anything else was unthinkable.

But once in the air, the 150 miles an hour felt like a crawl. Michael willed the copter to fly faster, willed the miles of frozen land to speed by, waiting in unbearable agony to see if the Silver Storm would still be there.

As they approached the cliff, Michael's eyes scanned the landscape, looking for the shimmering light of the Silver Storm, and his heart nearly stopped when he saw it. ''There it is! Hurry. It could disappear any minute.''

As the helicopter set down on the same spot where Michael had first seen Sheena in her wedding gown, the same spot where he had married her, his heart filled with hope that everything would be all right. ''Thanks, Tony. I can never repay you for this.''

''Hey, I was happy to do it. Oh. I almost forgot.'' Thrusting a white envelope in his hand, he said, ''Carolyn wanted you to have the pictures from the photo shoot. She forgot to give them to Sheena earlier. Now get the hell out of here. You've got a storm to catch.''

Clutching the envelope, Michael saluted the pilot, then climbed out of the cockpit and started running toward the vortex, eating up the distance, running as though his life depended on it, and oh, God, it did. He kept his gaze focused on the swirling snow, afraid that if he looked away it would disappear.

When he was no more than six feet away, he was horrified to see it begin to fade away. ''No! Oh, God, no!'' Before he could realize what was happening, it was gone.

Devastated, he came to a halt on the very spot where it had disappeared, looking up to the heavens as if in hope of calling it back. Still panting from the hard run, he drew the scent of ozone into his lungs, and knew he had been no more than a heartbeat away from achieving all his dreams.

How could it end this way? With him and his true love not only in different centuries, but the *wrong* centuries. What kind of sick joke was God playing on him?

But what use in cursing an uncaring God? What use in anything anymore? If he had any guts at all, he'd walk over to the edge of the cliff and jump. A bitter laugh escaped his throat and tumbled over the surrounding boulders, coming back at him in a mocking echo. He'd probably botch that too, and only maim himself.

The echo of his laughter went on and on, ringing in his ears, and he imagined it was mocking him, calling his name in a voice much higher than his own. It sounded so real he almost swore it was . . .

He froze, listening, praying it was true. Daring to hope the voice belonged to Sheena. Dazed, he slowly turned to look behind him, and there she was, running toward him from the direction of the standing rocks, her hair floating around her face in the wind. The most beautiful sight he had ever seen.

He thought, at first, he must be imagining her. But no, she was as real as the day he first saw her standing on the cliff in her wedding gown. He had thought her just a waking dream then, but she was real, and she was most assuredly real now. Anything less would be too heartbreaking. In a trembling voice he called her name. "Sheena!"

"Michael! Oh, Michael. What took you so long? I've been waiting here for over an hour."

Michael felt his knees give way. She was *real*.

In an instant Sheena was there to hold him up. "Never mind. It doesn't matter. You're here—that's all I care about."

Holding tight to his wife, Michael covered her face with kisses. "You don't know what I've been through. I thought I was too late. I thought we'd never be together again. Oh, baby, you don't know how scared I was."

"No more than I was. Oh, Michael, I was frantic thinking I had missed you. When I went back through the portal, your mother told me you had gone to the twenty-first century, and I fell apart. I was afraid I would never see you again. Thank goodness Snow Eagle was there to ride me back up to the cliff on Pale Warrior, because my legs wouldn't function anymore. I waited right here, watching the portal, afraid to take my eyes off it, afraid even to blink, for fear of missing you again. And here you are. Oh, here you are. And there's so much I need to tell you I don't know where to begin."

"Sheena, angel, it's all right. We have the rest of our lives to talk. Do you realize that? *The rest of our lives.*"

"It sounds too wonderful to be true. But, Michael, there's something I have to tell you right now. It can't wait a moment longer. I'm pregnant. We're going to have a baby."

Michael's face suddenly became solemn. "To think I might never have known I had fathered a child. Might never have seen it, held it. Sheena. I've been such a fool, but I swear things will be better now. I'll be a good father to our son."

"Daughter. Don't you remember Old Lucy's vision? She said it would be a girl."

"Even better. But when? When will it be born?"

Sheena laughed. "It'll be born on Winter's Solstice—can you believe that?"

"Of course I can. What other day would a child of Winters's bride be born? You are truly a miracle, Sheena."

Sheena stared up at her husband with eyes shining with tears. "Our love is a miracle."

Sweeping her up in his arms, Michael carried his winter's bride to the helicopter and set her inside. And as it rose over Lost Mountain, Michael and Sheena gazed down at the bare cliff that didn't seem quite so barren anymore.

Something caught their eye then, fluttering and soaring, as if on wings, a shiny photograph that had escaped the confines of the white envelope. Floating on a current of air, the image of Sheena, dressed in the wedding gown, was caught halfway between the earth and sky. Winters's bride in all her glory. Her spirit free at last.

A COLD DAY IN PARADISE

KATHRYN HOCKETT

CHAPTER ONE

The scaffold was a gruesome reminder. Christina Phillips couldn't help but shiver as she stared at the gallows rope that had sent the infamous outlaw Lance Meredith to his death.

Lance Meredith. He had been the last gunfighter of any importance in the nineteenth century, an icon to those too often exploited by the powerful and the greedy. He had been a symbol of defiance, a gunslinging Robin Hood on horseback, striking out against those who had preyed upon the weak and the needy. Hero or not, however, he had been hanged.

"A hundred years ago today!" she whispered. Christina's instincts for journalism prompted her to tell Lance Meredith's story. He had become a legend and, like all folk heroes, larger than life.

Today was not only the hundredth anniversary of the outlaw's death; it was also the beginning of a new century. Today marked both the end and the beginning.

For Christina it was a unique opportunity after years of struggling up the journalistic ladder. In just a few moments she was going to be given her shining moment to bask in the limelight as the anchorwoman of a network television newsmagazine, *Century Twenty-One*. The main segment was being broadcast from the ghost town of Paradise, Colorado. Today's story would depict the life and times of the famous gunfighting "Robin Hood" on this, the anniversary of his execution.

Christina had suggested broadcasting the segment live from Paradise instead of taping it at the studio. The camera was going to zoom in on the noose that had taken the outlaw's life, at the exact minute he had been executed a century ago. An actor who bore a remarkable resemblance to the outlaw would read from a script depicting the outlaw's final thoughts and words at the critical moments. Later the actor was to give Christina and the television audience a tour of "his" town as he told about "his" life and times.

Having been born and raised in Paradise, Colorado, a tiny mountain town west of Denver where the outlaw had lived, Christina was familiar with the town's most infamous and intriguing citizen; she knew everything there was to know about the outlaw. The epitome of the Western man, he had loved cigars, whiskey, women and adventure. A handsome devil of a man, so his lady friends had said.

Lance Meredith had moved from Philadelphia with his brother to run a chain of cigar and tobacco stores in Central City, Black Hawk, Georgetown and Paradise. The lure of quick riches through mining had soon changed the focus of their vocations, however. Through hard work and a clever strategy of buying and selling mining property, the Meredith brothers became wealthy. Then tragedy struck: Thomas Meredith was found dead—suicide, the law authorities claimed. Lance, however, insisted that his brother was murdered by the very men who now held deeds to the Meredith mines. In his quest for justice Lance Meredith became impoverished, then outlawed, and finally martyred.

"What would have happened if he had been saved . . . ?"

Christina shook her head. There was no use pondering the matter. It had happened a long time ago and the outcome couldn't be reversed. Even so, Lance Meredith fascinated her because of the paradox of his profession versus his strong code of honor. He had been called an "honest" outlaw.

Meredith supposedly never told a lie, never stole from someone in need, and always gave a share of his ill-gotten riches to those in dire straits. He was said to be the handsomest and most beloved man whose image ever stared out from a wanted poster. Hero to the common man or not, however, he had been hanged on the cold night of December 31, 1899.

Christina wondered what he had been thinking as they placed the noose around his neck. Had he felt any remorse for his chosen "profession?" Had he felt fear? Anger at his betrayal? Had he lamented the error of his ways? Or had he grinned at the hangman and faced death with his usual cocky arrogance?

Blinking against the snowflakes that brushed gently against her eyelashes, Christina shivered again. It was strange . . . eerie . . . and yet. . . . For just a moment she could almost feel the outlaw's presence.

"Hey, Christy, turn around."

"What . . . ?" Startled, Christina whirled to see Bob Easton, the television station's lead cameraman, staring at her.

"We need to get a final reading on these lights before the broadcast," he said with an upraised brow. "We're on in ten minutes."

The broadcast. For just a moment Christy had been so swept up in the past that she had forgotten why she was here. She looked at her wristwatch, synchronizing it to the countdown. "Ten minutes. Ten!" She tensed as a young makeup man powdered her nose.

"Smile so I can get a reading on those gleaming white teeth of yours." Bob winked as he and the multitude of people it took to create a television show bustled about.

Christina forced a smile to hide her sudden case of nerves. It was the first time she had done a show live. There would be no chance for retakes. She could only hope that everything "clicked" perfectly into place. If it didn't, there would be millions of people to view a mistake.

Glancing down, Christina took a last look at her interview questions. The television station referred to the segment's reenactment in the ghost town as an "interview," supposedly with the outlaw's ghost. It was a clever publicity ploy that had brought a great deal of media attention.

"If only I could go back in the past and interview the real Lance Meredith," Christina thought, "what a story *he* would have to tell. And who knows, perhaps I could have gotten him a good lawyer and saved him!" In Christina's opinion, Lance Meredith had deserved better than a quick kangaroo-court trial followed by his hanging. He hadn't been an angel, but despite his many indiscretions, it had been said that he was innocent this time.

Christina strongly suspected that Lance Meredith had been framed. Indeed, there were historians who insisted that Marshal Jim Roundtree had had a personal vendetta against the outlaw. Then again, other writers had suggested that the marshal had an affinity for working on the wrong side of his badge.

The more she read about Marshal Roundtree, in fact, the less Christina liked him. He was obviously cruel, greedy and as stubborn as a mule. A man with no pity. History had revealed him to be a man far more worthy of hanging than the outlaws he had sent to Boothill. It was even suggested that . . .

"Five minutes to broadcast!"

Bob's reminder brought Christina back to the present. Reaching up, she brushed her fingers through her long blond hair, licked her lips, and readied herself for the moment to come.

The clock at the courthouse displayed the time as 11:56. There were just four minutes before she was scheduled to begin. She stared at the hour and minute hands. Tick, tock, tick, tock. Had Lance Meredith heard the very same "ticking," knowing that each minute that passed brought the moment of reckoning closer and closer?

In grim fascination she looked up at the noose that dangled so ominously within her reach. She stared at it for just a moment, then lifted her hand to touch it.

"Lance Meredith, you have been tried and found guilty of robbery and murder by the territorial judge of Colorado. May God have pity on your soul!" she whispered, remembering the words she had read in the Western research books. "Do you have any last words?"

Any last words? A rapid succession of thoughts stormed through her brain. Emotions welled up inside her. Strange, but it was almost as if she could suddenly know the intense feelings *he* must have felt. Anger. Fear. A sense of helplessness.

"Get ready, Christy! Ten, nine, eight . . ."

Hardly daring to breathe, Christy waited. A drumroll sounded, mimicking the drumroll of a hundred years ago, as the cameras moved in. Her fingers brushed against the noose as she poised herself for the signal. She took a step forward, then another . . .

The trapdoor of the gallows must have been loose, the wood rotted through, for suddenly she started to fall. Helplessly her hands groped for anything to hold on to, but it did no good. She was falling through empty space. Down. Down. Down.

He didn't want to die! He wasn't ready. Not yet. He had only tasted of life. There was so much more to enjoy. "Isn't there a way out of this?" Wasn't there a bargain he could make to buy himself a little more time?

Always an optimist, Lance Meredith stared out at the gawking crowd, hoping for a miracle. It didn't happen. As he heard the drumroll, he knew that the end had really come this time!

"Damn!" He flinched against the rope around his neck that was already choking him.

He grimaced as he waited for the end, wondering if the fall through the trapdoor would break his neck or if he would suffer a slow strangulation. He could only hope that God in His mercy would make his death quick. A hanging was always a grisly end even for the worst outlaw.

In just a fleeting moment he contemplated a great many things he'd hoped not to have to think about until he was into old age. Just where did a man go after he died? Was there really a heaven and a hell?

It looked as if he was going to find out sooner than he had expected. Even so, there was no anger in him now, only a feeling of suspense. Any moment something was going to happen, but he didn't know exactly what, when or how.

"Help me!" he rasped. "For the love of . . ."

As if in answer to his unfinished plea, he saw her. A golden-haired angel materializing right in front of his eyes. Was she real? Had she come to save him? Or was he already dead?

The excruciating pain he felt as her body rammed into his just as the trapdoor opened answered that question. Lance felt a tug and pull as he slid into empty air. He felt as if his neck was going to be stretched beyond its limit.

He was choking. He couldn't breathe! That damned rope was strangling him, robbing him of air. His eyes felt as if they were bulging out of his head! His head was going to explode. And the angel was clinging to him, adding her weight to his own.

Let go of me! It was a silent plea that Lance was certain was going to be the last thing he ever thought.

In a state of utter confusion and panic, Christina let loose of the man she was clinging to and reached for the rope. "Dear God!" Her fingers gripped tightly around the coarse hemp, knowing it was the only thing that kept her from a ghastly fall. Ignoring the burning pain in her hands from the rope, she kept a death grip.

Suddenly the rope broke! Cristina fell with a thud.

"Omph . . . !" The groan came from two mouths as the collision of bodies knocked the wind out of Lance's and Christina's lungs. For what seemed an eternity they both lay on the hard ground gasping for air.

What on earth had happened! A miscue, obviously. Christina could only suppose that the actor had been at the wrong place at the wrong time. He wasn't supposed to be on the scaffold! Damn his mistake. It would cost her dearly.

"You blew it!" she scolded as soon as she could catch her breath.

Choking, gasping in the precious elixir of life, Lance stared at the woman. Who in hell was she? Where had she come from? At the moment he didn't care. Whether by intent or by accident, she had answered his prayer. Now he had to make the most of it.

"Hurry up! Untie me," he choked out. He had to think and act quickly before those idiots figured out their little hanging had gone amiss. Right now the confines of the scaffolding shielded them from view, but knowing Roundtree it wouldn't be long until he came forward to ghoulishly relish the results of his handiwork.

Although angered by the actor's bossy attitude, Christina complied, untying both the rope around his neck and the bonds that held his wrists securely behind his back. They had to hurry. Perhaps they could still salvage the broadcast.

"You weren't supposed to—"

Before she had time to give him a piece of her mind, he had twisted her arm behind her back and was forcing her to walk with him toward the opening of the scaffold.

"I don't suppose you have a gun, do you?" he rasped in her ear.

"A gun?" she gasped with indignity as he frisked

her. Broadcast or not, she would see to it that he was immediately fired!

Lance was disappointed that the woman wasn't armed with a pistol. He did, however, find something of interest in her pocket. "What's this?" He pulled the small leather-sheethed cylinder out and studied it with curiosity. It looked oddly like some sort of weapon.

"That's my pepper spray. If you don't let me go . . ."

He ignored her anger, pleased by her unknowing revelation of his suspicion. It was some kind of weapon. "How do you use it?" Before she could answer, he had figured it out. Desperation, they said, was the mother of invention. Aligning the mechanism, Lance aimed it at the deputy who was lowering himself down the scaffold opening to investigate.

"Be careful with that!" Christina screeched.

Rubbing his eyes and coughing, the deputy was rendered helpless long enough for Lance to divest him of his gun.

"Hmmm. Think I'll keep this. It comes in handy," Lance exclaimed, putting it in the left pocket of his shirt. Cautiously he moved up the inside ladder of the scaffold, bringing Christina with him.

It was at that moment that Christina knew something was terribly wrong. "Where are the cameras? The crew? Who are these people?" As if by some kind of magic, the entire scene had been changed. Gone were the cars, trucks, bikes and paved streets. They had been replaced by horses, wagons, a wooden sidewalk and dirt streets. And the lawmen and citizenry of Paradise.

"I must have hit my head." It was the only rational explanation. She had to be dreaming.

"Stay back. Don't anyone make a move." Lance pushed Christina toward the nearest horse.

"Get him. He can't shoot us all!" Marshal Roundtree was livid with rage.

"No, not all. But I can shoot you." Lance pointed the

pistol right at the marshal. "And take great delight in that act!"

Trying to hide his cowardice, Marshal Roundtree used Christina as his excuse for letting the outlaw get away. "We can't take a chance on his shooting the woman!"

"Ah, yes. The woman," Lance repeated. As if he would harm a hair on her precious head. Whoever this woman was, he owed her a debt of gratitude. Even so, he had to take her with him. She was an assurance that he wouldn't be shot, at least near town. "Can you ride?"

Christina had never been on a horse but had ridden behind her brother on his motorcycle. How different could it be? "Yes," she said, little realizing how soon she would come to regret that answer.

"Good. Come on!"

Hurrying to the horse, Lance grabbed the reins and vaulted onto the saddle, bringing Christina up with him in a daring show of horsemanship. Leaving the marshal behind in the dust, they headed east and to freedom.

CHAPTER TWO

Christina grimaced, trying to ignore the soreness in her backside. Shifting her weight in the saddle, she thought to herself that whoever this damned man was, he knew his stuff. A motorcycle couldn't have covered any greater distance or traveled at as frantic a pace as they were galloping now. Her companion seemed quite accomplished at getting away from any pursuers.

Or any rescuers, she lamented. She was being abducted. That was the only explanation. The question was, why? She wanted to ask her kidnapper that, along with many other questions, but all she could think about at the moment was how uncomfortable she was.

"No sign of them," Lance said as he looked behind him for the umpteenth time. "I know how to lose lawmen."

He heaved a sigh of relief as they left Paradise far behind. As experience had taught him, however, the danger was just beginning. All too soon Roundtree and his men would be hot on the trail. There wouldn't be an inch of ground between Paradise and Denver that they wouldn't search. He'd have to be on his guard.

Christina was annoyed by his self-confidence in wake

of the fact that his actions had undoubtedly ruined her career. She couldn't help verbally sparring with him by saying, "There's no sign of them now, but no doubt they'll find us any moment. There will be a dozen helicopters out looking for us once your little escapade is reported."

"Helicopters?" Lance shrugged. "Whatever that is, I'll soon put them far behind, just like I did Marshal Roundtree." The most important thing now was finding a place to hide out.

Christina turned her head just enough so that she could see him out of the corner of her eye. "Kind of cocky, aren't you?"

He answered quickly. "I suppose you could say that. But then I've been accused of worse." A smile crinkled his eyes.

Oh, he was irritating, Christina thought. "You're in big trouble," she warned.

He answered matter-of-factly, "Not as big as I was in before you came along. I owe you a debt of gratitude for saving my life, lady." At this moment he felt a special bond with her.

"Saved your life, indeed!" She was still confused by everything that had happened but she wouldn't have admitted that to him for the world. When all was said and done, she could be cocky too. "After the stunt you just pulled, don't count on me for any job references."

She swiveled in the saddle so that she could get a better look at him. He needed a shave and his face was streaked with dirt and sweat, but nonetheless it was a handsome face, one she had seen several times in the pages of Western history books. The actor looked exactly like Lance Meredith. So much so that it was spooky.

"Job reference!" Lance laughed. "I think you just might say my reputation speaks for itself." Surely she had to know who he was. Everyone in Colorado had seen his face on the wanted posters Marshal Roundtree had distributed.

"Oh, you'll definitely have a reputation now," Christina countered, feeling certain that this man's escapade would be carried on every news station in the country. "One that even the best résumé in the world won't rectifiy."

This woman said some strange things. Even so, Lance had to admit that she was damned pretty. Perhaps once they got out of this mess they might have a chance to get better acquainted. Right now, however, all his attention was centered on getting as far away from Marshal Roundtree as he could. He'd had his neck stretched today. It was not an experience he wanted to relive. Ever!

They rode all night at a punishing pace, splashing through streams, kicking up dust, galloping through the wild grass. They passed abandoned mining claims and cabins, dodged in and out of trees, rode over rough gravel and rocks. Uphill and down they rode, with no time even to talk about discomfort.

"Please ... I'm so cold ... thirsty ... and ... and tired ..." Christina said again and again. Alas, her complaints were ignored. The man forced her to go on until her body ached for rest and she was certain that she was on the verge of collapse. At last she couldn't help collapsing against the horse's neck.

Lance could see that he had driven both the horse and the woman too hard. Besides, it was a time for questions. First and foremost, he wanted to know who she was, how she was able to get past the marshal's men to come to his rescue, and most of all *why* she had wanted to rescue him.

"We'll stop here."

Helping her down from the horse, Lance was attentive, showing his appreciation in small ways for what she had done. Ignoring the stiffness in his own neck and arms, he picked her up and carried her to a spot beneath a tree. Taking a canteen from the saddlebag, he filled it from a nearby creek and gave her a drink.

"Thanks." Christina took a long gulp, too thirsty to worry if the water was pure, then pulled her mouth away.

Strange, it had been snowing earlier but now there wasn't even a flake of snow. It was cold, however. Trying to get warm, she tugged at her coat.

"It's chilly out. Sorry, but I can't take the chance of starting even a small fire. You'll just have to brave it."

Christina was cold. Even so, her curiosity won out over her discomfort. "Why did you sabatoge the television broadcast?" It was the most important question on her mind.

"Sabatoge *the broadcast?*" The question totally flabbergasted him.

"Are you a spy from a rival network?" She strongly suspected that was the case. The ratings war was becoming ruthless.

"Spy?" Once again Lance was taken off guard by her strange questions. He shook his head, determined to regain the upper hand. "Look, lady, I'm grateful as hell for what you did and all, but I'd like to ask *you* a few questions. Like who you are and how you just seemed to come out of thin air."

"Thin air?"

He sat down beside her. "Yeah. First you weren't there and then you were. Like magic. How did you do it?"

"The magic of television," she answered glibly. The truth was, now that he had asked, she could only wonder what had actually happened. She remembered reaching out toward the noose, then falling. "Well, I was listening to the drumroll, waiting for my cue, when suddenly I . . . I started falling," she said more to herself than to him. "The next thing I knew, I was sprawled on top of you." She supposed that she must have hit her head. How else could she explain her disorientation after the fall?

He seemed to be satisfied by her explanation. "Well, whatever you were doing, you certainly arrived in the nick of time." He looked her in the eye. "You saved me from a hanging!"

"Hanging?" She laughed. "Right." For just a moment she thought he was joking. The expression in his face told her, however, that he was deadly serious. "Oh, come on now. Aren't you taking your role a bit too seriously? I've heard about you actors, but—"

"Actor?" Lance was beginning to wonder about this woman. She certainly said some strange things. "I'm no actor, except when I'm claiming my innocence after a bank robbery." He grinned.

So, by his own admission he was a thief. And what else? "You're trying to tell me that you weren't hired to play Lance Meredith for the broadcast?" Christina asked, suddenly fearing the worst.

He shook his head no.

"Then who are you?" She had an eerie feeling about his answer.

"My name is Lance Meredith." He reached for her hand as if they were being properly introduced.

"Lance . . ." Panic raced through her. *Oh, my God,* she thought. This man not only was a criminal of some kind but he was also insane. He actually believed he *was* Lance Meredith. She could only hope he wasn't too dangerous.

Sensing her fear, Lance laid a reassuring hand on her shoulder. "Don't be afraid. I've robbed my share of banks and done some things of which I'm not proud, but I have never and would never harm a woman."

"Really!" She wasn't certain that she could believe him but did see the wisdom of humoring him. "How reassuring."

Although she had quit smoking several months ago, Christina felt the sudden urge for a cigarette. "Damn!" She still carried half a pack in her purse as a reminder of her newfound willpower. Trouble was she had left her purse in Paradise, along with all her other possessions. Reaching into her coat pocket, she fumbled around, quickly taking inventory. She had her lipstick, compact, a tiny pocket calculator, a pencil-size flashlight, her Visa card and her car keys. Small but important items.

Lance watched her, noticing the clothing she was wearing. He had been much too preoccupied with escape to notice before. Now, however, he realized that the garments she wore were as strange as she was. She was dressed in a tan overcoat that reached to her knees, dark green pants with a matching suit coat, and a colorful shirt. She was *not* wearing a dress. It was unfeminine attire, yet striking on her. She was very pretty. Perhaps that was why he couldn't keep from staring.

His steady gaze unnerved her. "So, just where do we go from here?" she asked.

"I haven't decided yet." The muscles of Lance's neck were sore. At first it hurt to swallow, but his thirst was greater than his discomfort. He took a mouthful of water from the canteen and forced it down his throat. "I don't want to ever have a rope around my neck again, even for a moment."

"No, I wouldn't imagine that you would." Christina looked out at the horizon, wondering how far they were from the main road. "I don't suppose it's even worth asking if you intend to take me back."

"I can't! I'd be shot on sight."

His answer doubly dismayed her. So, he was an even worse criminal than she had suspected. Nervously she surveyed the area. She was completely lost in the darkness. Where was the main road? Was it within hiking distance? If so she could go against her better judgment and hitchhike back to Paradise. Or if she could find a motorist with a cell phone she could call the studio. That is, if she could escape in the first place.

"So I'm your hostage . . ." Despite her fear, Christina was aware that she just might have quite a story here.

Lance's voice was soft. "I'd prefer to think of you as my fellow traveler."

Fellow traveler indeed, she thought but did not say. She had to get in touch with the station right away. She had to find out who this man was and if she was in any real danger. But how was she going to get away from him when all he did was stare at her?

"So what is it that you want? Ransom? What?"

What did he want? Lance wanted a chance to prove his innocence, at least in the matter of the murder Marshal Roundtree had pinned on him. He hadn't shot Pete Winthrop, but he thought he knew who had.

Lance looked long and hard at the woman who had rescued him. Perhaps her timely entrance upon the scene had bought him some time. "You're very beautiful."

He liked the light golden color of her hair, the slight curve of her brows, the tiny mole by her mouth, the proud set of her chin and the way her blue eyes widened when she was listening to him.

Christina was flustered. "I'm not." She didn't like the direction the conversation was taking. Considering the circumstances, his attentions were disconcerting. Quickly she stood up. "It seems to me that we've rested long enough." She had the feeling that she was safer when they were on the move.

She was right. "Yeah, we have to get going," Lance said. The danger still lurked on the horizon somewhere. The marshal's men would be following. He knew that, and yet a part of him wanted to stay. Now why was that?

Christina ran toward the horse. Maybe if she hurried she could mount up and leave him far behind. Putting her foot in the stirrup, she pulled herself up. Alas, she wasn't quick enough.

"Such enthusiasm." Reaching up, Lance grabbed hold of her. "But you have to wait for me."

Christina was determined to ride alone this time. Somehow she'd get the hang of it. As he started to climb into the saddle, she kicked out at him. A struggle followed. In the ensuing tussle her keys fell out of her pocket and tumbled to the ground.

"My car keys!" she exclaimed just as Lance pulled her from the saddle. She fell to the ground with a thud, scrambling for her keys. She wasn't fast enough.

Lance plucked the keys from the dirt, hefting them in his hand. Even her keys were unusual. Rubbing his thumb against them one by one, he studied them carefully. It wasn't the keys that unnerved him, however. It was the piece of metal that was attached. "Honda Accord," the letters said. There was a picture of a horseless carriage. It was the numbers embossed on the metal that mesmerized him. The numbers looked like they formed a year: 1998.

Christina noticed the way he was staring. "That's the make and year of my car," she whispered. "I can't quite afford one of the new twenty-first-century models yet. So if it's ransom you're after—"

"Car?" Slowly Lance handed the keys back to her.

"A far more comfortable way of making an escape, wouldn't you say?" she taunted. Certainly it would have saved them both a lot of aches and pains.

Lance shook his head. This woman wasn't like anyone he had ever met before. She was like someone from a different place. Or a different time. He remembered the way she had popped into sight so suddenly. But no, it wasn't possible. Still he asked, "Who are you?"

"I'm Christina Phillips, anchorwoman for the television news magazine that was filming in Paradise. That is, until you dragged me off." She brushed dirt off her coat. "Our segment was celebrating the historical transition from the twentieth to the twenty-first century with our story on Lance Meredith's hanging."

"Twenty-first . . ." Lance took a step back. "Don't you have your centuries mixed up a bit?" This woman was saying such strange things. "Don't you mean the change from the nineteenth to the *twentieth* century?"

"Nineteeth to twentieth . . ." One of them was crazy! Christina was certain that it wasn't she. In the cause of self-preservation, however, she decided to play along with him. If he wanted to think he was back in the Dark Ages, she'd humor him. "Anything you sa—"

She gasped as the man suddenly grabbed her, covering her mouth with his hand. "Shhhhhh," he warned.

At first Christina didn't hear anything except the loud

beating of her heart. Then as they both stopped breathing for a moment, she heard the sound that had alarmed him, a faint clip-crop.

"Damn. Horses."

Lance tried to figure out where the sound was coming from, how far away they were, and thus which way he should go. They were coming from the northeast, were about twenty minutes behind him, which meant his best chance was to go in the opposite direction. Back toward Paradise. They wouldn't be expecting that!

"Come on!" Bringing Christina with him, he moved toward the horse, first helping her up, then climbing up behind her.

CHAPTER THREE

Daylight was just peeping over the tops of the mountains as Lance and Christina approached Paradise. Just as Lance had suspected, there weren't any lawmen in sight. They were all in hot pursuit of him on down the canyon. He chuckled as he thought how daring he was to come back to the scene of his escape.

Riding hard and fast, doubling back, weaving in and out amidst the trees and scrub brush, Lance had done his best to dodge his pursuers, and he had indeed lost them. It was a victory that he freely relished. Taking a deep breath, he at last had a chance to calm down and take a look around him.

Never had it felt so good to be alive.

"Life is beautiful."

A colorful world of unusual rock formations, trees of several varieties and clear twisting streams met his eyes. There was a certain exhilaration in this vast space. The air was clean and fresh, the water cool and inviting. As at most times in his life, he figured that determination and keeping a level head would work to his advantage. It always had.

"Where are we?" Christina was tired and miserable. Combing her fingers through her hair, wiping the smudges from her face, she surveyed the area.

Lance pointed. "Paradise is right over there. See the sign?"

"Paradise, population 135," it read.

Christina remembered having seen the sign on her drive up the paved road, a road which was somehow unpaved now. Squinting her eyes, she stared in confusion. Something was wrong. Not only the sign but everything around it looked different.

"Where did all these trees come from?" They hadn't been there when she had driven by the sign on her way to Paradise. What's more, the sign had read, "Population 5." Paradise had been reduced over the years to a ghost town with only a caretaker and his family in residence.

Reaching in her coat pocket, she touched her car keys. Her car was parked less than a mile down the road. If she could only persuade her traveling companion to ride in that direction, she might be able to break away.

"Someone is coming?" she lied. "Quick, ride that way!"

She remembered the terrain very well now. She had turned left at the rock that looked like the face of a bear, then followed the stream to a small clearing that had been roped off to form a temporary parking lot. It was there that she had parked her car.

Straightening her back, holding up her head, she stared at the clearing so hard she thought her eyes would bug out of her head. There was no sign of her car, or anything else that was familiar.

"No, it can't be!" Christina fought the flicker of fear that flashed through her. Fear that she had lost her mind.

Lance sensed her panic. Damn. The last thing he needed was a frantic female. "Calm down. You'll get us into a whole heap of trouble." Tightening his arms around her waist, he tried to reassure her. "Everything is fine. You'll see. I know of an old abandoned mine not too far from here where we can hide out until I can get in touch with my men.''

An abandoned mine! Christina thought he must be kidding. As she soon found out, however, he was all too serious. "The Gold Dust," the sign read. By the looks of it, it had been abandoned quite a while.

"The answer to our prayers!" Lance got down off the horse. Tugging Christina down beside him, he gripped her hand. They hurried to the opening; then remembering that where there were tunnels, there were also shafts and therefore danger, he slowed down. Cautiously he entered. He hadn't escaped the noose only to go plunging to his death. "Easy. Easy."

Reaching in his pocket, he swore violently as he remembered that they had taken his matches. No doubt they had been afraid he would burn down the damned jail. "We'll just have to get used to the darkness and inch our way along until we find a comfortable place to settle down," he cautioned.

Fumbling along, carefully testing each and every step to make certain there was solid ground beneath him, he led Christina into the black, musty tunnel.

"Wait!" Reaching into her pocket, she remembered the tiny flashlight. "We can use this." Taking it out of her pocket, she flicked it on. The light wasn't very bright, nor did it illuminate a very big area, but it was better than chancing the darkness.

"What is that thing?" Lance eyed the tiny lantern with trepidation. She hadn't even struck a match.

"My pocket flashlight. We're lucky I brought it with me." Since she was the one with the light, Christina now led the way. "Come on. Let's go this way."

"You lead and I'll follow," Lance responded cheerfully. When he considered all that had happened since meeting this woman, he counted himself a very lucky man. He'd escaped with his life, at least for the time being. But where did they go from here? He had to formulate a plan. They had no food, and although he had learned to be a mediocre hunter he wasn't at all fond of raw meat and berries. Somehow he had to get in touch with his gang.

Reaching up, Lance massaged his temples with his fingertips. He had a roaring headache, brought on no doubt by that bone-jarring ride. Every muscle in his body ached. He was dead tired. To add to his discomfort, hunger was gnawing at his belly and he had no way of soothing it. He imagined that the woman with him must be just as miserable. Even so, Lance's sense of humor overtook him and he threw back his head and laughed, chuckling all the more as the sound echoed over and over in the tunnel.

His laughter unnerved Christina. "What on earth do you find humorous?"

"I was just imagining the look on old Roundtree's face when he realized I was going to get away. My only regret is that I didn't see his expression."

Finding an old length of canvas, he unrolled it on the ground, then sat down. Christina sat as far away from him as she could and still share the canvas. Desperate men were dangerous. That he remained silent for the moment, his eyes gazing at her as if he were looking straight through her to her very soul, only confirmed her need for caution.

"I'm not going to!" Lance moved a foot closer to her. Christina moved an equal distance away. He moved again. She moved again, slipping off the canvas.

I have the upper hand, she thought. *I have the flashlight.* Without it he would be helpless in the dark. She knew it. So did he.

"Give me the light!" He held out his hand.

"No!" Stubbornly she clutched it in her fist.

Lance sighed. "Look, I owe you for saving my life and I want to keep our association friendly, but . . ." With a lunge he was on her, struggling to get the flashlight away. To Christina's dismay he was successful.

"So, brute strength wins out!" she conceded.

Lance was fascinated with the contraption. Thomas Edison had brought the electric light into homes back east, but this was something strangely different. This light was an entity all on its own. It wasn't plugged into anything. Like a little boy he toyed with it, holding it up to his face, then turning it round and round in his fingers.

"How does it work?"

"The switch is on the side, just like on the larger models," she answered, puzzled that he seemed so entranced by a simple flashlight.

He clicked it off, then on, then off, then on again, laughing as he did so. "Amazing!" And so was she. Whoever she was and wherever she came from, he suspected that she would be more than a match for any man.

Unlike Lance Meredith, Christina wasn't in a jovial mood. She wasn't used to being at someone else's mercy. Not at all! But for the moment she was! The man had "her" flashlight and he had a gun.

"So, what do you plan to do now?" she asked, in much the same tone she used when conducting an interview.

Lance tried to make himself comfortable by leaning back against a rock. "We rest for a while." He grinned at her. "And while we're resting we get better acquainted."

"Rest?" Christina's whole body throbbed with aches and pains, thanks to this man. As for getting better acquainted, she tensed at the very thought. She knew enough about him to know that he was trouble!

"Are you married?"

The question took her by surprise. "No!" she blurted, realizing how foolish her honesty was the moment she had spoken. If he thought she had a strong, angry husband out looking for her, he might not be so determined to hold her hostage.

"Good!" That made things less complicated. "Seeing how pretty you are, I suspect you're a spinster by choice."

"Spinster!" She choked against her indignity. "I'm a career woman who values her independence. A successful career woman, I might add."

Lance could see that he had tweeked her ill will and obviously struck a raw nerve. He hurried to make amends. "I'm certain that you are." He moved the beam of the flashlight so that it illuminated her face. "As a matter of fact, I'll bet you've left a whole trail of broken hearts behind."

Christina didn't want to talk about her failure to find the deep and abiding love she had always longed for. Her friends told her that she just picked the wrong men. Christina suspected that the kind of man she was looking for didn't exist anymore. All her life she had been a hopeless romantic.

"What about you?" She focused the questioning on him.

"I've probably left a few broken hearts behind as well, though I didn't mean to." He sighed as he thought about one lovely woman in particular. "Poor Mary."

"Mary?" Christina made a mental note of the name in case she needed it for a future story—the story she hoped to tell after her rescue. "Mary who?"

"Mary Margaret Van Horn. She was as steadfast as—"

"Van Horn!" Christina recognized the name immediately. The love between Lance Meredith and the schoolteacher was as tragic a tale as that of Romeo and Juliet. The ill-fated Van Horn had been shot and killed by Marshal Roundtree's deputies in their quest to find the infamous outlaw's hideout.

"It's just one more score that I have to settle with the marshal," Lance said between clenched teeth. "And I will, when I find him."

Christina was unnerved by the reference to a woman and a lawman who had been dead nearly a hundred years. Still, her instincts for a story urged her on. "So that's what this whole escapade was all about? Your desire for revenge?" She could only wonder how she fit into his scheme of things.

"That and self-preservation!" Reaching up, he massaged his sore neck; then, suddenly weary of conversation, he lay down on his side. He shut his eyes. They'd hold out in here until it was dark again, then resume their travel. Jim, Bart and the boys knew about this mine shaft. If he was lucky, they'd put two and two together and realize this was where he would go after his escape. That would save him a whole lot of trouble finding them.

Keeping her eyes on him the whole time, Christina also lay down on her side. If she was patient she could lure him into a false sense of confidence. Then she could pounce and take the gun and her flashlight away from him.

Shadows created by the flickering light danced upon the wall. The inside of the tunnel suddenly looked eerie, unnerving. The expression on the man's face took on a demonic look as the shadows danced over his nose and chin. Well, she wasn't afraid. Not of him. Not of any man. Still, she was cautious as she moved to within an arm's length of Lance.

"That's better," he whispered. "You'll soon see that I'm not the desperado that you expect me to be."

Christina decided to make the best of a bad situation. She might as well try and be comfortable. Taking her arm out of her left coat sleeve, she formed a pillow for her head while using the right side of the coat as a kind of blanket. Strange, but it was surprisingly warm in the tunnel despite the chill outside. She closed her eyes, pretending to fall asleep.

Lance turned over on his other side only to find himself staring directly at the well-rounded breasts just a few inches from his face. A most tempting part of a woman's anatomy, particularly when they were just the right size. He wondered if they would be as soft to the touch as they looked, then shook his head to clear it of such a thought. Under different circumstances this might have been an extremely provocative situation, but not when a man faced such serious consequences. He turned off the flashlight, took a deep breath, and gave vent to his total exhaustion. He'd catch a few winks, just enough to keep up his strength for the harrowing moments he knew were ahead of him.

Although she was totally exhausted, Christina wouldn't allow herself to sleep. She had to get her hands on the gun. It was her only chance for escape. "Patience," she said to herself. "Wait until you're certain that he's asleep."

At last the soft sound of snoring gave her a signal that it was time to act. The gun was well within reach. All she had to do was reach out and yank it from his hand.

"Easy . . . easy . . ." she breathed.

Riveting her eyes on the rise and fall of his chest, she crept closer, stopping as still as a statue when she saw his hand move. He was going to wake up . . . but no, he was merely brushing at his face. His soft snoring gave proof that he was immersed in slumber.

Gathering her courage, she stretched out her hand, feeling jubilant as her fingers closed around the cold steel of the gun. Wouldn't he be surprised when he opened his eyes.

Lance Meredith, indeed! How dared he claim to be her Western hero? The real Lance Meredith would never have been so easily overtaken.

She held her breath as she tugged the gun away from his hand. Rising to her knees, she let the air out of her lungs in a sigh of relief. So far, so good. The flashlight was next. Standing up, she carefully turned it on, letting the light illuminate his face as she pointed the gun. She laughed triumphantly. Oh, what a story this was going to be for the evening news.

With her finger firmly on the trigger, she loudly cleared her throat. "Ahem!"

For a man who bragged about being a famous outlaw, he slept as soundly as the dead. Christina cleared her throat again, feeling a deep satisfaction when at last he opened his eyes.

At first they exchanged a series of glances. Then they both smiled, although for different reasons.

Christina was puzzled by his lack of fear. He couldn't possibly know that she had never shot a gun before. Could he? "Maybe you don't think I'll shoot. But I will!"

"Go ahead!" His grin dared her to pull the trigger.

What else could she do but call his bluff? Trying to ignore her trembling fingers, she aimed the gun at his arm. No one would blame her for firing at him. He was holding her hostage.

"I don't want to kill you. I just want to go back—"

"Taking you back would mean my death. So, the way I see it, I might as well die at your hands." He shrugged. "You're much prettier than Marshal Roundtree." As if taunting her, he started to get to his feet.

Though Christina abhorred violence, she pulled the trigger. The moment she heard the impotent click, she knew she'd been tricked.

"Damn! You actually pulled the trigger." He was genuinely surprised. "And here I thought you liked me. At least a little."

Christina had been through experiences involving danger before but never anything like this. Even so, she answered truthfully, "I might have liked you, if things were different, but. . . ."

Suddenly Christina sensed that they were not alone. Whirling around, she was startled by the man standing there. He was holding a gun!

"Thank God!" She assumed that help had come at last.

"Are you all right?" The man's tone resonated with concern.

"I'm fine." She moved toward him. "Just a bit bruised and—"

The man walked right past her. "When I heard you

had escaped, I had a hunch I'd find you here, Lance. Thank God, I was right.''

Christina was stunned. ''Who . . . ?'' She focused the beam of the flashlight on the newcomer's face. The curly red hair and beard, the broken nose, the scar across a wide forehead were familiar. ''James Cleary!'' No, it couldn't be. He, like Lance Meredith, was the stuff of legend.

''You came just at the right time, Jamie! I was counting on the fact that you'd remember.'' Lance paused. ''No doubt every lawman from here to Denver is out beating the bushes for me.''

''Yeah. Damn telephone! Alexander Graham Bell didn't do us any favors with his fool contraption.'' Jim Cleary's expression mirrored his disgust. ''Brings the posse that much quicker.''

''We'll have to hurry!''

Jim Cleary eyed Christina up and down. ''Who's she?''

''The woman who saved my life.'' Lance brushed himself off. ''I owe her a debt of gratitude. Go easy on her.''

''I'll treat her as gently as my own mother.'' The red-haired man gave Christina a little push toward the opening of the mine shaft. ''She'll save our hides for sure. They won't shoot at us while she's with us.''

Lance shook his head. ''I wouldn't be so sure. Don't forget what happened to Mary.''

In a gesture of remembrance, Jim Cleary took off his hat. ''I'll never forget. Damn Roundtree's soul to hell!'' Replacing his hat, he gestured for Christina to walk towards the tunnel entrance.

Christina didn't say another word. If she wanted to get out of this nightmare alive, it would behoove her to do exactly as she was asked. Meanwhile, she would hope against hope that somehow, some way she'd get a chance to break away before they arrived at their destination.

CHAPTER FOUR

The next few hours of Christina's life proved to be an experience she would not forget for a long time, if ever. It was just like being caught up in some old-time Western movie, only she knew that this mesmerizing drama was real. The blisters on her backside gave proof of that.

"I guess the first thing we've got to do is get her a horse," Jim Cleary was quick to point out, nodding in Christina's direction. "The two of you riding together will only slow us down."

"So, horse theft is the next order of business," Christina whispered beneath her breath.

Overhearing her remark, Lance was quick to come to his own defense. "We aren't going to *steal* a horse. Just borrow it for a little while."

Stopping by a small frame house a few miles from the mine, he paid good money for the use of a cream-colored horse he found grazing nearby.

"I make it a practice never to take from those who will be hurt by my actions," he said. "I only steal from rich bankers or greedy bastards like Roundtree." Quickly saddling the horse, he helped her mount up.

Having grown up in the area, Christina knew of all kinds of places where she could hide if she could only get away from her two companions. Get away? The farther they rode, the less important escape mattered to her. Besides, Lance Meredith, or whatever his name was, kept watching her like a hawk.

He can't really be Lance Meredith, can he? To even think for a fleeting moment that he might be made her question her sanity. And yet . . . .there was the matter of the other outlaw, Jim Cleary. Was his resemblance to a man who had lived a hundred years ago also a coincidence? Or were they impostors, hell-bent on the most bizarre practical joke of all time?

The identity of her riding companions was like a disturbing riddle. They looked exactly like the two famous outlaws, and yet how was it possible? A hundred years separated them from Christina. Unless they were ghosts or she had lost touch with reality, how in the world could she be riding and talking with them?

Either they have suddenly materialized into the twenty-first century or I have zoomed back to the days of the Wild West. Christina laughed aloud as she thought about those who had sarcastically suggested solving the Y2K problem by turning back the clocks to the year 1900. Perhaps in some way that was exactly what she had done! Perhaps . . .

No! Christina fiercely shook her head. She had never believed that any person could go beyond the parameters of their own time, no matter what the scientists theorized. And yet no one had believed in cloning or DNA until it had actually happened.

Christina's eyes were drawn to the handsome, dark-haired outlaw. Watching him ride, scrutinizing his manly physique made her wish that things could be different. He was the kind of man she'd always longed to meet. What a cruel hoax fate would have played if he really was Lance Meredith, for history revealed that Lance Meredith was going to die. There was no getting around it.

"Are you all right?" Riding up beside her, Lance reached out and gently touched her hand. "You look troubled."

Christina thought of how many times she had wished she had lived a hundred years ago, just so she could save Lance Meredith's life. "I was just thinking that I really don't want to see them hang you," she answered.

"They have to catch me first." He grinned. "If I can't outshoot, outride and outmaneuver a few of Roundtree's louts, then I don't deserve my reputation."

"Oh, yeah?" Jim Cleary pointed over his shoulder. "Looks like you'll get plenty of chances to live up to your words." Taking out his Colt .45, Jim Cleary took aim. One of his pursuers' hats went flying off his head and into the dust.

Lance looked behind him. "The posse." He swore beneath his breath. "They've come back looking for me much sooner than I had planned!" Lance felt his heart sink all the way down to his boots. He had misjudged the marshal. "We've got to lose them."

Christina hung on to her horse's reins, hoping the animal would follow the other horses with a minimum of horsemanship on her part. No matter what happened, she had to stay in the saddle. Now was not the time for a mishap. Not when she was actually being fired upon.

"With real bullets!" Her voice sounded remarkably calm, belying the utter terror she felt.

"As real as they get!" Lance's blood ran cold. He was afraid, not so much for himself as for his female companion. The men who rode with Roundtree had no scruples when it came to murdering females. He didn't want another woman killed because of him. Especially not this woman!

The thundering hooves of the pursuing horses echoed ominously. Christina shivered. "What are you going to do?"

Lance had no other choice. A gunfight was out of the question. They were outnumbered. "Ride. Ride like hell!" Somehow, some way, they had to outdistance the ruthless posse.

"That's . . . that's what I *am* doing!" And in the process she was being jiggled to death.

"Then do it even better and faster. Come on!"

If ever Christina's life depended on her strength and tenacity, it was now. Thus, with determination she set aside her fear and did her best to keep up with Jim Cleary and Lance Meredith.

Like a swarm of angry bees the pursuing lawmen came, closing the distance little by little. Worse yet, there wasn't anyplace where Lance, Christina and Jim Cleary could conceal themselves.

Christina felt a lump in her throat and swallowed hard. What if they couldn't escape? What if she saw Lance Meredith killed before her very eyes! "No!" She didn't want that. Somehow she had to be of help. "Throw me a gun!"

Despite the danger, he laughed. "What for? You probably don't know how to shoot it!"

"I don't, but then I didn't know how to ride a horse either," she shouted at the top of her lungs. "I'm a fast learner!"

In a daring exhibition of horsemanship, Jim Cleary guided his horse to within inches of hers. Leaning over in the saddle, he put one of his Colts into her hands. "There are four bullets left. Make them count."

She did, somehow causing two of their pursuers to slump in the saddle.

Lance and Jim Cleary unhorsed three more horsemen. Even so, the odds were still in the posse's favor.

"Faster! Ride faster!" she heard Jim Cleary's frantic voice order.

"I am! I am!" *Oh, how do you put this animal into high gear?*

"We're going to have to split up. It's our only chance,"

Jim Cleary yelled. ''I'll go to the left. You two take the road to the right. We'll meet up back at camp.''

''OK!''

They galloped across the uneven ground for what seemed an eternity. Her teeth seemed to rattle in her head, her muscles ached, she feared that her horse might stumble and she would find herself lying on the ground, yet somehow she managed to appear calm despite her rapidly drumming heart.

With Christina right behind him, Lance made his way from the trail and across the hills, dodging in and out among the trees in a manner cleverly designed to confuse his pursuers. He'd give them a run for their reward money! In the meantime, he prayed for another miracle.

''Head for the trees. It's our only chance.'' The foliage would offer a haven from the gunfire that was exploding into the air. ''Follow me!''

''I'm right behind you.'' Lance had chosen an intelligent horse for her, one that needed minimal guidance. She took a deep breath as they plunged into the greenery and trees. The posse followed.

''Damn! We can't lose them. We're going to have to fight it out!''

''Fight?'' Her voice was tinged with desperation and the awareness that what was happening could mean her death. Still, she was in no position to argue.

Lance reined in his mount next to a clump of tall trees. Helping her dismount, taking her hand, he made his way toward a big log, ducking behind it. He flattened himself to the ground. Ignoring the discomfort, Christina did likewise.

''How many bullets do you have left?''

''One, I think.''

''Make it count!''

Christina held the gun in both hands, trying to stop her trembling. Her favorite historical period was of the gunfighting West. She had read about gunfights. It was

the accepted method of settling an argument in the West.
Now she was going to be a part of it.

Most gunfighting was done at close range; the posse
would try to get as close as they could. Lance told Christina not to fire until he gave the word.

"I know you're scared, but remember, more than anything else a man's state of mind is the key."

"I-I'm n-n-not s-scared!" She was not a very good
liar.

Bullets whizzed through the air, pockmarked the dirt
and struck the log they were hiding behind with such
force that they sent wood chips flying.

"Hey, Meredith! Who's the pretty little lady? Another
schoolmarm?" Lance recognized Dan Bradshaw's voice.
He had been Mary's murderer. Well, he wouldn't kill
anyone today.

"She's my avenging angel, Bradshaw. If I were you
I'd show proper respect!"

"Angel. Ha!"

Lance tallied up the men who had followed them into
the woods. There were four. Jim's ploy had worked. The
odds had improved.

"She is an angel." Reaching over, Lance gently
touched her hand. "You're my good luck. Somehow I
feel as if nothing can harm me when I'm with you."

Christina smiled. Oh, how she hoped he was right.

"Well, good luck or not, we're gonna get you, Meredith."

Once again the air was riddled with gunfire. Seeing the
silhouette of one of the gunmen trying to move closer,
Lance took aim and fired. He turned to Christina. "Get
ready. If I don't miss my guess, their next move will be
to rush us."

He was right. Moving through the brush, three men
came on the attack.

Lance fired. "Now. Shoot!"

Christina pulled the trigger. Her heart hammered with
adrenaline as she realized that she had hit one of the

lawmen in the leg. His howl of pain was a strangely reassuring sound. Even so, the men kept up the assault. It didn't look good. Once again Lance wished for a miracle. In the next moment his wish was granted when a shot behind the lawmen rang out.

"Jimmy!" Somehow he must have doubled back to help them. The odds had evened up.

Another shot split the air.

"Too bad for you, Bradshaw. You see my whole gang has come to my rescue."

"The hell you say!"

"It's true! You're surrounded," Jim Cleary called out. "Better say your prayers."

Thinking themselves outnumbered, the remaining lawmen retreated to their horses. Lance fired again just to hurry them up. "When the odds are in a man's favor, even the cowardly can be brave. And then again, there are those people that can really be surprising." The woman's courage in the face of this peril was astounding. "Like you!" He winked at her. "Welcome to the Meredith gang."

In an instant he caught and held her tightly in the protective circle of his arms. She could feel his hard muscles, could hear the rhythmic beat of his heart, could feel the warmth of his body.

Lance was likewise drawn up in the moment. He could feel the fullness of her breasts as he pulled her closer, felt a fierce stab of desire pierce through his loins. She was quite a lady. He had never met anyone quite like her.

Locking her hands around his neck, surprising herself by her daring, Christina pulled Lance's head down to hers, initiating a kiss. His lips were soft as they caressed hers. His tongue moved across her lips, gently nudging them open in a way that was gentle yet passionate. His hand moved to her lower back, pressing her against him, as the fingers of his other hand combed through her hair.

Christina couldn't have spoken at that moment even if she wanted to. All she could do was to cling to him as the world seemed to blur into a haze. There was a roaring in her head. A warmth that enveloped her from head to toe. As the kiss deepened, Christina felt her heart race, then seem to stop beating entirely. She couldn't think, couldn't breathe; she could only feel

How long they kissed, she didn't know. When at last he drew back his head, she stared in surprise. Their gazes locked and held for a long moment, then Lance broke the spell. "Come on. We had best get going before ole Jim gets impatient." He was not in such a hurry, however, that he could not wipe the dirt from her cheek with fingers that were incredibly gentle. In that moment she knew that this was where she belonged. Here, with him.

CHAPTER FIVE

The shadowy outline of the mountains was a deep purple against the dark pink of the sky as Jim Cleary, Lance and Christina neared the hideout on Lookout Mountain. It was a secluded spot, difficult to find even for the wiliest Pinkerton agent, or so Jim Cleary insisted. For Christina it was irrefutable proof that she had stepped back in time. All the familiar houses she remembered had now vanished. In actuality they hadn't even been thought of yet. There were no traffic sounds, no steady hum of cars zooming up the highway.

"It's so peaceful," she whispered to Lance. And it was.

"I love this time of evening when the sun is preparing to sleep and the moon takes its turn to watch over us," Lance said. "Somehow I always feel safer at night."

Strange, Christina had always felt safer in the daytime, but that was because of the constant rise of the crime rate in the city. It was something she wouldn't have to worry about now. For the moment, her concerns were far different: fundamental and primal worries like survival. She had shot members of a posse. She was riding with two wanted men. That made her one of the hunted now.

Lance Meredith seemed to read her thoughts. "Ole Roundtree has been searching for my hideout for years. He'll never find it. And even if he does, we'll pick his men off one by one." The road to the ridge was a narrow strip, accessible only on foot or horseback. "Wagons can't pass this way but have to take the long way around."

Another thought troubled Christina. How was she going to fit in at the outlaw camp? A hundred years of progress seperated her way of thinking from that of the women holed up with their husbands and lovers. What would they think of her modern ways?

Once again Lance Meredith read her thoughts. "You're going to be just fine. You'll like them and they'll like you. It's not as different from other places as you might think."

He went on to explain that far from being a lawless place, the outlaw "oasis" as he called it was a group of people who took care of each other. They had formed a systematic, rough social order that worked for them.

"We probably have a lot stricter discipline than in some of the towns," he said with pride. "There's a code of honor we live by. Take care of each other and those who can't take care of themselves." First and foremost, any member of the hideout had to pull his weight and treat the others fairly.

"Yes, I know." Christina had prepared herself for her broadcast by reading everything she could about the Meredith gang. Even so, as the small encampment came into sight and three of the "boys" came whooping out to meet them, she could tell that she was in for a few surprises.

Lance had cleverly constructed a cabin up on the ridge, beneath an overhanging ledge of rock and well out of sight. It commanded a view of the area for miles in all directions and was the perfect lookout point. These three men had seen the threesome from a long way off.

"Damn, but you are a sight for sore eyes, Lance. We never thought we'd see you again."

"Nor did I." Lance touched his neck. "Let's just say that I got a little closer to a hanging than I ever want to again." He nodded in Christina's direction. "This pretty lady saved my hide."

The three men looked at Christina, studying her critically; then they all smiled. "Guess we owe you a real debt of gratitude."

The tallest of the men cocked an eyebrow. "Is she off limits, Lance?" His grin was villainous. He was the only one of the outlaws Lance was wary of. There was something different about Matt Denahay, a cruelty the others did not exhibit. Whereas the others showed restraint, he seemed to enjoy shedding blood. Lance always kept an eye on him.

"Definitely off limits." The look the two men exchanged was like a silent duel. *She's mine*, Lance's expression seemed to say.

Matt enjoyed riding into Denver on a Saturday night, hurrahing up the main street, carousing in the saloons and the cribs. He'd get liquored up and shoot up the town, leaving bullet holes in the walls and ceilings. One time he had wounded a man and would probably have killed him if the other gang members had not intervened. Was it any wonder that Lance had insisted that he be watched like a hawk so that he didn't bring calamity to the others? Now Lance had even more reason to keep an eye on him because of Christina.

"And just what does the lady have to say about the matter?" Matt cocked an eyebrow in question as he looked at Christina, brushing his fingers against the handle of his gun as if just itching to draw.

"I'm already spoken for," she replied, moving her horse closer to Lance's. She tried to remember what she had read about this particular outlaw, but for the moment her thoughts were hazy. Even so, her woman's intuition warned her to stay far away from him.

Oh, yes, she would avoid him, Christina thought. He was dangerous. Even now, though her coat hid her curves from sight, he seemed to be looking at her as if imagining what lay beneath. His attentions made her flesh crawl.

"Let's get going." Lance was eager to be home. "Be careful," he cautioned. Lance had traveled this same route more times than he could count, but even so, he still felt queasy as he looked over the side where the hill dropped off sharply to the boulders below. Taking Christina's reins, he carefully guided her along. "It can be treacherous here."

They rode together until the road narrowed and they were forced to ride single file. At the top of the mountain they came to a clearing hidden from sight by various rock formations. A huge cave acted as a stable for the horses.

"We have to hike the rest of the way," Jim Cleary instructed. He quickly took care of the horses, then caught up with Lance and Christina as they climbed the hill. At the top, Jim Cleary turned to the right, Lance to the left. Christina knew instinctively which cabin was Lance's. Hesitantly she followed.

It was definitely a man's abode decorated with wood, leather and brightly woven blankets at the window as curtains. A large wood-burning stove, used for heat as well as cooking stood in the center of the cabin. Lance hurried to light it, striking a match on the sole of his boot. He fed the fire with wood from the woodpile just outside the front door, then stood watching as the flickering flames danced about. "I'm so hungry I could eat my gun. How about you?"

She laughed. "Well, I don't think I'm that hungry but I wouldn't say no to some real food." She could only hope that he wouldn't expect her to do the cooking because she was a woman. TV dinners and the microwave were Christina's specialty.

Lance picked up an iron skillet. "How about hash? Jim was neighborly in seeing to my supplies. There's a whole bag of potatoes and onions in the crawl space under the cabin and some beef strips in the icebox outside.'' As she moved toward the stove, he shook his head. ''You're my guest. Just wash up and sit down. This won't take me long.''

She watched as he greased the skillet with lard from a tin can near the stove, then set about grinding the meat and vegetables in the hand grinder affixed to the table top. It was a different side to the infamous outlaw, one that hadn't been written about in the history books. A human side.

''Do you cook much?'' Somehow he didn't seem much like the house-husband type.

''Let's just say that for me cooking is a matter of survival.'' He laughed. ''I try to survive my cooking. How about you?''

Christina was honest. ''The same. I can't make the claim of being Betty Crocker.''

He looked puzzled. ''Who?''

She shrugged. ''Never mind.'' Determined to help out, she searched the cabinets for plates and utensils. She found clay plates and cups and knives and forks of silver, then set the table.

It wasn't fancy cookery, but as famished as she was it tasted delicious. There was little suppertime conversation. Both ate quickly and hungrily. Certainly Christina had enough thoughts stampeding through her mind. So much had happened to her. Perhaps that was why she didn't notice the knock on the door until Lance got up to answer it.

''Probably Jim. He can smell cookin' a mile away.'' Wiping his hands on the tablecloth, he opened the door, expecting his friend on the other side. Instead it was the blue eyes of another infamous outlaw. ''Johnnie!'' If Lance was Robin Hood, John White was Little John, an outlaw who had always fascinated Christina.

John White had been working in the boom town of Telluride, Colorado, as a mule master, packing high-grade ore down the treacherous mountain trails. Then he met up with Lance and joined the Meredith gang. He and Jim Cleary had both ridden with the gang, pulling off jobs in Colorado, Utah and Wyoming. He was caught with rustled cattle and sent to Wyoming State Prison, although he always contended that he was not guilty. The Laramie, Wyoming, sheriff liked him and released him if he would promise not to rustle cattle in Wyoming again. John was a man of his word, and never again pulled off any cattle-rustling job in Wyoming after his release from the penitentiary in January 1896.

"I can see that you're eating, so I won't stay. Just wanted to give you some news, Lance." The corners of his mouth dipped up in a smile, his blue eyes danced at her. "While you were gone we planned the biggest, most spectacular train robbery you ever dreamed of, and now that you're back you'll—"

"No!" The exclamation slipped out of her mouth before she realized it.

Lance wasn't angered at her outburst; he was curious. "Why do you say no?"

"Because you'll be caught. I know. I saw . . ." The old newspaper clippings she had read told the story. In 1900, two days after Lance Meredith was hanged, John White led the outlaws on a train hijacking. Marshal Roundtree ambushed them, shot half of them down in cold blood, and displayed their bullet-ridden bodies in the town square of Paradise. Christina couldn't stand the thought of Lance escaping death by hanging only to be gunned down.

"Don't listen to her, Lance. What does she know? She's only a woman." John White was not at all congenial when crossed.

"She's not just a woman." From across the room Lance's eyes connected with Christina's soulful gaze. He had a gut feeling that somehow she foresaw a tragedy concerning his people. "She *does* know. More than you could ever imagine." It took only a moment for Lance to make his decision. "We're not going to rob that train!"

"What?" John White was furious. "What are we going to do? Sit and knit doilies?"

"We're going to do as *I* say." Lance realized he had to regain his command. "Now that I'm back, I say what we will and won't do! Either you go along with that or you go your separate way. Which is it?"

A primal growl escaped John White's lips, but he agreed to go along with Lance's wishes. Even so, Christina had the feeling that a schism had been formed between Lance and this big man. A rupture that would have dire consequences for them all.

Nothing was spoken about the incident with John White as Christina helped Lance clear the table and wash the dishes, but there was an unspoken tension in the air. Lance was silent and brooding. He looked troubled. At last Christina couldn't stand it any longer.

"What is it? What are you thinking?"

He took the clean plates and cups from her outstretched hands. "Nothing is the same for me since I met you." He tapped his temple. "Not here." He touched his chest. "Not here."

It was as if he were a different man. He didn't feel the same, he didn't think the same, he didn't want the same things out of life. Once, being Lance Meredith, outlaw extraordinaire, had been all he wanted. Now all that had changed. The life he had been leading suddenly seemed empty.

"Do you think things are the same in *my* life now that I've met *you?*" Christina swallowed the lump in her throat. Her whole world had been turned topsy-turvy. Everything that had been routine in her life was suddenly gone. The impossible and unthinkable had happened. Whether she wanted to or not, she had to readjust her life to this new environment.

"Who sent you?"

His question took her by surprise. "No one."

"You aren't some angel sent to give me back my life and show me the error of my ways? Some being answering a dying man's prayers? Or some celestial ambassador here to make a bargain?" Although there was teasing in his tone, Lance was deadly serious. "Who are you?"

Christina braced herself for his disbelief. "I'm from your future." Or her past. "Another century." She wanted to answer as truthfully as she could, even though she could hardly believe the events herself. "In my century I was a newswoman. We were doing a newscast on the hundredth anniversary of your . . . your hanging when—"

"The hundredth . . ." He struggled to comprehend what she was telling him. "So that's how you know so much about me." If it hadn't been for the tiny lantern she had used in the mine tunnel, he would have been certain that she was touched in the head.

"You and your outlaw gang became part of our Western lore. I read all about you. I was fascinated." She touched his arm. Strange, but even though a century separated them, she had cared about him. Perhaps that was one of the reasons she had been thrown back in time.

"And just what did your Western stories say about me? Did they hang me?" He knew the answer before she answered.

"Yes."

"And the others?" He could well imagine that Roundtree would have done everything in his power to destroy them all.

"As I said earlier, John White took over as leader here. He and several of the others robbed a train headed from Leadville to Denver. Marshal Roundtree and some Pinkerton agents ambushed them outside Denver. They were shot." She hated to tell him the gruesome details but thought he would want to know. "Their bodies were put on display on propped-up boards in front of the mortuary as an example of what happens to those who live outside the law."

Lance paled. "Damn him!" And yet, was it all Roundtree's fault? Or should he share some of the blame? "I never meant to put any lives at risk. I only wanted to help people who, through no fault of their own, fell on hard times." He spoke with passion. "I robbed from the rich to help widows and orphans and men unjustly accused. People who had been robbed of any dignity! I wanted to give them hope."

"And you did." Moving closer, Christina touched his arm. "But the world you knew changed, and those changes made a big difference in everything. The Old West underwent a metamorphosis," she explained further. "The twentieth century saw new inventions that were just beginning at the end of the previous century." She tried to make him understand. "Roundtree used the telegraph and telephone among other things to bring reinforcements by train to capture your gang members. John White and the others didn't stand a chance. Not really."

Putting his face in his hands, Lance thought about what she had said for a long, long time. He had to do something to avert the tragedy she foretold. But what? He looked up. "Can you help us?"

"I can try!" Somehow she had to figure out how her knowledge of the future could save Lance and the others. "I have to believe that I came to be here for some reason."

CHAPTER SIX

Lance had started a fire in the fireplace. Sitting beside him on a large leather sofa, Christina was surprised by how right it felt to be with this man. Even though they had just met, she felt comfortable with him. It was as if she had known him all her life. Perhaps in a way she had.

"You know everything about me, but all I know about you is your name." In a tone of endearment he spoke the name she had revealed to him. "Christina."

She leaned her head against his shoulder. "There isn't much to tell. I grew up in Paradise; then after high school I moved to California determined to become famous." It sounded hollow. "The twentieth century brought hundreds of changes for women: the vote, equal rights. Total emancipation. I suppose you could say that the next few years were centered on my ambition and determination to succeed." She didn't want to talk about it. "And now I'm here."

He kissed her gently on the forehead. "Yes, you are. Thankfully."

She smiled. Oh, yes, she was here to view firsthand

the things she had only read about. But oh, how ironic it all was. Her experience was the story of a lifetime. Yet, here she was trapped in time without access to even a primitive camera. Even if she somehow managed to get back to her own time, who would believe her? *If* she got back. She wondered if she would ever be able to return to the twenty-first century. It didn't matter. For the moment at least, she was content.

"Christina . . ." For once in his life Lance felt awkward and unsure of how to proceed. He wanted to make love to her but didn't know what to say. "I want you to feel at ease with me," he said. "I want you to be comfortable. You aren't my prisoner. You're my guest." He couldn't help looking toward the small bedroom. "I like having you here with me, but if you would rather stay in one of the other cabins . . ."

Christina had always been a woman who said what she wanted. "I want to stay here with you." There was a shiny brass bathtub by the stove. She eyed it longingly. At that moment she would have given practically anything for the luxury of warm water and soap.

"You're hankering for a bath." So was he. The filth of the jail covered him from head to foot. "Allow me!"

Setting up the tub, then heating several buckets of water on the stove, he prepared the amenity for her. All the while amorous thoughts threaded through his mind. He eyed the tub. "You'll never know just how tempting that water looks."

"Oh yes, I do!"

They faced each other, both strangely silent. Christina made the first effort. Coming to him, she put her arms around his neck. There wasn't time to play it coy. She didn't know what might happen tomorrow, or even if there were many tomorrows. She could be whisked back to her own time and never have the chance to know what it was like to be loved by him.

"Lance . . ."

Gathering her into his arms, he touched his lips against

the side of her throat His fingers were gentle as he removed her garments piece by piece until they fell in a heap at her feet. The sight of her firm breasts, narrow waist and gently curved hips was well worth his ordeal.

"Perfect." Bending down, he kissed each soft peak.

Christina uttered a moan as his lips and hands moved over the curves of her body. "I love the way you touch me. . . ."

It seemed as if her breath was trapped somewhere between her throat and stomach. She couldn't say any more. The realization that he was going to make love to her brought forth a heady feeling as he brought his lips to hers. Such a potent kiss. It was as if she had never been kissed before.

When at last he drew his mouth away, he stared at her intently. "You know, in spite of everything, I wouldn't trade one minute of what happened to me, because it brought me you."

"Are you serious? You mean you would even experience the rope around your neck?"

"Yes!" He said it with conviction. It was the nicest compliment she had ever had.

He stepped forward, standing so close that there was barely an inch between them. Just enough space for him to take off his shirt and let it fall to the floor at her feet His boots and pants followed. Like Christina, he knew that their time together was precious.

Picking her up in his arms, he deposited her in the warm water. She leaned back in the soothing depths and closed her eyes to the tantalizing sensation of his scrubbing her back. Then his fingers moved to her breast, touching the sensitized skin. Christina shivered with pleasure, the warm, pulsating feeling in her loins becoming stronger and stronger.

Watching her in the bath aroused Lance even more, and he joined her quickly. The water nearly overflowed as he settled into the already brimming tub. With a grin he handed her a washcloth. Christina tugged it out of his hand and set about lathering him with soap.

Her eyes devoured him, noting with pleasure the broad chest, the muscles of his abdomen, and the throbbing maleness that seemed to have a life of its own. Whoever wrote the history books hadn't even guessed how magnificent he was. But now she knew.

"Touch me," he said huskily, noticing her stare. She did, with gentle, probing hands. Slowly his manhood began to stiffen. Because of her.

"Christina . . . !" The expression on his face was akin to pain. A torment she knew only she could take away. Her hands closed around his shoulders, pulling him to her. In the small confines of the tub it was difficult maneuvering her body, but she managed, crushing her breasts against the wet sleekness of his chest in the ultimate caress. Their lips met in a kiss. Then another. And another . . .

Every inch of Christina's body tingled with an arousing awareness of his body. His slightest movement sent a shudder of ecstasy rippling deep within her. Driven by emotions she'd never felt before, she arched up to him as he kissed her. When at last his lips reluctantly left her mouth to travel like liquid fire along her jaw line to her ear, she knew she was completely his.

"I think we're steaming up the water. It's growing much too hot in here." Reaching for a large linen towel he had placed near the tub, he pulled her to her feet, then began caressing her with the soft length of the linen. Slowly, leisurely, he dried her off, then used the towel on himself. His hands cupped her buttocks, pulling her up against him as he buried his mouth passionately on hers.

Lance had the feeling that he was doing everything for the very first time as he made love to her. All memories of other women faded from his mind. Her softness was the only reality in this hostile and dangerous world. Burying his face in the silky soft strands of her hair, he breathed in the fragrant scent of her hair and was lost to any other thought.

Christina caught fire wherever he touched her, burning with an all consuming need. Lance! A shudder racked through her. Christina took her turn to appraise him. The image of broad, bronzed shoulders, wide chest, flat belly and well-formed legs would forever be branded in her mind. Reaching out, she touched him, her hands sliding over the hard smoothness of his shoulders, moving to the crisp hair of his chest.

"Lance. . . ." Closing her eyes, Christina awaited another kiss, her mouth opening to him like the soft petals of a flower as he caressed her lips with all the passionate hunger they both yearned for. Christina loved the taste of him, the tender urgency of his mouth. Her lips opened to him for a seemingly endless passionate onslaught of kisses. It was if they were breathing one breath, living at that moment just for each other. They shared a joy of touching and caressing, arms against arms, legs touching legs, fingers entwining and wandering to explore.

Mutual hunger brought their lips back together time after time. She craved his kisses and returned them with trembling pleasure, exploring the inner softness of his mouth. The most enticing experience of all was the feel of his lips, on her mouth, at her throat, on her breasts, on her stomach.

"Christina . . . !" Desire writhed almost painfully within his loins. He had never wanted anything or anyone as much as he did her at this moment. It was like an unfulfilled dream just waiting to come true.

Carrying her to the bed, he stroked her all over. Then his hands were at her shoulders, pushing her gently down on the bed. Bending down, he worshiped her with his mouth. His fingers entwined in her pale golden hair. His teeth nipped gently at her lower lip as he kissed her. He pulled her closer, rolling her over until they were lying side by side.

He kissed her again, his knowing, seeking lips moving

with tender urgency across hers, his tongue finding again
the inner warmth and sweetness of her mouth. His large
body covered hers with a blanket of warmth. They took
sheer delight in the texture and pressure of each other's
body.

"Lance . . . love me . . ." she breathed.

"Not yet. . . ."

His hands caressed her, warming her with their heat.
Sensuously he undulated his hips between her legs, and
every time their bodies caressed, each experienced a shock
of raw desire that encompassed them in fiery, pulsating
sensations. Then his hands were between their bodies,
sliding down the velvety flesh of her belly, moving to
that place between her thighs that ached for his entry.
His gentle probing brought sweet fire, curling deep inside
her with spirals of pulsating sensations. Then his hands
left her, to be replaced by his maleness, entering her just
a little, then pausing. Every inch of her tingled with an
intense arousing awareness of his body.

Bending his head to kiss her again, he moved his body
forward pushing deep within her, fusing their bodies.
Christina was conscious only of the hard length of him
creating unbearable sensations as he began to move within
her. Capturing the firm flesh of her hips, he caressed her
in the most intimate of embraces. His rhythmic plunges
aroused a tingling fire, like nothing she had ever experienced before. It was as if they were falling over the edge
of a cliff together. Falling. Falling. Never quite hitting
the ground. She arched herself up to him, fully expressing
her love.

Lance groaned softly, the blood pounding thickly in
his head. His hold on her hips tightened as the throbbing
shaft of his maleness possessed her again and again.
Instinctively Christina tightened her legs around him, certain she could never withstand the ecstasy that was
engulfing her body. It was as if the night shattered into
a thousand stars bursting within her. Arching her hips,
she rode the storm with him. As spasms overtook her,

she dug her nails into the skin of his back, whispering his name.

A sweet shaft of ecstasy shot through Lance and he closed his eyes. Even when the intensity of their passion was spent, they still clung to each other, unable to let this magical moment end. They touched each other gently, wonderingly.

"Making love *is* strenuous no matter what century it is." She touched his lips in a smiling kiss, then cuddled up against him, closing her eyes as Lance stroked her hair.

For a long, long time he was contented to just look at her. "I don't want you to ever leave me," he whispered. Even if he had to make a pact with the devil himself, he knew he couldn't live without her.

Christina awoke to the sound of children's laughter outside the door. The Taylor twins playing baseball next door, she thought. Hopefully, they wouldn't break another window. Stretching out her hand, she made contact with the thick hair of the head curled up at her breast.

"I better let you out, Max, so you can keep an eye on them." Thinking herself to be back at her apartment in San Diego, she yawned and sleepily opened her eyes. It was not the black lab nestled against her, however, but another familiar dark-haired head.

"Lance Meredith!" In a whirlwind of remembered sounds and visions, the events of yesterday and last night came back to her. "Oh, my God!" It hadn't been a dream. It had really happened. She was with him, in his cabin at the outlaw camp!

Lance's arm lay heavy across her stomach, the heat of his body warming hers as she lay entangled with his legs and arms. All the details of their lovemaking came back to her in vivid detail, the kissing, his stroking, and teasing her with his tongue the moment he had brought her to a heart-stopping crest of pleasure.

His face had the calm peace of a delightedly satiated man. Breathing a sigh, she remembered his kisses, his caresses, the awe-inspiring moment when he had made her his woman. She remembered his eyes bright with desire, his lips trembling into a smile as he kissed her.

"My lusty outlaw!"

Shifting from his embrace, she turned so that she could watch him as he slept. He looked like a contented man without a care in the world. Could it be because of her? *"I love you,"* he had said and though she had always been taught to be wary of those impassioned three words, she had believed him. Last night had just been too special, too out of the ordinary. She had felt it and she knew that he had too.

Love. What a potent word that really was, encompassing so many things. Christina didn't think she would ever forget the way Lance had looked at her last night, his eyes bright with desire. He had learned every inch of her body, had whispered her name with a husky cry of passion that had made her heart sing. But what they shared went even deeper than that. Their love went beyond the physical gratification of the moment. She deeply cared about Lance, enough so as to risk her life and well-being, and she knew that he felt the same.

"So where do we go from here?" Just what did a successful television journalist do in a world where television hadn't been invented? How did they keep the world at bay?

Determinedly she shoved aside her misgivings and clung to optimistic feelings. She had crossed an uncrossable barrier to be with him. Their love was time-less. Right now that was the only important thing

The pleasant sound of soft snoring told her how deeply Lance slept, and she smiled, reaching out to touch a lock of his dark hair. "So where do we go to from here?" she asked herself again.

The answer was obvious. Somehow she had to help clear his name so that he could go on with his life and secure a future that did not include swinging from a rope. But how was she going to do it? How was she going to use what information she had on Marshal Roundtree to ensure Lance's freedom? There would have to be undeniable evidence that proved Roundtree's unscrupulous dealings. But how was she going to get her hands on any evidence?

"Christina?" Lance cherished the blessing of finding her cradled in his arms, her mane of long blonde hair spread like a cloak over her shoulders. He felt an aching tenderness and drew her closer. "So I wasn't just dreaming."

"No, unless we're sharing the same dream." She snuggled into his arms, laying her head on his shoulder, curling into his hard, strong body. His hand moved lightly over her hip and down her leg as he spoke. Her body had been pure heaven, her genuine outpouring of love a precious gift.

"I'd like to wake up every morning and find you next to me," he confided, nibbling at her earlobe playfully. But he was not sure just what the future had in store for him. "Christina, we need to—"

"Hush!" She didn't want to spoil the morning by letting reality intrude. "We've got a lot to talk about, but we'll do it later. Please!"

"OK!" Cupping her chin in his hands, he kissed her hard. Pleasure jolted through him, a rush of emotion. As she arched her body and sighed, he knew it to be the same for her. Her response to him gave him a heady feeling. He had been able to bring her deep satisfaction not once but several times during the night.

Lance moved his hands over her body, stroking lightly—her throat, her breasts, her belly, her thighs. With reverence he moved his hands over her breasts, gently and slowly, until they swelled beneath his fingers. He outlined the rosy-peaked mount, watching as the velvet flesh hardened.

Christina closed her eyes to the sensations she was becoming familiar with now. Wanting to bring him the same sensations, she touched him, one hand sliding down over the muscles of his chest, sensuously stroking his flesh.

Their eyes met and held as an unspoken communication passed between them. In a surge of physical power he rolled her under him. Then they were rolling over and over in the bed, sinking into the warmth and softness. Christina sighed in delight at the feel of his hard, lithe body atop hers.

A flicker of arousal spread to the core of her body. Being with Lance encompassed every emotion she had ever known.

"Christina ... oh, Christina ..." he said again, his voice thick with desire. But kissing didn't satisfy the blazing hunger that raged between them. Slowly, sensuously, Lance let his hand slid up her thigh, his fingers questing, seeking that most intimate part of her. His legs moved between hers and pressed to spread her thighs.

Christina moved her body against him, feeling the burning flesh touching hers. He inflamed more than just her body. Indeed, he sparked a flame in her heart and soul. The touch of his hands caused a fluttery feeling in her stomach. A shiver danced up and down her spine. She leaned against his hand, giving in to the stirring sensations.

Caressing her, kissing her, he left no part of her free from his touch, and she responded with a natural passion. Her entire body quivered. She would never get tired of feeling Lance's hands on her skin, of tasting his kisses.

A loud pounding at the door interrupted their pleasure. "Lance, it's me."

"Damn!" Lance was in a surly mood. He was tempted to let Jim Cleary stand outside the door all morning if need be, but knowing how stubborn Jim could be, he bolted out of bed, hurriedly got dressed, and opened the door. "What do you want?"

Jim raised his brows. "Don't want to intrude, but we have some serious talking to do! It's about Johnnie."

"John!" Lance remembered the confrontation last

night only too well. "He's planning a train robbery. I told him we weren't going to do it. You're here to tell me that he's going to tell me to go to hell!"

"He's gone. He and several of the others."

"Gone!" Lance hadn't foreseen that. "The damn fool. He'll get us all killed!" He grabbed his gunbelt. "Come on. We've got to stop him!"

CHAPTER SEVEN

Dressed in a pair of Lance's denims, cinched at the waist with an old leather belt, his flannel shirt, Stetson hat, boots and leather jacket, and armed with one of Lance's guns, Christina rode with Jim and Lance despite their objections. She had found Lance, and wasn't about to lose him.

"We'll find John before he gets into any mischief and somehow talk some sense into his fool head," Jim Cleary suggested.

"Or bail him out if he gets himself into trouble!" Although Lance was angered by the mutinous act, he still was determined to avert the tragedy Christina had prophesied.

"You're both going to get yourselves killed or captured! You'll be recognized the moment anyone lays eyes on you." Christina had tried repeatedly but couldn't get either man to change his mind. It seemed that no matter what century it was, men could be stubborn.

"Even if they see us, they'll never be able to catch us!" Lance could only hope that his prowess matched his bravado and that his instincts would guide him to the other members of his outlaw band.

They rode hard, pushing on until Lance's persistence was rewarded. As they rode over the ridge, puffs of black smoke and the pulsating roar of a train clattering over the tracks told them they were going in the right direction.

"There it is!" From a distance it looked like a toy train, Christina thought. The masked gunmen riding alongside the last few cars of the long train, keeping well out of sight, appeared to be motorized miniatures. They were all too real, however.

"We're too late!" Christina knew what was going to happen now. Marshal Roundtree was using the train as a trap. He had spread the rumor about a shipment of gold being aboard. There was no gold. What there was, however, were thirty-five armed and mounted men waiting in the boxcars. As soon as the outlaws held up the train they would be ambushed, shot and killed.

"We're *not* too late!" Lance knew he could never run from a fight just to save his own skin.

Christina shouted a warning, pleading with both men to turn back. "There are armed gunmen inside the railroad cars. It's going to be like a shooting gallery."

Feeling a sense of helplessness, she watched as the nine bandits rode beside the train. She could recognize John White as he leaned from his horse, caught the rail of the last car, and pulled himself up. Two others followed. Once on board, they climbed the ladder leading to the top of the train and were now running along the top, jumping from car to car. Their loud whoops of revelry were carried by the wind.

Christina could hardly believe her eyes. It was a daring thing to do with the train moving so rapidly, and yet they were successful. She remembered what was going to happen. John White, Cleophas Dowd and Bud Green planned to work their way up to the engineer and make him stop the train. Meanwhile, the other masked riders were to enter the passenger cars to rob any wealthy passengers they found. Pete Donner and Greg Lewis would remain outside to cover them.

Christina had seen a diagram of the train in one of the Internet computer encyclopedia programs she had logged on to. The passenger cars were the second and third cars after the engine and coal car. Altogether there were about twelve cars on the train. There were cattle cars, express cars carrying merchandise, and a mail car in addition to a caboose. There was no gold shipment!

"Lance, the train is going to stop unexpectedly, the cars are going to open, and John White and the others are going to be sitting ducks. There isn't anything you can do." As she rode beside him, she continued her tirade. "Please stop this suicidal mission before it's too late."

He couldn't! Lance had never been one to run from a fight no matter what the circumstances. Even when the train began to slow down as if confirming her words, he knew he couldn't do anything else but try and save his men.

Christina heard a shrill whistle blast while the metallic shrieking of the wheels on the rails rose above the rattle of the coach-couplings. A hand extended from one of the windows waving a red flag. The train screeched and came to a stop.

"The signal!" Marshal Roundtree's men were ready to pounce.

Christina acted on blind instinct to protect Lance. Riding up beside him, she raised the gun she had brought with her and slammed the handle of it down upon his head. The impact of the metal striking his skull made a sickening thud.

"What the . . ." A searing pain flashed through Lance's head. He slumped in the saddle, trying to focus his eyes to an all-consuming darkness, struggling against the blackness that pressed down on him. Then he could fight it no longer and gave in to unconsciousness.

"What have you done?" Jim Cleary's eyes focused on Lance's crumpled form. "Whose side are you on?"

"Lance's side!" She reached for the horse's reins. "Whether you want to believe it or not, I just saved his life—and yours if you come with me."

For a moment Jim Cleary was torn. Proving that he was just as stubborn as Lance, however, he rode in the direction of the train.

Christina's heart rose in her throat as she knelt down and bent over the still form. She touched the knot on his head with tenderly examining fingers. Dragging him behind a large cottonwood tree, she watched the chess game between the outlaws and Marshal Roundtree's men from afar.

It was like watching a movie or the footage on a news station, only the action was real. With a lot of shooting into the air and hollering, the lawmen broke out of the cattle cars and took aim at the stunned outlaws. Without a shred of mercy they gunned every outlaw down one by one.

"No. Not him. Not James Cleary. I want him taken alive!" Roundtree cried out. Though the red-haired and bearded man put up quite a fight, he was subdued.

The ground beside the train tracks was littered with dead bodies. Even from afar, Christina could see Jim Cleary's expression of anger mixed with desperation. Slowly, cautiously, he raised his eyes, focusing them in her direction. She held her breath, fearful that he might purposely give her whereabouts away.

"When Lance hears about this, you'll be as good as dead, Roundtree!" Jim Cleary spat on the ground at the marshal's feet.

"That's just what I'm counting on. That's why, and only why, I'm keeping you alive. You're rat bait, Cleary. I'm going to catch a rat."

So, Christina thought, Roundtree knew his adversary well. He had captured the perfect hostage to lead Lance into a trap. She might have saved Lance this time, but she knew that sooner or later he would do everything in his power to rescue his friend.

"Come on. Let's get these bodies loaded and get the hell out of here. I don't want to tangle with Lance Meredith here. I want him to have to come to Paradise!"

Christina watched as the bodies were dumped unceremoniously aboard the train. Gray clouds of smoke puffed up from the locomotive's smokestack like a winsome ghost as it moved down the tracks The train began gaining speed, at last vanishing into a long, sweeping curve in the roadbed.

Christina looked down at the still form before her, wincing as she saw the lump on his head. With gently exploring fingers she examined the damage she had done. She would have a lot of explaining to do when she got back to camp. *If* she got back. She had to find the way back herself, for there was no one to help her.

Trying to get Lance back in the saddle presented her first obstacle. He was well over six feet tall and weighed close to 185 pounds.

"Lance . . . wake up." She must have hit him harder than she realized. "Lance . . ."

Spying the rope coiled on the saddle, she thought of a plan that might work. She would tie the rope around Lance's waist and use the pommel of the saddle as a pulley. If she could get him near enough to the saddle, lift him to a standing position and then get him up on the horse's back, the rest would be easy.

Springing to her feet, Christina grabbed the rope and knotted it around Lance's lithe form. "I've got to get you back to camp. Somehow!" The nagging fear that Marshal Roundtree might come back to search the area prodded her on. Perhaps that was why she was able to accomplish the task at hand.

Placing the free end of the rope around the pommel so that it slid easily when she pulled on it, she tugged and tugged until she had him in a seated position. Leaning on the horse for support, she slid her hands under Lance's armpits and managed to lift him to his feet, put her arms around his waist to support his sagging body, and shove him over the horse's back just in front of the saddle.

It was quite a struggle, but after two efforts at balancing his bulk had failed, she accomplished her task. Lance's limp body was draped facedown, hanging across the horse's back in front of the saddle. He looked to be in a secure though uncomfortable position. Placing her foot in the stirrup, swinging herself up, she mounted her own horse, nudged his flank with the toe of her boot, and guided him toward the distant hills. She did not pressure the horse into a fast gallop but let him select his own pace.

If I'd known I was going to have to find my way back I would have paid more attention to the landmarks, she thought "I hope *you* know the way!" she said, letting up on the reins of her horse. She had heard that animals had a homing instinct. She'd put it to the test now.

The journey was far more tedious coming back than going out. There was no access from the east, only the west, up a steep incline, which made traveling difficult. The cliffs, caves and overhangs gave excellent shelter from a posse, however. Most lawmen did not want to follow any outlaw into this area. It was steep and it was dangerous. Nevertheless, Christina headed in that direction.

All along the way Lance remained unconscious, which was beginning to worry her. Pausing, she felt his pulse and examined the bump on his head. He was going to have quite a goose egg thanks to her, but his pulse was strong and from time to time he mumbled. She saw that as a favorable sign that he would soon come around.

Lance groaned, opened his eyes, and suddenly sat up in the saddle. Damn, his head felt as if someone had tried to split it wide open. "What . . . ?"

"You got hit on the head." She didn't say by whom. Lance mumbled few obscenities beneath his breath.

"Yeah, well I wish I could get my hands on the person who hit me." He looked around. "Where are we going?"

"Home." Strange, but that was exactly how it felt.

"Where's Jim?"

The moment she had dreaded had come. "He's gone."

"Gone?"

Christina wanted to prolong the moment of truth as long as possible. The more time that passed, the closer they came to the hideout, the less chance there was of Lance doing something risky. Lance asked again and again, but she didn't respond to his question until they had dismounted and were leading both horses up the path.

"After you were . . . were hit, Jim rode right into trouble. Roundtree has him." She didn't want to say any more than that.

"Roundtree has him. . . ." Lance started to turn his horse around.

Christina lashed out. "Don't be a fool. You aren't going to do Jim or any of the others any good by getting yourself killed. That's exactly what the marshal wants you to do."

Although he wanted to argue, Lance knew she was right. The intelligent thing to do was to wait and plan.

CHAPTER EIGHT

The boundaries of the camp were a welcome sight. Christina wondered if she would have been able to find her way back to this haven of safey if Lance had not regained consciosness. She wanted to believe that she could have. People were capable of doing amazing things when the need arose.

"You're back!" A young red-haired boy ran to greet them, looking forlornly down the road. Christina recognized his resemblance to Jim Cleary and knew at once it had to be his son. "Where's my pa? And the others? You said you were going to bring them back."

Five other people had run out to greet them. Their eyes turned in Lance's direction. One glimpse at his face told them that something had gone awry.

The red-haired boy's eyes reflected all their fears as he asked. "Is my pa dead?"

Christina answered. "He's not dead but. . . ."

"Nooooooo!!" The boy's wail said it all.

Lance's head throbbed as he got down off his horse. Sadly his eyes scanned the perimeters of the camp and his people. Some of the men had been rescued from prisons, some from the gallows. Three of the camp's ten women had come to be with their men. Three had grown up there from childhood. Four had been rescued from brothels. He had given them a home where the troubles of the world could be at least for a time forgotten. Now reality was going to intrude with a big thud. The news he had was going to bring a lot of pain.

"We rode out to try and stop the train robbery. We failed." Though he knew it wasn't his fault that John White and the others had ridden into an ambush, he felt an overwhelming sadness and sense of responsibility. He had wanted to create a shelter for those who had been put off their lands by greedy men and self-seeking political leaders. He had wanted to be a modern-day Robin Hood. Somehow he had failed.

"What went wrong?" Matt Denahay pushed his way forward with a scowl.

"John and the others rode right into an ambush. They were killed. Jim Cleary was taken."

"But you came out alive!" There was accusation in Denahay's tone.

"Lance was hit on the head," Christina said, feeling a twinge of guilt at the reminder of what she had done. "I dragged him into the bush or he would have been captured too."

Lance had suspicions as to who had hit him on the head, but he wasn't angry. The blow had undoubtedly saved him. Now he would have a chance to rescue Jim, not share his jail cell.

"But he escaped!" Matt Denahay spit on the ground. "How lucky for him."

Sadness prevailed as the word was spread about the ambush. For the moment Lance was too caught up in plans for freeing Jim Cleary to think about anything else. Once his friend was saved from the hangman, there would be time to mourn those who had been killed.

"I say we ride into town and storm the jail." As usual, Matt Denahay wanted to rush right in without letting tempers cool down. In between gulps of whiskey, he managed to strap on his gun belt and shove a short-barreled Peacemaker revolver inside his holster.

"That's exactly what Marshal Roundtree wants you to do," Christina shot back at him.

There was something about Matt Denahay that deeply troubled her. She knew so much about the Meredith gang and yet she couldn't remember Matt Denahay's name being mentioned in the books at all. Why was that?

"Roundtree is a cold-blooded killer." She revealed her eyewitness account of the shooting, relying in part on what she had read in Western lore.

"But by all means go ahead and ride into town half-cocked. Then you can be exhibited outside the undertaker's front door," she continued.

"Maybe I'll do just that!" Matt took a step forward as if threatening her, but Lance stepped between them.

"She's right! We have to use our heads. It won't do any of us any good if we walk into a trap." Now it was up to him to see that the others held their tempers in check and didn't act too quickly.

"Well, I for one am not going to wait." The whiskey bottle, now empty, was dropped on the ground. After drawing the back of his hand across his mouth to remove the wetness, Matt Denahay moved toward his horse. Lance stopped him just in time.

"Don't be a dolt! You can't do anything all by yourself. You'll end up just like John White. He'd be alive now if he had listened." Trying to keep the peace, Lance patted him on the shoulder. "If we use our heads, we can rescue Jim and still come out with our skins." For the moment, it seemed that reason prevailed.

Christina nestled against Lance's strong form. "Do you forgive me?"

He knew what she meant: the blow to his head. "I'd probably forgive anything you would do. Love does that to a man." He teased her ear with his tongue, then whispered, "I have to free Jimmy, even if it means risking my own happiness." And his life. "I hope you can understand."

"I do understand. Just as I've always understood that our moments together are precious." Reaching up, she touched his mouth.

"I wish I could give you the world. I wish—"

"You give me your love. That is all I ask." Her lips trembled in a smile. "Though I might ask for another kiss." He complied most willingly. His lips were soft and gentle. There was a sadness in the caress of his mouth, as if already he was mourning what might have been. Reaching up, he threaded his fingers in her hair.

Christina could feel the rhythmic movement of his fingers as he stroked through the strands. The touch of his hands in her hair caused a fluttery feeling in her stomach. A shiver danced up and down her spine. She leaned against his hand, giving in to the stirring sensations.

Lance's fingers left the softness of her hair. He clasped her shoulders, contenting himself just to look at her for a long moment. "Perhaps I'll never understand how it was possible for us to be together, but I want you to know this. Even if I have to die to fulfill some kind of destiny, having been loved by you will help me to die a happy man."

His words tore at her heart. "You won't die!" She had to believe that they were meant to be together for a long and happy life. Fate couldn't be so cruel as to show her such happiness only to take it away.

He didn't answer, but deep within his heart he made a silent promise, to whatever powers that be, that if he was allowed to live a long and happy life with this woman he would spend the rest of it inside the law.

"Are you warm?"

"Mmmhmmm."

Staring up into the mesmerizing depths of his eyes, Christina felt an aching tenderness for him. She hadn't been wrong about him. Outlaw or not, he was the kind of man who had a good heart and wanted to do what was right. Reaching up, she clung to him, drawing in his strength and giving hers to him in return. She could feel his heart pounding and knew that hers beat in matching rhythm.

"I wish. . . ." He wished so many things. Most of all he wished that they could just stay like this forever

Caressing her, kissing her, he left no part of her free from his touch, and she responded with a natural passion that was kindled by his love. Her entire body quivered with the intoxicating sensations his nearness aroused in her.

Before when they had made love, Christina had been a little shy, holding a small bit of herself back from her pleasure. Now she held nothing back. Reaching out, she boldly explored Lance's body—his hard-muscled chest and arms, his stomach. His flesh was warm to her touch, pulsating with the strength of his maleness.

"Christina!" Desire raged like an inferno, pounding hotly in his veins. Her skin felt hot against his as he entwined his legs with hers.

"My time with you is the most precious gift I have ever been given," she whispered. For a long, long time they contented themselves just in lying side by side; then Christina slowly guided him to her.

They made love as if it were both the first time and the last time. Writhing in pleasure, she was silken fire beneath him, rising and falling with him as he moved with the relentless rhythm of their love. Sweet, hot desire fused their bodies together, yet there was an aching sweetness mingling with the fury and the fire. They spoke with their hearts and hands and bodies in the final outpouring of their love.

In the aftermath of the storm, when all their passion had ebbed and they lay entwined, they sealed their vows of love with whispered words. Sighing with happiness, Christina snuggled within the cradle of Lance's arms, happy and content.

At first she thought she was dreaming. Then she imagined that the sound she heard was caused by the beginning of a storm, but it was *not* thunder. Too late she realized that the explosions were dynamite and the sharp cracking sound came from guns and rifles, not the sky.

Lance was awakened by the noise. "What in hell?" He bolted out of bed, hurrying to get dressed and grab his guns.

Christina sat up, fumbling for her garments.

"No, you stay inside. I don't want you to get hurt."

Though he was right to urge caution, Christina didn't listen. She was a journalist. She had to know what was happening, and she had to be there to protect him. Stubbornly she followed him toward the door.

"Christina!" There was no reasoning with her. All Lance could do was to shield her with his body as they went out the door.

The night exploded around them. Sounds of battle echoed all around. Christina felt her heart stop. This attack wasn't part of anything she had read in the history books. Was it happening because of something she had done?

She tried to sort it all out. By saving Lance's life not once but twice, she had changed everything. She could only guess at what had happened. Roundtree had somehow found the camp and was here to destroy the last remnants of the Meredith gang. But who among them had turned traitor? It was one answer she wouldn't get from history books.

Lance stood there for a fleeting moment, stunned; then his instincts honed by years of facing danger took over. Waving his arms in the air, he shouted his orders.

"Matt, Danny, Lou, take your places on the rise. Thomas, see to the women and children. Ted, come with me. Frank, cover us." Grunting, Ted jerked his pistol from his holster.

Bullets struck the ground all around Lance as he moved forward, but he barely noticed. His thoughts were on one thing only, saving these people who trusted him.

What had gone wrong? How could this have happened? Roundtree and his men were closing in all around them. He could see them now and gasped at their numbers. A veritable army encircled the camp. Someone had led them here. A traitor.

"When I find out who betrayed us, I swear I'll kill him."

All around he could hear the curses of his men, accompanied by staccato gunfire. Dust began to rise, blending with the smoke from the fires Roundtree's men had set about the camp. Soon not even one building would be left standing. The marshal was being very thorough.

From the corner of his eye Lance saw Christina bustling about, gathering up the women and children, leading them to an area of rocks and safety. Fear that she would be struck with a bullet made him go temporarily insane with anger and fear. Forgetting his own danger, he ran forward.

"Christy . . . watch out!"

Lance could not keep from crying out as a bullet struck him in the shoulder. The impact sent him sprawling, yet he struggled to his knees. Another gun was fired; this time the bullet hit him in the hand, knocking the gun from his grasp. It was as if a fire had been ignited in his whole arm. Instinctively he reached up to close his fingers over the wound, feeling blood pour over his hand. Through a haze of agony he could hear Christina's frantic screams, watched as several men held her immobile, pinning her to the ground.

"Leave her alone! I'm the one you want! She has nothing do with all of this!" With superhuman strength he dragged himself along the ground, trying to maneuver himself to where she was being held. It was then that he saw Matt Dehaney standing not with the outlaws but with the lawmen. In that moment he realized.

"You!" So Christy and his own gut feeling had been right after all. "Damn you to hell!"

Christina looked toward the lawmen and Matt Denahay. Again she wondered why she hadn't read about Denahay being one of the outlaws. Of course, it was because he had sold Lance and the others for money and had thus escaped his own punishment. Undoubtedly he would live out a long life, invisible to future generations. Oh, how she wished she could make him disappear now.

"Damn me?" Matt Denahay laughed.

Somehow Lance managed to get to his feet. He lunged toward the traitor in their midst, determined to get his hands around his neck. "You'll pay. . . ."

Lance heard a loud cry, a howl of anguish, and realized that it was he who had uttered the sound.

In horror Christina saw him struck down again. "No!" A voice inside her screamed that this was proof that you couldn't change the past. There was nothing she could do. Lance's death seemed to have been ordained. "No!" she cried out again. She wouldn't give in to fate. She wouldn't let him die.

It was like a nightmare. Wounded and whimpering people lying on the ground, people who had been Lance's friends, men, women and children. Roundtree had no mercy. She watched as his men put torch to everything in their way. Like a flock of vultures they destroyed everything.

Christina watched in horror as Lance was subdued. For just a moment she felt dizzy, the same kind of dizziness she had felt when she had been drifting through time.

''No, I won't go! I won't go back!'' Stubbornly she shook her head, determined to stay here in body, spirit and mind. She had saved Lance once. She was determined to save him again!

CHAPTER NINE

He was right back where he started. Lance grumbled as he looked down at his bandaged hand and arm. Oh yes, Roundtree had been ''merciful'' all right. He had called in a doctor so that Lance would be all in one piece when he swung by a rope for all of Paradise to see.

''What a peach of a guy!'' Roundtree had even given him back his old cell, complete with the calendar Lance had scrawled on the wall. This time he had five days before he would be hanged. He doubted that Christina would be able to save him this time. Miracles didn't happen twice. Did they?

Christina! At least there was a silver lining to his cloud. He had told Roundtree that she was a hostage, being held against her will at the hideout. At least he knew that she was walking around free. Christina! Her face seemed to dance before his eyes, and he ached with the longing to hold her again.

It was cramped in the cell with barely enough room for a man to move around. A miserable way to be treated. Worse yet, Roundtree had tripled the number of deputies guarding him, so any thought of escape was little more than a dream. No, he was trapped all right—there was no getting around it. The thought that at least he was alive didn't quell his anger.

"Damn Matt Denahay!" He wondered what he was doing right now and figured he was undoubtedly out celebrating somewhere, spending his blood money.

What hour was it? The minutes moved so slowly that he wasn't really certain of the exact time. There was no clock near the cell. He looked out his window. The sun was still out. It must be around ten o'clock. He couldn't have been in the cell more than just a few hours. A few hours! And already he was going crazy. Still, he tried to keep his calm. Christina had insisted on finding him an attorney. She had said she knew some things that could prove Roundtree had been involved in several unscrupulous dealings, including murder.

"Roundtree!" he scoffed. As if calling out the name was some kind of spell, he looked up and saw the marshal standing in front of him.

"Well, looks like I'm finally going to see you hang." Roundtree's eyes narrowed to resentful slits.

"Don't count on it. I've cheated death a few times in my life. I'm counting on at least one more."

"Sure. Sure." Marshal Roundtree made it a point to smile. Then as suddenly as he had appeared, he left.

"What I wouldn't do to send him into the twenty-first century," Lance said aloud. "Permanently."

A tapping sound came from the other side of the wall that separated his cell from Jim Cleary's. Lance answered his friend's taps with a code of his own, speaking in their voiceless language. It was as if they had their own private telegraph.

"We have to find a way to break out of here," Jim Cleary tapped. "Before they put a rope around our necks."

"When are you scheduled to hang?" Lance asked.

"In two days." It seemed that Roundtree wanted to hang Lance Meredith all by himself.

Lance didn't have the heart to tell him that he had tried to escape the last time he was here, only to feel the sting of failure. "Then we must move quickly. At least it will give us something to do." He stopped his tapping. He heard footsteps, heavy and rapid. Someone was coming.

His body tensed as the door swung open, creaking from the strain put on the rusty hinges. The rifle pointed his way squelched any thought of escape, at least for the moment.

"What do you want, you ghoulish bastard? I'd bet my last dime this isn't a social call." Lance did not even try to hide the loathing stamped on his face. "If you have come to shoot me down in cold blood like you did the others, do it quickly."

"Shoot you and be merciful?" Roundtree shook his head. He slammed the door in Lance's face. "Oh, no. I've waited too long to see you dangle from a string. And this time there won't be any of your friends alive to come to your rescue!"

Thinking about Christina, he answered, "I wouldn't count on that!" He could tell by the look on the marshal's face that he had worried him.

"What do you mean?"

Lance shrugged. "Only that I might have a few more friends than you know."

Lance regretted his foolish bravado the minute the words were out. His bragging might have somehow put Christina at risk. Roundtree left for a moment, and when he returned there were four ugly men accompanying him. "This one is too big for his breeches, boys. What are you going to do about it?"

Lance looked at the men the marshal called "boys," a rough-looking bunch if ever he'd seen one. The bald one was lanky, trigger-happy, and had the face of a lizard. The one with a scraggly beard and gap-toothed smile looked undeniably mean. Then there was the pair who walked so close together that they reminded him of bookends, a humorous fumbling duo as stout as they were tall.

"He thinks he's going to make a fool out of us. He says someone is gonna come and spring him from our nice little jail. Now what do you say, boys?" Suddenly four guns were pointed at Lance, as if it was feared he could walk right through the bars.

The man with the scraggly beard pushed forward while the others aimed their guns to cover him. "Watch him."

As if I would be fool enough to try and escape when I'm a walking target, Lance thought, watching as the man unlocked, then wrenched open the door.

"What are you doing?" As if he didn't know. Though Lance had wanted to be set free he wasn't foolish enough to think that was what was going to happen.

With a sick laugh one of the men grabbed his injured arm, twisting it cruelly.

"Who's going to try and rescue you, Meredith? Tell me and I'll stop the pain," Roundtree said.

Lance bit his lip to help him bear the burning agony, but he wouldn't cry "uncle," and above all he would never even whisper Christina's name.

"Vickery and Jamison," the sign read, the last name appearing in the tiniest of letters. Lance needed a lawyer and he needed one *now,* but so far every lawyer Christina had visited had turned the case down. They were afraid to go up against Marshal Roundtree.

"Well, let's give it one more try."

Dressed in her pants suit and coat, Christina ignored the stares of the townspeople as she crossed her fingers and walked through the doorway. Reaching in her coat pocket, she touched her credit card out of habit. It wouldn't do her any good here, but oh, how she sometimes missed the future's amenities. Still, she had to make due with no money and an awkward awareness of her surroundings. Remembering the dizziness that had come over her when Lance had been taken, she was reminded of how tenuous her presence was here.

"I can't go back now. Not until I've helped him!" And then what? Deep in her heart she knew that as long as Lance was alive, her place was beside him. Alive! It seemed that his future was in her hands.

Entering the small office, she looked around. If lawyers were known to make a more than respectable amount of money, this drab, plainly furnished room did not give a very good recommendation of the occupants. But perhaps that was all for the best. Christina didn't have a penny to her name. She would have to make some kind of arrangement to take care of Lance's legal bills. She would also have to be thrifty, clever and resourceful to get by in the coming days.

"Interesting decor," she said aloud.

There were no rugs on the wooden floor, no large leather chairs, no chandeliers, no paintings or wall hangings. The only furniture was a large mahogany table with two straight-backed wooden chairs and a bookshelf loaded to the ceiling with books. One lone oil lamp gave the room any light. Its flickering flames illuminated a hunched-over figure busily scribbling on a small piece of paper. Had the situation not been so desperate, Christina would have turned around and headed back toward the door.

"May I help you?" A petite tawny-haired woman wearing a suitcoat, tie and spectacles addressed her politely.

Christina spoke right up, anxious to get this matter over and done with. "I'm looking for either Vickery or Jamison," she stated, looking around for either one of those attorneys.

"I'm Jamison," the woman said.

"You?" Christina voiced her surprise. According to what she had read, there hadn't been very many professional women in Paradise in the year 1900. She seemed to have stumbled on one of the few.

"Yes, me." The woman laughed good-naturedly. "I'm Anne Jamison, a bona fide lawyer, I assure you." Putting her small-fingered hand to her temple, she smoothed the tendrils that had escaped from her chignon. "I hope my being female doesn't put you off."

Christina smiled. "To the contrary. I would imagine that you must be twice as good as any male lawyer in town and ten times as gutsy. Being a professional woman myself, I know the rules."

"And just what profession, might I ask?"

"I. . . .I'm a journalist."

"Aha! A newspaperwoman?"

"I suppose you might call me that. I have a degree in journalism. My specialty is doing stories on the life and times of the famous and infamous."

Anne stated her own qualifications. She had studied at Hastings College of Law in San Francisco. More importantly, however, since few lawyers ever graduated from a law school, she had apprenticed herself to Arthur Findley, a noted lawyer. Absorbing all the knowledge that she could from that association, she had passed the California bar examination.

"Alas, despite my accomplishment, California law restricts the legal profession to 'any white male citizen' who can satisfy the requirements of age, moral characater and legal knowledge. Thus I have come to Colorado to establish my career. I want to be more than a glorified legal clerk. I want to be a lawyer in every meaning of the word." She pointed to the sign. "Edward Vickery has given me that chance."

"Then God bless him," Christina declared, feeling an instant kinship with this woman. Quickly she revealed the reason for her visit. "As you know, Lance Meredith has been recaptured. Marshal Roundtree is planning on hanging him in five days. I want a trial."

"A trial? But he has already had one. He was found guilty."

"I know of new evidence that can prove his innocence. Are you brave enough to go up against the marshal and help me?"

Anne responded without hesitation. "I am! It will give

me a chance to make a name for myself.'' Enthusiastically she reached for a piece of paper and a pencil. ''And to tell you the truth, I've always secretly admired Meredith. I think he got the short end of the marshal's stick, if you know what I mean.''

''I know exactly.'' Christina had a very positive feeling about this woman. Together they would win. It just had to turn out that way!

The walls of the jail seemed to be closing in on him. Lance felt helpless and frustrated. How was he ever going to clear himself? He had played cards enough to know that the deck was stacked against him. Just when he had found everything he had ever wanted, when life looked as though it was going to come up with a winning hand, everything had fallen apart.

Through the tiny window of the jail cell Lance could hear the sounds of Paradise, the clatter of wagon and buggy wheels, tinkling piano music and drunken laughter from the saloons, barking dogs, gunshots and hollering from those whooping it up. Lethargically he just lay on his cot, not even bothering to get up until one sound pierced through the ruckus.

''Lance!'' It was Christina's voice, coming from outside.

Lance bolted to his feet and ran to the small barred opening. Clinging to the bars he looked out at her. ''You shouldn't be here. I told the marshal a lie so that you wouldn't be in any trouble. If anyone sees you—''

''He'll hang me too? Good, then we can hang side by side.'' Reaching up, she touched his hand, holding it for a long poignant moment in time. He looked so tired. There were deep circles under his eyes and the stubble of a beard on his chin.

''I've hired a lawyer just like I promised, one who is going to try and get you a retrial.''

''I hope this lawyer knows his law.''

"*Her* law," Christina corrected. "And she does."

"What?" Lance was taken aback.

"Your lawyer is a woman, Lance. Anne Jamison." Motioning to the attorney to come forward, she introduced her to him.

"Christina. . . ." His whisper seemed to ask her if she had suddenly lost her mind. "I've always been in favor of women's suffrage but—"

"But you have your reservations about my qualifications," Anne Jamison said softly. "Don't. To put it bluntly, I'm the best."

Lance started to protest, then thought better of it. This was one argument he just wouldn't win. After all, Christina was a female. From experience he had learned that they stuck together like glue

"I hope you can prove that boast by saving me from the upcoming necktie party."

"I'll do everything I can."

His attitude softened. "I'm sure you will." He had to trust Christina's judgment. She had saved him before. He couldn't believe that she would hire anyone to help him who wasn't top-notch.

Taking out a notebook and pencil, the lawyer wrote something down. "Now, for the record, just where is the money that you and your gang got from the train robbery?"

"Money?" Lance was incredulous. Not one penny had been taken. "There wasn't time to take any money. My men were shot down before they had time to blink, much less open up the safe."

"Ten thousand dollars is missing. The marshal insists you took it and hid it somewhere."

"Bull roar!" The truth hit him right between the eyes. "The marshal must have taken it himself."

Anne turned to Christina. "If we could tie the marshal to the robbery, I think we might have a chance."

"What do you need? Being a journalist had helped me perfect the art of being a snoop." Christina said lightly.

"Just tell me what kind of evidence you want and I'll find a way to come up with it."

"The marshal's ledgers would be a start. He might have some explaining to do if he has more money than a marshal is entitled to."

"The ledgers. . . ." Of course. She remembered from her research that those ledgers had revealed his guilt when they had been found fifty years after his death. Well, she would hurry their discovery.

Christina had often heard it said that "hindsight is twenty-twenty vision." Armed with her knowledge of the marshal's dishonest transactions and unscrupulous dealings, she was determined to prove that saying true. Furthermore, as soon as she had proof, she was going to make certain that the *Paradise Daily* ran the story for everyone in town to see. Nothing was as powerful and persuading as the media. The only problem was, she was running out of time.

"I have to cram a week's worth of detective work into a few hours," she said to Anne, "but I'll get you the proof you need. The rest is up to you."

Christina knew that she had found more than just a lawyer in Anne. She had found a friend and a kindred spirit. Anne had a spare room above the office that she insisted Christina use until she was settled in Paradise. More importantly, Anne wanted to see justice done. She believed in Lance's innocence and didn't want to see him hang for a murder he hadn't committed.

"Lance Meredith was the only man brave enough to go up against a tyrant. He gave people hope. But don't put yourself in any mortal danger. The marshal has proven himself to be a lethal enemy," she advised.

"I'm a journalist. I've gone up against dangerous men before, but I will be careful." The marshal had murdered several men in cold blood. She doubted he would have any qualms about murdering her if the need arose. Still, that wouldn't keep her from paying his home and office a late-night visit.

Armed with Lance's pistol and a hairpin to unlock doors, Christina kept to the shadows as she moved through the streets and alleyways. An eerie silence had fallen over the town of Paradise in the late hours of the night. Only the faraway tinkle of the saloon's piano and the trod of her shoes on the boardwalk sliced through the quiet. She had never felt so alone, so desperate in all her life.

Passing by the scaffold, she averted her eyes, not wanting to give in to the despair such a sight initiated, but the image danced before her eyes nonetheless: Lance dangling from the rope.

"They're going to hang him." She repeated it over and over until at last the reality pounded into her head. *It was really going to happen unless. . . .*

She only had a few hours—so little time to successfully come up against the mockery of justice that had been planned—yet she had to make use of them.

She forced herself to concentrate on the image of Lance safe. Lance free. Lance alive and in her arms. "There must be a way. There just has to be." With that thought in mind she blended into the shadows. According to what she remembered, Roundtree had a secret drawer in his desk where his most intimate papers were kept. She had to find it.

CHAPTER TEN

Lying on his cot, Lance once again contemplated life and death, heaven and hell. And love! How ironic it would be if he found Christina and learned what was important in life only to have to leave it all.

"I won't let them hang me!"

He'd fight every step of the way. He'd denounce Roundtree on the very steps of the scaffold if need be. He wouldn't let them hang him. He had too much to live for.

"Oh, Christina. I can only hope that you and your lawyer friend will be able to come up with *something*." In the meantime, he and Jim Cleary hard tried everything they could think of to break free. Unfortunately, everything they had tried had been thwarted.

"Hanging day is just around the bend, Meredith," one of the jailers announced cheerily, eyeing Lance's discarded hat as if already laying his claim. "Your friend Cleary is scheduled to die tomorrow morning. Then it's only a little longer until it's your turn."

"Yeah, my turn," Lance answered. As the hours dwindled, so did his faith.

"Any last wishes?"

Lance laughed. "Yeah, how about the key to my cell?"

"The only way I'd give it to you was to make you swallow it," was his answer.

An idea was slowly taking root. Lance spoke up. "How about a cigar and a match? I feel the urge for a smoke. Surely even a condemned man has a right to a cigar and some matches."

"Well . . ."

Lance said a silent prayer. "Please . . ."

The jailer thought a moment, then left, returning with one cigar and one match. Fewer than what Lance had wanted but better than nothing.

"Thanks, I'm mighty obliged." Striking the match on the sole of his boot, Lance lit the end. Puffing, he blew the smoke into the air. "Ahhhhh." Leaning back, he watched the jailer settle down in a chair, put his hat over his face, and slip into a nap. Punching a hole in the cot, Lance held the hot tip of the cigar to the straw inside, then blew on it, igniting a fire. It was a fire that spread slowly but it just might be his salvation nonetheless

The smoke choked him as the flames turned into a blaze.

"What the hell?" From the other side of the wall he heard Jim Cleary cough. "What are you doing over there?"

"Trying to get us out of here alive." Lance coughed as he spoke, and so did the jailer as he ran forward.

"What in tarnation do you think you're doing?" His eyes bugged with anger. "Why, you. . . ." He ran forward, his ring of keys in hand. There was no way for him to put out the fire without opening the cell, which was exactly what Lance was waiting for. The moment he stepped inside, Lance jumped him.

"You bastard!" The jailer swung his fists but Lance was stronger. He was fighting for his life and for Jim's. He had nothing to lose.

The two men rolled over and over on the floor, first

the jailer on top, then Lance, struggling for the gun. Pinning his adversary around the neck by way of a stranglehold, Lance choked him until he gagged. "Give me the gun! Quickly! Do it or I'll squeeze until your eyes pop out!"

Fearful that Lance might well make good on his threat, the man gave up his revolver, throwing it to the far side of the cell. And all the while the flames grew higher and higher. "For God's sake, let me out of here!"

"Jim, get ready. We're walking out of here!"

Lance's jaw ached where he'd been hit, but he ignored it as he crawled on his hands and knees on the floor toward the gun. His hand grabbed it and squeezed it as he held it up.

"We'll burn to death!" the jailer cried.

"Not we, *you*. Jim and I are going, but I'll leave you here," Lance threatened, but not being a cold-blooded murderer, he reneged on his vow and therein came his defeat. Reaching down to give the man a hand up, he was caught in a bear hug. His hope of escape was put to an end when the jailer yelled at the top of his lungs. The marshal and the other two guards heeded the call in an instant.

Lance was easily overpowered and beaten and kicked into submission. He could only watch from his sprawled position on the floor as the marshal doused the flames. Then he was shoved back in the cell.

"If you know what's good for you, you won't try to escape again."

Lance's lips curled into a rebellious smile. "To the contrary, Marshal. If I know what's good for me, I will."

It was great to be back in the newspaper business, Christina thought as she watched the printer apply ink to the type form with a roller. She'd wanted a miracle and she had been given one. After breaking into the marshal's office, she artfully had used a hairpin to unlock the drawer of his desk and had found enough evidence to put him where Lance was. In jail. Better yet, she had found the bag with the money in it. Now all she had to do was set the marshal up for a fall by having his little stash of money confiscated. In the meantime, she had talked the editor of the *Paradise Daily* into letting her write an article that would set all of Paradise on its ear.

How she loved the sense of anticipation that crackled in the air, the smell of the paper and ink, the clanking sound of the Washington Hand Press as the blank sheets of paper became newsprint. It made her feel invigorated. Useful. Alive! Made her feel empowered. She'd found a place for herself after all in this century.

"Well, roll up your sleeves and let's get to work." Bart Mathews, the editor of the *Daily,* took off his coat and tie and did just that, keeping his white linen sleeves in place with elastic. He handed Christina a large apron, then, with both arms moving up and down like pump handles, he gave instructions to the *Daily* staff that would turn Christina's scribbling into an article, one she was sure would raise more than a few brows. If all went well, she would be able to get Lance a new trial.

"I think Roundtree is in for one big surprise," Mathews exclaimed, punctuating his sentence with a large puff of smoke.

"His game is up," Christina said with exultation. What's more, Mathews had hired her on as a reporter. He wanted an article a week. It was his plan to expose Roundtree and his operation bit by bit, story by story, knowing it to be a way to increase his readership.

"I'll help you and you help me. We'll pat each other on the back and both come out winners," Mathews stated.

"With all that I've found out about Roundtree, I could be writing stories for a long, long while."

Christina was amazed. Even the history books had not fully exposed all that the dishonest marshal had done, dipping into the profits of saloons, gambling houses and other businesses, and even peddling laudanum to the houses of prostitution. Not to mention cold-blooded murder, extortion and thievery. Mathews hoped that some of the townsmen would be so brave as to come forward with their own stories.

"With all I've found out, I know Lance will be given a new trial. It's Roundtree that should hang, not him!" Christina felt excitement surge within her as she joined in on the actual printing. She placed the sheet of paper on the hinged wooden tympan, folded it over the type, and then slid the bed bearing the form into position beneath the cloth-covered platen. By pulling the lever she caused the plate to press the paper against the type and produce an impression. A system of toggle levers kept the plate from moving and smudging the print when the bar's leverage forced it downward.

"There!" Taking the paper off the tympan, she was careful not to ruin the ink. "A complete detailing of the marshal's finances."

Taking into account Roundtree's salary as marshal, minus his expenditures and the value of properties and goods, he should have come out severely in the red. That he did not meant only one thing. Even so, Christina was wise enough to know that you just can't call a man a thief unless you can prove that he is. Thus, with the help of Anne, Mathews and the widows of the men Roundtree had murdered, they had employed a spy to do some nosing around in Central City and Golden. It seemed Roundtree's evil had deep roots. Deep enough to hang him!

CHAPTER ELEVEN

Marshal Roundtree, fearful that somehow Lance would escape, had moved the hanging up. Lance and Jim would hang together. In less than half an hour.

The clock on the jailhouse wall displayed the time as half past eleven. There were just thirty minutes left before they were scheduled to die. Lance stared sullenly at the hour and minute hands. Each minute that passed brought the moment of reckoning closer.

"She doesn't know. She won't have time. . . ." Somewhere along the line he must have angered old Father Time. Now he was exacting his revenge.

Lance had just finished cinching his buckle and was tucking the collar beneath the neck of his shirt when one of the jailers came to the door of the cell. "What are you doing?"

"Just making sure I look presentable," Lance answered sarcastically. "A man wants to look his best at his hanging."

The jailer was dubious. "Yeah, well ain't that nice."

Moving his hand up to his chin, Lance ran his fingers over the stubble. "Don't suppose you'd let me take time for a shave? So I'd look nice for the ladies present?"

"Yeah, me too. I'd like a shave." Jim Cleary was likewise anxious to buy some time.

Lance laughed. At least he had his sense of humor. "That thatch of red will take more than just a razor. How about an ax?"

"An ax will be just fine."

The jailer wasn't in the mood for a joke. "Where you're both going it won't matter if you're clean-shaven or not." The barrels of six guns were aimed at Jim and Lance as the jailer opened the door. "Now, come on. The time has come."

Bad news always seems to travel fast. Nevertheless, Christina was stunned by the disasterous turn of events. Her face was ashen as Anne informed her of Marshal Roundtree's new hanging schedule. "The hanging has been moved up."

"What do you mean?" Christina's heart skipped a beat.

"It's today!"

"No!" Time had seemingly run out! Even so Christina tried to remain calm. "Tell me what's going on, Anne. What have you heard?"

"Marshal Roundtree is going to hang Jim Cleary and Lance Meredith side by side. There'll be two nooses instead of just one."

Christina's hands and knees trembled in unison. Her stomach seemed to coil up in a knot and stay there. "When is the hanging?" How much time did she have?

"I'd say in about fifteen minutes."

Christina forced herself to remain calm. Dissolving into a blubbering, quivering display of womanly weakness wouldn't do Lance any good at all. "Oh, Lance," she breathed.

She had to move quickly. Somehow she had to move heaven and earth to get a stay of execution.

Escape was impossible with so many guns and eyes trained upon them, but then even the best-laid plans were often prone to failure. Intellectually Lance was prepared for the possibility that there would be no last-minute reprieve, but emotionally he could not help but be on edge. He didn't want to die! Hadn't prepared himself to meet his Maker just yet. He had thought. . . .

Above his head Lance could see a spider hanging from its web and he shuddered as it reminded him of his own fate. "Well, I guess at least we're in good company, Jimmy," he said, trying to make light of it.

"Would you like me to say a prayer?" One of the guards pulled out a Bible.

"Yes, say a prayer for me that Roundtree will change his mind." Roughly his hands were tied behind his back. "I seem to remember enacting this scene once before."

"Yeah, but this time there won't be anyone to whisk you out beneath our noses." The jailer took out his keys and opened first one creaking door, then the other. Lance and Jim were led out into the corridor. Sandwiched between the guards, they walked in their gruesome procession. It was a death march and it felt and looked like one, but Lance walked as slowly as he could. He needed more time, had to buy himself as many extra minutes as he could.

"Christina. . . ." He wanted to see her one more time. Then perhaps he could die a happy man. A jab to his ribs hastened him along.

Lance shivered as he stepped through the outer door. The sun was at its zenith. It was unseasonably warm. "A fine day for a hanging," Lance heard one of the guards declare as they walked by the scaffold. "A mighty fine day, indeed."

"Up the steps, Meredith. You too, Cleary!"

They walked up the twelve makeshift wooden stairs of the scaffold very slowly, searching the crowd that was quickly gathering. There was no sign of Christina. Lance could only assume that she didn't know

"Lance Meredith, Jim Cleary, you have been tried and found guilty of robbery and murder by the court of Paradise, Colorado. May God have mercy on your souls!" Marshal Roundtree sounded authoritative, the very epitome of justice, but his composure faltered for just a moment as he looked around him. People were staring, not at his prisoners but at him.

"What in blazes are they gawking at?"

"I don't know."

"They're pointing their fingers and staring."

It seemed to trouble the marshal. Even so, he continued, "Do you have any last words?"

Any last words? A rapid succession of emotions stormed through Lance's brain. Hell, he thought, he had enough of a speech planned to take all day, all on the injustice of a system that allowed men to be cheated of their lives while people like Roundtree walked around free. "People of Paradise, I declare to you that I am innocent, but I wonder if your marshal can say—"

"Enough!" Lance was quickly silenced, though at least he had caused even more people to stare.

"The rope."

It seemed they were in a real hurry to hang him. Lance looked around for Christina again but didn't see any sign of her. Fear that she had somehow been called back to her own time chilled him. Seeing her again was important to him.

A drumroll sounded as the hangman looped the rope over Jim Cleary's neck, then another rope around Lance's neck. "I just want you to know that I'm proud to have been your friend," Jim Cleary croaked. "I always said I'd follow you into heaven or hell. Guess we'll soon see where we end up."

"Wait!"

All heads snapped around to look at the blond woman and her companion.

"I have a document. There won't be any hanging. Unless it's yours, Roundtree!"

"Really?"

"Really." Anne Jamison thrust the document to within inches of the marshal's face. She turned to the guards. "Arrest this man."

Christina used the moment of confusion to hurriedly cut the ropes from around Lance's and Jim's necks. Then she put her arms around Lance's neck.

CHAPTER TWELVE

The courtroom was packed wall to wall. It was warm in the room despite the chill of the day—so warm that Christina had to loosen the collar of her blouse so she could breathe. She felt dizzy. The excitement of the moment, she supposed. And who wouldn't be excited? She was witnessing the unfolding of a historical event that she had initiated.

People had come from miles around to witness the trial of Lance Meredith, the last great desperado. For the last few years, outlaws who could remain at large for long enough to brag about it were becoming about as rare as a white buffalo, some whispered.

Newspaper reporters from such places as Denver, Georgetown, Central City and Leadville elbowed each other out of the way for an interview with the infamous outlaw leader. Alas, it did them no good. Christina had been granted an "exclusive" interview for what some were calling the "trial of the new century."

"Ha! A woman reporter and a woman lawyer. What is the world coming to?" she heard one irritated male citizen of Paradise say.

Christina just smiled, though she wanted to tell him that he hadn't seen anything yet. She was determined to handle herself with poise and professionalism. Dressed in a fashionable jacket and skirt, she looked slim and almost fragile, but her expression showed that she definitely knew what it took to be a top-notch reporter.

Lance sat at the defense table. He looked tougher, leaner and surer of himself than he ever had before. Looking back over his shoulder at her, he boldly winked as if to say that everything was going to be just fine.

You're going to win, Lance. The people of Paradise are sympathetic to your cause. They know you did a lot of good. To them you're a hero, Christina thought. The *Paradise Daily* had taken a poll. Eighty percent of the people thought Lance Meredith was more philanthropist than thief.

"I don't think you've talked with any of the bankers," Lance had replied when she told him. "I just hope there aren't any on the jury."

"It doesn't matter," she had said. "The people admire you for your courage in trying to stop that train robbery. You'll be freed. Bravery is rewarded. You'll see." Even so, it irked her that there wasn't even one woman on the jury. The subject promised to become the topic of a story in the coming days.

There was a buzz of voices as everyone discussed the upcoming proceedings but they all hushed as the large double doors at the far end of the room opened. There was a stir in the courtroom. People stood up as the judge entered. Christina assessed him. Dressed all in black, he looked awesome and unforgiving. Hastily she scribbled down for her readers a vivid description.

"You may all be seated," the judge ordered sternly.

Christina assessed the lawyers on the case. Anne Jamison, dressed somberly in a suit of dark brown, looked knowledgeable and formidable. The prosecutor was all smiles.

Let him feel confident, Christina thought. He was obviously amused by the turn of events, certain that no one would take a woman lawyer seriously, or a lady reporter for that matter. *Little does he know.*

Indeed, Anne had a few surprises up her sleeve, such as insisting that Marshal Roundtree be called upon as a witness. Neither he nor his lawyer knew that she had likewise called upon a mystery witness, none other than the marshal's better half. As for Roundtree's banker, a warrant for his arrest had been issued, making certain that he too would be at the trial today.

The prosecutor went first, offering evidence against Lance. He called several bankers to the stand who described the bank robberies the Meredith gang had committed. His voice was loud and clear, carrying throughout the hushed courtroom. Christina leaned forward with a curiosity that turned to anger at the blatant ties he told. Lies that were quickly made evident when Anne took her turn.

"I have a copy of Marshal Roundtree's savings accounts. From the figures I'm looking at, it is apparent that he has amassed quite a significant fortune in the span of three years. Considering the fact that his salary as marshal is ten dollars a week, how can you explain that?"

"The marshal is very thrifty?"

Before he was excused from the witness chair, Anne had managed to expose not only marshal Roundtree's double-dealings but the banker's dishonesty as well. Now there were two men in hot water.

Lance focused his attention on the woman who held his life in her hands and the men who would decide his fate. For the first time since this had all happened, he actually felt that he would be freed. Anne's sharp mind had been trained to notice everything at once, a gift that she exercised now in the crowded courtroom.

The trial was short and sweet. What touched Lance's heart most was that Christina stepped forward as a witness in his defense, telling about his honesty, his caring, his bravery in riding into danger in order to stop the train robbery. When the prosecution tried to belittle him, calling him another Jesse James, she was his fiercest advocate, showing her love for him with every word.

"Mr. Meredith borrowed from the rich in order to help those in need," he heard her say. "If in fact he were the scoundrel you insist, he would be a wealthy man. I saw for myself that he was not. But someone sitting here in the courtroom is. He is the real thief, as can be proven." She revealed her search of his office for evidence, informing the listeners about the money from the train robbery. "Lance didn't take it. Marshal Roundtree did."

Several of the widows were called upon next. They all spoke highly of Lance, told of how hard he had worked and of his integrity. Each and every one of them proclaimed him to be a saint. He had given them understanding and hope.

It was then that Anne pounced. All eyes swept toward the back of the door as a mystery woman appeared. Dressed all in black, her bright red hair hidden under a hat, Angelica Roundtree was nonetheless breathtaking.

"Why, you doublecrossing. . ." James Roundtree sputtered his outrage when she enumerated several wrongdoings her husband had initiated against the citizenry, only to blame it on the Meredith gang.

"Sorry, darling," she calmly replied, "but I'm not lying for you any longer. I know for certain that I wouldn't like to be in jail."

Pandemonium broke out in the court as Marshal Roundtree's misdeeds came to light. Despite the prosecution attorney's indignant statement that Lance Meredith and not the marshal was on trial, it was apparent that he soon would be.

The excitement was only beginning, however. When she perceived that the time was right, Anne called Lance Meredith to the stand. Armed with clever questions, she soon convinced both onlookers and the jury that he and his outlaws were the Western equivalent of Robin Hood and his band.

The jury debated for less than ten minutes, and when they returned a verdict of not guilty was read. *Not guilty.* The courtroom broke out into wild applause and hoots of congratulations. Though they had first looked upon Anne as doubting Thomases, it was clear that all of Paradise now admired her tenacity and wisdom. It was a certainty that she would have no trouble getting clients.

The judge rapped his gavel. Not only was Lance freed, but Jim Cleary and the surviving members of the gang were given amnesty as well, on the condition that they would give up their outlaw ways.

What might have ended in great sadness ended in a triumph.

Looking up, Lance's eyes were filled with love as he saw Christina coming toward him. Wordlessly he gathered her into his arms. "So, as of this moment I'm no longer an outlaw but an honest man. From now on I'm going to have to make an honest living. Any ideas?"

"How about becoming a lawyer. Anne is going to be so busy now she could use a partner."

"Hmmm. Work on the other side of the law." The idea appealed to him. It would be a way to help people in need. He was silent a moment, then asked, "What about you?" He was concerned that she might miss her own time period, now that the excitement in Paradise was over. "If you could, would you want to go back?"

"Never! My heart is here with you." Even so, she had an overwhelming feeling that her time with Lance was coming to an end. She felt it all the way down to her toes, that same feeling she had the day of his hanging. That surrealistic feeling, as if she were viewing the world through a thin strip of gauze.

"And my heart is with you. I owe you so much." Oblivious of the people around them, he kissed her and murmured over and over again how much he loved her.

"You're going to live to be a ripe old age, I just know it." And she had wanted to grow old beside him. "You have it in you to do great things. I always felt that. If you were only given the chance.''

"Together. We'll do great things.'' Lance had it all planned, knowing how much she inspired him.

Christina looked up at him. Her fingers brushed against his face. "I'll love you forever.'' She took a step backward, fighting against the wave of dizziness that swept over her.

Through a fog she heard a voice. *"Hey, Christy, turn around. We need to get a final reading on these lights before the broadcast. We're on in ten minutes."*

Helplessly her hands groped for Lance's hand so that she could regain her balance, but it did no good. She felt as if she were falling. . . .

"Careful, Miss Phillips. It's slick. Here, let me help you up!''

Tears stung Christina's eyes. She knew where she was without bothering to look.

"There's just a few minutes before the broadcast. Let me help you up,'' a husky male voice said again.

Christina looked up. Her heart pounded. "Lance?'' For just a moment she thought it was him. But no. Something about the eyes. They were different. Brown, not blue. It wasn't him. And yet. . . .

"My name is Lance. How did you know?'' The dark-haired man smiled. "Lance Meredith. I'm named after my great-grandfather.''

"Your great-grandfather. . . .'' The words stuck in her throat. So Lance had married someone else. And yet, what did she expect?

"We don't have much time to talk now, but I'd like to get to know you. Perhaps after the broadcast. . . .''

Christina didn't have time to answer. The cameras were rolling. She read the script from the teleprompter. "Welcome to *Century Twenty-one*. Today's story celebrates the life and times of Lance Meredith on this anniversary of his acquittal. Please join us while we honor him by renaming Paradise . . .''

She couldn't help but smile as she read her lines and finished the segment. She was proud of him. Proud of herself. Paradise, Colorado, was now going to be called ''Meredithville'' in honor of its greatest philanthropist, a man who had devoted his life to helping others. A man who had made a positive difference in so many people's lives.

''Oh, Lance, you kept your promise.'' And then some. Her visit to the past *did* have positive consequences. Still, it grieved her that the man she loved was now only a memory. He was part of the past. She was part of now. They'd had so little time together. And yet she had loved him!

''Miss Phillips, that was an excellent show. I'm impressed.''

Turning around, Christina was once again fascinated by the resemblance this Lance Meredith had to the other Lance. ''Christina. My name's Christina. Please . . .''

''Christina!'' Lance Meredith smiled. ''Strange, but you remind me of someone.''

''Who?''

''There was a woman who actually saved my grandfather's life. A newspaper reporter for the *Paradise Daily* took her picture the day of that trial.''

Christina held her breath, then let it out in a whisper. ''What happened to her?''

He shrugged his broad shoulders. ''She disappeared without a trace. My great-grandfather insisted that she had come from the future and that she had gone back to her own time.'' He looked embarrassed. ''It was the only time anyone ever questioned his sanity. He was a wise man.''

''From the future . . . Really . . .''

''I know it sounds . . . well . . . strange . . . but . . .'' Reaching in his coat pocket, he pulled out an object the size of a pencil. He handed it to Christina. "How else can you explain this?"

Christina gasped as she recognized her flashlight. The one they had used in the mine tunnel. *A hundred years ago . . .*

"It was his greatest treasure. An heirloom he held, to be priceless. I really can't explain how he came to have it before flashlights were even invented but. . . ."

There was something about this man. The way he looked at her, the way he held his head. His smile! Somehow, despite the fact that she had just met him, Christina felt warm and secure in his company.

"I haven't eaten. Would you like to have dinner with me?"

"I'd love to!" Christina reached in her pocket for her keys. They were still there. "I have my car."

"So do I. I'll drive!"

As they walked to his car they talked about many things. Just like his great-grandfather, he was easy to talk to. It didn't take Christina long to realize how much they had in common. They liked the same kind of music. Read the same kind of books. Were glued to the TV when the Denver Broncos were playing. Had a passion for Western lore. And yet there were subtle differences too.

Christina had friends who talked about "soul mates." She hadn't belived such a thing existed, until now.

"What were you thinking just then?" It seemed to be the most natural thing in the world for him to reach for her hand as he asked the question.

"Oh, I was just thinking about the Meredith gang. Their hideout was up on Lookout Mountain." It was a place that held both good and bad memories for her.

There was a look of pride on his face as he said, "I have a house up there, built on the very same spot." He stopped and looked deep into her eyes. "I don't want to rush anything, but I'd like for you to see it one of these days."

She laughed. "I don't want to rush anything either, but

I'd love to see it!'' She wondered what he would think if she told him she had been there before, a hundred years ago.

Someday she'd tell him. Someday . . .

WINTER SONG

LISA PLUMLEY

*To my editor, John Scognamiglio
whose enthusiasm and creativity
inspire me to reach farther and write
better
and
to my husband, John Plumley,
whose love makes romance real, every
single day*

CHAPTER ONE

New Year's Eve
Present Day

The Old West owed its legends to dance music, jalapeño buffalo wings, and margaritas, Jolie Alexander decided sometime after midnight. Or, more specifically, to the lack of them.

Any one of the triumvirate would have felled the old-time gunslingers and pioneers she'd spent the past nine months learning about. Taken together, the techno-revved beat, blistering food, and frosty alcohol would have squelched their urge to tame the frontier in a heartbeat. Especially in a place as raw and inexplicably desolate as the mountainous former ghost town of Avalanche, Arizona, in the middle of a snowbound January night.

But snow and stars and pioneers aside, the celebratory vibe-wings-and-'rita trio had definitely done its work *inside,* at her supposedly sedate investors' New Year's gala.

With mingled pride and watchfulness, Jolie surveyed the scene. Below her vantage point on the second-floor

landing of her newly constructed faux saloon, partygoers
thronged the dance floor, dressed in everything from
beaded designer evening gowns to cowboy hats. Her investors, assorted FantaSee, Inc. colleagues and supervi-
sors, and recently hired Wild West cast members mingled,
danced, and tossed back hors d'oeuvres with a practiced
ease, mixing business with pleasure even more enthusiastically than she'd dared hope.

In their midst, the caterer's uniformed staff glided
across the sawdust-strewn laminate floorboards, offering
trays of cactus coolers, sarsaparilla, and green gecko margaritas. Multicolored lights twinkled from the exposed
rafters, and the spicy aroma of chili-laden Southwestern
cuisine filled the air. Thanks to the exclusive Los Angeles
chef Jolie had coaxed into appearing at her attraction's
launch party, the appetizers' kick was unrivaled—except
by the music.

No less seduced by its pulsing rhythm than her guests
were, Jolie rocked her hips back and forth, feeling her
strappy black cocktail dress shimmy higher up her stockinged thighs with every gyration. She wanted to feel deca-
dent. Wanted to dance and drink and celebrate the
accomplishment of more than a half-year's work. Wanted
to step out of the shadows—literally—and bask in the
approval she must surely have earned with this project.

She couldn't. Instead, remaining half-hidden in the
shadows outside her second-floor office, Jolie nodded her
head in time with the DJ's latest selection and watched
the party's progress a little longer. As much as she yearned
to join in, she knew she would stay on the outside. For
now. Soon, she would be so accomplished that nothing
could keep her from the spotlight, she promised herself.

Until then—until she'd earned the accolades she longed
for—there was work to be done.

Dozens of tasks still vied for her attention. There were
supplies to order, additional cast members to hire, insurance to select and pay for. Costumes to purchase, tickets
and brochures to be printed, advertising to arrange. She'd

come to the mountains of northern Arizona to launch the latest in a series of award-winning theme parks, not to party amidst strobe lights and a lot of schmaltzy back-slapping.

She could do without all that. Sure, the Go West! theme park's plans were drawn. Yes, the prototype saloon's construction had been finished with time to spare, just before the first snowfall. But Jolie hadn't become Fanta-See, Inc.'s youngest and most successful exec by waiting around for somebody else to see to the details.

There had been hints of a promotion, if all went well with tonight's schmooze-fest. More responsibility. More travel. More pole-vaulting up the rungs of the career ladder she'd been eyeballing since graduating from college two years ago, with nothing but an MBA and ambition to keep her warm at night.

Jolie raised her curvy margarita glass in a toast to the glittering revelers below. "Congratulations, Alexander. You've hit the big time at last!"

No one looked up. The music swallowed her self-made tribute, leaving her with a slippery glass and a trembling grasp on her sense of accomplishment. Funny how making a toast to yourself didn't have quite the same élan as someone else's acknowledgment did.

Memo to Jolie, she thought with a twist of her lips. *Hire somebody to compose toasts and perform other ego-boosting activities. No references necessary.* What were career experience, a stock portfolio, and an expense account good for, if not for making her feel fabulous?

She'd sure as heck given up plenty to get them.

Frowning, Jolie sipped the margarita her assistant had shoved into her hand on the way upstairs. *Enough with the gloom-and-doom squad,* she told herself. She'd created the life she had all by herself, and had done it knowingly. Nobody had strong-armed her into postponing a personal life for the sake of a career. Nobody had glued the cell phone to her ear or the day planner to her hip . . . or forced those frequent-flyer miles' worth of business trips onto her laptop's accounting program.

But nobody had warned her it would be this lonely, either.

Oh, boy. Wincing at her uncharacteristically maudlin thoughts, determined to work herself into a festive mood, Jolie swallowed more of her margarita. Its icy tartness slipped between her lips with the ease of a kiss, then traced a path to her belly. That was better. Who said drinking on an empty stomach was a bad idea?

With the same deliberation with which she did everything, Jolie drank a little more. Everyone was entitled to a few regrets, especially on New Year's Eve. The secret was in not going crazy trying to undo them all at once.

Halfway through her drink, she sneaked a glance at her platinum watch bracelet. Just before one o'clock in the morning. Nearly time for the festivities to wind to a close. And nearly time for the hostess's encore appearance. With a decisive gesture, Jolie drained her margarita and left her glass atop the banister.

New Year's Day was a time for new beginnings, she told herself as she clicked her way downstairs in her high heels. A time for starting over.

Who knew what the days to come might hold for her? Suddenly, the possibilities seemed endless.

By the time Jolie had shepherded the last party guest onto the last chartered bus headed for the college town of Flagstaff, several miles distant, the night seemed more endless than those possibilities she'd been thinking of earlier. Only the promise of the Snowbowl skiing trip she'd already arranged for tomorrow had been enough to coax her investors and colleagues onto the bus and into the darkness toward cozy lodgings and civilization.

It definitely paid to plan ahead.

Huddled in her hooded down-filled parka, Jolie watched with relief as the bus chugged onto the snowbank-bordered road. On either side of it, white-shrouded pines rose into the night sky. At this altitude, and with the sky so icy clear, the stars looked close enough to touch. They glittered over the pine and oak forest by the millions. The sight of them never failed to steal the breath from even the most jaded of tourists—including tonight's guests.

And Jolie.

Having never thought of herself as the type to stand still and gape at constellations, Jolie had to smile. She guessed everybody had to stop to admire beauty like that at least once in a lifetime. Even ambitious tourism execs with more degreed initials after their names than lasting relationships to their credit.

Besides, could she help it if ambition and romance didn't exactly cozy up together at night?

Ahead, the bus paused at the turn onto the winding two-lane highway. Its taillights shone through a plume of hazy exhaust, then dipped out of sight. With a final wave, Jolie turned her gaze from the road to the snowy clearing around her. Her domain, her staff jokingly called it. Twenty acres of pines and meadows and possibilities, just waiting to be transformed into another of the tourist attractions she was rapidly becoming known for in the industry.

The sound of footfalls tromping through the snow broke the stillness. With a muffled exclamation, Erin Delaney skidded to a stop beside Jolie.

She raised the clipboard she held in mittened hands. "That's the last one, boss. Sheesh, I thought they'd never leave. Who'd have thought a bunch of stuffed-shirt investors and FantaSee bigwigs would have that kind of staying power?"

"Anybody who's golfed with them," Jolie said, holding back the edge of her faux-fur-trimmed hood to grin at her assistant. "I barely wrenched them from the golf courses in Phoenix as it was. I'd swear they jumped off the plane from Boston with putters in their hands."

Of course, when she'd arrived from Boston last April,

Jolie had all but jumped off the plane herself—with a swimsuit in her hand. After a damp springtime back east, Arizona had felt like a sun-baked heaven on earth. With no family to lure her back home—other than distant relatives of the parents she barely remembered—she had been tempted to stay in the Southwest forever.

Still was tempted, in fact.

For some reason, Arizona felt like home to her. She couldn't explain it any more than she could resist it. The magical sensation of homecoming had persisted all during her stay here . . . and had only increased when she'd first stepped onto the rocky soil that had once housed a ghost town called Avalanche.

A brisk, snowflake-sprinkled wind swept through the pines, ruffling the papers on Erin's clipboard. Jolie reached for it, and cast aside her whimsical thoughts. "I'll take care of this, Erin. You've done a great job tonight. Thanks for all your help."

"You're welcome. It was fun, wasn't it?"

Jolie nodded. "Sure. Lucrative, too. Did you see how fast everyone snapped up those raffle tickets?"

It seemed everyone had wanted a chance to win the saloon piano they'd found in one of the dilapidated ghost town buildings and painstakingly restored. Even Jolie had succumbed, and bought two tickets for herself.

"Anything for a good cause, I guess," Erin said. "That was a brilliant idea you had, to use the raffle winnings to send inner-city school kids from Phoenix to Go West! when it opens next year."

"Well, ideas like that are why I earn the big bucks," Jolie said with a teasing smile. "Too bad I won't be here when they visit."

Turning, she gestured for Erin to accompany her back to the saloon. They walked together through the moonlit snow, their knee-high boots packing the drifts into an improvised pathway.

"You're right." Beneath her cropped red hair, Erin's face scrunched in a frown. "By then, we'll be visiting investors, drumming up enthusiasm for the next FantaSee attraction.''

Jolie murmured her agreement . . . but kept the sudden sadness she felt to herself. There was no point in burdening Erin with whatever New Year's angst had struck tonight. After all, as her oldest college friend—and all that passed for family in her life—Erin deserved better.

Inside the saloon, warmth and dazzling light blasted them both, stealing some of the melancholy from Jolie's heart.

"Thank God for central heating and electric lights," she said, peeling off her scarf as she tromped to the brass-trimmed faux-mahogany laminate bar. She propped her booted foot onto the bar rail and looked at Erin, watching her pull her car keys from the depths of her purse. "I don't know how the pioneers survived without them."

"I don't know how you survive out here *with* them. Sure you don't want to drive into town with me, instead of shacking up on that cot in your office tonight?"

Jolie yawned, pausing in the act of unbuttoning her parka. "Nah. Thanks, anyway. I've still got more work to do."

"Now?" Erin crossed her arms and gaped at her. "Not even you could be that much of a workaholic."

Well . . . actually, she could. Jolie winced. But in her defense, at least work promised rewards—unlike the rest of life, which was about as predictable as a lotto winner and as controllable as the weather. Judging by the obvious disbelief on her friend's face, though, tonight wasn't the time to compare philosophies.

"I'm not. But I don't mind staying here. I know my office digs aren't fancy, but . . ." *But they feel closer to home than anywhere else.* Jolie shrugged. "But they'll do. You go on. I'll see you tomorrow."

"Okay, see you then." With a smile and a wave, Erin tramped to the saloon's exit, then paused on the threshold with one hand on the door. "Don't forget that New Year's wish I told you about. My granny always said it was good luck to make a wish before sunrise on New Year's Day.''

''Sure. Make a wish. Gotcha.'' Jolie waved her assistant out the door, then dropped her scarf amongst the scattered confetti and empty cocktail glasses littering the bar. Propping her elbows on the laminate beside the puddled red knit, she rested her chin in her palms and looked around the re-created saloon that months of work had wrought.

Her gaze stopped on the ornate gilt mirror behind the bar. Spying her image in it, Jolie remembered Erin's words and frowned.

''Who are you kidding, hotshot?'' she asked her reflection. Her dark-haired likeness scowled defiantly back at her, backlit with multicolored lights and incongruously dressed in a padded parka and skimpy evening dress. ''*You* make wishes like you stop to look at the stars. Once in a lifetime.''

CHAPTER TWO

Sighing, Jolie heaved her elbows from the bar. She clomped across the saloon and locked up, checking the fire exit and windows as a matter of habit, then set the security system. Her snow boots kicked up cheerful drifts of confetti as she crossed the room again, headed for the staircase. She batted a rafter-strung balloon, wove around a stack of empty serving trays waiting for the cleaning crew tomorrow . . . and found herself thinking of Erin's parting words once more.

Once in a lifetime. Well, it only took once to make a wish come true, she reasoned.

With sudden decisiveness, Jolie stopped in front of the saloon's piano. She plunked onto the polished wooden bench. Looked around with a surge of unwelcome self-consciousness. Her staff would have the laugh of a lifetime if they caught their no-nonsense boss indulging in anything so unlikely as a wish.

The question was—what to wish for? Mulling over the possibilities, she gathered several pages of Go West! character specifications from the piano's surface, then tapped the pages to square them and lay the stack aside.

The townspeople's roles they described wouldn't be filled
for weeks, after a lengthy interview process spearheaded
by Erin. Looking at the papers now, Jolie smiled. Design-
ing the Old West characters had been fun. Too bad she
couldn't design a new beginning for herself just as easily.

On the other hand, that was what the wish was for,
wasn't it? Thoughtfully, Jolie ran her hands over the
restored saloon piano's keyboard. The aged ivory felt
smooth beneath her fingertips. Cool. Savoring the sensation, she pressed a little harder.

Discordant notes filled the air, chosen too much at
random to be called a melody. All the same, she grinned.
There was something comfortable about sitting at the old
piano. Something joyful in playing it, without a goal in
mind or an evaluation at the end of it. Feeling her smile
broaden, she let her fingers flow over the keys.

As though the music had whipped up all her unfulfilled
yearnings, she thought of things to wish for. Security.
Success. Health. Friendship. Respect.

She had them all, Jolie realized with a sinking feeling.
Had everything people typically wanted . . . and still felt
unsatisfied. What was the matter with her, that she could
have so much and still want more? Dispirited, she stopped
playing.

A flicker of movement at the upright piano's top captured her gaze. One of the papers from the stack of character scripts and specifications fluttered, then drifted over
the edge.

It dropped onto the keys, a sheet of manila-colored
paper with curled edges and lines of music imprinted on
one side. Jolie stared. *That* hadn't been in the stack she'd
straightened. She touched it, meaning to examine it more
closely. Instead, the unexpected fragility of the paper
made her pause.

Where had it come from? The sheet of music looked old
enough to disintegrate with a sneeze—unfortunate, considering the faint line of dust along one edge. It must have

been wedged beneath the piano top somehow, although how the restorer had missed finding it, she couldn't imagine.

Carefully, Jolie straightened it. Above the lines of bars and notes, elaborately lettered script proclaimed the music as a "Winter Love Song."

Her heart pounded. *Love.* That was what she wanted. What she'd yearned for. What she'd never found. And in that moment, she knew without a doubt what her wish would be.

With trembling fingers, she propped the sheet music above the keys. This time when she poised her hands atop the ivories, a new sense of excitement filled her. *I wish for love,* Jolie thought. *I wish for the love of a lifetime.*

Feeling immeasurably cheered, she played the first notes. Their beautiful sound rose to the rafters, filling the whole saloon with a melody unlike anything Jolie had ever heard before. Listening in wonder, she went on playing. Jolie barely glanced at the sheet music. Barely needed to. Never had she played so well, or so effortlessly. It was almost as though the song took on a spirit of its own . . . almost as though it needed her, and only her, to set its magic free.

"I wish for love," she whispered. "Love!"

Tears stung her eyes and blurred the page before her. Even so, Jolie went on playing. The music grew stronger, filling the party-cluttered space around her. The glossy laminate-and-particleboard furnishings receded, beyond Jolie's notice as the poignant melody swept her to a place of wonder.

Beneath her fingers, the piano's keys slowly brightened. The ivory took on a new gleam. Almost imperceptibly, the keys grew straighter, as years' worth of stroking vanished from their worn surfaces. The changes lent a new gracefulness to Jolie's playing, and coaxed her into continuing the winter song.

Love, love.

"I wish for love!" Jolie yelled, raising her face to the

multicolored lights strung above. Lights which, a part of her noticed, seemed to have gone inexplicably dim. A power outage? Maybe. She didn't care. Something told her this wishing business of Erin's had merit—and Jolie was not a person who did things halfway. "Love, love, love! I wish for love!"

"Love be damned!" A hoarse-sounding male voice shouted the words, straight into Jolie's ear. "All I'm wishing for is some blasted peace and quiet!"

A large masculine hand clamped over hers. It squashed her fingers against the piano keys, sending several notes wheezing into the air. With a shriek of surprise, Jolie quit playing.

She jerked her head upward, sucking in a breath in preparation for the confrontation to come. No doubt a partygoer—one of the construction laborers, judging by the size of the work-roughened hand still covering hers— had been left behind when the buses pulled out. And wanted to blame her for it. Well, she'd be damned if she'd be pushed around like this. Especially by one of her own employees.

Jolie rose, heedless of his restraining hand, and faced him with her knee propped on the bench for balance. Momentarily distracted by the cushioned feel of it, she stared downward. When had the wooden bench been upholstered with red velvet?

It didn't matter. All that mattered was the burly interloper in front of her. At least he'd stepped back a pace when she rose . . . but how dared he disturb her like this, anyway? Her wishing had been going so well!

She lifted her chin. "That macho crap went out with the gunslingers, he-man. And you don't look like one of the attraction's actors to me, so . . . ."

In an expression meant to be dismissive, she let her gaze travel from his bare feet—*bare feet? In January?*— to his pants legs—*long johns? In the saloon?*—and up to his face. Halfway there, the unexpected sight of bare skin, muscle, and a scattering of coarse curly hair struck her dumb. *A bare chest? Now?*

Shivering with sudden unease, she tried to gather her wits. Maybe he was a homeless construction worker. Maybe he camped someplace on the site, and had drunk just enough green gecko margaritas at the party to confront her over the piano music disturbing his sleep.

Sure. And maybe the next Hershey bar she treated herself to would be magically calorie-free.

Ha! And maybe she'd find sawdust beneath her boots right now, too, instead of the confetti she'd kicked up on her way to the piano. Fat chance.

Shifting her weight into a fighting stance, Jolie looked down, past the inexplicably upholstered bench.

And saw sawdust.

No. It couldn't be. It only looked that way, in the power-surge-altered lighting. She looked at the rafters. Her vision filled with darkness, and she could have sworn she heard bats flapping within its depths. Where were the electric lamps? The festive strings of multicolored lights?

Feeling slightly hysterical, she fisted her hands. "So, so, I guess you'd better leave."

"Leave?"

"The door's over there." She tipped her head to the left—where the incandescent red exit sign was supposed to be. It was gone. Ohmigod.

The mystery man leaned closer. She had the sense he'd been scratching his head in confusion.

"Because I'm not an actor?" he asked.

Because you're a figment of my imagination! the rational part of her screamed. She was sure she'd locked all the doors. Positive she'd set the alarm. So how had he gotten in here?

"Yes. No." *Look at him,* Jolie ordered herself. *Look him in the eye and make him go away.* Her fists tightened. "Because you don't belong here. This is private property, and I'd appreciate it if you'd leave."

There. She'd said it. Feeling encouraged by her undiminished ability to take command, she looked into his face.

He frowned. Shoved a hand through his pillow-creased mass of dark blond hair and frowned even harder. His face looked . . . lived in, Jolie decided instantly, with a bristly jaw, sleepy hazel eyes, and an assertive nose that was surprisingly attractive when combined with the rest of his features. With relief, she noted the intelligence in the mystery man's assessing look. Despite his beefcake-worthy body, at least the guy had a brain.

"I belong here," he said. "I own this place."

On second thought . . . that brain of his was obviously two cans short of a six-pack. Jolie sighed. Why were the gorgeous ones always so dim?

"No, you don't!" she blurted.

"Ma'am." His husky voice turned smooth as hot caramel on Häagen-Dazs. "I most surely do."

"You don't!"

"I do."

"Don't."

"Do." With a concerned expression—the kind of concerned expression a person wore when confronting a certifiable nut-job, Jolie guessed—he came closer. "And much as I ordinarily take to a good argument, I'm not up for jawing with you after the night I've had. You'd best skedaddle."

"*Skedaddle?*" Jolie chortled. Either he was a refugee from *Gunsmoke* or she was going insane. Maybe both. She folded her arms over her parka in a gesture that was one part defiance and one part protectiveness, wishing she'd thought to stick her cell phone in her coat pocket. Nine-one-one was looking better all the time.

"Do I look like the type of woman who's going to 'skedaddle' anyplace?" she asked.

He assessed her. "Maybe not. And you look too fleshy to pick up easy." He scratched his beard stubble and let his gaze rove over her again, more thoroughly this time.

Doubtfully, he added, "But I'm strong enough to do the job."

Fleshy? He meant fat! Thoroughly affronted, Jolie snapped, "It's just the coat, birdbrain. It's padded. See?"

Driven beyond reason by his stupid accusation, she thrust her hands to her hips. Just as she'd intended, the motion swept her parka aside and bared the black cocktail dress beneath it.

His eyes widened. *Ha!* she thought victoriously. *I'll show you fat, buster.*

Quick as a heartbeat, his arm swung upward. Her first glimpse of the rifle he held killed Jolie's sense of satisfaction instantly. Evidently, he'd thought she'd been making something other than a body consciousness statement. He'd thought she'd been drawing a weapon of her own.

With a surge of unreality, she stared at the rifle, then at the hard-featured man behind it. Next time, she was phoning in her damned New Year's wish. That was all there was to it.

"I insist you leave," he said, gesturing with the gun.

A moment later, everything went black.

CHAPTER THREE

Avalanche, Arizona Territory
New Year's Day, 1887

"Dammit, Lillian! I told you that was too much laudanum." Cole Morgan gazed helplessly down at the woman
sprawled crossways on his bed, then turned his attention
to his elderly neighbor. "How long will it take her to
wake up?"

"Can't say." Lillian pulled her wrapper, scarf, and coat
more tightly around her body. Her nightclothes' scraggly
hems swished above her boot tops, then settled. "Might
be better for you if she's out a good long while. That
one's trouble. With a capital T."

Cole sent a skeptical glance toward his unwelcome
guest. Without her huge coat—a castoff from some hulk-
ing brute of a man, he'd guess, judging by its size—she
looked much smaller than before. Carrying her upstairs
to his living quarters above the Second Chance saloon
had been easy as hauling a barrel of ale to a table of
thirsty men.

"You know what this means, don't you?" Lillian had

asked last night, trailing him into the bedroom with a lighted oil lamp in hand. "You carried her over the threshold, boy!"

"So?" Scowling over Lillian's knowing tone, he'd laid the woman atop the quilts and tugged off her shiny boots. He couldn't help but notice how thin her stockings were— transparent enough to show that whoever she was, she'd somehow painted her toenails red as a pair of long underdrawers. Crazy.

"So that makes this woman your choice for a bride," his neighbor had continued. "Finally, Avalanche's most eligible bachelor has got himself hooked."

Now, in the daylight streaming through his upstairs bedroom's frost-tinged mullioned window, Cole remembered their conversation and scowled anew. Only a lackwit would get himself hitched to a woman like the one snoring softly in his bed.

"She looks cold," he muttered, reaching for the bunched-up quilt. It had been a gift from a hopeful mailorder bride, only one of many who had responded to his early—and woefully misguided—newspaper advertisement. Sewn in shades of red, white, and blue, the coverlet looked too cheerful to cover a woman so pale and so drably dressed. He tugged it over her anyway.

"You just let me do that." Lillian shouldered him aside. "Keep that beefsteak on your eye like I told you."

"I had planned to eat it, not wear it."

"Do you more good fixing up that fine-lookin' face of yours, 'stead of filling up your belly." She jabbed him in the gut, poking into his layers of green flannel shirt, knitted undershirt, and long underdrawers. "You want to scare her away?"

"Maybe, seeing as how she's the one who socked me in the eye."

"Pshaw."

Lillian fussed over her patient, looking all-fired tickled to be doctoring up somebody new. Ever since her husband, Doc Delaney, had passed on last year, she'd been moping around the Delaney Pharmaceuticals shop next door like a book without its pages. Unchanged on the outside— empty on the inside.

She squinted through the morning light at him, swiping at the dust motes dancing in the beams. "I hate to say it, Cole. Seein' as how she walloped you and all. But I get the feeling this gal here is your destiny."

Only if I'm cursed.

He couldn't say it aloud. Not so long as Lillian stood there, looking bright-eyed and hopeful. Cole smiled at her. "If anybody would know about something like that, it's you," he said instead, thinking of the abiding love she and Doc had shared. "Thanks for helping her like you did. I'm obliged to you."

Gathering her things, Lillian shrugged. "Don't be thanking me yet. You'll need more help with her, I'd say. Maybe more'n I can give. But I'll be right next door if you need me."

After a hasty, surprising hug, she clattered downstairs and was gone. The saloon's front door opened and closed on the chill morning, and Cole shivered beneath the gust of wintry air that swept upstairs. It snaked past the potbellied stove in the corner, then fluttered the pages of the calendar tacked to the wall in his office across the hall.

Sourly, he regarded the illustrated dated pages, torn from a periodical by one of his barkeeps. Two years later, two years since his foolhardy New Year's resolution to find himself a wife, and he still hadn't found the woman he wanted. Half the town had known about his quest. Since last night, the other half—the *female* half—was enlightened, too.

Hell. He would never know a moment's peace again.

Strangely, the thought drew his gaze to the woman. What had possessed him to bring a she-devil like her into his home? Sure, she looked ordinary enough. For now. At least as ordinary as a woman could look drugged up on laudanum and obviously without resources.

He figured her for a woman down on her luck, with

no family to turn to and no connections in the Territory.
Otherwise, why would she have turned up like she had,
playing his piano in the dead of night? Maybe she was
one of those traveling entertainers. A lady singer, or an
actress. Cole had seen such performers several times,
working in places like Tucson and Tombstone. Maybe
she'd been angling for a job last night.

Or maybe her madness is catching, a part of him prodded. *You know damn well that piano has been broken for
months now.*

Frowning, Cole shoved aside the thought that had
plagued him since he'd first awakened to the strains of
a melody both familiar and unidentifiable. There was
no point in dwelling on the impossibility of what had
happened. Not when the proof of it was right in front of
him, monopolizing his carved, special-ordered, cherrywood bedstead.

He'd vowed the only female to sleep in that bed would
be his wife. But there was no help for that now. The
woman needed him. It wasn't in his nature to turn her
away.

Cole crouched closer. Above the quilt, the thin straps
of the woman's bizarre black chemise curved around her
bare shoulders. Because of its color, Lillian had been
certain the woman was in mourning. Cole wasn't so sure.
She didn't look like someone who had suffered a loss.
Her demeanor had been too feisty last night, her dark
eyes too damnably filled with spirit . . . her stance too
purposely provocative.

She'd been wearing next to nothing beneath that ugly
coat, he recalled. Just snow boots and a thin dark shift.
And she'd brashly displayed herself all the same, just as
though daring him to look away.

He hadn't been able to. He'd been dumbstruck. Seized
with unexpected interest and undeniable lust. For a crazy
woman!

His wife hunt had obviously driven him 'round the
bend.

'Course, his reaction had lasted only as long as it had taken her to bat her eyelashes and fall into a swoon. She'd wavered. He'd grabbed an armful of sweet-smelling, monstrously padded female, and wound up catching her moments before she would have slumped to the sawdust-covered plank floorboards.

Just in time to get punched in the eye when the hellion awakened.

Surveying her closely, lest she repeat the maneuver today, Cole adjusted the wrapped slab of cold meat Lillian had given him and pressed it against his swollen cheekbone and eyelid. He'd have a shiner, to be sure. What would his barkeeps—not to mention his friends and neighbors—say when they spotted *that?*

He'd wrestle with that problem when he got to it. For now, he had enough to think about—like what to do with *her*.

Asleep, she looked almost sweet. Entirely unlike the vixen who'd ordered him off his own property, brazenly flaunted her feminine charms, and then thanked him with a fist when she'd awakened from her swoon. Christ Almighty. Maybe she wasn't an actress at all, he decided with a shake of his head. Maybe she was one of those reformers, wanting to wear bloomers and smoke cigars and do a man's work.

Oddly enough, Cole didn't care. For some reason, he felt a powerful urge to protect her. To keep her near and safe. Setting aside the beefsteak, he washed and dried his hands with the basin of water, soap, and linen towel Lillian had left on the table beside the bed. Then, breath held, he leaned near the woman and touched his fingers to her forehead.

Her skin felt as soft as he'd imagined. Cool to the touch. "No fever," he muttered, hoping to convince himself it had been a need to gauge her temperature that had drawn him to touch her . . . rather than an overwhelming urge to feel her softness beneath his work-callused palm. He could not. He'd never been a man to lie to himself.

No point in starting now.

Cole swept back a stray lock of spiky black hair from her forehead, savoring its silky texture between his fingers. It was plain she'd been ill. Her shorn hair lay against the pillow in lengths no longer than his little finger. 'Twas unusual-looking to be sure, but when contrasted with her delicate features and lush mouth, the woman's cropped dark hair seemed surpassingly feminine. Cole had never seen its like.

His gaze slipped lower, past her neck and chest to the quilt-covered curves he knew lay beneath. She hadn't seemed particularly frail—especially not when her continued hysterical struggles had necessitated help from Lillian's medicine bag—and yet he sensed a vulnerability in her. He found himself wondering if she'd yet recovered from whatever ailed her, wondering what sickness had brought down a strong woman like this.

Her eyes opened. Cole stilled his hand, waiting while her slumberous dark gaze focused on the raw lumber walls, functional furnishings, and piled-high quilts surrounding her. Her attention centered on his chest, then moved upward. He knew the exact moment when she recognized him. Her eyes widened. She opened her mouth and released a scream loud enough to peel whole months from a man's glory days.

Whatever ailment she'd suffered from to necessitate lopping off her hair, Cole concluded in that moment, must have been an illness of the mind. The woman acted like a damned loon.

She heaved herself from the mattress just as he clapped his hand over her mouth. With a muffled grunt, she fell back into the pillows and feather ticking, clawing at his wrist with those underdrawer-red fingernails of hers.

"And to think I thought your caterwauling last night was pitiful." Cole did his best to deliver his remark along with a reassuring smile, just so she'd know he was joking. "This is even worse than that love song of yours."

Her reply was a barefooted kick to his thigh. Looking

determined, the woman arched against the mattress and readied a second blow. Above his restraining hand, the wicked gleam in her eyes promised her next kick would be higher, better-aimed . . . and likely struck directly at a most highly prized spot on his anatomy.

Cole winced and turned sideways. Obviously, she had no sense of humor.

Neither did he, when it came to matters like that.

"Shhh. I won't hurt you," he told her, ladling as much comfort as he could into his voice. "You're safe here. I won't hurt you."

As a good-faith gesture, Cole lifted his hand. She stared at the hand as it moved away from her lips, looking as if she wanted to chew off a finger or two, just for spite.

"That's what they all say, you psycho!" she cried.

"Say—what?"

"Don't play dumb with me, Brutus. I want out of here. Now."

She thrust herself into a sitting position, agonizingly mindless of the way the movement made the quilts fall away . . . and the tantalizing bounce it put in her small, pert breasts. His imagination caught hold of the image, making him wonder what she would look like bared completely. What she would feel like, filling his hands. What she would sound like, moaning when he touched her.

Desperately, Cole reined in his wonderings. Thoughts like these would only earn him another shiner . . . and a permanent empty space beside him in bed at night.

Damnation. When had he begun thinking of her as a potential wife?

In defiance, he sent her a stern look. "My name isn't Brutus. It's Cole. Cole Morgan. And you're . . . ?"

"Leaving."

She shoved away the remaining quilts and knee-walked to the edge of the mattress, then vaulted onto the rag rug beside the bed. Ignoring his protests, she strode to the chair upon which he'd stored her ugly coat and boots. The woman grimaced when she first set foot beyond the rug—a reaction to the January cold that permeated the room down to the floorboards—and then bent to retrieve her things.

The motion was enough to make Cole's head swim. Her black chemise rode up her thighs, baring several appealing inches of skin clad in those remarkable stockings of hers. He decided that his wife, whenever he finally found her, would wear nothing but see-through stockings. Maybe, if he let this woman play his broken piano again, she would tell him the name of the merchant who'd supplied them.

The sight of her struggling into her snow boots, hopping on one leg in the warm spot beside the potbellied stove, shoved his lusty thoughts aside. His conscience stepped in instead. No matter how unwilling she was to admit it, it was plain the woman had no place to go. No belongings other than the ones he saw in her hands. He couldn't let her leave.

Not yet.

CHAPTER FOUR

"Wait," Cole said. "Don't go."

The woman rammed her foot into her boot at last, then grabbed the second one. Shafting him a single withering look, she ducked her head and set to work outfitting herself for a snow-shrouded world—and a sleepy mountain town—that she'd never survive in.

"Sorry if this wrecks your evil plans, mister. I'm not sticking around." She quit struggling with her boot long enough to swab her tongue around her mouth, then made a face. "I don't know what you gave me to knock me out like that. Some kind of date-rape drug, I guess. It tastes nasty."

Magnanimously, Cole allowed her ridiculous rape accusation to pass. 'Twas plain she was out of her head with desperation. Everyone in town knew he'd never hurt a woman.

"Laudanum."

She quit moving altogether. "What did you say?"

"Laudanum. That's what I gave you. You were plumb hysterical, and I—"

"—thought the best thing to do was drug me?" She

shook her head, her tone filled with incredulity. Muttering something about "definitely two cans short of a six-pack," whatever that was, she resumed her battle with the boot. A moment later, she stopped again and peered at him. "Did you really say 'laudanum?' "

He nodded.

"Where in the world did you get it?" The instant the words left her mouth, she let loose an inexplicably rueful smile and raised her hand. "No. Never mind. I don't want to know the sordid details."

Cole shrugged. "It's not sordid, nor hard to find. My neighbor Lillian owns Delaney Pharmaceuticals next door."

He moved toward her, determined to keep her safely indoors no matter what kind of stealth it required. The woman was a danger to herself and the community of Avalanche alike.

"Right." More wrestling with her boot followed. "So you just plucked a can—"

"Bottle."

"—of laudanum off the shelf and rattled out a couple of tablets—"

"Drops. In a glass of water."

"—to keep me quiet." She glanced up; then her mouth gaped open. "You're serious."

" 'Course." What kind of lunatic would think a discussion of medicinals was funny? He took several slow steps. "And you're staying."

As though she'd just realized he'd nearly crossed the width of floor separating them, the woman gasped. She raised her boot like a shield. "I—I should warn you. I know karate."

"He's not here right now." Cole put his hands to his hips and assumed his most protective manner. *"I am."*

Incredibly, she rolled her eyes. "Self-defense, you moron. As in karate, judo, jujitsu . . . garlic bread, bad perfume, discussing bridesmaids' dresses on the first date.

Sheesh, what's it going to take to get you to leave me alone?''

More than a pile of nonsensical woman's talk, he reckoned, examining her closely. She looked slightly less scared of him. Slightly less ready to bolt downstairs and run shrieking through Avalanche about how Cole had raped, drugged, and misunderstood her. Good.

He grinned. "You don't really want to be alone . . . do you?"

The boot sagged in her grasp. A haunted look came into her eyes. He wondered at its cause, even as that glimpse of unexpected vulnerability vanished.

Her chin rose at a stubborn angle. "Nobody wants to be alone."

"I agree."

She narrowed her eyes. The suspicious gesture stole some of the sparkle from their dark brown depths—but couldn't diminish their beauty. For a homeless waif with flailing fists and too few clothes, the woman was damnably attractive.

"If you're making fun of me," she said, "I swear I'll—"

"Clobber me with your boot?" Cole nodded toward the limp leather in her hand, then came closer. "Smother me with your hideous coat? Slice me up with that shrewish tongue of yours?"

Frowning, she stepped back a pace. He touched her arm to keep her from treading upon the potbellied stove at her back, and was gratified to find that she no longer jerked away from his touch.

"I've already sampled your right hook, angel." Cole grinned, being sure to keep himself turned partly sideways in case she took a mind to end his chances at fatherhood with a well-aimed kick. "Why should I tempt fate by teasing you? It's plain to see you want me to keep my distance."

"And it's plain to see you can't take a hint." She gazed

pointedly down at his booted feet, only inches away from her half-undressed ones.

He shrugged. "I don't believe you really mean it."

"Of course I mean it! I—" Her protest ended on a gasp as she looked up at his face. She started to reach for him—to stroke his swollen cheek, Cole guessed—then curled her fingers at her sides instead. "I always mean what I say."

"And I always say what I mean." Patiently, he pried the boot from her fingers and readied it. "I don't believe you're getting very far with this footwear of yours. It's as obstinate as its owner."

"How dare you!" She grabbed for her boot and missed. "You don't even know me."

True. But more and more, he wanted to. The woman intrigued him, beyond all good sense. Cole knelt to the floorboards and patted his thigh. "Let's get this boot on you before those cute toes of yours freeze clean off."

"I can do it myself."

"Not while I'm holding your boot."

She didn't move. What sort of cockeyed fate had sent him a mule-headed woman like this for a New Year's surprise, anyway? He grasped her hand and guided it to his shoulder for balance. Then he wrapped his fingers around her ankle and lifted her foot to his thigh.

The woman sucked in a breath. Reflexively, her toes curled against the muscle beneath her foot, and her fingers tightened on his shoulder. Cole glanced up at her.

Her shrug stood at odds with her fiery red cheeks. "You—you surprised me. You're, ahh, really warm," she mumbled.

From her, it sounded like high praise. "Thank you."

"For a bossy, chauvinistic—ouch!"

Cole finished ramming on her boot, then stood her slightly apart from him, and rose. "I liked your punch better. At least it was honest."

Looking chagrined, the woman stared at her toes. He

decided a little regret wouldn't kill her, and crossed the room to drag one of the quilts from the bedstead.

"You're shivering," he said, wrapping the soft tufted cotton around her shoulders. He drew the ends tight in his fist, then nudged her chin up with his knuckles. Her expression was mulish—and wary. "I meant what I said. I'm not going to hurt you. Don't be scared."

The woman gulped. Tears shimmered in her eyes, then were dashed away beneath a merciless twist of her palm. "I am scared. I can't help it. I—I can't believe I'm admitting it, but there you go. Guess I'm not up on my hostage protocol."

"You're not a hostage."

"You won't let me leave." Her gaze met his. "That makes me a—"

"A guest."

She gave a short laugh. "Right."

"A surly, bad-tempered guest . . . but welcome, nonetheless." Cole grinned.

Astonishingly, the woman did, too.

"You look beautiful when you smile," he said.

All at once, he felt a powerful urge to bring more smiles to her face. To see her happy and at peace. Despite the sooty smudged face paint around her eyes and the knowledge he held of her harpy's disposition, Cole was drawn to her.

This gal here is your destiny.

"You look as though you mean that," she said.

"I do."

Her eyebrows dipped in apparent confusion. "Why would you . . . oh, criminy. Here I am, getting jazzed over a compliment from a lunatic. What's the matter with me?"

Jerking the quilt from his grasp, she paced to the frost-covered window. She stood on booted tiptoes to breathe on the glass, rubbed a clear circle in the center, then looked outside.

Cole knew what she'd see. Avalanche's main street,

slushy and frozen and bordered by a few shops, saloons, and restaurants, plus miles of pine and oak forest and a backdrop of snowcapped mountains. He'd awakened to the same view for four years now, ever since retiring from his army surveyor's post and coming to the northern part of the Territory to start a new life.

He'd thought that life would include a wife and children by now. A family to love. Instead, he had a prosperous business, property interests, a share in the Avalanche newspaper, the respect of his friends and neighbors . . . and more socks knitted by hopeful spinsters than a man could use in a century of cold winters. Cole couldn't in good conscience wear them. Not when he'd chosen none of the ladies for a bride. But that didn't stop new pairs from arriving on his saloon's doorstep with alarming regularity.

He gazed sideways at the woman, hoping she didn't knit.

Instead, he found himself contemplating the remembered wonder of her see-through stockings. Were her garters transparent as well?

Her gasp rattled the lusty musings from his brain. "I thought I dreamed all this!" she cried, wheeling from the window with amazement writ upon her face. "I thought— I thought—"

She looked outside again, fingers splayed against the glass. "How long was I passed out?" she cried.

"Four, five hours."

"Oh, God." She rested her forehead against the windowpane, then stared through it with apparent misery. "That green gecko margarita was definitely too much for me."

Curiously, Cole watched her. Had she missed an appointment? A performer's audition of some kind? If old man Shaw at the tavern down the street had wrangled some kind of arrangement with her, he'd . . .

Well, he'd get her some damned decent clothes before letting her leave, that was for certain.

"Are those real wagons?" she blurted.

On second thought, he wouldn't let her out of his sight. Not for Shaw. Not for anyone. She needed help. *His help,* Cole decided.

Had she fallen last night? Struck her head on the piano? Or was she still unwell from whatever illness had assailed her? Maybe that was why she'd fainted at the mere sight of his rifle last night.

"Yes, the wagons are real," he said cautiously.

"The people too?"

She sounded forlorn. At the notion of people in the streets? "Yep. We might not have much commerce here in Avalanche, but we've got plenty of fine folks who—"

"Avalanche?"

She swayed. Cole, recognizing an impending swoon as well as the next man, lurched closer and pulled her into his arms. The crown of her head fit neatly beneath his chin, with only a few stray strands of cropped hair to tease his lips. Even through the quilt her body felt made to be cradled against his.

How long had it been since he'd held a woman this way?

"Avalanche. *No.* It's not possible," she said, drawing the last word into a moan. "It just can't be."

"'Tis. You're here, aren't you?" he pointed out, endeavoring to sound reasonable for her sake. Perhaps, in the dark and snowy New Year's Eve night, she hadn't noticed the sign at the edge of town. "There's no arguing with that."

"Ha! Who knows?" She waved her arm toward the window in a dramatic gesture that seemed perfectly suited to her performer's nature. "Maybe there is. Suddenly, anything seems possible."

Cole scoffed. "It seems possible that you're not here?" Either she really had hit her head or the woman was a pitiful jokester. Whichever it was, he somehow needed to ease her worries. Gently, he pulled her closer. "You're here, all right."

"You don't understand," she protested as she pivoted

within the confines of the quilt, then flung herself back into his arms. "I don't belong here. Maybe I'm not really—"

"You are." He looked at her seriously, then cupped her cheek in his hand. "This is not my imagination I'm touching. It's you. Soft and warm and sweet."

"But—"

"And it's not some dream that's got me feeling like this. Wondrous and chowder-headed as a boy with his first schoolyard fancy. It's you. All you."

Oddly enough, her response was a pinch. On her own arm. She seemed surprised to find herself still beside him when it ended.

He smiled. "And no quilt ever sewn could make me hunger to hold it tighter. Nor spur me to fancy speeches like this one. 'Tis only you."

Weakly, she pushed at his chest. "You're—you're joking. To make me feel better about having gone loony overnight."

Cole's smile broadened. "I'm not. I mean every word." *God help me.*

She looked dazed. Skeptical. Heartbreakingly hopeful. "But I've never . . ." Her voice wavered, then strengthened. With a question in her eyes, she gazed up at him. "I've never even dared to *wish* for that much, and now—now—"

"Now?" He caught hold of the quilt's edges. Slowly, he pulled them apart, then sheltered them both together within its warmth. "Now what?"

"My wish!" She gaped at him. "You're my wish!"

With unabashed interest, she scrutinized his face, then as much of him as she could see beneath their shared quilt. The woman was brazen, he'd give her that much.

He liked it. Despite her daft "wish" claims and her evident stubborn streak and her inexplicable arrival. If details like that were important, they'd reason them out together, Cole decided.

"Wow," she said at last.

Her tone was an awestruck whisper that warmed Cole's

heart—and eased a worry he hadn't known he'd been harboring. To judge by her wide eyes and daffy grin, the woman he'd gone soft on felt somewhat the same for him.

She looked up. "I didn't know I'd wished for anything *this* big."

"I'm only around six foot. There are bigger men about."

Her laughter was joyous. With a shake of her head, she regarded him again. "Sheesh, you'd think Erin might have warned me."

Another of her indecipherable comments. Cole's head began to ache. "Erin?" he asked.

"My best friend. From . . . back home. Erin Delaney."

Delaney. Probably a relation to Lillian. That explained why she'd arrived in Avalanche. With that settled, he realized, there were only two things remaining to be discovered.

And both could be unearthed nearly at once.

He angled her face upward, then stroked the smooth line of her jaw with his thumb. "Tell me your name."

"My name? I—"

"Mmmm-hmmm." Nodding, he lowered his head. "I've never kissed a woman I didn't know."

"Never?"

Her lips parted softly. At the sight, anticipation poured through him like liquid fire. "Never. But I'm passing close to trying it right now."

"To k-kissing a woman you don't know?"

Cole drew her closer. "To kissing you. Tell me your name," he murmured, "else run the risk of a reputation past repair . . . when I kiss you all the same."

CHAPTER FIVE

Jolie trembled in his arms, staring wide-eyed at the man who'd somehow dragged her through time, scared her into unconsciousness—and then sweet-talked her half past bearing.

Wow, she thought again, taking in the amazing rugged perfection of his freshly shaved face, tousled hair, and hard-angled body. He looked like a billboard for healthy outdoor living, crossed with a dose of pure masculine sex appeal.

His smile was remarkable all in itself. And best of all, Cole Morgan had aimed that sensual smile of his straight at her. If this was a dream, she never wanted waking up.

If this *wasn't* a dream . . . well, she was in trouble. Big trouble. Because she wanted to believe in everything he'd just said. Wanted to believe he'd found her soft and sweet. Wanted to believe in the sappy expression on his face and the close warm circle of his arms.

She couldn't. It wasn't possible Cole had really meant all those things he'd said . . . was it?

No. Much as she longed for them, his kind words and tender touches couldn't really be meant for her. Not the *real* her, the woman she was underneath the MBA and cocktail dresses and credentials that were her protection against disappointment.

Jolie sighed, looking him over again. Maybe if she was really lucky, she mused, this wish-come-true business was her big chance to prove herself. To herself. And to him. And maybe her reward in the end would be the kind of love she'd wished for while playing an incredible song on an impossibly powerful piano.

Or maybe she'd just gone round the bend. *After all,* Jolie told herself, *you know perfectly well you never learned to play the piano.*

Or even to read music.

"Hmmm?" Cole prompted. His gaze lowered to her lips . . . and lingered in a way that sent her pulse through the roof.

Wowsers. He still meant to kiss her! The gentle upward tilt of her face in his hand left no doubt of that. So did the slow, seductive way he drew her closer.

Their bodies pressed tightly together beneath the quilt, defying the wintry weather—and common sense, too. Jolie had never fallen for a man this quickly. Had never even considered kissing someone she'd met only hours before.

Until now.

Her only defense was a good offense. Desperately, she recalled the challenge he'd offered her.

"Whose reputation will be ruined?" she managed to ask, hoping she sounded half as confident as he looked. "Mine, for letting you kiss me? Or yours . . . for failing to do it?"

Cole's puzzled frown said plainly that he wasn't used to being questioned while only inches from a woman's lips. No doubt he was the Casanova of territorial Avalanche, stealing kisses right and left from eager pioneer gals—and then breaking their hearts when he moved on again.

Careful, Jolie told herself. Maybe Cole Morgan was

her wish come true, made real with big strong hands, a
killer grin, and an outdoorsman's cozy flannel-and-cotton
wardrobe. But on the other hand, time-traveling wasn't
exactly small potatoes. What if she'd been brought here
for some other, bigger purpose?

It was best to step cautiously.

At least as cautiously as she could while wearing her
clunky snow boots, anyway. Jolie wiggled her toes within
their rigid leather confines. It was just her luck to be
trapped in the past without so much as a cute pair of
slingbacks or a comfy pair of sneakers to slip into.

He hesitated. His thumb caressed her jaw once more,
then Cole smiled. "I'd say you're the type of woman
who doesn't give a fig for her reputation. Or her man's,
either."

"You make that sound like a compliment."

"It is."

Weren't women supposed to be demure in the olden
days? Although she didn't know the exact date, Jolie
estimated that she'd landed sometime in the late eighteen
hundreds, judging by the wagons and horses in the streets
outside—and the predominately calico wardrobes of the
women she'd glimpsed on the snowy raised board side-
walks. It was the era of maidenly virtue and modesty.
Not the era of locking lips with anybody who looked
appealing.

No matter how tempting the idea might be.

At the renewed descent of Cole's mouth toward hers,
another possibility occurred to her. Feeling panicked—
and more eager to kiss him than she wanted to be—Jolie
whipped her hand upward to stop him.

"I get it," she said quickly. "Taking advantage of the
new girl in town, huh? I'll bet you thought I'd fall for
this in a New York minute."

Evident confusion wrinkled his brow. "I don't know
about New York. But if you mean the kiss . . . sure. Most
women are happy to be kissed."

I'll bet. "By you?" she asked aloud, trying to sound unaffected by the idea.

When his arrogant expression returned, she knew she'd failed.

"Sometimes by me." He released her jaw and caught hold of the hand she'd raised to ward off his kiss. "Unless the ladies can't quit flapping their jaws with harebrained questions long enough to enjoy it."

With a wink, Cole brought her hand to his mouth. Tenderly, and with a seductiveness she wouldn't have believed without experiencing it, he kissed the tip of her index finger. His warm lips nuzzled her sensitive skin, then moved to her middle finger. Then her ring finger. Shivers raced up Jolie's arm, lodging someplace near the heart she was determined to protect.

Mindlessly, she watched as he smiled up at her, then tilted his head in the sunlight shining through the window behind them. The motion revealed shiny strands of hair in shades from warm honey to caramel, cut to collar's length. Would they feel soft? Or thick-textured and strong-willed as the man beneath them?

Before Jolie could sneak up a hand to find out, Cole resumed his explorations. He kissed her little finger, then nipped it and kissed once more. Amazingly, her knees weakened. From a kiss on her pinkie? Oh, boy. She'd obviously been dateless for far too long.

"That's enough!" she cried, whipping her hand from his grasp. "For Pete's sake, we barely know one another."

"That's easily mended." Cole's hand slipped beneath the quilt and wrapped around her waist. "Starting with you. Since you won't tell me, shall I guess your name? Rumplestiltskin, maybe?"

"Do I *look* like a warty little man from a storybook to you?"

"No, ma'am. You look like heaven wrapped in a quilt." He squeezed her waist, rubbing his fingertips over her dress as though fascinated with the lycra and rayon blend's smooth texture. "You feel that way, too. A little on the scrawny side, maybe—"

"Scrawny?" He actually thought her ten-pounds-more-than-ideal self was too skinny? This *was* a dream. Jolie brightened.

"—but mighty fine, all the same." Cole smiled. "For a woman of mystery. What's your name?"

For one panicked instant, she was afraid telling him would send her magically hurtling through time again. But that was ridiculous. More and more, she felt sure it was the mysterious piano music that had done it—combined with the strength of her wish, perhaps.

"It's Jolie. Jolie Alexander."

"It's my pleasure to know you, Miss Alexander."

"Jolie." Geez, was she actually on the verge of giggling over her name? *Get a grip,* she commanded herself. So what if he was the greatest-looking man she'd ever seen up close? So what if he was looking at her like she was a nice toasty fire—and he was an icicle-bearded man just come in from the cold?

He was only a man.

And she was only a woman. A woman with wobbly knees, a hidden romantic heart, and too much yearning in her soul.

Funny how that didn't make her feel any more courageous.

"Now that that's out of the way," Cole said briskly, "let's move on to finer things."

His wolfish grin predicted that his definition of finer things included kissing. Lots and lots of kissing. And God only knew what other seductive minefields for her to leap over.

"Not so fast, buster."

"It's Cole, remember?"

His eyelids lowered partway as he examined her mouth with rapt interest. Extremely flattering rapt interest. Just in time, Jolie's befuddled brain zapped her with an impending kiss warning. Cole's lips barely grazed her cheek as she stepped backward.

The close-wrapped quilt stopped her before she got far. Scowling at it, she flung back one corner and ducked away before her foolish heart could persuade her to do something stupid.

Like kiss him back, for instance.

From the safety of the warm area beside the potbellied stove, Jolie folded her arms over her chest and glanced at him. Her erstwhile abductor—strange how she'd thought *he* was the out-of-place one, when it was really her—gaped at her with obvious surprise.

Then his face took on a new certainty. "Aha," he said in a voice turned husky and knowing. "You want wooing, don't you?"

"Wooing?"

What a charming word. None of the gelled-hair yuppie business types she'd dated could have uttered it with a straight face. Somehow, it sounded wonderful coming from Cole.

"Yes, wooing. Courtship," he explained in his nut-case-sensitized voice. With a powerful throw, he abandoned the quilt to a rocking chair in the corner, then regarded her thoughtfully. "Like when a man pursues the woman he fancies."

Despite the fact that he apparently still suspected she was mentally confused, Jolie couldn't keep a goofy grin from her face. "I know what it means. That's not what I—"

He held up his hand. "Say no more. I know women have fancy notions about falling in love. I don't mind. Truly." Doubtfully, he added, "It will be passing strange to court a woman I've never kissed, but—"

Jolie almost interrupted him to ask if he locked lips with every potential girlfriend before "wooing" her. The charmingly openhearted look on Cole's face kept her silent.

"—but if that's what you want, Jolie, then that's what I'll give you."

Something told her she hadn't seen the last of his kissing attempts. Something still stronger warned her that Cole Morgan was far more sincere in his determination to woo and win her than his playful manner implied.

It looked as though life in the past could become very interesting, indeed.

Just to be sure Cole realized he had a worthy opponent, Jolie smiled. If her experiences in the business world had taught her anything, it was the importance of maintaining an advantage in all situations. Especially when those situations happened to be challenging. New. Or fraught with high stakes.

This situation definitely qualified. No less than her heart was at risk.

With her best approximation of a seductive walk, she took full advantage of her cocktail dress getup and sashayed toward him. "Give it your best shot, big boy."

His eyes bugged in a most satisfying way.

"Meanwhile," Jolie went on, "I'll be out and about, seeing what else this burg has to offer."

Boldly, she looked him over once more, trying not to show the quiver of anticipation that raced through her as she did. Then she tossed her head, started to walk toward the hallway behind him . . . and paused to land a pinch on Cole's taut, trouser-covered behind.

His yelp of surprise followed her all the way to the stairs leading to the saloon below.

Jolie wasn't sure what she'd expected to find upon finally setting foot in Cole's Second Chance saloon almost an hour later. A dark, gunslinger-filled set piece straight out of *Bonanza*, she guessed. Instead, she'd found something surprising. Something bright and clean and, at noon on a snowy day, nearly deserted.

Stranger still, she'd found a place that was almost

exactly like the *faux* saloon she'd had constructed at Go West! The differences between the two were small, but significant. Here, no electrical outlets punctuated the whitewashed walls. No informational plaques adorned the entryway, and no red velvet ropes divided the fully stocked bar—also something different—from the rest of the room.

In this saloon, Jolie's snow boots struck real hardwood planks as she stepped from the staircase to the open area below. Here, the acrid odors of whiskey and stale tobacco were authentic—not manufactured by a scent company specifically to enhance the saloon's ambiance. And here, laminate and particleboard were unheard of. The tables, chairs, and bar were all obviously fashioned from solid carved and lacquered wood, as was the staircase banister.

She ran her hand along its length and then abandoned its stability to walk amongst the saloon's tables and chairs. With a growing sense of exactly how different this time was from her own, Jolie noticed that the lanterns hung over each table held wicks and, presumably, kerosene—not light bulbs and hidden electrical cords.

In place of the ever-present hum of modern electrical generators and heating units, a serene silence cloaked the room. The stillness was broken only by the sound of Cole's footfalls behind her as he followed Jolie's progress from table to table, past another black potbellied stove, a billiards table, and a pair of snowdrift-embossed multi-paned windows, and then to the edge of the brass-railed bar. Raising her hands to her hips, she gazed in amazement from the rafters to the furnishings around her. It couldn't have been more identical to the Go West! saloon.

CHAPTER SIX

Wonderingly, Jolie shook her head. "I just can't believe it."

"What?" Cole glanced upward as well, then frowned. "Ahhh, let me guess. You want me to put new glass chimneys on the chandelier lamps. Probably with little flowers painted on them. Am I close?"

"Flowers? No, I ..." She stopped, at a loss for what to say next. "I wasn't thinking about flowers at all."

"Ribbons, then," he guessed. "Painted on china chimneys with gilded edges and—"

"No!" Jolie interrupted, feeling exasperated. What was his deal, anyway? "Contrary to your obviously misguided beliefs, Mr. Neanderthal, and with flowers, ribbons, and gilt aside, women are *not* fixated on lamp chimneys."

He looked puzzled. Then his knowing expression returned—the same one he'd worn when proposing courtship to her.

This time, it was somewhat less engaging.

"It must be the walls, then," Cole said, nodding.

"The walls? What about them?"

He gestured toward the plain plaster walls, embellished

with only a few racy Victorian-looking prints and a chair rail. "You're yearning to slap on some pink wallpaper with angels and trumpets and God only knows what else."

Jolie gaped at him. "I have *never* 'yearned' for wallpaper in my life."

The skeptical arch of his eyebrows told her Cole didn't believe a word of it. Great. She'd been tossed into the territorial saloon of a man obsessed with decorating.

"I'm not putting down any damned fancy rugs, either," he warned with a suspicious scowl. "The sawdust is fine."

"It's very practical," she agreed, nudging a clump with the toe of her boot. *Much more so than confetti.*

Evidently, he thought she needed convincing, because he went right on talking.

"Have you ever seen a drunk try to walk on top of tassels and doodads? Do you know what pink angel wallpaper would do to my business?" Looking aggrieved, Cole swept his hand through his hair. "Christ, no man would dare to lift a whiskey glass with the likes of cherubs staring down at him from all sides."

Jolie stifled a smile and propped her boot on the brass bar rail. "Your saloon is terrific," she reassured him. "Much cleaner than I expected."

His answering look could have melted the snowdrifts outside.

"I mean, much cleaner than anyplace I've ever seen," Jolie backpedaled. Sheesh, the man was touchy about his saloon. "I don't think the Second Chance needs new lamp chimneys, or wallpaper, or anything else."

Cole grunted. "You're the only woman in town who doesn't."

"Fine with me," she said, shrugging. "I wouldn't change a thing."

"Hmmph."

"Neither would I!" said an enthusiastic masculine voice from behind her.

"You keep out of this, Rick," Cole snapped. "And shut your mouth, too. You look like a damned half-wit."

Jolie whirled. They weren't alone after all. The dark-haired, bearded young barkeep behind her wore a Henley-style shirt, suspenders, a pair of twill pants . . . and a stupefied expression. Despite the fact that she'd turned to face him, he ogled her with all the chutzpah of a downtown construction worker on a coffee break.

A construction worker unexpectedly confronted with a whole contingent of Playboy bunnies.

The glass and linen towel in his hands went slack. Unrepentantly, Rick gazed from her breasts—only the merest bit revealed in her dress's straight-fashioned neck-line—to her bare arms and back again. He grinned.

Obviously, Cole's barkeep hadn't been commenting on his reluctance to change the saloon's décor. No, that look of his said something else entirely, and it wasn't the least bit Victorian or proper in nature. *Hubba, hubba. Get a load of the boss's half-naked new babe.*

It seemed that human nature—human *male* nature—didn't change much with time, after all. Jolie sighed.

Beside her, Cole smirked. He leaned closer to murmur in her ear. "Can't say I didn't warn you."

Well, that much was true. He'd predicted this reaction during the hour they'd debated her first appearance down-stairs . . . after he'd recovered from her appreciative pinch and hauled her back into the bedroom, that is.

Cole had thrust his neighbor Lillian's castoff gingham dress and breath-stopping underthings at her, spouting some macho idiocy about not going out in public until she was decently clothed. In reply, Jolie had stubbornly stuck to her own perfectly respectable black cocktail dress. After all, she'd reasoned, when worn with her snow boots, the dress didn't reveal much more than her knees.

What woman on earth had lust-inspiring kneecaps?

Apparently, she did. Frowning, Jolie gave the barkeep a leer-dampening glare of her own, then shoved aside a

woven basket piled with multicolored knitted socks and
sat on a bar stool.

"Fine, I won't say it," she muttered.

The wisecracking reply she expected never came.

Looking up, she caught Cole staring in fascination at
her legs, revealed more than usual thanks to her high
seated perch. No wonder he hadn't gloated over being
right. He was too busy ogling her himself.

With a ridiculous surge of feminine giddiness at his
interest, Jolie straightened. "But I will say this much.
Corporate policy begins at the top, Mr. Morgan."

"Hmmm?"

Like a caress, his gaze touched her calves and swept
along their stockinged curves. Her body tingled beneath
his scrutiny—but Cole didn't have to know that.

Deliberately, Jolie crossed her legs. Her skirt rode up
a few inches. "Heard of the pot calling the kettle black
much?"

"What?"

"Black," she repeated, teasing him. "The pot calling
the kettle—"

"Mmmm. I like black," Cole said slowly. "I didn't
realize how much until right now."

His mouth curved in a sensuous smile. His gaze turned
dreamy, moving in a lazy arc past her miraculously allur-
ing knees and touching her thighs instead. A look like
that would have been enough to ignite a more fearless
woman's every passionate impulse.

Who was she kidding? Another few minutes, and she'd
go up in flames herself.

Across the polished bar, the barkeep set down his glass,
loudly breaking the spell. He picked up another one, and
his movement sent splinters of sunlight dancing along the
mahogany bar.

"I reckon she wants you to quit gawking at her naked
legs, boss," Rick remarked without looking up.

"Don't you have work to do?" Cole shot back, frowning.

The barkeep shrugged. "She's got that wrathy tone,"

he explained with a helpful air, "like Lillian gets when she's strung up in a new mail-order corset."

"Hey!" Jolie glanced over her shoulder. "Let's truss you up in a pair of whalebone britches two sizes too small and see how happy you sound, buster."

He winced and resumed polishing with more vigor.

Cole nudged her, looking inexplicably worried. "Do they really have britches like that in the future?" he whispered.

While they'd been arguing over her wardrobe, she had explained to him her theory about having traveled back in time to the tune of the piano music. At the time, Jolie had been sure he hadn't believed her. Now, she saw doubt in his face.

She gave his arm a reassuring pat. "No, not really."

His expression eased. He lowered himself onto the bar stool beside her, then irritably swatted the basket of socks further down the bar's gleaming surface.

Jolie watched it slide away, then bump to a stop against Rick's stack of clean glasses. First the decorating obsession, and now this. What problem could he possibly have with a basket of socks?

Whatever it was, it would only be charitable to distract him from it, Jolie reasoned. And she couldn't think of a better excuse for giving in to the humongous urge she felt to tease Cole just a little more.

Casually, she smoothed her dress over her thighs. "Actually, the men in the future wear their pants only *one* size too small."

His eyes bugged.

"And," she added nonchalantly, "I've heard the *real* men don't mind the whalebones a bit. What's a little discomfort, compared with looking good?"

"A *little* discomfort?"

Thoughtfully, Cole pursed his lips. They were fine-looking lips, she noticed. Masculine and perfectly shaped. The man beside her had the kind of mouth that had set hordes of women screaming in adulation at movie idols and rock stars for generations. He'd wanted to use that mouth of his to get better acquainted *with her,* Jolie remembered. And she'd turned him down.

What was she, crazy?

In a gesture that fairly oozed Lord-of-the-Saloon assurance, Cole spread his arms along the bar behind him and leaned back. He gave her a decisive look.

"Men in the future are crazy," he said.

So were women in the past, for subjecting themselves to torture devices like corsets and the kind of pointy button-up shoes Cole had tried to foist off on her as standard attire. But Jolie could hardly tell him that—at least not without reigniting the Clothing Debate.

"No, they're not. And they treat their women wonderfully, too," she went on, embellishing her vision of the future for him. "They compliment them, help them, listen to their every word with complete attention."

Cole quit frowning at the sock basket and fixed her with an attentive look worthy of any fourth-grade staring contest. "They do?"

She nodded. "And they shop with them, too."

"Men in the future have no backbone," he grumbled.

He couldn't possibly be this easy to bait. Could he? With a shrug, Jolie swiveled on her stool. "They have plenty of backbone."

"But no jobs," Cole guessed. "How else could they have time for all those—those"—his nose wrinkled in a distasteful expression—"*women* things?"

She laughed. "Of course the men have jobs. It's just that, where I come from, their women are more important to them." It had to be true of some men. Even if it hadn't been especially true of the ones she'd dated.

Cole and Rick exchanged a look of puzzlement.

Whoa. If that piano worked both ways, she was in trouble.

As long as she was already in hot water, Jolie figured she might as well go all the way. "But that's not even the best part," she said.

Both men's gazes swerved back to her face. Cole's looked especially attentive. "What's the—"

"I don't think we want to know, boss," Rick interrupted. "The whole thing sounds *loco* to me."

Jolie gave him her best "you-can-trust-me" smile. With a Doubting Barkeep like Rick on hand to goad her, how could she resist laying it on a little thick? After she'd gone, no doubt the women of Avalanche would thank her.

"In the future," she said, "all the men give their, ah, womenfolk gifts every week. Nothing fancy. Just little 'I love you' kinds of trinkets. Except for on birthdays and wedding anniversaries and . . . and bad-hair days"—geez, she was really reaching now—"of course, which demand a little fancier sort of—"

Their jointly horrified expressions stopped her midstream. Whoops. Maybe she'd pushed it too far.

Rick cocked his head. "Bad-hair days?"

"Trinkets?" Cole narrowed his eyes. "What kind of trinkets?"

She couldn't help it. Jolie took pity on them and held up her fingers, pinching them in midair a few inches apart. "Teeny-tiny ones. Nothing big."

They continued to stare at her.

"For Pete's sake! It's the thought that counts, remember?"

Muttering to himself, Rick went back to work polishing and stacking. On the stool beside her, Cole rubbed his fingers slowly over the bar, appearing lost in thought.

"Good thing I'm the man in town with the most caboodle," he finally said.

"I'll say." Propping her elbow on the bar, Jolie rested her chin in her palm and looked him over. From boot heels to flannel shirt collar, the man looked good enough to eat. *Hubba, hubba to you, too, Mr. Morgan.*

Cole caught her looking. His devil-may-care smile widened. "Caboodle as in money. Don't play dumb with me, angel. There's a reason you turned up at my place first, and not Shaw's Tavern down the street.''

''Oh? And what reason is that?''

He remained silent, giving her a look that made it plain he thought she was trying to pull one over on him. Since when did she look like little Miss Innocent?

Especially in her vampiest cocktail dress?

''Do you pay the best?'' she guessed.

Rick burst out laughing. He had loaded the glasses beneath the bar, and now he paused amidst inventorying the liquor bottles shelved beside and below the saloon's gilt-edged mirror to shake his head. ''It ain't that, I can tell you for sure.''

''What, then?''

Inexplicably, Cole whisked the basket of socks toward her. ''What do you think these blasted things are for?''

''I dunno.'' She nodded her thanks to Rick for the drink he slid over the bar to her, then raised her eyebrows. ''Barefoot drunks?''

With a twist of his lips that might have passed for amusement in a less sock-hating kind of man, he shoved the basket to the bar's end once more. ''Never mind. If you want to keep on like this, you just go ahead and try.''

''I will!'' *I would, if I knew what the heck you meant.* ''Good.''

Perversely, Cole seemed pleased at her defiance. He had the same look in his eye as the really hard-core investors did when she approached them about a new FantaSee attraction. Intrigued. Interested. But perfectly willing to let her run through her whole spiel before committing to anything.

He crossed his arms. ''So,'' he asked, ''these future men of yours—what do they get?''

''Get?'' Jolie choked on a sip of her sarsaparilla. Helpfully, Cole rubbed her back while he waited for her answer.

''What do they get?'' she repeated.

"In exchange," he explained, "for all that compliment-ing and helping and listening—"

"And shopping," Rick put in. "Shopping, too."

Cole's frown deepened. "—and trinket-giving."

"Oh." Great. Her tall tales needed a payoff, too. Think-ing it over, Jolie gazed at Cole's expectant face, and said the first thing that came to mind. "Love."

"Love?"

"That's what the men get in return. The women love them. It's not as mercenary as it sounds, of course. But the nice guys, the really caring, thoughtful guys . . . sure. Their women love them to pieces."

The whole idea suddenly filled her with a longing that was strangely—and increasingly—familiar. *Love, love . . . I wish for love!*

With a wholly unrevealing sound of understanding, Cole examined her face. His gaze touched her like the softest of caresses, and for one crazy instant, she realized how easy it would be to believe in something as idiotic as love at first sight.

Too easy.

She couldn't possibly be falling for him, Jolie told herself fiercely. He'd been born more than a hundred years before she had. She'd known him less than a day. And she'd never been in love before, anyway. What were the chances it would magically happen to her now?

About the same as the odds of finding herself in a snowbound nineteenth-century Arizona Territory town without so much as a cell phone, a plug-in for her PDA, or a way to get back home again.

About a gazillion to one.

Slowly, Cole rose from his stool. Here it was—the inevitable retreat. Cue one commitment-wary male. What had she been thinking, to mention the "L" word?

She had to give him credit, though. At least he balked from love and commitment slowly, with his customary strength and surety and proud male grace.

"Love, huh?" Amazingly, he winked at her. "I reckon

the love of a good woman sounds like the best reward in the world to me. And I'll be damned if those men in the future are going to keep it all to themselves.''

Bedazzled by his unexpected response, she couldn't manage anything more than, ''Huh?''

''Love, Jolie.'' Cole leaned forward, smiling, and squeezed her hand tenderly in his bigger, stronger palm. ''You sang about it. I want it. And if your heart is pounding anywhere near as hard as mine is right now, just from being beside you, I'd say we have a fine chance of finding it together.''

She blinked. Realized that at some point she'd raised her free hand to her heart and it was, as he'd said, pounding like mad. And knew that, incredibly, he might be right.

Holy cow, Jolie thought. *I just hope I can find a way to deserve it.*

CHAPTER SEVEN

By the time January gave way to February, the pine forest looked as if it had been sugared twice over and set to freeze. Wintry winds scrubbed the warmth from the sunshine and blue skies overhead, and in the distance, the San Francisco peaks wore thick white blankets of snow.

Closer to home, the powdery drifts had climbed halfway up the clapboard sides of most buildings in Avalanche, including Cole's Second Chance Saloon. Icicles sparkled from their eaves like rows of grinning teeth, and their roofs were wreathed by the ever-present wood smoke drifting from chimneys and stovepipes all over town.

Most days, the best place to be was inside, wrapped in layers of long underdrawers and wool. Most days, nothing warmed a man better than a mug of steaming coffee, a fragrant strawberry pine fire, and the knowledge that he was where the universe intended.

"Most days" were not the kind of days he had much anymore, Cole mused, sipping a fresh cup of Arbuckle's. Not since Jolie had turned up—and turned his life upside down. Between her smiles and sassy chattering, her off-key bathtub singing and her endless "to do" lists, his woman from the future had done an indecently good job of stirring up even the most taken-for-granted parts of his life.

And turning them sweeter.

Folks in town loved her, of course. She'd hit it off with everyone from Lillian and old man Shaw to the minister at Avalanche Unified Church and the lumbermen's wives who lived with their hardworking men along the abandoned railroad route. Jolie had charmed one and all with her energy and wit. Including Cole. And despite what he assumed were her future-related eccentricities, somehow she'd managed to blend right in.

Without a doubt, Miss Jolie Alexander had woven herself straight into the fabric of the life he'd lived comfortably for the last several of his thirty-two years. It should have been perfect. And it would be. Once he convinced her to give up her stubborn, harebrained insistence on leaving before winter's end.

Once he convinced her to stay with him.

Sighing, Cole tipped back his customary chair beside the Second Chance's warm potbellied stove and watched his new saloon hostess perform her self-proclaimed duties. Jolie cleaned up right well, he had to admit. Clad in a deep blue calico dress—one of several she'd bartered for from Thompson's Mercantile on Main Street—she moved with feminine grace between tables filled with saloon customers. Stopping often, she spoke with equal ease to grizzled miners, ranchers, and suit-wearing businessmen, including the mayor, John Westley.

The woman had a knack for jawing to folks. Her pretty brown eyes brightened with genuine interest, no matter who had captured her ear. Her smile could have lit the murkiest, most low-down place on earth.

It lit up your damned gave-up-hope heart, now didn't it? Cole asked himself, and had to smile over the answer. 'Twas true that Jolie had brought him new hope of finding a woman to love. Unfortunately, she wasn't ready to admit that the woman he wanted to love was her.

As though in answer to his thoughts, she headed toward him with a fresh smile. He doubted she was aware of the way every man's eyes followed the womanly, side-to-side swoosh of her skirts as she stepped toward his place beside the stove. And she couldn't have been aware of the way his turned-to-mush heart seemed to swell in his chest as she approached. But Cole felt pretty certain that, after working nearly three weeks in his saloon, Jolie finally understood his wealth and standing in town.

And that was the crux of the problem, wasn't it?

Her expression sobered as she dragged over a ladder-back chair and seated herself beside him. "I see you're still doubtful," she announced.

"Huh?"

"Even after I told you how I could bring in more customers to your saloon. Even after I proved the bigwigs in town would come flocking to this place, once it had a little more curb appeal and consumer-added value, well . . . you're still doubtful."

Sometimes she had a plainly incomprehensible way of putting things, Cole thought. "Now hold on," he said aloud. "I was never—"

"And don't try sweet-talking me, either. I saw your face a few minutes ago. I saw the way you were watching me before, making sure I wasn't scaring away the customers."

"You're anything but scary, angel."

"Hmmph." Tapping her high-buttoned shoe, Jolie took in his undoubtedly soured expression. In typical woman's fashion, and with a damnable lack of faith in herself that was starting to set his teeth on edge, she had mistaken it for a sign she'd failed somehow.

"And I was never doubtful." He smiled at her, and felt his heart turn over at the sight of her worried face, framed by soft dark pixie hair. She really was afraid she'd failed. Afraid he didn't believe in her. Silly woman.

"How could I be doubtful about you," Cole teased, "when you've pointed out your successes so often?"

She quit nibbling at her lips—lusciously full lips, he noticed, bare of the paint she'd worn on the day she'd appeared at his piano—and frowned at him. Doubtless she figured he'd forgotten all her endless talk about her MBA and "corporate executive" work, because Jolie treated him to a new course of it, delivered with her hands waving in the air for emphasis and her eyes holding his in an earnest fashion.

When she'd finished, Cole captured her hand and gave her fingers a gentle squeeze. "I'm duly impressed," he told her, "with all your accomplishments in the future. But I don't need to know about what you've done to realize how fine you are, Jolie. I've got two eyes of my own to see that for myself."

She blew an exasperated breath. "I'm talking about more than the fit of my *Little House on the Prairie* dress, you lunkhead. I'm talking about being fine on the inside."

"So am I."

Her snort of laughter made it plain she didn't believe him. So did the way she withdrew her hand. He felt the loss of the contact between them like a physical ache— one that grew fiercer with each day spent in her company. He hadn't tried kissing her again since the morning they'd met, when he'd realized she wanted wooing. But he'd been sorely tempted to, all the same.

It was up to Jolie to take the next step. He just wished she'd quit moseying and start running outright.

" 'Course, your outside is mighty appealing, too," Cole added, grinning at her. He'd never known a woman he loved to tease more. Never known a woman who was more sheer fun to be with than the one scowling suspiciously over his last remark. "Now that you've given up flaunting yourself all over town in that black chemise of yours, that is."

Jolie looked wounded. "You can hardly claim you didn't like it, buster. I won't believe it."

"Matter of fact, I'm experiencing a powerful nostalgia for it right now." Letting his gaze speak the rest of the truth, he slowly took in her curvy waist, wonderfully round breasts . . . determined and beloved face. "And for the way it felt. Smooth as silk in my hands, so warm and soft. You know, it even smelled nice. Like cinnamon sticks dipped in sugar and berries."

"My dress smelled nice?"

"Sure."

Her arched brows pulled a smile from him. Leaning closer, Cole pretended to think on it a minute. "Or maybe it was the woman underneath who felt so good beneath my hands." He nodded. "Yep. I was wrong. It wasn't that scandalous dress at all. It was you who felt so perfect in my arms."

"Cole—"

"You who'd feel perfect there again, if you would only admit it."

Jolie shook her head. "You just don't give up, do you?"

"Not when I'm this close to wooing a certain mule-headed female from the future."

"Oh, Cole!" Despite her laughter, a certain sadness touched her eyes. "You know I can't stay here past winter. I—I think I was brought here to do something important—"

"Love isn't important?"

"—and when I've done it, I'll have to go. Don't you see?"

He finished his coffee and set aside the mug. With a long look, he took both her hands in his, ignoring the murmur of conversations surrounding them, the scrape of chairs and the muffled clank of billiard balls knocking against each other in the corner. All that existed was Jolie. And himself.

Together.

"What if *I'm* what you were sent here to find?" he asked.

For a long moment, she only looked at him through

enormous eyes, her gaze awash with longing and something else he couldn't identify. Then she slowly shook her head.

"Sometimes I wish—" She broke off with a laugh, slipped her hands from his, and started again. "Well, I already wished, didn't I? And—"

"And look what it got you." He spread his arms wide in indication, his gesture taking in the form and fittings of the most prosperous saloon in Avalanche, the well-paying and jocular customers who filled it, and most of all . . . himself. "You said yourself I was your wish come true."

She twisted in her chair, for all appearances consumed with folding foot-long pleats into her floor-sweeping calico skirt. Another woman might have blushed, or tried to deny the outrageous claim she'd made more than four weeks earlier—weeks during which they'd become friends. Jolie did neither.

"That doesn't mean you're *willing* to be mine," she said, raising her chin in that direct way she had. "My wish come true, I mean."

Sweet blazes, but he would be if she would let him.

"Let me decide that for myself."

She only slanted him a dubious look. "Come on, Cole. It's not as though you had a choice in the matter. I just appeared at your piano—poof!—and dropped all this in your lap. You've been terrific about it, letting me stay here until I find that sheet music and all, but you don't have to pretend something you don't really feel."

Damnation, but the woman could prattle on about senseless things. He couldn't take her constant doubting any longer. His jaw fairly ached from grinding his teeth in frustration, just listening to her. For diversion's sake—and to retain his sanity—Cole nudged his elbow against the small, ribbon-wrapped box on the table beside him.

"Open it," he said. "It's for you."

Her gaze lit on the crooked pink bow. A wondrous wide smile filled her face. "Again? Oh, but I—"

"I want none of your nonsense," he warned with mock sternness. "You told me and Rick plain enough what wooing gestures were expected of a man in your time. Did you think I couldn't manage the same here in Avalanche?"

"No, but . . . but I don't deserve it. Thank you, really, but I—" Jolie leaned forward and gave the box a pitiful halfhearted shake of her head. "I shouldn't accept any more gifts, wonderful as they are. Not when I'm—"

Leaving. He didn't want to hear it. "Open it."

Hesitating, she touched her fingertip gently to the curve of the pink ribbon. Was that guilt he spied in her expression? Surely not.

"Would you rather go shopping again?" Cole asked.

Her laughter astonished him.

"You would take me shopping again, wouldn't you?" Giving him a look of giddy disbelief, Jolie straightened in her chair. "Even after we've been through every mercantile, dry goods store, news depot, and dress shop in town."

"There was only one of each," he felt compelled to point out in his defense. It wasn't as though he'd gone completely spoony over her. Yet. "Avalanche is a small town."

"And it will stay that way, too," she interrupted quickly, "or worse! Unless—"

"Arrgh!" Spying the familiar fervent gleam in her eyes, Cole held up his hands in mock surrender. "Not that ghost town business again. I swear, Jolie, if anyone can change the future, it's you."

She seemed cheered at his praise. Pride glowed in her face, powerful enough to nearly stand her cropped hair on end.

Or maybe that was just some future hairstyle she'd whipped those spiky dark strands into for the day. There was just no telling with Jolie.

"But," he went on, returning to the topic at hand, "I can't put together the picture you gave me of Avalanche with the reality of what's outside. This town has been thriving since I got here—''

"—and doubly so with your help."

He frowned over her reference to his investments in the saloon, newspaper, and other town property, then doggedly continued, "And I can't believe it won't stay this way for a long while yet."

"But it won't!" Urgently, she gestured toward the frost-covered windows at the other side of the saloon, beyond which false-fronted buildings huddled in the snow and townspeople hurried by outside. "It won't stay this way, not unless something is done to save it."

"Another time." He caught hold of her outflung hand and kissed it. "Another day."

Another woman, he wanted to say, suddenly fearful Jolie's quest would take her from him somehow. After all, he couldn't explain how she had come to him from the future. Nor could he doubt the truth of her presence there. The fact that she was beside him, touchable and lovable and *real,* made a lie of any disbelief he might have had.

He had to accept it. Plain as that. And Cole did.

But he didn't have to like the implications of it.

Jolie's sigh called him back from his thoughts. He looked to see her regarding the saloon with something very near wistfulness, and wondered at its cause.

"Don't you see?" she asked. "All these years, I've been creating fantasies. Empty imitations that people could visit, clutter with popcorn and soda cans and wadded-up attraction maps, and leave behind with nothing but a few memories and a souvenir."

"And you were good at it," Cole ventured, remembering her talk of all she'd been in charge of as a "corporate exec." He could tell she was upset, but he couldn't begin to reason why. Who could, when faced with feminine logic? So he settled for giving her his best "attentive listener" expression.

He wrinkled his forehead thoughtfully. "You made

those fantasies come true over and over again, like you said.''

Somberly, she nodded. ''But this place is different. This, Avalanche . . . oh, Cole!'' Jolie clasped her hands at her heart and closed her eyes for a moment. ''This is my chance to create something *real*. Something lasting. It's my chance to finally do something really good.''

When she opened her eyes, the eagerness he glimpsed there made his breath catch in his throat. How could he combat the kind of naked need he sensed in her? Especially when what she wanted was so blasted impossible?

CHAPTER EIGHT

"I know you want to," Cole said, as gently as he knew how. "But how can you fight something that's not there to see? How can you stop this, when it hasn't even begun? Let it go. Be with me, and we can—"

"No!" Jolie stood, making the table wobble when she butted her hip against it in her haste to be away. The ribbon-wrapped box slid with the movement, then stopped a few inches from the edge. "I can't stop this! How can I—how can *you* ever care for me if I don't prove . . ."

With a muffled sob, she turned away. Cole lurched to his feet, pushed past bearing with her inexplicable, ever-changing woman's moods and her obstinate insistence on having done with a job any fool could see didn't need doing at all. Saving Avalanche! He'd be damned if he'd let her weep herself into misery because of some foolish ghost town notion.

"I already do care for you, you stubborn female," he said, dragging her reluctant, stiff-necked body into the circle of his arms. With a self-conscious glance around the saloon—where knowing, half-cornered grins met his gaze—Cole awkwardly raised his big arm and patted her on the back, trying to help her relax. "Believe me, and let's go on from there."

"Mmmmph." She burrowed closer against his chest, and he could feel her cheeks moving against his warm knit sweater and shirt as she spoke. "Mmmmph."

Smiling, Cole angled her head sideways.

"You just don't believe I can do it," came her sorrowful reply.

Such a misguided notion surely didn't need a reply, he reckoned. 'Twas obvious enough that if he didn't believe Jolie could accomplish whatever she set out to do, he wouldn't have been trying to dissuade her.

Instead, Cole contented himself with snuggling her a bit closer—and had the wicked, unconscionable wish that they were alone in the saloon now, as they'd been on New Year's Eve. Jolie felt so good in his arms. So right. So feminine and curvy and soft . . . exactly the woman he wanted.

He whispered as much to her, moving his lips close to her ear.

With a little cry, she shuddered in his arms. Her response drew him closer, near enough to nibble on her warm, delicate earlobe. Mmmmm. Blissfully, Cole closed his eyes, shutting out the intrusive saloon and its damned busybody customers, and nuzzled his lips lower to her neck.

"Ahhh, Jolie. You taste so good. Don't fight me anymore."

With a frustrated yelp, she jerked backward and stamped her foot, narrowly missing squashing a few of his toes in the process. "It's not fair! Why did I have to find you *here*"—her louder wail encompassed the Second Chance saloon, Avalanche . . . hell, probably the whole of Arizona Territory—"where an MBA counts for less than a wedding ring, and—and—a woman like me, who can't sew a stitch or milk a cow or work the stupid water pump, is about as useful—and as common—as snow in Arizona."

"It does snow in the Territory, here in the high country." Pleased that he'd shot down at least one of her arguments—he thought—against staying in Avalanche with him, Cole smiled. "And if you were common, you wouldn't be you. Any more addle-headed philosophies you want me to take care of?"

Her answering smile flashed, but he saw the gleam of tears in her eyes, too.

"Everything I pride myself on is useless here," she said. "How am I supposed to earn some respect, and, and—"

And what? Cole wondered.

"—and stuff—" she warbled, sniffling.

"Stuff?" Skeptically, he raised his eyebrows. If he had been uncertain she'd meant to say more before, he wasn't now. Jolie was hiding something. He wanted to know what it was.

"—when all the things that make me who I am are gone?"

Cole shook his head, at a loss to help her. "You're still you. On the inside."

"Ha!" Her rueful expression could have broken a man's heart. "Maybe that's the problem."

"Awww, Jolie—"

"No. No pity party for me," she interrupted brightly. With a patently false, pasted-on cheerful expression, she smoothed his heavy wool sweater over his chest. "I've done enough of that for myself, haven't I? Besides, it's not your fault. It's not fair of me to take this out on you."

It was even less fair of her to take it out on herself. But if he said as much, Cole had the feeling she really *would* squash his toes. And maybe other, more vital parts of him as well. He decided to remain silent.

Jolie worked her hands down his blue knitted sleeves, absently patting and tugging. Her fingers rose to his neckline and fussed some more. She looked upward, and he felt her breath tickle the hollow of his throat. For a woman who claimed she wasn't even supposed to exist in his time, Jolie was doing a pretty good job of making him want her to stay there forever.

"Did you get this sweater from the same place all those baskets of socks come from?" she asked.

He grimaced. "No. This one came straight from the Bloomingdale Brothers mail-order catalog that Verna keeps down at her general store."

"Oh."

"And what's that smile of yours for?" Cole demanded, reminded by her straightening and smoothing—and her mention of the dreaded spinster socks—of the reason he hadn't settled down with any of the ladies in Avalanche.

From their skinned-back hair buns to their parasols and high-buttoned shoes, every last one of them was the same. The marriageable females in Avalanche would rather run their fingers through his bankbook than cozy up with him through the Territory's long winter nights.

He hoped like hell Jolie wasn't the same.

Especially when she'd come so close to making him believe in love again.

'Course, she hadn't taken him up on his offers to redecorate the saloon, he reminded himself. Not even when he'd tried tempting her with flower-painted lamp chimneys, pink cherub wallpaper, and geegaw-bedecked rugs. Any of the other gals in town would have flown at an offer to spend his money on fripperies like those. But if he knew women—and Cole had known a few—Jolie might change her mind at any time.

"I just didn't know Bloomie's existed already," she explained, abandoning her sweater-ly efforts. She tweaked a lock of hair behind his ear instead. "And I didn't know *you* were such a man of fashion."

Laughing over his undoubtedly disgruntled expression, she gazed over her hostess's domain, where glasses of whiskey and ale and mescal traveled from tabletop to mouth in practiced arcs, and men hunched over games of chance ranging from Faro to poker to chess. Behind the bar, Rick paused in the act of doling out foaming beer mugs and wielding liquor bottles to meet Jolie's watchful glance. He nodded. Then winked. The rascal.

With an unreasonable urge to draw Jolie's attention back where it belonged—to the man who was wooing her, dammit—Cole cleared his throat. She turned with a questioning look.

He decided a concession was in order. A goodwill gesture, to begin one of those "heart-to-heart" talks that future women were apparently so fond of.

Recalling the feel of her nimble fingers against his neck, Cole touched the same strands Jolie had. "You can cut my hair if you want," he offered.

Her reaction to his generous proposal was more laughter. As compensation, though, she pushed her fingers into his hair as though mulling over the idea, first rubbing the strands, then making little caressing whorls against his scalp. His knees went weak. At a touch to his hair? Lord Almighty. He had obviously waited too long to find himself that wife he wanted.

Waited too long to make Jolie see how much he cared for her already.

"Just call me Vidal Sassoon," she said with an impish grin.

Whoever that was.

Then she rose up on tiptoes and ruffled the strands at his temples, inciting another ridiculous bout of wobbling . . . and a powerful urge to haul her back into his arms and demonstrate exactly how a nineteenth-century man went about winning himself a woman from the future.

Jolie crossed her arms and regarded him with puzzlement. "Seriously, though. Why would I want to cut your hair?"

Despite her patient expression, something about the upward quirk of her mouth told him she found the whole idea vastly amusing. Mulishly, Cole crossed his arms as well and said nothing.

"Isn't there a barber in town?" she prodded.

A logical reply, he groused to himself. How un-womanlike.

"Mulligan's got a barber at his hotel down the street," he relented.

"Then why would I . . . ?"

In annoyance, he noticed the absence of mug lifting, billiard ball knocking, and general conversation in the area of the saloon surrounding them.

"Don't you think it ought to be changed?" Cole burst out. He shook his head, deliberately mussing his hair, and gave her a defiant look. "Don't you think my hair is too shaggy, too wild, too long or too short—"

"Well, 'too short' can't be fixed with a haircut, Mr. Morgan."

"—too *something* for your refined feminine tastes?"

Silently, Jolie shook her head. To her credit, she must have sensed his frustration, even if she couldn't understand it, because she didn't laugh.

A brash male voice broke the momentary stillness. "Mebbe the gal wants to slick you up with some pommade, Cole, like that widow woman did last year."

"*Ja!*" put in the German butcher from three doors down. "Or could be, Morgan, that the lady wants a pair of long mustaches on you, with wax on the ends to tickle her fancy. Like that old bluestocking did at the edge of town."

Guffaws filled the air, and glasses clinked in agreement.

Reminders like these Cole didn't need. Not even from friends. And especially not with Jolie there to hear them all. Both of the women they'd mentioned had delighted in Cole's misguided courtship . . . until he'd refused to go along with their plans for the made-over, fancy lives his money could have bought a new bride.

Then the two of them had skedaddled after likelier prospects. Literally. Within a year, both the widow and the bookish gal had gotten hitched to prospectors passing through town.

He didn't know how he could have been so blind to

the women's true interests. And he didn't care to have his past mistakes hurled in his face like yesterday's bar slops.

"The next man who wants to set out an opinion"—he scoured the room with his most no-nonsense glare—"had better be prepared to settle up his bar tab."

Gasps rose from the tables' occupants.

"In full."

Every head ducked, as each customer found himself overwhelmingly involved in a game, a brew, or whatever conversation he'd abandoned. Cole surveyed the restored order with temporary satisfaction, then turned again to Jolie.

"It's my whiskers, isn't it?" he asked.

Her face softened. She reached up, gently cradling his jaw in her hand, and shook her head.

He couldn't help but persist. There had to be something about him she wanted to change. Some part of his life Jolie wanted to take charge of, muddle up with far-fetched, highfalutin priorities, and then use to wheedle open his bankbook. There was no reason she would be different than the other women he'd known since his search for a wife began.

Except she is different, the hopeful part of him whispered.

Cole squashed that mush-hearted voice and concentrated on the crux of the problem instead.

"You don't have any whiskers," she said. "I saw you shaving this morning while I was buttoning all those zillions of buttons on my shoes, just like every other day."

Her reminder of the easy intimacy they shared in their common rooms upstairs—platonic as it was—made him yearn for that closeness to deepen. The renewed stroke of her thumb over his cheek made him close his eyes. Just for an instant.

"I know," he muttered, wishing he could cast aside his need to test her, and simply trust her instead. "That's just it. You want me to grow a beard."

"Oh, Cole."

In that unguarded moment, he opened his eyes to see her looking at him. With love. Amazingly, it shined in her pretty, fine-boned face, and lit her skin from within like sunlight soaking into new snowfall at midday. It caught him so off guard he could have been blown over with a breath.

"There's nothing about you I want to change," Jolie whispered. "You're wonderful, just as you are."

In the face of all that had happened . . . in the face of her resistance and her tears and her refusal to open the beribboned gift he'd slipped into his pocket for later . . . Cole could hardly swallow such a declaration at once. *She's not the only stubborn one,* he realized just then. But he couldn't help how he felt.

" 'Course," he said gruffly. "Not every man can claim my saloon and properties and—"

Jolie's fingers against his lips stopped him midsentence.

"I'm duly impressed," she said, all seriousness as she repeated the words he'd said to her not an hour before, "with all you've done here in Avalanche. But I don't need your investment portfolio to realize how fine you are, Cole."

She had two eyes of her own to see that for herself, he thought in completion of the declaration he'd coined for her today. And Jolie, his mystifying, aggravating gift from the future, was unafraid to use those eyes. Her sultry perusal started at the top of his head . . . and left him breathless by its end.

If he was to do anything but lift her in his arms, take the stairs two at a time, and finally lay her in his bed again—and join her there, this time—looks like that one had to stop. Or, at the least, they had to take place somewhere less accessible to warm flannel sheets, downy pillows . . . and the lovemaking he yearned to share with Jolie.

With a desperation Cole wished he could deny, he drew the box from his pocket and held it toward her. ''Open it,'' he said. ''There's something I want to show you.''

CHAPTER NINE

"This isn't quite what I expected," Jolie said to Cole almost an hour later. Speaking loudly to be heard over the wintry wind that whisked between them—and, of course, the clomping hoofbeats of the rather shaggy paired brown horses he was controlling at the head of their sleigh—she added, "But you were right about these. They're perfect."

She held up her hands in demonstration and waggled her fingers inside his latest "just-a-little-trinket" gift, a pair of sky blue knitted mittens.

Between his flat-brimmed hat and forest green knit scarf, Cole's face broke into a grin. "I'm glad you like them."

"I do!" she yelled back from the depths of her parka's hood, lurching sideways a little as the sleigh picked up speed. Its squeaking runners sent a spray of snow over the low carved and red-painted wooden chassis. "I haven't had a pair of mittens since I was a little girl in Boston."

Even so, tugging them over her hands had made her feel just as cozy and ready for playing as the pairs her mother had safety-pinned to her coat sleeves as a kid. Jolie had resisted the confinement of a hat, just as she'd resisted the endless combing and fussing and braiding that had come with her long girlish hair. But she'd always been game for a new pair of mittens—and the inevitable snowball fights, snow fort-building, and snowman-making that had followed.

Too bad she was too old for those things now. She'd be willing to bet Cole could make a monstrous snow fort.

Beside her, the builder in question went right on driving, guiding them toward whatever destination he had in mind. With a mysterious half-smile, he gazed across the leather traces that stretched from his gloved hands to the harnesses around the horses' fast-moving bodies. Despite his layers of wool clothes and the two red-and-black plaid blankets they shared, somehow he still looked powerful. Manly. Irresistibly attractive.

She swallowed a sigh and stared down at her mittens.

He caught her movement, and misunderstood. "In case you're wondering," he offered, "those didn't come from the same place the baskets of socks do, either."

And inexplicably aggrieved, she added to her mental description of him. Aside from powerful and manly and irresistible, now he looked aggravated, too. It was the mention of the sock baskets that did it. As always. Jolie didn't understand his reaction, but just now she felt too happy to dig deeper. There would be time enough for that later.

If she magically managed to prove her value to Cole before her time here was finished.

The enormity of that *if* left her feeling scared and needful and woefully inadequate. Everything that had ever drawn people to her in the future was worthless here. Career accomplishments, educational achievements . . . even the lures of expense-account traveling and well-connected friends. Here in the past, Jolie had none of those things. Being stripped of them left her bare and unsure.

What if Cole had only befriended her—had only begun to "woo" her—because he pitied her?

The possibility yawned like an icy chasm between them. If she had been the least bit unsure of her plans before, Jolie wasn't now. Saving Avalanche from its future demise as a ghost town was the only accomplishment big enough to erase the self-doubt that had followed her all the way to the nineteenth century. It was the only thing impressive enough to earn Cole's respect.

And, if she was enormously lucky, his love.

Of course, he didn't think she could do it at all. Despite the fact that she wasn't sure of precisely how she would accomplish the task herself, his lack of faith in her stung. *How can you fight something that's not there to see?* Cole had asked her this morning. *How can you stop this, when it hasn't even begun?*

His final, damning advice still rang in her ears.

Let it go.

But she couldn't. She had never been a quitter, and Jolie didn't plan to start now. She would save the town. Somehow. For the sake of all the townspeople she'd come to know and care about. For her own sake, as well. And she would win Cole's love in the process, too. She had to. It was plain as that.

Unwilling to linger on the depressing alternatives if she didn't succeed, Jolie looked for something else to focus on. Smiling, she raised her hands higher and examined her mittens. Their homespun style and cheery color clashed horribly with her modern parka's high-tech neutral fabric and streamlined design.

Not that she cared. They were from Cole. That made them cherished, all by itself. And he'd given them to her with generosity and maybe even a little love in his face. That was all that mattered.

Why blue? she'd asked him upon pulling the mittens from their pink-beribboned box.

Because it reminds me of you, he had answered, smiling as he watched her try on his gift. *And how good I feel when I'm with you. Like I could touch the blue sky with a single reach.*

Geez, she had nearly melted on the spot. The gentleness in his eyes, the sexy smile on his face . . . they'd nearly been her undoing. Whatever resistance she might have had against him, Jolie figured she'd lost the minute he started "wooing" her. In spinning her outrageous tales of those attentive, complimentary, listening, shopping, trinket-giving Super Men of the future, she had accidentally given Cole all the ammunition he needed to win her heart.

Now she was just hanging on through sheer desperation, afraid to let him know how much she cared for him. Already. After only a little more than a month spent in his world, in his time . . . in his home.

For the life of her, she couldn't figure out why he was so dead-set on 'courting' her. Here in Avalanche, Jolie had nothing to recommend her. She had left behind the things she relied upon to win people over—her job, her education, her glamorous travel-packed life. They'd vanished at the moment she had propped up that enchanted sheet music, made a wish at the old piano, and started to play.

So what in the world did Cole see in her?

Jolie wished she knew. Wished she could believe all the wonderful things he said. A lifetime of wariness held her back, just when she most wanted to break its bonds.

As if on cue, he turned to her. His smile still lingered, then broadened in the moments before he spoke. "Your coat—is it from that Bloomie's place, too? Like my sweater?"

Her spirits lightened. "No. It's from someplace far more accessible. The mall."

"Maul? Like a bear?" He snorted and shifted the traces in his fingers. "What a daft name for a shop. That has no curb appeal, I can say for sure."

Jolie smiled over his reference to the oft-repeated marketing terms she'd used to talk him into her hostess position at the saloon. "It's got plenty of appeal. At least for a woman."

"Not a bear."

His sideways wink told her he'd been joking all along. The rat. She explained the concept of a mall to him anyway.

"Ahhh," Cole said with a nod. "A marketplace nearly as big as Avalanche, filled with shops. Doubtless a woman's paradise."

You're this woman's paradise, Jolie wanted to blurt out, filled with the same kind of wicked urge that had made her pinch his behind on the day they met. What was it about him that brought out the wild woman in her?

"You must miss it," he remarked.

Not on your life. "Not as much as I thought I would."

He frowned, staring straight ahead as they traveled. The forest whooshed past, filled with snow-covered pine trees and unexpected silvery meadows. Midafternoon sunlight filtered through the pines and gnarled frosty oaks, shedding too little warmth with its Arizona-Territory-strength light. Above the treetops, the mountains jutted skyward, dividing the horizon into peaks and valleys. Closer, one of their horses shook its head, setting the bells along the harness jangling.

Yes, their sleigh actually had jingle bells on it. The clear musical sound of them delighted Jolie as much now as the sight of them had when she'd first stepped into the vehicle. Underlaid with the swish of the runners and the rhythmic, muffled stamps of hoofbeats through the snow, the pealing bells lent a certain fairy-tale quality to their ride.

"Well," Cole said, breaking the stillness with his rough, low voice, "mall or not, have I told you how much I like that strange coat of yours?"

"No. You do?"

He squared his shoulders as though girding himself for a difficult—or revealing—task. "Yes. I do."

Naturally, he hadn't said why. "You're going to make me drag it out of you, aren't you?"

His answering look was endearing. "And miss an opportunity for complimenting the woman I'm wooing? No, ma'am."

For the next few minutes, their sleigh swooped in small bounces over the snow. The jingle bells jingled. Birds flew from the oak trees in chirping, flapping groups.

Still he made her wait.

At last, Cole raised a gloved hand to her parka's hood. " 'Tis a fine coat for an uncommon fine woman," he said. "And that's why I like it." He touched his fingers to her wind-whipped cheeks, a caress far too moving for its slight duration. "Your hood frames your face like the mountains frame the sunset . . . showing its beauty with contrast and shadows."

Jolie felt her mouth drop open. Grinning, he swept his fingers sideways and tipped her chin up again.

"I'd cross whole canyons just for a glimpse." Smoothly, Cole brought the team and sleigh to a stop beside a sun-spangled snow bank.

Jolie scarcely noticed. *Beautiful as a sunset.* How like him. And how sweet.

He dropped the traces atop the plaid blanket in his lap and swept his arm forward. "Canyons just like that one. Look, Jolie."

She glimpsed the sudden break in the trees first, then looked beyond it and realized why he'd waited for that precise moment to say what he had. Straight ahead, just past the horses' steaming bodies and a snowy outcropping of rock, sprawled the very canyon Cole had mentioned. Its peaks and valleys were formed of orange and gray rock, dusted with snow and shadow. Between the blue-white drifts, the canyon was golden with shafts of sunlight.

"Oh, Cole! It's beautiful."

"Very beautiful," he agreed.

Smiling with the postcard-perfect surprise of it, Jolie turned to face him again. She was startled to find his gaze fixed on her, rather than the gorgeous sight before them. "But you're not even looking at it!"

"I know."

He traced her cheek with his fingers once more. She felt the buttery texture of his glove's napped surface, sensed the earthiness of the suede and the clean scent of the air surrounding them. The warmth in his smile made the frost-tinged breeze and swirling snowdrifts insignificant.

"And I can tell you truly," Cole murmured, "this place has never looked more beautiful to me than it does right now, with you in it."

"Oh."

His eyebrows rose, and his face took on the familiar, teasing cast she'd come to love so well. " 'Oh?' That's all you can say?"

"I can't come up with anything more. I think my brain is still stuck on the first 'beautiful.' " To her horror, Jolie felt tears well in her eyes. She tried to swipe them away, and only managed to dampen her mittens instead. "That's not the kind of thing a girl hears every day, you know."

"It should be. Especially in your case."

Somehow, he actually managed to make a sappy sentiment like that sound real. Absolutely believable. Utterly sensible. The expression on his face proclaimed his belief in it.

On a shuddery indrawn breath, Jolie stared at her mittens and then—when she felt strong enough—at him. He smiled. Her heart broke all over again. Why had she found Cole now? Now, when she had no chance in the world to make him love her back?

"Unless it makes you cry," he amended quickly, looking alarmed at the renewed tears in her eyes. "Then it should never be said at all. Ever."

She heard him swear beneath his breath, searching his pockets for something. A handkerchief, she guessed. Always the gentleman, Cole was. It was one of those nineteenth-century things that, to her surprise, she found so charming about him.

On the other hand, handkerchiefs themselves she found somewhat less charming. Yuck. She was a Kleenex tissue woman all the way. Before he could finish his chivalrous maneuver, Jolie dug into her parka pocket and withdrew the pocket-sized packet she kept there. Casting him an apologetic glance, she wiped away her tears, blew her nose, and refastened the packet's self-stick closure.

The sound of crackling plastic caught Cole's attention. With a wondering look, he gestured for the packet. ''May I see it?''

''Sure.'' It was just like a man to be interested in the technology of the thing, even more so than the function. She handed over the tissues.

He turned them over in his hand, then crumpled the packet in his fist and watched in amazement as it sprang back into a tidy rectangle. Cole looked up. ''It's clear, like glass. But so thin it can bend.''

''It's a kind of plastic. Cellophane, I think. In the future, lots of things are made of plastic.'' *Like tourist attractions. And all the temporary, artificial things she'd taken so much pride in.* ''Even furniture and dishes and things for your house.''

Cole eyed the cellophane dubiously. ''Sounds cold.'' He rubbed his fingers over the packet, then returned it to her. ''I'd rather have furniture of pine and oak.''

I'd rather have you. Suddenly, the world she used to live in did seem cold. Cold and lonely. No place to return to . . . much less to call home.

Of course, unless she found the missing sheet music that had transported her to Cole's saloon, going back home to the future wouldn't be a problem. But Jolie couldn't stay there, loving him—and knowing there was no hope he could love her back. She had to find that magical music.

She had to win his heart somehow.

"Well, *I'd* rather have some fun!" she said with forced cheer. "Come on!"

Intent on enjoying all the time she did have with Cole, Jolie pushed aside the blankets they shared. Wintry air swept instantly over her. Beneath the layers of her parka, a big wool sweater borrowed from Cole, a calico dress and all its underpinnings, and, underneath everything else, a layer of vivid red long underwear, she was warm enough, though.

She teetered on the edge of the sleigh, grasping its edges with her mittened hands for balance. With a bounce and a smile that felt a little steadier than before, she jumped sideways atop the snow.

And sank.

CHAPTER TEN

Cole, oblivious to her predicament, happily bounded from his side of the sleigh. He clomped with powerful strides through the drifts at the edge of the canyon, his hands filled with what looked like burlap sacks, then stopped beside the horses.

Feeling silly, Jolie tried jerking her right foot free. It stuck fast. So did the left. Her borrowed boots kept her feet toasty enough, especially when combined with her stockings and old-fashioned tightly buttoned shoes. "Cole?" she called.

The sounds of jangling harnesses—and their slightly *less* enchanting bells—drowned out her voice. He must be caring for the horses, she decided. Probably giving them feedbags of oats or something.

Her stomach growled in response. Wonderful. She was stuck, hopelessly in love, and all her body could think about was having a snack. Things oatlike and delicious drifted through her mind. Hot oatmeal with maple syrup and raisins. Oatmeal cookies. Oat-apricot scones from the coffee shop in Flagstaff where she'd gotten her occasional double-decaf-skinny-mocha fix.

Yum. Desperately, Jolie fished in her parka pocket for a forgotten mint, a stick of gum, *something* to tide her over. Her hand touched something slick and folded, and she pulled it out.

It was a sample Go West! brochure. As the designer of the piece, she was intimately familiar with the tri-fold, full-color brochure and it did, unfortunately, not have the advantage of being edible. With a sigh, Jolie started to refold it and return it to her pocket.

A flash of alien color on the brochure's front caught her eye and stilled her hand. With a sense of mingled dread and curiosity, she raised the brochure closer. The corner photo, included on every FantaSee, Inc. attraction brochure as a nod to the site's creator, no longer featured Jolie's flashy publicity picture.

Instead, her assistant's face smiled from the corner, happy and confident beneath her stylishly cropped red hair. Beneath her photo, the caption read, "Erin Delaney, Go West! creator and developer."

Shaken, Jolie reread it. Rubbed her mitten's sky blue thumb gently over the glossy photo. Raised her head and stared unseeing at the silent pine trees and empty canyon beyond.

What did this mean? Happy as she was for her friend's obvious success, Jolie couldn't help wondering at its cause. Had Erin taken over at Go West! when Jolie had turned up missing on the morning of New Year's Day? Or did this mean that time-traveling had somehow wiped out her existence altogether?

The idea was an unsettling one. Feeling dazed, she examined the rest of the brochure. Everything else remained as she'd designed it, right down to the choice of font used in the paragraphs describing the ghost town of Avalanche and the re-creation of the city as a tourist attraction.

"What's this?" Cole asked, suddenly appearing in front of her.

She looked up. At the sight of him standing so near,

her breath escaped her on a startled puff of white. While she'd been engrossed in the brochure, Cole had finished with the horses, tracked a path round the sleigh, and stopped only a few feet from where she stood.

"It's nothing." Hastily, she tried refolding it. The last thing he needed was to see the proof of his town's downfall, laid out in full color. Or maybe that was exactly what he needed—but Jolie didn't have the heart to deliver it.

She folded too slowly. His head ducked closer as he read rapidly. "It's about Avalanche. And one of your attractions." Cole reached for it. "Maybe I ought to see it."

"Another time." Mustering a smile, she shoved the brochure in her pocket. She thrust both hands in her pockets, too, hoping the gesture seemed less the defense it was and more a simple need to ward off the cold. "Another place."

"Another woman," he rejoined. "Jolie, can't you leave off this quest of yours? We might not have much time together. I want—"

"Then we'd better use the time we have," she interrupted, propping her hands on her parka-covered hips. "Wouldn't you say?"

"Stubborn woman."

"Stubborn man." She couldn't help but grin. "If you weren't every bit as bad as me, you'd quit pestering me about it."

As a joke, her effort fell flat. Cole's face sobered.

"If it means keeping you with me, I'll pester you night and day," he said gruffly. "Stay. Please."

He really seemed as though he meant it. Because he truly wanted her? Or because he knew that, without the missing sheet music, she had no place else to go? Until she was certain, Jolie couldn't risk the "yes" she wanted so much to give him.

"Stay? No problem." With a shrug of her shoulders,

she stared down at her boots. Now they were wedged to midcalf in the snow. "Looks like I'll be here awhile."

He took in her predicament with a swift glance. Then he grinned, his face filled with devilment. "I'll get you out."

"You will?"

" 'Course."

She didn't trust that look of his. "Then why don't you?"

Thoughtfully, he examined the stands of pine trees, the runners of their sleigh, and her half-buried boots. "Answer a question first."

"As soon as you get me out."

"You're in no position to bargain." Stepping the merest few inches closer, Cole gave her boot top a meaningful nudge with his boot's big snow-powdered toe. "Are you?"

A brisk wind rose, ruffling the faux-fur-trimmed edge of her hood . . . and sending his appealing leather-and-castile-soap scent wafting toward her. Jolie tried to ignore it.

She succeeded about as well as she succeeded in ignoring his lighthearted, expectant look. Not at all.

Raising her chin, she said, "Actually, I'm in a very good position to bargain." Never let it be said that Jolie Alexander had let a challenge go unanswered. "Come closer, and I'll tell you what I mean."

"I'm intrigued."

"You're still standing too far away," she pointed out. "*I* think maybe you're scared."

Cole's confident masculine laughter warmed her from the inside out. It also increased her resolve to gain the upper hand with him.

"Ha. It's you who should be scared," he said, folding his arms.

"Of you? Never."

"Hmmmm. Brash words. Especially coming from a woman who's so . . . ."

He paused in overly obvious thought, tapping a gloved finger against his lips. His eyes sparkled with good humor. With zest for life and all it had to offer. And with passion. For her?

The hot, head-to-boot-tops perusal he gave her would have her believe it. Nevertheless, Jolie could not. The beliefs of half a lifetime were about as pliable as the straight-set, broad shoulders of the man in front of her.

". . . so hard to resist," he finished.

The husky timbre of his voice told her that maybe, just maybe, Cole had resisted all he wanted to. And was ready to give in.

It was a feeling she understood well. Too well. She struggled against it even now. From her racing heart to her suddenly wobbly knees, her whole body urged her to take the chance she both feared and longed for.

"Then why resist?" she asked, all reckless invitation and foolhardy challenge. "Come closer."

Slowly, he shook his head. "If I do, I might never leave."

Oh, God. That sounds perfect. "I'll take my chances."

Still, he hesitated. If she could have, Jolie would have beckoned him with the appreciation in her eyes, the warmth in her arms . . . the fast-growing love in her heart. But those were things she doubted Cole would want from her. So instead, she offered only bravado.

And prayed it would be enough to draw him near.

"After all," she goaded, "it's not as though I can come to you."

"Would you?" He took a step forward. "Would you come to me if you could?"

The question was lightly said. And fully felt, she was certain. In this, Jolie realized, Cole was as serious as the nights were long and lonely.

She had only the truth to give him. "I already did come to you. On New Year's Eve, remember?"

He leaned forward, just barely. From across the few inches of chilly air dividing them, his warmth touched her. Insensately, she shivered. Wanting more, she knew a sense of sharp disappointment when he didn't move again.

"And when you did," he asked, "did you know about me already? From your research for that attraction"—his gaze went to her parka pocket, where she'd stowed the telltale brochure, then returned to her face—"or from meeting folks in town? Did you know about me, Jolie?"

The answer mattered fiercely to him, she could tell. Without thinking, she reached for him. Captured the thick woolen lapels of his coat and tugged him close. With a sound of surprise, Cole came. His coat brushed against hers, and their combined warmth tingled through layers of coverings and sweaters and clothes.

"Is that your question?" she whispered.

He nodded, and waited with unblinking patience for her reply. Proud. Gorgeous. And, she sensed, in some small way that was deeply hidden, almost as needful as she was.

Oh, but over and above all those things, her mind was wickedly occupied with the thrilling, bluntly sensual impact of having Cole near, exactly where she wanted him. Tight against her, the lean strength of his body tempted her to push still closer. She only barely resisted, letting her greedy gaze take in all the details she'd tried so hard to seem nonchalant about until now.

The hard angle of his jaw, shaded with the faintest beginnings of beard stubble, begged for the stroke of her fingers. Beneath the shadow of his hat, his eyes looked deep and mysterious, a darker hazel than before. The curiosity she glimpsed there sparked an answering awareness in her . . . made Jolie wonder how he would look as those eyes drifted shut in passion.

Finally, Cole was close enough to touch, to savor . . . to taste. Jolie's gaze dropped to his mouth, lingered there. She wondered what he would do if she kissed him. Wondered if she possessed the courage to find out.

"Did you know?" he asked hoarsely. "About my

money, my property, my saloon? Was that why you came
to me?''

Was that why you stayed? his beseeching gaze asked.

"I didn't know," she murmured, and decided to answer
the rest with her body—not words. Jolie rose on tiptoes,
frustrated when her feet would only budge a few measly
inches in her stuck-fast boots, and cupped his jaw in her
mittened hands. "I didn't know any of that when I came.
And I didn't know how much I would want to do this,
either."

Before she could lose her nerve, she lurched upward.
Her mouth touched his, tentatively. It was the smallest
of kisses, unsure but heartfelt. It was the bravest thing Jolie
had ever done. And even at that faint contact, excitement
thrummed through her, tightening her belly and leaving
her breathless. She edged back. She opened her eyes.

And discovered exactly how perfect a man could look
in the midst of a passionate moment.

Especially when he was the man she loved.

Within the frame of her sky blue mittens, Cole's face
was drawn with restraint, yet curiously softened with what
could only be affection. His cheeks were flushed. As she
watched, he opened his eyes.

" 'Bout time you did that," he said. "I thought I'd go
crazy with waiting."

Relief flooded her. Giddy with the knowledge that he'd
wanted to kiss her, too, Jolie rose upward again. This
time she let her kiss linger, slowly rubbing her mouth
back and forth over his. She delicately nibbled the fullness
of his lower lip, using every ounce of restraint she had
not to throw caution to the snowbanks and overwhelm
him with too much at once.

Cole was a nineteenth-century man, she reminded herself. He probably wasn't used to sexually assertive
women. Or to being ravished in the midst of a white-
muffled woods on a long afternoon. Sucking in a deep
breath, Jolie kissed from one corner of his mouth to the

next, savoring all the hot, intriguing textures she met along the way.

A moan rose from inside her. Bliss. Kissing Cole was pure bliss, sweetened with love and poignant with the knowledge that their time together could never last. All at once, she wanted to throw him into the snow, press herself against his warmth, sear the imprint of his body and soul on hers for all time. Awash in sensation, Jolie offered all she had in the next union of their mouths. Her love. Her life. Every joyous experience she would ever have. Everything was for Cole.

For him to remember when she'd gone.

As though he'd sensed her urgency, he tightened his fist in her hair and took control of the kiss. His mouth slanted over hers, tasting and probing and silky hot, and it was all she could do to hold on. For an instant, her broken heart healed, and Jolie could almost believe it might stay that way forever . . . if only she could keep Cole by her side.

Wetness touched her cheek. Then her closed eyelids. Her forehead. *Snowflakes,* she realized. As magically as if their kiss had conjured them, the flakes drifted lazily from the sky all around them, wrapping them in lacy white and lending a new stillness to the beauty of the woods.

When at last the kiss ended, Jolie found herself clinging to him. Wide-eyed, she brushed away starry snowflakes from her hood and stared upward. "Wow."

Cole's smile mirrored her own. "I guess that means the wooing is working?"

"It worked from the moment I met you."

Through the falling snow, he gave her a look of mock astonishment. "Then all that shopping, all that listening—"

"Was nice. *Really* nice."

"—all those compliments and those 'little trinkets' of yours, those were all—"

"Also very nice. But not the least bit needed to win me over," she confessed. "You had me from the start."

"Wicked woman," he said, but his eyes were filled with teasing and love.

He kissed her again, holding her still with both hands on the edges of her parka's hood, then went right on kissing her until Jolie sagged against him in delight. Lord, but the man could kiss. She felt hot enough for July beneath his hands and mouth and heated gaze.

"You know," he said, "I have half a mind to leave you stuck there in the snow. It would serve you right for all that wooing business."

She laughed. "No problem. I think that last kiss melted the snow right off my boots."

Cole gazed downward. He shrugged. "Oh. In that case, I guess you don't need me anymore."

He turned and started clomping away, leaving big boot prints in the snow. Arms flailing, Jolie yanked him back.

"I do need you," she whispered, all banter cast aside as she drew him up against her with her hands on his shoulders. She gazed with love into his face, and knew in that moment how very true it was. She did need him, whether fate meant her to or not. "And I—I—" *I love you.* "I need you with me, right now. Here."

"Here?" Cole arched his brow with curiosity, but came nearer all the same. "You've got me, angel. For as long as you want. Don't you know that by now?"

"Oh, Cole." A promise like that could have filled all the empty spaces she'd kept hidden for so long. Did she dare claim it?

If not with words, Jolie decided, then with her body and heart and soul. She would claim Cole's promise for as long as she could, seize the time they had together, and treasure it later, after she'd gone. There could be nothing wrong in that. And the risk was something she'd have to accept.

"Get me unstuck," she said, smiling as seductively as

she could. "And let's see if we can find a new way to make those sleigh bells jingle."

For the space of a heartbeat, he only frowned at her, uncomprehending. Then disbelieving. Then dumbfounded. With satisfying speed, Cole dug the snow from her boots and held out his hand.

"I promise," he said, "with all my heart. 'Twill be a music of those bells like you've never experienced. A winter song so beautiful you'll never forget it."

Silly man. He couldn't have known that it already was.

CHAPTER ELEVEN

A mere two weeks' time saw the changes in Cole's life made complete. The sweet, incredible ringing of the jingle bells on his and Jolie's snowy sleigh ride had set into motion something he'd never expected . . . and had always wanted.

Love.

And he couldn't have been happier about it. His wife hunt was over, Cole reflected as he rounded the upstairs saloon landing on Sunday morning and headed below. He'd found the woman he wanted. Jolie. With each passing day, it seemed more and more likely that she'd decided to stay in Avalanche for good.

Because she loved him.

She hadn't said the words. Not yet. But as they had come together beneath the blankets on that flurry-dusted afternoon, her body and heart had all but shouted out her love for him. And since then, Jolie had woven herself deeper into his life until he couldn't imagine being without her.

Finally, he'd found a woman who wanted him for himself. Not for his money, nor his influence in town. 'Twas a freeing thought. And a happier twist of fate than he'd ever have imagined.

From the saloon below came the sounds of feminine chatter and shuffling feet. Cole descended the stairs with a smile ready-made to greet the group of Avalanche wives and widows and spinsters Jolie had organized into a ladies' reading group.

He stepped onto the lower floor and stopped dead at the sight that greeted him.

Abandoned straight-backed chairs—cadged from the Second Chance's tables, which had been shoved against the walls—circled an open space in the center of the floor. Each chair held a single leather-clad book. All lay unopened. Feather-plumed hats and scarves and ladies' coats rose in a sacrilegious heap atop the billiards table in the corner. Mountains of small, kid-leather snow boots trailed away from the mess, as though they'd been tossed off in haste and left where they lay.

In the middle of the circle of chairs, frozen in the chaos of Cole's blessedly closed-to-the-public Sunday afternoon saloon, stood the prim and proper ladies of Avalanche. Grouped in pairs with their arms outstretched, they appeared to be stopped amidst some sort of ... Cole scratched his head. He could only describe it as he saw it.

An exotic tribal dance.

A dance the likes of which he'd never seen. Skirts rose in plump little fists, exposing yards of petticoats and lace. Stocking-clad feet poised in midair. Sassily tilted hips stopped in midsway, with skirts still swirling from earlier exertions. No less than a dozen faces stared toward him in shock. Every last one of the jaces was covered in some sort of pasty pink goo.

Beneath its concealing swirls, Cole recognized Lillian, several of the old-maid sock-knitters with their long wooden needles haphazardly shoved through thick hair buns, Miss Verna from the mercantile, and—in the center of them all—Jolie.

She made a self-conscious swipe at the goo. "You weren't supposed to be finished with the bookkeeping yet."

He made a mental note to finish all his tasks early in the future. God only knew what interesting events he might stumble upon, with Jolie around to brighten his days.

"I was just headed out for more pencils," Cole said, pulling on his coat to hide a bemused smile that would surely put her dander up. He stuck his arm through his sleeve and waved toward the ladies. "Don't let me stop your . . . ahhh, whatever this is."

"Miss Jolie's teaching us a new dance," one of the women piped up. He recognized her as a lumberman's young widow from the edge of town. "It's called hip-hip."

"Hip-hop," corrected Lillian. Her smile grew broad, making tiny cracks in the goo on her face. "It's called hip-hop dancing, Marjorie."

"Oh, that's right."

The widow's voice trailed away, fraught with a sudden reticence that doubtless was due to the button-your-lip looks she'd been receiving from her dance instructress, Jolie.

"Dance lessons." Pretending to consider the notion, Cole wound his knitted scarf around his collar. Thoughtfully, he headed toward the bar to retrieve his flat-brimmed brown hat. With it in hand, he paused and looked again over the pink-goo-wearing ladies staring back at him. "No wonder you wanted to hide your faces."

Jolie frowned and strode to the front of the group. Toe to toe with him, she put her hands on her hips and looked upward. "It's a beauty treatment."

Doubtfully, he examined the stuff at close range. No question. She looked better bare-faced. "If you say so."

"It is!"

Clearly, a concession was called for. "The color is nice," Cole offered. "Like a . . . a flower."

"That's my contribution!" said Ursula, the butcher's wife. "Smashed-up beets."

Cole shuddered.

All the ladies looked impressed. The gal nearest Ursula gave her a pat on the shoulder. Their enthusiasm made him afraid to ask what else might be in the concoction.

"I'd better be going." Hat in hand, he hastened toward the door. For all he knew, Jolie might take it in her head to slap some goo on him, too.

God knew, he couldn't refuse her much of anything. Cole didn't want to know exactly how low he'd sunk.

"Wait!" A pair of feminine hands grabbed him. "You're just what we need for the hip-hop dancing. A partner!"

He turned to confront the originator of that horrific idea, and found himself staring into the enthusiastic face of Abbie Farmer, one of the former sock-knitters.

In shock, he looked at her more closely. "Abbie, what in blazes did you do to your hair?"

She smiled beneath her goo and patted the shorn blond strands he'd at first mistaken for a spinsterish bun—and now recognized as a suspiciously familiar close-cropped haircut.

"Do you like it?" she asked. "Lots of us gals are having it done. Mr. Mulligan's barber was happy to oblige."

They all aimed adoring glances at their obvious inspiration. Jolie grinned back.

Lord, his whole world was coming unraveled. What would be next? Dozens of skimpy black chemises, designed to torture the unsuspecting men of Avalanche?

Cole gave Abbie—and her hair—what he hoped was an encouraging look. "It's very . . . modern."

"Thank you!"

Whew. He stepped toward the door, ready to make his escape before the dance-partner idea could be reborn. "I'll be back soon, Jolie."

As if on cue, all the ladies moved backward. Cole frowned in confusion—until Jolie stepped through the

space they'd made. Her arms came round his neck, and
he forgot everything else. Lord, but she looked beautiful
to him. All he wanted for the rest of his days was to see
this woman smiling up at him. Even if that meant gazing
at her through endless shades of goo.

"You're looking sappy today, Mr. Morgan," she said.

Because I love you. He thought of what she'd said, and
wondered what Jolie would do if he offered to make her
Mrs. Morgan.

"Sappy? Like a tree?" Cole grimaced. "Sugaring season's a ways off, you know."

"No, sappy like . . . what's that thing Rick always
says?" She snapped her fingers. "Spoony. Besotted. *In
love.*"

He winked. Sometimes she was so easy to bait, future-
talk and all. "I know."

"Arrgh!" His delicate little woman socked him in the
shoulder. "You'd better leave before I make you get
funky with us."

Cole laughed. "I'm afraid to know what that means."
He leaned closer and kissed her, then whispered in her
ear. "But you can show me in private later on."

"I will." Jolie raised her chin and all but smirked with
feminine satisfaction. "So long as you promise to keep
looking at me that way."

"What way?"

Suddenly, he felt as though every thought he had was
plastered on his face for the world to read. Hastily, and
despite the bad manners it implied, Cole slapped his hat
on his head. In its concealing shadow, he felt a little
better.

"You big galoot." To his relief, Jolie kept her voice
low. "You know perfectly well what I mean. You're
doing it right now."

"Doing what?"

"Looking at me like you love me," she whispered.

"Oh, that." As nonchalantly as he could, he swiped a
smudge of pink goo from the corner of his mouth—a

remnant from their kiss—and licked his finger clean. It
didn't taste half bad. "Don't you know by now? I do
love you."

Her astonished look made him realize he hadn't said
so nearly often enough. If at all. Damn. What kind of
wooer didn't include the most important part of all?

Jolie pointed a shaky finger at her goo-smeared face.
"Even with this?"

"Even with that." Smiling, he gave her another kiss
good-bye, then squeezed her waist with the same hands
that had loved her so gladly this morning in their newly
shared cherrywood bed. "Even if your concoction had
peas smashed up in it." An involuntary quiver whipped
through him. Peas were his most-hated food. "I would
love you no matter what, Jolie. Top to bottom and all in
between. 'Tis true."

Applause broke out behind them. One of the ladies—
Lillian, he thought—even whooped. Cole tried to give
them a quelling glance.

He felt too happy to carry it off.

Jolie rose on tiptoes and kissed him once more, then
gave him a little shove toward the saloon door. "If that's
true," she said, "then you'll love me double by tomorrow.
Just wait and see."

Another of her surprises, Cole guessed as he stepped
onto the iced-over, snowy sidewalk outside. That was
fine. 'Twas for certain by now—he was ready for anything
she could deliver.

He hoped.

There couldn't be that many places to hide something
in a place the size of the Second Chance saloon, Jolie
told herself the following afternoon. So where was the
damned sheet music?

Frustrated, she raised the oil lamp she'd lit and gazed
with rapidly fading hope over the assorted books, sheets
of music, and scraps of paper she'd already looked

through. It had to be here someplace. It couldn't have just vanished after sending her into the past. Could it?

No. Some part of her knew the music still existed. Felt sure that it did. And Jolie intended to find it.

Now that she'd discovered such happiness with Cole, the last thing she wanted was for that magical music to turn up unexpectedly. With visions of a saloon musician innocently playing those notes—and accidentally sending Jolie back through time—she set the lamp atop the piano and resumed her search.

Long minutes later, she'd still discovered nothing. Sighing, she sank onto the red velvet piano bench and stared mindlessly at the snowflakes scuttling past the windowpanes, then at the empty saloon. They'd locked the doors early today, just after lunchtime, in preparation for her surprise. Now, with the tables unoccupied and the bar cleared of glasses and liquor bottles, the place looked eerily reminiscent of the Second Chance saloon she'd found herself in on New Year's Eve.

The realization sent a chill through her. Hastily, Jolie swept her gaze to the front door, half expecting to see an incandescent red exit sign there. To her relief, she saw nothing but Cole's plain plaster walls.

"There you are," Cole said, coming in from the back room with a pine box in his arms. He set it atop the table nearest the piano, then stepped over the papers left by Jolie's search to squeeze her waist in greeting. He kissed her. "I thought you'd be upstairs getting ready for your surprise."

"I will be. Soon." She smiled up at him, at the way he towered protectively over her place on the piano bench, and hoped he would be pleased with what she'd planned.

Grinning, he nodded toward the scattered papers. "Once you've finished destroying my saloon, I guess. Lots of work for a small woman. I'm impressed with your far-reaching abilities."

"I was looking for the sheet music," Jolie explained. She didn't have to tell him for which song. His fading smile made his knowledge of that plain enough. "Somehow, I felt it was important to find it today."

"You don't need that music." He put his hands on his hips and looked at her seriously. "In fact, I don't care if you never find it. You can stay here as long as you want."

More charity from him? It had to be. It saddened her to realize it, especially after all they'd shared. She wanted to come to him freely. To love and be loved as equals.

"I don't need your charity," she said stubbornly. "I need that *'Winter Love Song.'* "

He gave her a long look. "I thought we'd already found it. Together."

His reference to their sleigh ride—and the sensual music of the snowy jingle bells that had followed it—only strengthened her resolve. "We did," Jolie whispered. "And I want to make sure it lasts."

"Nothing is sure. Not the way you mean." Cole turned back to his box and pried it open with the crowbar he'd carried in along with it. His arms strained with the effort, working hard, as though he could pry loose her need to have her way back to the future secured, along with the box top. "Leave off, Jolie."

"I can't."

"You need that music like you need to save this town." The lid came loose in a squeal of nails wrenched through wood. He set it out of the way and pulled the first two whiskey bottles from the nest of excelsior inside. "Not at all."

Jolie didn't understand how he could say such a thing. She did need to save Avalanche. For herself. For him. For the people who lived there. And how else was she supposed to accomplish something important enough to make him love her?

Oh, he'd said he loved her yesterday. The memory of his gruff admission still lingered in her heart and soul, making everything she'd planned for today twice as important. But for all she knew, Cole had only said it out of kindness. In his old-fashioned time, the lovemaking they'd shared demanded a commitment. It was perfectly likely, Jolie reminded herself, that he'd only been trying to spare her feelings in front of the other ladies.

In any case, Cole could only love her more if he respected her. If he didn't feel sorry for her because she'd been stranded alone in the past. Jolie was sure of it. After today's surprise, he would be, too.

CHAPTER TWELVE

"Never mind the music," Jolie said, endeavoring for a lighter tone as she slipped from the piano bench to follow him to the bar. "Don't you want to know about my surprise?"

He put away the gleaming bottles of liquor, then headed toward the box for more. With two in hand, Cole grinned up at her, " 'Course. After all, the whole town's in on it, except me. I'd say it's about time I knew."

Jolie gathered her courage, along with a deep breath, and began. "Remember that man who came in here earlier this week? The one who had his bills sent to Mr. Mulligan's hotel?"

"The citified-looking fella with the spectacles and the fondness for applejack toddies?" He made a face over the sweet drink's combination of brandy, hot water, and sugar. "I remember him."

"Well, he was only passing through Avalanche, delayed by a snowstorm on his way north." Cole's movements quickened, as though he'd turned impatient with her story, and she decided to cut to the chase. "Thanks to my hostessing job, I found out he was a railroad executive, on his way to meet with investors for a potential route through the middle of the Arizona Territory.''

She'd hit it off with the man, Townsend, instantly. Two birds of a feather, landing by chance on the same shaky, snow-laden branch. Jolie didn't want to think of how his presence there would have been overlooked completely had she not been acting as hostess on his first visit to the saloon.

"We've had railway men through here before,'' Cole said stonily, reaching into the shipping box's fine wood shavings to withdraw the remaining whiskey. "Half the ladies in your reading group live along the line they started. And abandoned.''

"They won't abandon it this time,'' Jolie told him, gripping the bar's smooth edge in her enthusiasm. "Not if we make them see what a good investment it will be.''

"More curb appeal?''

"Sort of. Cole, a railroad would be perfect for this town! It would bring in industry, and supplies, and more people. Maybe even tourism. I think it's the lack of a railroad that lets Avalanche die, only a few years from now. Not even one whole generation.''

"It's as prosperous as it ever was.''

"It won't stay that way. Think of it—Lillian's place will be gone. So will Verna's mercantile. Ursula's children will never get to grow up in the house their parents built. They'll never work in the butcher store, or take their place in the family business.''

Slowly, he shelved the bottles behind the bar. In the gilded mirror, Cole's expression turned thoughtful.

Then he shook his head. "You can't know all that.''

"I can. I do.'' Sensing his resistance weakening, she went for the knockout punch. "And I know *your* children will never even see the town you helped grow. Never see the Second Chance. Except in the middle of a ghost town, as a falling-down shack.''

He shook his head. "Jolie—''

"*I've seen it.* It was terrible.''

With a kind of grim patience, he turned and spread his palms over the bar, facing her. "What does this have to do with your surprise?"

"Didn't I say?" She must be losing her edge, to begin pitching a deal without asking for what she needed in the end. "Everyone is meeting down at the church. It's the only place big enough to fit so many people."

"How many people?"

Jolie blinked. "Everyone. Everyone is going, to help persuade Mr. Townsend to make Avalanche a stop on the new railroad. Working together, we can all make it happen."

"And you put this whole thing together?"

This was it, she realized. *The moment when he'd understand exactly what good things she was capable of.* "Yes!"

Silently, with an expression she'd never seen from him before, Cole crossed the room. He stowed the crowbar in the box, gathered up fallen scraps of excelsior, then replaced the lid.

Bewildered by his response, she could only watch as he lifted the box in his arms. What was the matter with him? He hadn't said a thing. Instead, he only took a few measured steps toward the back room. She'd known he wanted her to abandon her efforts to save Avalanche. But this? Now, in the face of her accomplishment . . . well, there was no way around it. His indifference stung.

"I—I hope you'll be there," she said quietly. "It would mean a lot to me if you'd come."

His hands tightened on the box. All at once, she saw how his knuckles had whitened against the knotty pine, and knew a terrible sense of foreboding.

"I'll bet it would," Cole said, his voice strangely hoarse. He stopped a few feet away from her.

It might as well have been a few thousand miles.

"Your—your support means everything to me!" Jolie cried, desperate to make him understand. "If you can't be at the meeting—"

''The meeting to save Avalanche.''

''—then there's no point in having it at all.''

His suddenly cold gaze pinned her, freezing in its intensity. ''No. I'm not going.''

''What?''

''I'm not going to your meeting.'' Hefting the box more securely in his arms, Cole headed for the back room.

Jumping from her stool, Jolie followed him. He couldn't be serious. ''You have to go. The whole town is going.''

''Not me.''

In the chill of the storage room, far from the saloon's potbellied stove, he stacked the box atop the others in the corner. For a few moments, she could only watch him work, his back and shoulders flexing as Cole lifted boxes and sorted them into various parts of the room.

''Why?'' Jolie asked him at last. ''Why won't you go?''

His reply was silence. Wood rasped against wood as he stacked another box, his back turned to her.

''Cole, you're the most important part of this. I need you to be there.''

''No.''

''Won't you at least look at me?'' Desperately, she crossed the space dividing them and grabbed his arm. He wrenched away, leaving her more confused than before. ''What's the matter?''

With no warning at all, he dropped the last box and turned to confront her. His voice was bitter when he spoke. ''You're not the woman I thought you were,'' he said. ''Let's leave it at that.''

''Leave it at that? What . . .''

Suddenly, realization struck her. *Not the woman I thought you were.* He didn't believe she could do it! Didn't believe she could save Avalanche, no matter how hard she tried or what she planned. Cole didn't believe in her. Surely didn't respect her.

Couldn't possibly love her.

Oh, God. It was worse than she'd imagined. And far

more painful to accept. She couldn't make him love her. Couldn't prove herself to him. Trembling, Jolie stared up at him through tear-filled eyes.

"I understand." She had to get out of there. Had to leave before she did something really stupid—like beg him to love her anyway. Blindly, she headed for the door. "I've got to get ready."

She swung around the doorframe, feeling unsteady. It seemed as though the familiar grooved floorboards had shifted beneath her feet . . . as though the caring she'd taken for granted had been yanked irretrievably out of reach. Cole didn't love her. Never would. What kind of cruel fate had sent her here?

"Wait."

At the sound of Cole's voice behind her, Jolie stopped. She thrust out her hand for support, and struck the cold smooth keys of the saloon's piano. A cacophony of notes wailed up.

She glared at it. The damned piano ought to be hacked apart and burned for firewood.

Cole stared at the piano, as well. "That piano has been broken for months. Did you know that?"

"No, it's not." In demonstration, she dashed the tears from her eyes and ran her fingers over the keys. Rising and falling notes filled the silence. "See?"

He came to stand beside her. Holding her gaze, Cole pressed his hand over the keys. There was a dull thud as the ivories descended, then . . . nothing.

"The music came from you," he said. "I don't know how, or why. I only know it did."

Jolie backed away. She didn't want to think about the piano, or whatever force had sent her there. She only wanted Cole.

And he didn't want her back.

"It can't happen without you." Cole grabbed her hand, tugged her beside the piano again. "When you finish your damned mission to save the town—when you leave— the magic goes with you."

"I don't care about the piano!" Her vision blurred with tears. She cupped his face in her hands. "Won't you change your mind? I can do it, I swear. You only have to see it. Just come to the meeting, be there when I—"

"No." He lowered his head. Slowly, he slipped from her grasp altogether. "Lord, Jolie. This is hard enough. Don't ask me again."

"Hard? But why—"

The pain in his features stopped her midsentence. His hand closed over hers; then she felt his fingers spreading open her palm. Something dry and tubular pushed its way into her hand.

"Because of this," he said, lifting her wrist.

She looked down at the rolled yellowed paper he'd pressed into her grasp. Its aged edges and faint lines looked familiar. The title it bore when she unrolled it confirmed her worst fears. "Winter Love Song."

"I hid it. The first night you came here," Cole said. "And I've kept it locked away in the back room safe ever since. That's why you couldn't find it."

"But why?" Jolie gestured with the sheet music, her movement encompassing the items she'd strewn about during her earlier search. "Why this, why now? Why would you give me this now, when we both believe it has the power to send me away?"

Tight-lipped, Cole stared back at her. "Why not?"

"Because I—" *Because I love you. And I thought someday you might love me back.* She couldn't say that. Not now. Through her tear-tightened throat, she forced out an excuse he'd believe. "Because I haven't finished what I was sent here for."

"Saving the town."

"Partly, yes."

The harsh set to his face told Jolie she hadn't delivered the reason he'd hoped for.

"And until I'm finished, I won't need this." Urgently, she rerolled the sheet music and shoved it toward him.

He refused to take it. Instead, Cole's fingers closed around hers, locking the music within her grasp.

"I can't give you what you want," he said hoarsely. "I can't, Jolie. But true as I'm standing here, I need you more than this town ever will. If that's not enough . . . then let the music take you someplace where you'll be happy."

And with that, before she could say a word, he was gone.

CHAPTER
THIRTEEN

It should have been raining, Cole thought as he trudged down an icy Main Street past shuttered windows and snowy, locked-tight storefronts. It should have been raining as if all of heaven cried out for a lost angel who'd fallen amongst men and had decided to stay.

Instead, snowflakes sifted from the sky. Like cold kisses, they touched his face. Like sorrowful tears, they melted on his cheeks and ran downward. He tilted his head to the sky and sucked in a wretched frost-filled breath, fighting off the damnable weak impulse to mingle real tears amid the snowy ones. All he wanted was Jolie.

And all she wanted was to use him.

Fiercely, he yanked his hat lower and tucked his chin in his coat collar. No point bawling over a woman. Especially not when she'd turned out just like all the others.

Cole tightened his grasp on the whiskey bottle he'd taken with him from the Second Chance. The liquor sloshed back and forth with his steps, its rhythm harsh with self-recrimination. Lord, he should have known better than to trust Jolie. Especially with all her talk of saving the town and hostessing his saloon. The words might be different, fancier and stranger on the ears, but her intentions were the same. And they were every bit as mercenary as those of the bookish woman and the widow from last year.

If you can't be at the meeting, then there's no point in having it at all.

Choking back a humorless laugh, Cole raised the whiskey bottle and took a slug. 'Course there wouldn't be any point to the meeting without him. She wanted his influence to help persuade the railroad man to bring the line through Avalanche. She wanted him for his money and his position in town. Just as he'd feared.

Slowing his steps, he recorked the bottle and kept walking. Far ahead at the end of the street, a sleigh and team came into view, just visible between the snowfall and the rapidly graying afternoon light. The driver was doubtless headed for Jolie's town meeting. He rounded the corner and drove in an arc toward the church, confirming Cole's suspicions.

Pulling the team to a stop, the driver jumped out and came round the sleigh to help his bundled-up wife and children to the ground. Moments later, they disappeared inside the church, letting slip a sliver of warm lamplight as they opened and closed the door.

Left behind, the horses stamped and shifted. The sound of sleigh bells drifted on a snow-laden breeze, leaving Cole even more bereft than before. How could Jolie have loved him so well and so sweetly on that day by the canyon . . . and want only to use him now?

She couldn't, the softhearted part of him insisted. *She's not like the rest.*

He couldn't listen. Not now. Instead, he walked further, past the butcher store with Ursula's hand-painted sign atop the windows. Past Mulligan's two-story, balconied hotel and accompanying barbershop. Looking inside, Cole imagined Jolie in the chair usually reserved for men, having her hair cropped in the style from the future he had somehow come to favor on her.

Frowning, he strode faster. The woman had changed his perception of things forever. How in hell was he supposed to forget her after she'd gone?

This gal here is your destiny, Lillian had said on that first day. Now, Cole grimaced to recall what his answering thoughts had been. *Only if I'm cursed.*

It seemed he was. Because no matter where he went, no matter what he saw ... Jolie was there. For nearly half an hour longer, he wandered the streets of Avalanche, swinging his whiskey bottle by his side. He thought of all he knew of her, remembered how eager Jolie had seemed for him to discover her surprise. He called to mind how sure she'd been that he would love her twice as well once he'd learned what it was. And by the time the church bell tolled, signaling the impending town meeting, Cole had come to the hardest decision of his life.

She was insane, Jolie told herself as she hurled the "Winter Love Song" sheet music onto the quilt-covered mattress of the carved bedstead upstairs. She had to be. What else explained letting the man she loved walk out on her?

Clumsy with desperation, she dragged her high-buttoned shoes from beside the washstand and shoved her foot into one, then the other. She had to hurry. There was no telling how many second chances fate might allow.

If it allowed any at all.

With trembling fingers, Jolie grabbed the button hook from the bedside table. She looked down at the twin rows of shoe buttons facing her, raised the hook higher ... then hurled it into a corner and pulled on her snow boots from the future instead. Time spent buttoning her damned shoes was time better spent finding Cole.

And telling him the truth.

She loved him. It was as plain, and as complicated, as that. All this time, she'd been too busy planning and working to tell him. Too afraid, and too consumed with trying to prove herself to him. But in those moments after he'd left her alone in the saloon, sheet music in hand, Jolie had realized something.

Impressing Cole wasn't what she needed. And making him love her was impossible—especially when he already did. She didn't need him to approve of her meeting with the railway man, or anything else she did. She needed Cole to approve of *her,* inside and out. And he already did. She'd just been too blind to see it.

I would love you no matter what, Jolie. Top to bottom and all in between.

He'd proven it when he'd given her the sheet music. When he'd given her what he thought she needed to make her happy. Cole had sacrificed his own happiness for hers . . . even when he'd thought she wanted to use him to save the town.

Jolie couldn't believe she hadn't realized it before. During their time together, Cole had referred so many times to his wealth and position in Avalanche. She'd thought he was trying to impress her—when really he had been trying to make sure he was loved for himself alone.

Just like her.

Heart pounding, she threw on her parka, then shoved the sheet music in one pocket and raced downstairs. Within moments, Jolie had stepped outside onto the snowdrift-covered raised sidewalk. Biting cold stole her breath, making her eyes water. Squinting through the falling snow, she raised the lighted lantern she'd brought and gazed down the winter wonderland that Main Street had become.

There was no sign of movement anywhere. The streets she passed were empty of all but snowdrifts and ice. The shops were closed, their windows dark in the fading afternoon. Everyone had taken her seriously, it seemed. The whole town must have turned out for the pitch meeting with Mr. Townsend.

Ahead, the church bell tolled, inviting latecomers to

hurry toward the end of Main Street. Raising her lantern, Jolie walked faster, packing snow tight beneath her heavy boots.

"Cole?" She raised her voice, forcing out another wobbly-sounding cry. "Cole!"

He had to be out here. God knew, he wouldn't have gone to the meeting, and all the stores and saloons—even Mr. Mulligan's hotel—were closed for the afternoon. She called louder, hoping against hope he would hear her.

No answering shout came.

At the far end of Main Street, lamplight beckoned from the windows of the church. Jolie looked toward it, then away. The meeting could wait a little longer.

It could wait until she found Cole.

Snow drifted steadily from the sky, dusting the rooftops and blurring the silhouettes of buildings and hitching posts. Within its drifts, she caught a flash of movement. Then another. As she watched, a coat-shrouded figure emerged from the shadow of the livery stables and headed toward the church. Away from her.

Picking up speed, Jolie followed.

And prayed fate had smiled on her once again.

CHAPTER
FOURTEEN

It wouldn't hurt to go inside, Cole told himself as he neared the church. If going to the meeting and convincing Townsend to lay his railroad through town would help keep Jolie's memory alive in Avalanche, that's what he would do.

She'd already gone. During his trek through town, Cole had circled back to the Second Chance, and found the place empty and cold. Not so much as a spoonful of pink goo, a scrap of "Winter Love Song" sheet music, or a hint of black chemise remained. It was almost as though he'd imagined Jolie's presence all along.

Except Cole knew better. The ache in his heart told him that much. And even if it hadn't, the emptiness in his arms would have been a powerful reminder.

He'd lost her.

All because he'd waited too long to realize that the love in her eyes had been for *him*. Not his bankbook or property deeds or anything else. Only him.

With measured paces, he ascended the steps leading to the paired church doors, following the snowy footprints of the many who had come here before him. On the landing, lamplight from the windows washed him in its glow. Despite its steady brightness, Cole felt nothing but the cold.

They had been two of a kind, he and Jolie. Both of them wanting to be loved for who they were on the inside . . . both of them too busy polishing up the outside to know when someone had.

From inside the church came the sounds of murmuring voices and feet clomping across the floor. Drawing a deep breath, Cole planted his whiskey bottle in a drift at the edge of the landing. He reached one gloved hand forward. His fingers touched the doorknob.

The wind rose, sending a swirl of snowflakes against the paired doors. For a moment, it almost seemed as though the breeze carried a song within it. As plainly as he stood there, Cole heard the gentle notes of a piano playing. The melody was what captured his attention the most.

'Twas a "Winter Love Song."

It couldn't be. Not unless fate was so cruel as to taunt him with memories of Jolie, now that she'd already left him. Steadying his resolve, Cole began twisting the doorknob.

"Cole! Cole, wait!"

At the sound of her voice, and the snow-crunching footsteps that accompanied it, he turned. A hooded figure emerged from the flurries. He blinked, and looked again.

Jolie. Here. *Still.* It couldn't be, and yet it was. Brandishing a lighted lantern, she strode through the snow with all the bravado he would have expected from her. She turned her face upward, watching him as she approached, and the joyous smile that lit her face at the sight of him made Cole's throat tighten.

"Jolie?"

"I couldn't leave," she said. "I'm so sorry."

She swiped her sky blue mittens at the moisture glinting on her cheeks. He hoped reverently those were melted snowflakes he saw—but knew it was unlikely they were anything but tears. At the sight, Cole wanted to bawl aloud himself.

"You're not apologizing for staying," he croaked. "Are you?"

"No." Jolie moved closer, letting the lantern swing at her side. "For everything that came before. For waiting so long to come to my senses—"

" 'Twas both of us," he assured her.

"—and for this."

She dipped her other hand toward the lantern, then raised her arm. In her fingers, Cole glimpsed familiar yellowed pages . . . now ablaze from the lantern's flame. They burned rapidly. Soon their blackened edges drooped toward the snow underfoot, and the lines and notes written on them were obscured with ash.

But not so obscured that Cole couldn't read the words of the title—and know that he'd just watched Jolie destroy her only chance of returning home.

He hardly dared breathe. "Awww, Jolie. I felt so sure you wanted to go back. I gave you the music because of it. Are you sure you wouldn't have been happier in your own time?"

With a decisive gesture, she dropped the sheet music into the snow. She looked down at it for a long moment, then set the lantern beside the blackened music and raised her head.

"How could I be," she asked, "when the man I love wouldn't be there?"

Smiling broadly, she bounded up the stairs and hurtled herself into his arms. The feel of her snuggled against him was all he needed to know she spoke truly.

Holding her close, Cole felt his gaze drawn again to the sheet music she'd left behind. The lantern cast a round circle of brightness over its charred edges . . . and illuminated something else on the snow beside it.

A quick retrieval revealed it to be Jolie's attraction brochure. He turned it over in his hands as the two of them read in amazement about the re-created Go West!

town—now run by Erin Delaney and located on the out-
skirts of "thriving Avalanche, Arizona."

"Looks like you did it," Cole said, smiling at her. "I
knew you could."

"Arranging the meeting with Mr. Townsend must have
been enough." Happily, Jolie settled into his arms again.
"But I don't need to know all that to know the most
important part."

"Which is?"

"I love you," Jolie said, punctuating the words with
a kiss. "I love you from top to bottom and all in between.
I do. And I've decided on a new plan of action, as well."

Thinking of the meeting in the church behind him, the
new mannish hairstyles of the town ladies, the hip-hop
dancing, the pink goo, the black chemise and—most
importantly—their jingling sleigh bells, Cole nearly
groaned aloud. "I don't doubt that you have. Are you
sharing, or is this another surprise?"

Her smile was like the sun breaking through the gray
skies.

"Nah, no more surprises from me," Jolie said.

"Somehow, I doubt that."

"Skeptic." She rose on tiptoes and kissed him. "My
plan is only this—to love you well and often. And to tell
you that I do, at least three dozen times a day."

Cole raised his eyebrows. "Three dozen?"

"Greedy man. I'll make it four." Catching hold of the
trailing ends of his scarf, she pulled him nearer. "Four
dozen, but no more."

"It could be only once," he bargained, "if . . ."

"If?"

". . . if it lasts for the rest of our lives. Say you'll stay
with me, Jolie."

"Stay with you?" She rose upward and gave him a
little nibbling kiss. "You couldn't get rid of me if you
tried, buster."

He made a mental note not to try. At all. "Is that a
yes?"

Jolie nodded. "Oh, yes. It's definitely a yes."

Her whispered assent warmed his heart. The close, top-to-bottom hug she gave him next heated up all the rest of him, too.

Suddenly, Cole thought, there seemed a lot to look forward to in the long winter nights still ahead.

Like loving.

Being loved.

And finding out exactly what Jolie meant when she offered to "get funky."

He looked forward to every minute.

Dear Reader,

As Jolie discovered, it really does snow in Arizona—and sometimes, magic abounds there, too. The town of Avalanche exists only in my imagination, but I truly believe that the kind of love Cole and Jolie found in the Old West still surrounds us today . . . just waiting to be recognized and returned. I'm thrilled to be part of *Timeless Winter,* and I had great fun sharing my *Winter Song* with you. I hope you enjoyed it just as much.

I'd love to hear from you! Please write to me c/o P.O. Box 7105, Chandler, AZ 85246-7105, send E-mail to *lplumley@home.com,* or visit me on the Internet at *http://members.home.com/lplumley/* for previews, reviews, sneak peeks of upcoming books, and more.

Very best wishes, and happy reading!

Lisa Plumley